WINTERLIGHT

BOOK ONE OF THE SILVERLINE CHRONICLES

SANAN KOLVA

Winterlight

Editor: Silven Read
Cover Design: www.damonza.com
http://sanankolva.com

❀ Created with Vellum

Only the most determined, desperate, or demented protesters braved the frigid winter chill to cluster outside the steel gates of the Silverline Power Cooperative complex. Bundled as they were in wool coats, rough-spun scarves, and wool or bearskin hats, Alistar couldn't tell man from woman, young from old, elf from human. Most probably wore every piece of clothing they owned, and still looked miserably cold. The clump of people barely even turned as he hurried past them, though lackluster curses followed him, a now familiar refrain.

"Thieves! Turning the gods' gift into something unnatural and then *selling* it!"

Protesters had been a persistent fixture outside the gates since spring. During the summer, their numbers had been strong enough that many Silverline employees had taken to using side entrances rather than the front gate to avoid harassment. Alistar normally arrived at work early enough that few morning protesters had assembled, but by the time he left for the day, the gathering had inevitably grown, and when the weather had been less forbidding, bolder protesters had attempted to physically accost Silverline employees. Alistar could have handled one or two in a fight, if needed—he'd not lost all his sailor's muscles since becoming an engineer—but he didn't fancy being mobbed. And any direct confrontation would have proven ready fodder for the city's scandal rags.

What do they hope to gain from this? Do they expect us all to burn oil for light and heat like paupers?

Alistar flipped up his collar and pulled his hat low to trap heat and give the wind less of a target, grateful for his seal fur coat and boots—gifts from his family that served him well even so far inland. The sharp wind sliced into every gap it found, and Alistar began to wish for snow to soften the bitter sting, despite his passionate hatred for the winter precipitation.

Over the heads of the protesters, a faint violet line shimmered in the clear winter air. Alone, it hardly seemed worthy of the vitriol spewed by those gathered under it, offering only a little light. Soon, though, it joined others, weaving a web of magic over Lewarden to bring power to all corners of the capital city. Alistar followed the mahiy line with his gaze for a moment before ducking his head again and hurrying down the street.

The Silverline Power Cooperative headquarters occupied a full city block. The gray buildings, utilitarian and uninviting in their appearance, contrasted with the company's function and mission —to provide the magic that made Lewarden not only the political capital, but the center of industry and progress in all of Calarand. Around the complex, carriages clogged the streets, giving the protesters wide berth. Those employees who could afford to maintain a coach and driver were hurrying to their vehicles. Others, like Alistar, had to rely on public transport. To his relief, Alistar managed to flag down an empty coach before his fingers went entirely numb.

The driver was so bundled in coat, lap rug, and fur cap that Alistar could only tell he was human by the bushy beard that bristled past the edges of his scarf. His team of horses snorted and pawed at the ground, objecting to stopping in the chill. The coach sported a fresh coat of white paint, and a steady hand had added flowers and vines in red around the windows and doors. Alistar clamored into the coach, calling "Shale Lane."

The driver nodded curtly, and the horses plunged into motion again. Alistar rubbed his eyes and sighed as he settled on the hard wooden bench. The coach was chilly, but better than the biting open air. He pushed open a curtain as the cab clattered down the street. Coaches and carriages crowded the streets as they left Silverline Power behind and entered the heart of Lewarden. Drivers cursed half-heartedly at one another, their anger sapped by the biting wind. Along the corners, beggars hunched around small rubbish fires. A swarm of urchins darted in and out among the coaches, dodging filth and looking for handouts.

Alistar's coach turned, then turned again, and finally rumbled to a stop. The driver jumped down and opened the door. "Shale Lane. Five chips."

Alistar stepped down to the cobbled street and handed the man an ivory mark. "Thank you."

The driver looked at the mark, then started to rummage in his purse for change, muttering something under his breath.

Alistar interrupted him. "Keep it. This is miserable weather. Get something to warm your bones and chase off the chill."

"Aye?" The driver eyed him with surprise, then tipped his hat to Alistar. "Thank ya kindly, sir." From the accent, Alistar thought he must come from Dockside. He might spend the extra on drink, but he was just as likely to spend it on feed for his team. Docksiders were like that.

When he'd first joined Silverline Power, five years ago, Alistar had been determined to live on his own salary rather than asking his father for the allowance that any firstborn noble son could reasonably expect. He'd quickly found that the housing Silverline Power made available for their workers was too loud, too crowded, and much too unwelcoming to him. Most engineers already lived in Lewarden before joining the company or received a stipend for housing from their noble families, leaving only the lower-ranking workers, predominantly elves, in the company housing. They had resented Alistar for outranking them, for being human, and for intruding into their domain. He had quietly persisted for the first several months, saving his funds until he could afford to rent a modest townhouse. Shale Lane wasn't in the best part of town, but it was a predominantly human neighborhood, and his neighbors were generally friendly.

Alistar walked toward a row of tall, narrow houses. Laughter and music rose from Madame Faybel's brothel as he passed, and the bouncer at the door nodded to him. Alistar returned the greeting, but didn't stop to chat with the man. He had never seen the inside of the brothel, but on more pleasant days, he sometimes paused to talk to the bouncers. He hurried past four more doors and one shadowed alley before climbing the steps and fishing the key from his pocket.

He unlocked the door and stepped into the welcoming embrace of light and heat that he called home. Alistar hung up his hat, uncovering short black hair. His seal fur coat followed the hat. He heard sounds of movement from the kitchen.

"Good evening, Mrs. Ke'lyn," he called to his housekeeper.

"Welcome home, Mr. De'seneth," she called back. "Your dinner will be ready shortly."

He climbed the stairs and walked down to his dressing room, unlacing his necktie and unbuttoning his shirt as he closed the door. Opening the wardrobe, he paused to consider its contents. Some of his colleagues expressed their condescending distaste for his clothes, as if *every* engineer in Silverline Power should wear silkweave suits and have their personal grooming done by an attendant. Sometimes he responded with a light jab about knowing how to trim his beard and button his own shirts, and most times he simply ignored the comments. The established nobles did not easily accept anyone they saw as an outsider, a lesson Alistar had learned long before he began his career at

Silverline Power. They took pride in having hands too smooth to do a day's labor, and had not grown up hauling sails and climbing a ship's rigging, which made their opinions worth practically nothing to Alistar.

"Your dinner is in the oven, Mr. De'seneth," Mrs. Ke'lyn said as he descended the stairs dressed down for the evening. "I finished the day's wash. Tomorrow I'll dust the parlor and polish the silver."

Alistar smiled warmly at his housekeeper. "Thank you, Mrs. Ke'lyn. As always, you are a rare gem."

She laughed, a rich, warm sound. She was a pleasant, tidy woman, and Alistar offered prayers of thanks to all the Reyker that her contract had been included in the lease when he first rented his home. In the five years he had lived on Shale Lane, Mrs. Ke'lyn had always ensured that he had a hot meal waiting upon his arrival, no matter when he came home from work. Sometimes Alistar wondered if she had hints of Oracle in her blood. She had the olive skin and straight chestnut hair, which she kept pulled back in a braid. Though she was old enough to be his mother, the only wrinkles on her face were the lines of smiles. Her accent was pure midcity, whatever her ancestry.

"Have you heard from your nephew recently?" Alistar asked politely as she pulled on her coat.

"Not yet, Mr. De'seneth. He and his young lady should be settled in Fallowood by now, so I expect to hear from him any day now. I'll tell him that you asked after him. The lad always was fond of your company."

"I'm glad that he's wed and settled. Joining the ranks of the Silver Prince's Forestkeepers is impressive, and it seems a good post for him," Alistar said. "He'll have a lot of opportunities there."

"He'd never have tried for it if you hadn't encouraged him, sir," Mrs. Ke'lyn replied, tying on her bonnet. "I do thank you for that."

Alistar smiled. "He has the talent; he just needed a little push.

But I had best let you retire for the evening. Thank you, as always. Be careful—there's a bitter chill tonight."

"I heard the wind howling. I'll take care," she promised. "A good night to you, Mr. De'seneth."

When Mrs. Ke'lyn opened the door, a blast of cold air swept into the room. Not for the first time, Alistar wished that the capital lay in a warmer climate. Summer was pleasant, but he had yet to grow accustomed to the winters, even after living in Lewarden for nearly five years.

A meat pie awaited him in the oven, the juices just starting to bubble around the edges of the crust. Mrs. Ke'lyn always seemed to know what food would best suit his mood, although it was likely not difficult to guess that he would prefer something hearty and hot on so cold a day. As was his habit, Alistar settled at the small kitchen table rather than the formal dining room. The dining room saw little use; he rarely entertained, and felt more at home eating in the kitchen.

Steam escaped the pie when he broke the crust. Alistar savored the first bite. The meat tasted like pheasant, complemented by a mix of tubers and spices. It wasn't traditional Rillwater fish stew, but still made a hearty meal. He relaxed, putting the day's work behind him.

He was halfway through the pie when his lights began to flicker. Alistar's head jerked up in surprise and he looked to the wall sconces. The gleams of white ghostfire jumped and danced erratically, as if they were flames hit by a gust of wind. Alistar pushed away from the table and rushed to the window.

"Blood and sand…"

In every street lamp, the lights performed the same flickering, fading performance, as if the magic seeped from them. Alistar's gaze rose to the sky and his breath caught. The purple glow of the mahiy lines dimmed, and as it did, lights flickered out on Shale Lane.

Atop a roof several blocks down, Alistar glimpsed a flash of violet, outlining silhouettes for an instant, but the gleam was as swift as lightning, then gone, leaving him to wonder if he'd seen it at all.

"What's going on?" he whispered, his gaze sweeping toward the nearest generator plant. *Did the protesters actually assemble? Did they attack the generators? The Silver Prince ordered company property be guarded at all times. Even a mob wouldn't be rabid enough to assault guard ogres, would they? I don't see any fires...*

Abandoning dinner, Alistar raced down the stairs, grabbing coat and hat in the darkness. He fumbled the door open. The nearest generator stood six blocks away, and if something had gone wrong, they might need help.

Across the street, a door crashed open and a woman burst outside dressed only in her gown. She dropped to her knees on the icy cobblestones, arms raised to the sky. Her voice rose in a keening wail. "Lord of Magic, Mighty Rechmal, preserve us! Grant us your light! Do not abandon your children to the darkness!"

Her husband hurried from the house, throwing a cloak over her shoulders and urging her to stand. She shook him off and continued her wailing prayer. Alistar hesitated, unsure whether to offer assistance or continue to the generator. Seeing Alistar, the woman's husband waved him off quickly. Respecting the silent request, Alistar nodded and jogged up the street.

In the windows of Madame Faybel's brothel, candles began to glow. Other areas of the city remained lit—Alistar could see the glow against the sky. But Shale Lane and the streets around it were dark. Overhead, for the first time since he'd come to Lewarden, Alistar glimpsed gleams of starlight in the sky.

"Rechmal is punishing us! He has seen our lack of faith, and how we have taken for granted the blessing he bestowed on us! Join me! Beg his forgiveness!" the woman continued. "Lord of Magic, look down on us! See us, how we prostrate ourselves before you!" She bowed down on the cold stones. "Forgive us for our sins, our ignorance."

A thin trace of violet etched across the sky as Alistar hurried down the street. At first he thought he imagined it, but it slowly grew in strength as monitors located the blackout, and the nearest generator plants poured magic into the depleted lines. First the street lights flickered, playing their dance in reverse. Then magic returned to homes, bringing back lights, heat, and power.

Alistar's gaze followed the lines in the sky.

That shouldn't have happened. The magic should not fail. Did something go wrong at the generator? At Silverline Power itself?

By the time he reached Shale Generator Plant, the lights were steady, leaving no signs of the incident. An ogre stood at the generator gate, arms folded across his chest. "No entry," the ogre rumbled.

"I'm Alistar De'seneth, Associate Engineer Third Degree," Alistar said quickly.

The ogre, a good three feet taller than him, frowned. "Not on the roster for tonight, Associate."

"There was an outage about half an hour ago. I want to make sure everything is stable and offer assistance if it's needed," Alistar said.

The ogre grunted. On the whole, they tended to be a people of few words, though they were far from stupid. "Come."

Alistar followed the ogre to the generator's entrance. The ogre knocked once, and the door opened quickly. A young man in a technician's uniform blinked into the darkness. "Yes?"

"Associate De'seneth here to check on generator," the ogre rumbled.

Alistar stepped into the light from the doorway. "Associate De'seneth, Third Degree. There was an outage on Shale Lane. Is everything all right here? Are you in need of any help?"

"Third Degree?" the technician repeated, stiffening with a hint of alarm. "Sir, I assure you, there's no need for you to—I'm going to write the incident report!"

"I live in the area," Alistar said, hoping to calm the technician's indignation. Relations between the technicians and the engineers of Silverline Power often carried an undercurrent of tension and departmental rivalry, and this man acted as if he thought Alistar would accuse him of attempting to cover up the incident.

The technician relaxed a little and shook his head. "It's under control now, sir," he said quickly. "No need to worry. We're running an analysis now to locate the hiccup in the lines. Thank you for taking the time to come out here, sir." The technician was closing the door even as he spoke. "I'm sure it's nothing serious. Have a good night, Associate."

"Are you sure—" Alistar started to ask, but the door clicked shut. "I guess you are." He frowned. The outage he'd witnessed had not matched the behavior of a "small hiccup," but the ogre looming over his shoulder discouraged pressing further.

He walked home once again, coat pulled tight against the frigid night. *I lived most of my life without reliable magic or the amenities of Lewarden. Five years here, and now I can't imagine living without lights on command and water hot from the tap. Losing those for ten minutes makes everyone panic. Even me. Am I so spoiled?* He shook his head, trying to force himself to see the absurdity of the situation.

And yet, his eyes returned to the glowing lines in the sky, and the pressing certainty that what he had witnessed should not have happened.

CHAPTER 2

Alistar arrived at Silverline Power before many of the protesters had assembled. A few clustered across the street from the main gates, and someone shouted at him.

"Scummer! Thief! You steal what the gods have given us freely and sell it for profit!"

Alistar ignored the shrill voice and approached the front gate. A thick stone wall, tall enough make even a mammoth hesitate, surrounded the facility, accessed by either the massive front gate, sized to allow the passage of supply caravans, or the much smaller side and back gates. Ogres stood guard at all entrances, though the back gate opened into a private street patrolled by the Silver Prince's personal guards—an understandable precaution, given that the Silver Prince had built Silverline Power beside his own estate, and that street ran between the two. The ogre on duty at the front gate looked Alistar over, leaned down, and sniffed him before declaring, "You can pass."

"Thank you." Alistar nodded politely and waited for the gates to swing open. It always paid to be polite to the gate ogres. They might be large and look less than bright, but they remembered courtesy. And they also remembered insults.

The gates moved smoothly in spite of their size, without a groan or creak of protest. As he walked down the footpath, Alistar pulled off a glove and patted one of the sneering garnet gargoyles that lined the way. His hand appeared to be the first to disturb the sheen of frost on the cold head. A tongue flicked over his skin, tasting and testing him yet again. If an intruder managed to pass the ogres at the gate, they risked being torn to shreds by the gemstone guardians on their approach. As he continued walking, Alistar patted a snarling figure of a winged cat, and it rubbed against his hand in response with a purr like two rocks grinding together.

"Good morning, Morath," he greeted the cat.

The gargoyle purred again, stretched, then settled back into place, wings folding against its back and tail curling around to cover its feet. Alistar didn't think that gargoyles actually got cold, but Morath acted like the feline it appeared to be, treating the weather with disdain no matter what it might be. Alistar pulled his glove on again and shoved his hands into the depths of his pockets, shivering as he hurried up to the massive steel door of the austere gray building.

"Alistar De'seneth, Associate Engineer, Third Degree," he said through chattering teeth.

The door opened, and he rushed inside. The entry lobby contrasted sharply with the utilitarian, imposing exterior of the expansive three-story building. The floor was tiled with polished marble, set with a mosaic in the center. The image of the bolt of violet lightning striking a sword wreathed in silver fire was familiar to the entire city—the symbol of Silverline Power Cooperative. Alistar stepped into the coat room to remove his overcoat and change his winter boots for indoor shoes. He noted a handful of additional coats and boots, telling him that he was not the first to arrive for the day.

His steps ticked on the marble as he crossed the lobby. Sconces shone with light, mixed with a few more traditional candelabras, all enchanted to radiate illumination without flame. Ornamental everblooms blossomed around the room to complement the paintings and hangings on the walls. Most of the images appeared abstract to Alistar's eye, though he knew that elves attributed great symbolism to certain shapes and combinations of colors.

He passed the front desk, nodding to Assistant Goldleaf. She sat perched primly on a low-backed chair of rosewood, three logbooks spread open before her on the desk, their pages filled with small, tight, neat script. When he had first joined Silverline Power, Alistar had been shocked to discover that the majority of the assistants and record-keepers stood no taller than two feet high, with wings like dragonflies and hair colored every shade of the rainbow. Before moving to Lewarden, every sprite he had met had been silly, flighty, and obsessed with flowers, or animals, or pranks. He had not imagined a breed of sprites that devoted that same obsessive passion to numbers and records.

Assistant Goldleaf looked up as she finished a notation, and she set aside a quill pen half as tall as she was. "Good morning, Associate De'seneth."

"Good morning, Assistant Goldleaf. Any news for me?"

"Let me check." She rose and crossed the desk in three strides, opening another ledger book. "You have a meeting scheduled for ten-thirty with Director Strey'mend, but otherwise nothing has been reported."

Alistar nodded. The meeting with the Director was a standard status report. Director Strey'mend was a personable man who projected an attitude of interest in the reports of his employees. He was also one of the highest-ranking humans in the Silverline hierarchy, and the man Alistar felt most comfortable reporting to about the previous night's outage. "Thank you, Assistant."

Beyond the front desk, two curving staircases swept up to the second floor. Under the balcony, another set of doors led farther into the depths of the first floor, to the research chambers and the botany department. Alistar climbed the nearest staircase and turned right. Coming to the second door on the left, he entered the room.

"The day begins," he said.

The words triggered a simple enchantment, and sconces bloomed to life around the room, illuminating neat rows of desks. The faintest shimmer in the air indicated the thin magical walls that divided the desks into individual spaces. Reaching his desk, Alistar lightly brushed his fingers across each of the four walls, activating the enchantments within them. At his touch, they shifted to a cloudy white color. They didn't obscure his view of the room entirely, though he could have done so with a heavier touch, but they did provide a sense of privacy. And equally important, when his fellow engineers began to arrive and settle in for the day's work, the clouded walls would tell them that he was in the midst of some task and did not wish frivolous interruptions.

Not that he had any terribly pressing assignments to attend to, but mornings were always filled with gossip—engineers were as bad as old women in a marketplace sometimes. The morning after any gathering or event, Alistar had only to listen for a few minutes to know the highlights, rumors, and scandals of the court. Most of the engineers were nobility of some level, and a few even mingled in the upper ranks. And some of them absolutely thrived on opportunities to pass on a choice bit of gossip.

Alistar opened his desk drawers, searching through files. He heard voices and laughter as other men arrived and settled at their desks, but tuned out the words. He looked for any records of other outages in recent months, or even complaints and unsubstantiated claims, but came up with nothing, to his frustration.

"De'seneth, don't you have a meeting with the Director soon?"

Alistar looked up and turned to see Veril Lamorage standing at the entrance to his desk area. A young nobleman, by elven standards he was the equivalent of a year Alistar's junior, and at work he was a cheerful soul, as if he had no cares in the world. Coming from the western mountains, Lamorage was almost as much of a political outsider as Alistar, a commonality that had proven the basis for friendship. Arching an eyebrow at the pile of paper on Alistar's desk, he asked, "Special project?"

Alistar shook his head. "Not yet. Just doing some research."

"Ah." Lamorage nodded. "Well, that can be interesting or dull as stone, but it's better than coming in and finding some ominous pile of papers waiting for you. Slee only knows, I hate finding those little surprises lurking in wait for me in the morning. But in any case, you haven't said a word all morning, and it's closing on ten-thirty. Didn't you mention the other day that you have a status meeting today?"

Alistar fumbled for his watch. "What? It's that late already?" To his dismay, the watch read ten-twenty. He quickly shoved papers back into a haphazard pile. "Thank you, Lamorage. I lost track of time."

Lamorage grinned. "Well, it's a first, *me* telling *you* that you're about to be late for something."

Alistar found a smile in spite of himself. Lamorage made an art of being late to anything that he possibly could. As Lamorage returned to his own desk, Alistar opened a drawer and stuffed the pages inside. He locked the drawer with his key-word, rose, and hurried from the room and down the hall, not quite running. Director Strey'mend's office lay around the far side of the building.

As Alistar approached, a chill of unease crawled up his spine. Guards always patrolled the building, and the Director had a pair who stood watch outside his office, but Alistar saw more uniformed men than he was accustomed to seeing, even near the Director's office. He didn't recognize most of them, either, and that unsettled him more. His stomach twisted in a knot, though he couldn't place a reason for his discomfort.

When he arrived at the Director's office, the usual pair of guards stood outside. One of them nodded to Alistar. "Associate

De'seneth, go ahead. The Director is expecting you." He opened the door.

"Thank you," Alistar said. He drew a deep breath, telling himself firmly that his worries stemmed from the outage, and walked inside.

Director Kalald Strey'mend, a stout human man of forty-seven years with thinning brown hair, sat at the desk. Alistar knew him to be even-tempered and a skilled administrator who had risen to his position through great personal effort. Alistar especially respected him for being a human who had risen to the rank of director in spite of his common birth.

"Alistar De'seneth, Associate Engineer Third Degree, sir."

"Right on time as always, De'seneth. Come in and take a seat," Director Strey'mend invited. As Alistar settled into the comfortable chair across the desk from the director, Strey'mend continued. "Do you have any concerns, De'seneth? Any issues to be brought to my attention?" It was his typical manner of starting a meeting—offering an opportunity for his workers to voice concerns and grievances. Alistar appreciated the practice, especially once he had seen that the director both listened and acted on valid complaints brought to him.

"I do have something, sir," he said.

"Go ahead."

"Last night around seven, Shale Lane, where I live, lost power," Alistar told him. "It lasted nearly ten minutes, as best I could guess."

Director Strey'mend sat up straight. "An outage on Shale Lane?"

"Yes, sir. The mahiy lines dimmed until they were nearly drained. I believe that the loss of power covered several blocks."

"Any surges? Fluctuations?" the director asked, frowning.

"No sir." As he said it, Alistar recognized how odd that was. "The lights dimmed, then went dark. I didn't notice any flaring or fluctuations. When power returned, it was much the same—the lights brightened until everything ran as normal. I made a trip to the nearest generator, but the technician I spoke to there gave no answers; he was more interested in sending me on my way than accepting any offer of assistance." He paused. "I didn't find records of other recent outages in my review this morning, but this concerns me, sir. There could be an unrecognized potential fault at the local generator." That was the thought he'd had the previous night, but Alistar was starting to doubt his guess now. A fault should have caused surges as well as dips.

Director Strey'mend's frown deepened. He thumbed through a stack of papers on his desk. "Shale Lane… ah. Arrived this morning. The technician sent a report, but it wasn't flagged correctly." He leaned back in his chair, steepling his fingers as he thought over something. "The information I am about to share with you is confidential, De'seneth, not to be discussed even with your colleagues."

Alistar looked at him in surprise. "Sir?"

"Though you did not find record of them, yours is not the first loss of power in the last month. They have popped up around the city, all quite similar to what you described. Small areas, brief times, no discernible cause in the equipment. We have been monitoring the generators and checking the lines for damage, so far without success. The technician you spoke to last night had likely heard some unfortunate rumors that imply Silverline Power is placing blame on the operators at the generators. Rumors, I will add, that are entirely untrue."

Alistar sat back. "This has happened other places?"

"Yes, primarily in the poorer districts of the city. By His Highness's orders, such incidents have been marked as confidential. Have you discussed your experience last night with anyone?"

"No sir," Alistar said numbly. "I don't know about my neighbors or who they might have spoken to, though." He thought of the wailing woman on the street.

The director nodded. "This situation is a growing concern for His Highness. I appreciate your discretion in the matter."

"Of course, sir." A wise man did not spread tales that he knew the Silver Prince wished kept silent, especially when he worked in the company owned by the Silver Prince.

Director Strey'mend's expression was grave. "The last thing Silverline Power needs is further scandal and more reason for protesters at our gates. His Highness has already ensured that none of the official news sources will report on the outages. Though we can't prevent all rumors from spreading by word of mouth, the Silver Prince wants to contain the damage as much as possible."

Alistar had seen the prince before, from a distance, but never personally met him—nor did he ever expect to. The elf Cero Feyblade was only slightly younger than his brother, Suleton Feyblade, High Lord and Ruler of Calarand. Alistar knew the tales, though the events had taken place nearly a century before his birth. When Suleton had been newly crowned, his brother Cero had revealed a plot years in the making that would have ended the new king's life and opened the throne to the Silver Prince. The court had been in turmoil at the revelation of the plot —not because there was a plot against the king's life, but because the person who revealed it was the one who appeared to have the most to gain from its success. People still debated over whether the revelation of the plot was a move of brilliance or insanity by him. Since then, the Silver Prince had been viewed as an uncertain force in the politics of the land, unpredictable and apt to break from tradition. His creation of Silverline Power was one example of his unorthodox actions. Alistar, like every employee of Silverline Power, knew that Cero Feyblade was a man devoted to his dream, and that dream was part and parcel of the company.

The fact that Silverline Power Cooperative had also made the prince fantastically rich and a force not to be ignored in the nation's politics could hardly be overlooked either.

Director Strey'mend gave Alistar several minutes to collect himself, then turned the topic to the status of Alistar's projects—all of which were nearly done, and mostly waited on input from one of the botanists to be complete. Normally, the director assigned new tasks at that point, to keep his employees occupied and not waiting on someone else's schedule. To Alistar's surprise, though, the director did not provide him with anything new from the stack of folders on his desk. He seemed thoughtful through the rest of the meeting, and when Alistar was dismissed, he couldn't help but feel that his report of the outage related to whatever was on the director's mind.

It was just past eleven thirty when Alistar returned to his desk, still numb from the conversation with Director Strey'mend. *Something is happening with the grid of mahiy lines. The Silver Prince wants to cover up the problem, and now I have some small part in it.* The idea left a bad taste in his mouth and made him wonder how much effort was being put into fixing the problem, and how much into hiding its existence.

He had barely sat down when Veril Lamorage walked to his desk. "Long meeting, De'seneth. You don't need to pack your desk or anything, do you?"

Alistar smiled. "No, nothing like that. But I'd like to stretch my legs. Ready for lunch?"

"My stomach hadn't *quite* started eating itself yet, but… yes," Lamorage said. "And it's my turn to pay."

Alistar stood. "In *that* case, I'm ready any time."

Alistar and Lamorage left by the side door, avoiding the protesters at the front gates. Alistar wondered if some of the people had been drawn to the protests because they too had experienced loss, even if temporarily, of the power they all depended on. Had they filed complaints, only to be ignored in the company's effort to suppress knowledge of the events?

Lamorage led the way to one of the small eateries around Silverline Power. Taverns and cafes had been equally swift to see the potential of a large group of workers in a stationary location. Lamorage favored a cafe that claimed to serve an assortment of dishes of Heiset origin—mostly noodles with mutton. Mutton was considered peasant food, just as wool was for those who couldn't afford decent textiles, but in the matter of Heiset cuisine, most people made an exception.

The patrons were equally split between humans and elves. They found a table and placed their orders with the server. Alistar looked around the room, recognizing most of the patrons as employees of Silverline Power. The dining room was decorated with replicas of Heiset-style art, mostly copies of familiar tapestries.

Lamorage smiled. "I do enjoy coming here. The atmosphere... some days I can almost forget that we are in the capital."

Alistar poured tea into the small porcelain cups and sipped his. "You do know, Lamorage, that none of us actually know what 'authentic' Heiset food or art are, don't you? We humans only started making such claims when we realized how fascinated your people were with our origins."

"Oh, come now, De'seneth, don't be so cynical! This food isn't part of *our* tradition, and it had to come from somewhere. I am not about to argue with the proprietress over the authenticity of her food when she tells me that all the meals prepared here come from recipes recorded in her great-grandmother's cookbook which was the sole treasure that said ancestor carried clutched to her chest when she passed through the portal. And I certainly have never seen references to braised mutton noodle soup that date from *before* your people stormed our borders." Lamorage added a heaping scoop of sugar to his tea before sipping it. "Certainly *we* would not expect someone to drink *this* unsweetened."

"We did not 'storm' your borders," Alistar said, willing enough to debate history three hundred years in the past, well before either of them had been born. "The Heiset humans came through that portal as refugees, fleeing from whatever drove us out of our lost homeland."

"Rather aggressive for refugees," Lamorage remarked. "I think that the initial list of demands might have had a part in our lack of immediate sympathy. Our texts use the word 'invaders' rather than 'refugees'."

"You don't want to know what *our* text called *your* people," Alistar told him. "Whatever drove us from our land apparently made our leaders reluctant to simply ask for help. Misunderstandings abounded. But you must admit, after the first few assassination attempts by both sides failed, our two sets of leaders did manage to hold a diplomatic meeting and discuss the matter like civilized people."

"That's true. I don't think the leaders of the day had ever met a people with assassins as skilled as our own," Lamorage agreed. "Assassins were expensive. Diplomacy was cheaper. To say nothing of the fact that they couldn't figure out who was actually the leader of your people."

Alistar chuckled. "And right there is one reason that an oligarchy is superior to a monarchy."

"Yet here we all are, under a monarchy," Lamorage countered.

Their food arrived. Alistar pushed up his sleeves before picking up the bowl and chopsticks. Lamorage pulled off his gloves, but didn't go so far as rolling up his sleeves. Elven taboos strictly forbade showing more skin than absolutely necessary. Shirts were always long-sleeved, the cuffs hugged the wrists even during summer. Collars rose high on the neck. Most elves wore thin gloves in public, and even removing them to eat was a touch scandalous, though less so when dining among humans. Strict traditionalists frowned fiercely on frequenting human eateries for that very reason.

Lamorage gobbled up noodles, then washed them down with a gulp of tea. "So, how is Miss Tan'shyo?"

Saskia Tan'shyo. Thinking about his fiancée always brightened

Alistar's mood. "She's quite well. We attended the theater last week, a comedy about a man who stumbles into the land of the trolls and ends up bumbling his way onto their throne. I was hoping to take her to another show in two nights, but I'm not certain that she'll have time."

"Oh? Is something happening at her father's clinic?" Lamorage asked. Like many elves, he was uncomfortable with the idea of doctors and the necessary indecency such work required, but Lamorage also knew that Alistar didn't share his cultural disquiet. "Don't you worry about her, De'seneth, in the midst of all the poor, treating orphans and vagrants?"

"I do, but she loves being able to help them. And if she didn't pursue her work, I would never have met her, and then where would either of us be?" Alistar countered. "As for any new crisis, I haven't heard, but she said things have been unusually busy."

"Well, even if Doctor Tan'shyo insists on focusing his practice on the wretched of Lewarden, at least he doesn't oppose His Highness's work. Can you believe, the other day a healer told me to my face that the restructuring of the mahiy lines and the flow of magic through the city is going to somehow poison us all? He seemed to think that our water will become contaminated and we will all fall victim to some plague or another. And perhaps there was some mention of frogs raining from the sky, the sun turning to blood, and Slee's mighty axe falling to smite the unrighteous. I stopped listening to him after a bit."

Alistar chuckled. "That is a prophecy of doom I have not heard before. It's an interesting theory."

"Bah, it's rubbish. All this, this is *right*. This is the way we should live, not cowering in the dark and hoping our lamps don't burn out, wondering what lurks and waits in the shadows," Lamorage said firmly.

Alistar nodded. He didn't know a great deal about Lamorage's past except that the elf came from the western mountains, where magic was scarce and monstrous beasts lurked in the dark, preying on elves and humans alike. And Alistar knew that Lamorage would never, ever, enter an unlit room.

Alistar changed the subject. "And how is life in court? Attended any balls lately?"

Lamorage's mood lightened and his characteristic smile returned. "Of course! Some friends and I visited an event at the Perchau estate two evenings ago. They have a fine ballroom, and the dancing was splendid. Afterwards, we were invited to join some of the other gentlemen at a much more exclusive gathering. I made the acquaintance of three fine ladies who I hope to see next time." He paused. "You should come with me sometime, De'seneth."

Lamorage had made the offer before, and Alistar had always declined. He had challenges enough dealing with the condescension of his coworkers. Voluntarily attending an event with the nobles of Lewarden went against both his father's wishes and his own. Still, the fact that Lamorage continued to extend the offer made him feel guilty about constantly refusing.

"I'll think about it," Alistar told him.

Lamorage looked startled for a moment, then he beamed as if Alistar had accepted. "Excellent!"

"I'm not making any promises," Alistar said hastily. "I don't know what project I'm going to be working on next."

"All the more reason that you need some time to unwind, De'seneth," Lamorage told him. "Trust me! I'll let you know the next time a good party is in the works, and you'll see. You'll be among friends, De'seneth, believe me."

His enthusiasm was so genuine that Alistar couldn't help but smile. Lamorage had not faced the same degree of rebuffing as Alistar had—he did, after all, bear a family name known to most, and he was an elf—but he had experienced enough slights to sympathize with his human friend. The Lamorage family was a branch of the Wyrud line, a powerful family whose wealth came from a lucrative trade in precious metals. However, while the head of the Wyrud family dwelt in Lewarden and maintained a massive estate, the Lamorage family lands were far from the capital. The young man sitting across from Alistar had come to the capital to join the court, but had struggled to find acceptance there, facing a battle against forces and factions well entrenched and wary of outsiders. The fact that Lamorage actually worked outside of his family trade only added to the opportunities for other, established nobles to ostracize him, no matter that a great many younger sons and daughters of noble houses found employ in Silverline Power.

"I'll think about it," Alistar told him again. He checked his watch. "But we had both best be thinking about getting back."

"Ah, Slee's Heart, is it that time already?" Lamorage checked his own watch, an elegant silver piece covered with intricate scrollwork on the case. "Now see, this is why I like you, De'seneth. You keep me on time! What would I do without someone who knows how to be punctual?"

"You would probably be late more often than you already are," Alistar answered with a smile.

"I'm hardly ever late!"

Alistar managed to turn his snort of laughter into a cough, but only barely.

"Well, not late enough to really matter," Lamorage amended, setting an ivory mark on the table.

"If you say so," Alistar said with a chuckle.

The wind was biting, and the cold sharper, when they left the eatery and hurried back to work. The lobby of Silverline Power was blessedly warm, and Alistar spent a few moments rubbing his hands together to warm them once he had hung up his coat. As he and Lamorage walked to the stairs, Assistant Goldleaf called his name.

Alistar turned in surprise. "Yes?"

"Director Strey'mend sent a message down a short time ago,

asking that I clear your schedule this afternoon. He wants to meet with you again at one-thirty today."

Alistar hastily checked his watch in an effort to cover his surprise. "Um, I don't believe that I had anything on the schedule for this afternoon, did I?"

"No, Associate De'seneth," she agreed.

"And I should expect this meeting to last the rest of the day?" he guessed.

"That is the impression that the director gave me, though he didn't say so," Assistant Goldleaf said.

"Thank you, Assistant." Alistar couldn't think of any other response.

Lamorage raised an eyebrow as they climbed the stairs. "Another meeting with the director?"

Alistar offered a helpless shrug. "I don't know. A new project, maybe? Something that needed more time than he had this morning? I don't want to make too many guesses."

He wondered about the meeting as he returned to his desk and completed paperwork. Alistar still didn't have any solid explanation as he walked back to the director's office. Once again he was struck by the sense that too many guards walked the halls. When he reached Director Strey'mend's office, the two men who had stood at the door in the morning had been joined by four more. The newcomers considered Alistar suspiciously, but the regular two just nodded to him as they opened the door. "They are expecting you, Associate De'seneth."

They?

Alistar stepped into the office, and the guard closed the door behind him. For a long moment, he stood frozen in place, unable to move. Two men awaited him in the office. One was Director Kalald Strey'mend.

The other man was Cero Feyblade, the Silver Prince, owner and creator of Silverline Power Cooperative.

CHAPTER 3

Alistar collected himself as best he could and bowed. "Your Highness. Director."

"Associate De'seneth," Director Strey'mend responded. "Come in."

"Thank you, sir." Alistar approached the desk and stood beside the plush chair. Both the Director and the Silver Prince remained standing.

Prince Cero's blue-gray eyes studied Alistar. The Silver Prince stood even with Alistar's nearly six feet. His hair had, supposedly, turned white in his childhood. Rumors claimed that his servants wove precisely two hundred and seventeen strands of silver thread into his hair every day. As rumors also claimed he maintained his vigor by feasting on the heart of a unicorn under the new moon, Alistar gave them little credence. In the Silver Prince's younger years, he was said to have been a skilled duelist. Now, nearing one hundred and forty years, he was still lean, and none would dare call him feeble, but he showed his age. The lines on his face and the set of his jaw gave him a stern air, and he carried himself with the unconscious poise of a man who knew himself to be superior to everyone around him—a fact that he assumed would be respected. He wore a black silkweave shirt, the collar rising to rest against his neck. His overjacket hung to mid-thigh, emerald green with panels of white and black trim. The clothing looked almost underwhelming on a man of his status—at least unless one knew that the clusters of delicate silver pearls that made the jacket buttons only came from a single island in the far south, and the number of them on the jacket represented at least two full seasons' harvests. Or one noticed the silver embroidery and the emeralds stitched into the cloth. He wore wyvern hide gloves, either dyed silver or made from the hide of one of the particularly rare silver variety.

The prince spoke. "Alistar De'seneth, Associate Third Degree. Director Strey'mend has spoken well of you."

"I… am honored, Your Highness," Alistar responded. *Why is the Silver Prince here? What is this about?*

"Of course, I would expect no less from a man of your lineage," Prince Cero continued.

Alistar's shoulders tensed and his voice tightened. "Is there some problem involving my family, Your Highness?"

"None have come to my attention. Since you went to such lengths to avoid tying your career to your family name, I have respected your family's evident wishes on the matter." Prince Cero continued to study Alistar. "As I have heard no reports of any falling out between you and your family, I was surprised when I learned, some months after the fact, that the heir to the As'enel house had left the family privateering fleet to become an engineer in my employ under an assumed name."

"De'seneth is my matronym," Alistar corrected. The Silver Prince's eyes narrowed in slight irritation at the implication that his information was not complete. "Given the reputation of my patronym, using a less known name has allowed me to better maintain my family's policy of non-involvement in Lewarden's court, Your Highness."

"Indeed—a policy you have maintained quite well, De'seneth,"

Prince Cero agreed. He leaned forward. "Director Strey'mend told me that you are aware that failures on the mahiy lines have taken place in Lewarden."

"Yes, sir," Alistar agreed cautiously. "Last night one occurred outside my home on Shale Lane." He caught himself toying uneasily with his watch chain.

"Given the recent protests and unrest regarding Silverline Power, we have been working to prevent word of these incidents from becoming widespread. However, that does not address the true task at hand: finding the cause." The Silver Prince sat in Director Strey'mend's chair, resting his elbows on the desk. "I have suspicions as to the source. Sit, De'seneth."

Alistar sank into the chair. "You do, sir? Then we have a solution to the problem?"

"Not so easily, no. If this were simply a failure of the mahiy lines or unstable growth, even a flaw in my design, I would have only to purge it and begin repairs. Time-consuming and costly, but straightforward. No, these problems are not natural outgrowths of the lines. You studied at Treanthlor Academy, De'seneth. Mahiy line theory is a required course—I designed the curriculum. You should know that a natural failure manifests certain signs—fluctuations, widespread loss of magic. Such failures ripple across the system; they do not remain confined to every line in two or three blocks."

The Silver Prince presented the matter like a logic problem. Alistar compared it to the theory he'd learned. "A talented channeler, or a group of them working in concert, could do so. Possibly also a high-powered unregistered device."

"Precisely." Prince Cero nodded curtly. "Someone is stealing great quantities of power from me. Their goal remains to be seen, but I have suspicions."

His pause was clearly meant as an invitation for Alistar to ask about those suspicions, and he complied. "What do you believe the thief or thieves want, Your Highness?"

"They want to see Silverline Power fall." The Silver Prince's voice was cold and hard.

Alistar rocked back in his chair as if shocked by a bolt of lightning. "Silverline Power?" he repeated weakly.

"My creation of this company was not welcomed by everyone, De'seneth," Prince Cero said, a fact that Alistar already knew. "It is no secret that I have enemies, and there are many who resent my control over the mahiy lines, especially among the highbloods. There have been petitions laid before His Majesty many times demanding that I release the monopoly on magic generation in Lewarden."

Alistar frowned. He had heard of the last such attempt, two years ago. The newsrags had been gleeful in their posting of King Suleton's answer: "If you wish to compete with Silverline Power, you have only to found your own generators and mahiy lines." Since anyone who understood the particular fluctuations and energies that generated magic already worked for Silverline Power, the answer had both the appearance of agreement and an air of mockery wrapped together.

The prince continued, "They have finally accepted that they will not wrest my work from me by open confrontation, so now they resort to sabotage."

"You suspect one of the noble houses, Your Highness?" Alistar asked, taking the pause to mean he could speak.

"At least one, perhaps several in concert. I have little trust that any of them would give up an opportunity if they thought the reward enough to offset the risk—even those who present themselves as allies."

Alistar nodded slowly.

"You worked on the investigation of the fire at Jalsine Automaton Factory. Your reports were thorough and complete, De'seneth. I also noticed that you were not intimidated by threats that drove away senior engineers," Prince Cero said. "Your work most certainly earned you the promotion from Second Degree to Third."

The factory fire, compounded by catastrophic failure of the fire suppression system, had been the incident that first incited protesters to gather outside Silverline Power's gates. Even though the company had been cleared of any fault, and the investigation pointed to sabotage rather than any problem with the mahiy lines, the scandal rags had rapidly perpetuated the myth that Silverline Power bore some responsibility for the deaths and injuries. Lacking any other solid target, the public had fixated on Silverline Power.

Alistar nodded again. "I try to do whatever task I am assigned to the best of my abilities, Your Highness, regardless of politics."

"Indeed. Your family's deliberate non-involvement in court politics is refreshing. Your dedication and neutrality are the reasons I have chosen to assign you to the investigation of these incidents."

Alistar jerked up straight in his seat. If he had not been sitting, he was sure he would have found himself on the floor. "What?"

The Silver Prince didn't blink at Alistar's startled and entirely improper exclamation. "Your only possible alliance is to a minor branch of a house in the western mountains, and while I do not completely discount involvement from the wildlands, I've deemed it unlikely, given their need for reliable light. I need someone who will look at all suspects with equal suspicion, not favoring one house over another. And I need someone who is qualified to analyze the results of the reports we receive from the monitor gargoyles regarding the outages. You fit those qualifications well, De'seneth, and you come with Director Strey'mend's recommendation."

"I…" Alistar fumbled for words. He took a deep breath, collecting himself with an effort. "Your Highness, are you tasking me with the overall investigation of this issue, or specifically with seeking signs that this is a political attack and discovering who might be involved?"

Prince Cero gave him a long, unreadable look. "I expect you to find the evidence and follow that evidence in whatever directions it leads. Even into the houses and gatherings of the nobility, if necessary." He raised a hand to forestall objections. "I respect your family's position, De'seneth. I do not expect you to begin forming ties within the court. However, if you present yourself as potentially being open to such, I suspect far more doors will open to you."

Blood and sand. You want me to be bait. Alistar ran his watch chain between his fingers. "Your Highness, this is an enormous undertaking for one man."

"You will have whatever resources you need for the task, De'seneth." Prince Cero drew a purse from his coat and set it on the desk with a clink of ivory marks, then set a silver-colored badge on top of it, sliding both to Alistar. Alistar hesitantly picked up the badge. The metal was too heavy to be silver, and it was cast in the image of a blooming kurowa blossom wreathed in fire—the Silver Prince's personal emblem.

A man bearing this badge could requisition any items he might need, with the understanding that compensation would be paid by the prince. He could gain access to places restricted even to most nobility. He could ask prying questions of nobles and expect answers. A man bearing this badge was a representative of the Silver Prince, and it could be assumed that anything he said came with the prince's backing, and anything said to him would reach the prince's ear. But a man displaying such a badge would not be subtle, or find it easy to make himself appear to be corruptible.

When he said I would have whatever resources I need, I didn't realize he meant he was granting me full access to the resources of his estate.

"Use my symbol as you see fit, De'seneth," Prince Cero told him. "As for your need for assistance, I have a solution. I do realize that few of my employees have experience or expertise in theft and sabotage of this nature. You will need the service of someone who does."

Alistar sat straighter in his chair. "Please excuse my asking, Your Highness, but if someone within Silverline Power is an expert in these matters, why do you need me as part of the investigation? I don't know what I could add."

"The expert is not in my employ, De'seneth. You are familiar with the name 'Tiyron Onyxflame'?"

Anyone in Silverline Power who was *not* familiar with that name had to be living under a rock. Onyxflame was one of the most notorious elven criminals of recent history, accused of countless charges of theft and extortion. Many of his crimes had targeted Silverline Power in particular. "Of course, Your Highness. You... intend to recruit him somehow? Does anyone even know how to find him? I've not heard reports of activity from him in months."

"No one has heard reports of his activities because Tiyron Onyxflame currently resides in Chirrod Prison, De'seneth. He was apprehended and sentenced this summer. His Majesty chose to keep the trial closed from the public to avoid inciting the protesters further," Prince Cero said.

Alistar absorbed the information in silence. Given the public opinion against Silverline Power the previous summer, sympathies could easily have been incited in favor of Onyxflame, and a trial could have led to rioting if someone applied pressure in the right ways. That didn't make the thought of secret trials any more palatable.

Prince Cero continued, "Onyxflame has the knowledge to understand how these thefts can be conducted, and perhaps who could perform them. I doubt he will be eager to cooperate without convincing." He nodded to the badge. "With my blessings, you are authorized to issue any punishment short of death, or any reward, even up to a promise of release once the investigation is complete, if necessary. Do what you must to ensure his assistance and cooperation."

"Yes sir," Alistar said, though his gut was tying into knots.

"I have sent word to Warden Mon'serrat at Chirrod Prison. He will release Onyxflame into your custody," Prince Cero told him. "Tomorrow, a carriage will take you there with an escort of guards."

There would be no arguing. The Silver Prince had made his decree, and now it was up to Alistar to find a way to make it work. "I will look for them first thing in the morning, sir."

"Good. I expect regular updates on the status of your work," Prince Cero continued. "Deliver them to Director Strey'mend unless you deem a matter worth my immediate attention." His eyes held Alistar's. "And if a matter *does* require my immediate attention, I expect you to make certain that it reaches me. The Director and any of my guards stationed here will know the proper channels for you to use."

"Yes sir," Alistar repeated. *He is granting me access to speak to him directly? At any time I have something of importance to tell him? Not only that I have access, but that he expects me to use it and will be displeased if I do not do so.*

Sobering and intimidating thoughts, in all honesty. The Silver Prince was one of the most important men in all of Lewarden, perhaps in all of Calarand. Only his brother the king held more power.

Prince Cero's eyes narrowed and he leaned forward. "I have no doubt you will encounter many who will obfuscate, lie, or simply pass on baseless hearsay. The As'enel heir should be capable of sorting the gems from the slag of court talk and of telling sabotage from accident. If you are not, I strongly question whether there is a place for you in this organization."

Alistar stiffened, then inclined his head in a small, polite nod.

Prince Cero rose, and Alistar pushed to his feet. The prince turned to Director Strey'mend. "I leave the rest of the details in your hands."

"Yes, Your Highness," Director Strey'mend responded, bowing.

Prince Cero retrieved his polished ivory walking cane. Once more the gray-blue eyes fixed on Alistar. "I look forward to your success, De'seneth."

"Your Highness." Alistar bowed deeply.

The Silver Prince nodded curtly and crossed the room. When he opened the door, the guards snapped to attention with a clatter of armor and weapons. Prince Cero swept out of the room, and the door closed behind him. Alistar stared after him, trying to force his thoughts to work properly.

"Why don't you take the rest of the day off, De'seneth?" Director Strey'mend suggested, not unkindly. "Let your head clear a little. You're likely to be very busy for quite a while."

"Yes," Alistar agreed. "Thank you, sir."

"I would not have recommended you for this task if I didn't think you capable of completing it, De'seneth. I hope that you will not prove me wrong."

"Yes sir," Alistar said quietly. "I hope the same."

My neck is not the only one on the line here. If His Highness is right, the entire city may be in danger.

CHAPTER 4

A listar stopped by his desk briefly, then locked the drawers. No one commented on him leaving early. Every one of them did so on occasion, and it was an unspoken rule that so long as no one began to abuse the opportunity, their colleagues wouldn't mention it. Lamorage gave Alistar a curious look, and Alistar stopped by his desk.

"I'm on a new project, and I'll likely be in and out of the office a lot. Don't know if I'll be in tomorrow or not, but probably not."

"Ahh!" Lamorage relaxed. "Field work in this weather? I don't envy you *that*, but if the director gave you a special assignment, congratulations—you're moving up."

"Only if I don't completely mess this one up!" Alistar replied with more levity than he felt.

"You'll be fine!" Lamorage assured him. "It's surely not *that* bad. Couldn't be worse than the fire investigation."

Alistar smiled, knowing he could not tell his friend that it *was*, in fact, "that bad," and appreciating the vote of confidence. "Well, if it is, maybe I'll see another promotion."

Lamorage raised an eyebrow and chuckled. "If you can move

from Second Degree to Fourth in a year, De'seneth, you'll put us all to shame."

Retrieving coat and hat, Alistar left Silverline Power by the side exit. The numbers of protesters across from the front gate continued to dwindle; now only a handful stood in a clump. Even as he watched, someone left, hunching in their coat against the wind.

Alistar flagged down a carriage. The driver was bundled to his beard, but he had a cheerful, gap-toothed grin. "Where to, mate?"

"Shale Lane," Alistar told him.

"Be there in three shakes of a wyvern's tail!"

As Alistar settled on the bench, the carriage rattled into motion. The streets were crowded as usual, but the driver seemed skilled at finding the gaps and squeezing through them, bringing Alistar home faster than usual.

"Which house?" the man called, slowing his team to walk up the street.

"712," Alistar said. "And if you will wait, I only need a moment, then I need another ride."

"At your service, sir!" The driver pulled to a stop at Alistar's house, then hopped down to open the carriage door. Alistar handed him six chips and ran up the five steps to his door.

"Mr. De'seneth? You're home early," Mrs. Ke'lyn said in surprise, turning from her dusting of the parlor.

"The Director gave me the rest of the afternoon off, but I'm only in for a moment," he told her. "No need to worry about dinner this evening."

"Ah. You're going calling on Miss Tan'shyo." The housekeeper gave him a knowing smile. "Have a good evening, then, Mr. De'seneth."

Alistar grinned like a schoolboy, then took the stairs two at a time. He dropped his satchel on his study chair. As he left the room, he pulled the door shut, whispering a quick incantation to bind the lock. At the top of the stairs, he paused, thinking about the task he'd been assigned. The implication of Prince Cero's words had been that Tiyron Onyxflame would be his responsibility for the duration of the investigation. And that meant that the criminal would need to be housed with him under some form of house arrest.

He spun a quick story through his mind as he descended the steps. "Mrs. Ke'lyn? I am probably going to have a guest, perhaps arriving tomorrow. I'm sorry for the short notice; I just received word today."

"Oh! A guest? How delightful! I'll prepare the guest room first thing tomorrow."

"Thank you so much. You are a wonder, Mrs. Ke'lyn."

The driver and carriage still waited when Alistar came outside, the horses nibbling on straw the driver offered them. "All set, mate?" the driver asked.

"I am. Thank you for waiting."

"Not a worry, mate. Where to now?"

Alistar answered without hesitation. "Coiled Dragon Clinic, on Redstone Street."

"Aye, I know the place. Most everyone who lives on my end of town knows the place. Hop on in, we'll have you there quick enough."

Most "respectable" men sought a healer rather than a doctor when they needed care. And even those who did visit a doctor didn't go into the poor part of the city to find one. Alistar's first visit to the Coiled Dragon Clinic had been one of necessity, though. While a newcomer to the city, he'd fallen ill from eating something bought from a street vendor. A stranger had helped him to the clinic, perhaps thinking Alistar one of the transients who drifted up the river alongside the boats. Alistar's first meeting with Nurse Saskia Tan'shyo had not been what he would have hoped, with Alistar feverish and on the verge of retching, but he had at least managed not to leave the lovely lady with a horrible first impression.

After recovering, Alistar had returned to the clinic to settle his bill. He learned *that* act left an impression far more favorable than the first. Saskia's father, Doctor Tan'shyo, had easily recognized Alistar as a misplaced upperclass man or noble rather than one of the impoverished patients he normally saw. The doctor had not, however, expected Alistar to actually return and settle his bill. Doctor Tan'shyo had no way of knowing where Alistar lived or how to send a bill to him, and it seemed that similar situations happened enough at the clinic that the doctor simply wrote off the occasional incident as debt that would never be collected. To Alistar, the idea that he could have simply vanished without repaying his debts went against every value his family instilled in him, and he had been shocked to discover that his return had not been expected.

Of course, if he had not returned to pay his bill, he would not have had another chance to see the doctor's lovely daughter, grown to know her better, or eventually propose to her.

The carriage rumbled to a stop, pulling him from his thoughts. The driver opened the door for Alistar. "Coiled Dragon Clinic, mate. That'll be three chips."

Alistar fished through his purse and pulled out an ivory half-mark. Marks eventually wore down to half-marks, then chips—it was simply the nature of the ivory currency. "Thank you, friend." Alistar handed the driver his payment.

The driver tipped his hat. "Always a pleasure, mate."

Alistar climbed down to the street and shivered, then hurried to the door. When he opened it, he heard a soft chime of bells. A few people huddled around the waiting room: a mother cradling her sniffling child, a bearded man of indeterminable age rocking and humming to himself, and a young street hooligan with a bandaged arm, who kept glancing sharply around the room as if daring anyone to demand an explanation for his presence. The hooligan glowered at Alistar, a look he received often enough from the protesters that he was immune to its attempted intimidation.

Doctor Tan'shyo hurried around the partition, wiping his hands on a cloth. "Please have a seat, I will be with you in a mome... Oh, Mr. De'seneth." He looked both surprised and genuinely pleased to see Alistar. The doctor was human, with short, slick black hair. Tall and lanky, he seemed to be constantly in motion, moving with boundless energy even after the longest day. Saskia said that he could practically eat his own weight in a meal, and Alistar could believe it. In fact, he thought the doctor practically had to in order to maintain his constant high energy.

"Good afternoon, Doctor Tan'shyo," Alistar greeted him. "I can see you have patients—I'll wait."

"I'll tell my daughter that you're here. Pardon me; she's assisting a patient."

"Of course." Alistar picked a chair and sat. The waiting room was clean, and the seats, if plain, were solid and sturdy. The air smelled of sharp chemicals that even the best freshening spell would struggle to mask.

After several minutes, Saskia stepped around the partition. She nodded to the young hooligan, signifying that he was the next patient. As the young man stood, Saskia looked to Alistar and a warm smile lit her face as a flush of color rose in her cheeks to complement her strawberry blond curls. He smiled back. She was beautiful, as always, with hints of makeup around her ever-so-slightly slanted eyes and brightening her red lips. Her dress was light green, of course, as all the nurses wore, with long sleeves that buttoned snugly just above her wrists.

Saskia vanished again, leaving Alistar with a pleasant glow of contentment in her wake. He hoped that the patients would be simple to care for and that she would be able to leave early. Doctor Tan'shyo tended to be lenient when Alistar came by in any case.

After the hooligan, the mother and child were called back.

Alistar relaxed, taking reassurance in the fact that no one else had come since his arrival. It seemed an auspicious sign.

He jumped when the door slammed open. Three men rushed inside, carrying a fourth between them. All were ragged, stinking of the streets, their hair matted and unwashed. The wild-eyed leader looked frantically around the room.

"Doctor! Doctor!" He looked at Alistar. "You ain't the doctor. Who are you? Where's Doctor Tan'shyo?!"

Doctor Tan'shyo hurried into the waiting room. "What's wrong? Who's hurt?"

"Doctor! It's Grenny, sir! He's sick! Fell over and started foaming and jerking all over the place!"

Doctor Tan'shyo's face paled, but his voice was firm. "Bring him back here. Mr. De'seneth, I hate to impose on you, but I may need your assistance to hold this man still."

Alistar stood quickly. "Of course." He felt tension surge through the air with this new arrival. He followed the grungy men as they carried their fellow around the partition and into the infirmary.

"Lay him here," Doctor Tan'shyo instructed, indicating a neatly made bed.

The patient moaned and thrashed as his companions lay him on the bed. His eyes were open wide, the pupils huge. Foam and spittle flecked his beard. His hands curled like claws, seeming locked into the position. His companions stood anxiously, unsure what to do, waiting for the doctor to perform a miracle.

Saskia was finishing with the little boy and his mother, but her back was tense, and Alistar thought she hurried, rushing them out of the clinic. The boy kept staring at the convulsing man, eyes big as saucers. Doctor Tan'shyo pulled a curtain between the beds, cutting off Alistar's view of the child and Saskia.

"Is your friend an elf?" Doctor Tan'shyo asked. The sick man jerked, tossing too much to be able to easily tell his race.

"No sir, he's human like us," one of the men quickly assured him.

"Good. I need you to get him out of his clothes so I can examine him."

The elven taboo against nudity was so great that even a doctor had to take precautions to avoid treading on sensibilities, though exceptions were grudgingly granted in life-or-death situations if there was no healing magic near at hand. The street men felt none of that hesitation, obviously, and began helping their companion out of his heavy, worn coat, then his shirt. A lump of horror settled in Alistar's gut. Black patches spread across the man's skin like ink spilling across a page, and around the edges of the black splotches, boils and sores formed.

Grenny shrieked as the men undressed him, and he flailed wildly at them. Alistar grabbed one of his arms and pinned it down on the bed. The skin was hot, slick with sweat. Grenny tried to pull away, and his strength surprised Alistar, who struggled to hold his arm still.

"That will be sufficient. Now, each of you take a limb, please," Doctor Tan'shyo ordered. "Hold him as still as possible."

"Is he going to be all right, Doctor?" asked one of the men anxiously.

"I don't know. He might—some have pulled through."

The doctor's words surprised Alistar. *He's seen this before? What is causing this? This man looks like something is eating him from inside.*

The other men looked at each other anxiously, but they took hold of Grenny's free arm and his legs. Grenny screamed as if someone stabbed him; wide, wild eyes fixed on something that only he could see. Sweat streamed down his face and soaked his skin. His mouth formed words, but they were so jumbled that nothing made sense. Spittle trickled from his mouth, then Alistar saw flecks of blood on the man's beard.

"Keep away from me!" Grenny shrieked, the first of his words to make sense. "You can't devour me! I am Ardum, Conqueror of the Six Heavens!"

"Delusions," Doctor Tan'shyo said quietly. Alistar barely heard him under Grenny's ranting. "He's near the end."

Alistar saw sorrow in the doctor's eyes, and he didn't need to ask what "the end" meant. Blood ran from Grenny's nose in a steady stream and bubbled at the corners of his mouth. The doctor tried to pour a dose of medicine into the raving man's mouth, but it dribbled out again as Grenny began to hack. All across Grenny's chest, the boils swelled and began to burst, releasing a stench of rotting flesh. Alistar made a sound of horror and disgust. He let go of Grenny's arm with one hand and covered his mouth and nose with a handkerchief, feeling the bile rise in his throat.

"Let go of him," Doctor Tan'shyo said. "I'm sorry, there is nothing more I can do for him now."

"But..." one of the men began, hesitant, and keeping his hold on Grenny's other arm. "But Doctor..."

Grenny jerked, released a gurgling scream, then fell still, eyes open and staring, face locked in a twisted cry of agony.

Doctor Tan'shyo bowed his head and closed his eyes. "Lord Starbinder, have mercy upon this man, and grant his soul peace in death. Carry him to your hallowed halls, where he shall dwell forevermore."

The other men, Alistar included, quickly bowed their heads with a murmured chorus of "And may it ever be so."

Doctor Tan'shyo closed the dead man's eyes, then pulled a sheet over the body, giving Grenny an illusion of restful repose instead of twisted agony. Grenny's companions didn't say anything, only stood with bowed heads.

"I will see him laid to rest in Planter's Field, unless you wish to bury him elsewhere," Doctor Tan'shyo told them.

One of the men jerked his head in a nod. "Grenny always hoped to be buried there, sir. Would be kind of you to do so."

"Will you want to attend the burial?"

All three shook their heads. "No, sir."

The rapid transition from death to discussion of burial rushed over Alistar like a runaway carriage, too abrupt, too sharp, but the men seemed accepting of it. Their friend was dead, and they wished only to be done and away from the specter that followed. The men dug in their pockets and found a nub of an ivory chip apiece. They laid the chips on Grenny's shrouded forehead, then turned and shuffled out.

Doctor Tan'shyo gazed down at the covered body for several minutes before speaking again. "You had best wash, Mr. De'seneth. I'm not yet sure how this disease travels."

With that, he pushed open the curtain and strode to the wash basin. Alistar followed, numb. Not until he had shoved up his sleeves and scrubbed his hands and arms nearly up to his elbows, trying to wash away the sensation of the dying man's skin, did he ask, "Disease?"

Saskia offered him a towel. "This is the eighth case we have seen so far. All but one have been fatal, and even the one who lived may never fully recover. We've begun calling it Rat's Disease."

"It seems confined to the poorest people of the city, so far," Doctor Tan'shyo said. "It's a horrible, horrible fate for any living creature to suffer. The only mercy I can see is that it's swift, rarely more than an hour between the onset and the end. But that hour is one of terrible agony. This disease… because I don't know what else to call it… devours the victim's body from within. If I were to perform an autopsy on Grenny right now, we would find almost nothing left of his lungs, heart, or gut. Only a vile sludge mixed with blood and the juices of his stomach." The doctor's face was pale as he spoke.

Alistar couldn't speak for several moments, too horrified by the thought. "This… Rat's Disease. You don't know what's causing it? Or where it came from?"

"No, not yet." Doctor Tan'shyo closed his eyes. "I wish to all the gods that I did, Mr. De'seneth. But I cannot find a connection between the patients I have seen. If it were a normal illness, I would expect his three companions to begin showing symptoms after being exposed. But... so far only two of those who have brought in victims have been struck themselves, and them shortly after the deaths of those first victims." He sank down in a chair. "I would think it a poison of some sort, but I've found no traces of that either."

"Is there anything I can do?" Alistar asked.

The doctor shook his head. "No. Only keep this to yourself, please. If rumor of a disease begins, there will be no stopping it, and that can only lead to panic. I've seen such things before. The panic kills more people than the disease itself will. People suspect one another, people seek a target. And there is just enough unrest, and fear, that I think some would turn to your employer as that target."

"What?" Alistar said in disbelief. "People would think that Silverline Power is somehow responsible for a disease?" *How can I keep this a secret? If there is an outbreak of a disease in the city, someone must be told, so that it can be contained. Haven't I been given enough secrets to carry for one day?*

"Some people would. Some would just be carried along in search of anyone to blame. It would be chaos." Doctor Tan'shyo shook his head. "Until we understand how this is spreading, and where it has come from, we need to limit how far word of it moves. It could be something as basic as a contaminated food supply, some poison accidentally released from an alchemical laboratory." He looked at Alistar's face. "Do not think I am attempting to conceal this entirely, Mr. De'seneth. All the cases that I have seen, and the handful that other clinics have had, we are reporting to the apothecary and surgeons' guild. Already they are working on medicines to treat cases, though so far they have had little success. It is the panic that I wish to avoid. Frightened people take foolish actions, and they can cause more harm and death than any outbreak. I have seen it before—I don't wish to see it again."

Alistar nodded slowly. "How many people have died in total from it?"

"Our poor friend Grenny here makes eighteen reported cases. It's possible that others have died on the streets without us knowing the cause."

"How many does it take for something like this to be labeled as an outbreak by the guild?" Alistar asked. The number wasn't large, really—not compared to the regular numbers of deaths among the vagrants and beggars, but it was unsettling.

"At least twenty-five." Doctor Tan'shyo let out a slow, deep breath. "There is something you can do for me, Mr. De'seneth."

"What is that?" Alistar asked.

"You can escort Saskia safely home. I must finish attending to matters here, but it is not work for a lady."

"Father, there's no need to send me home because of another victim of Rat's Disease," Saskia protested sharply. "I am no fainting *dreesha*."

"No, but you have a gentleman who would very much like some time with you, even if you do not need the smelling salts and a shoulder to weep on," the doctor replied. "I am certain that Mr. De'seneth would like some fresh air as well. He is looking a little green himself."

"I'm fine," Alistar said quickly—perhaps a little too quickly, given that his gut still twisted and churned.

"Oh. Oh! Alistar, I'm sorry!" Saskia said quickly, her eyes opening a little wider.

"It's all right," Alistar said, the heat of embarrassment spreading across his face. Still, he avoided looking to the shrouded body on the bed, and was grateful that the harsh odor of the chemicals in the air covered the stench that had burst from Grenny's sores.

Saskia found her coat and hat, though her expression was still troubled and her eyes guilty over leaving. Doctor Tan'shyo would hear no protests, though, and Alistar was glad—he longed to be away from the death before he thought too much on the symptoms the doctor had described.

Outside, the city was normal. Carriages clattered past, beggars called for alms, vendors hawked their wares. Inside the clinic, a man had died, but outside, people didn't know and didn't concern themselves enough with the plight of one vagrant to care. Beside Alistar, Saskia shivered, threading her hand through his offered arm and walking close to him. The winter chill somehow was more bearable with her at his side.

"Are you all right?" Alistar asked quietly, his breath rising in a cloud.

"I hate it when people die," she said as softly. "It always makes me feel like Kalyp is taunting me, like he's laughing at our efforts to save them." Her gloved fingers sketched a sign of protection in the air.

"This disease... it sounds like anyone who contracts it, there's nothing you can do," Alistar said, unsure what reassurance he could offer when his beloved was invoking the name of the god of pestilence.

"If Rodos had not left the clinic, or we had someone else who could use healing magic, maybe we could," she responded.

Alistar rested his hand on hers. "Rodos was a foul, selfish groper who couldn't bandage a hangnail. He had some healing magic, I know, but from all you told me, that was his one and only redeeming quality."

"On a day like this, I start to think that one quality might have been enough to make up for the rest."

Alistar shook his head sharply. "No. Your father was right to dismiss him. I don't want to imagine what might have happened if you hadn't walked in when he was 'attending' that girl."

Saskia nodded finally. "I know. Still, if we had someone with healing magic, then maybe… maybe we could save these people." She let out a long breath, and it danced in the air. "We can make so many tools and machines that can mimic the work of a channeler. You'd think someone would figure out how to make one that mimics a healer's abilities."

Alistar nodded silently. Only a small percentage of people could draw power directly from the mahiy lines and bend it according to their natural inclinations. Healing was, fortunately, one of the more common manifestations of a channeler's ability, but even so, healers were not common.

They turned onto another, busier street. The mahiy lines glowed overhead, and the street lamps shone with ghostlight, casting illumination without heat. Alistar looked at the lamps as they passed.

"What's on your mind, Alistar?" Saskia asked.

"In Rillwater, we still use oil lights for the street lamps. Less dependable, and they can burn out if not tended properly, but on a night like this, they are little bursts of warmth along the street, and people hurry between them just to get to the next one. Sometimes these lights just feel so cold." The words conjured memories of his home city, of cold nights spent with his siblings, returning home after an evening spent in the taverns celebrating another successful voyage with their father's or mother's crew.

"I know. It's strange to think that the same power gives us heat in our homes, gives us light, gives us so many things that we used to rely on oil for." Saskia shook her head. "We would be lost without it."

"We would," Alistar agreed.

They kept walking. When he had first headed over to Coiled Dragon Clinic, he'd thought to invite Saskia to a show, but that seemed wrong now. He'd lost his interest in attending some comedic play, and he didn't think Saskia would enjoy it right now either. Instead, Alistar guided their walk to a tea house. Inside was warm and quiet, with a bard playing quietly in one corner.

The air smelled of wood smoke and tea. As they found seats at one of the small, intimate tables, a server came to take their orders before vanishing into the mysterious depths of the kitchen.

Once they had mugs of steaming tea and bowls of hot squash soup, Alistar said, "I have a new assignment—an important one. I can't talk about the details, but if I can complete it, well… I could get a promotion." *And if I fail…*

Saskia's smile lit the room, his news banishing some of the lingering sadness. "Really? Oh, Alistar, that's wonderful!"

"I don't know how much free time I'll have," he warned. "It's hard to say, and I don't even know how long it will take to complete. The situation is complicated and very politically charged."

She nodded slowly. "So, it might be a while before we have much time together."

"You know that's not what I want," Alistar said quickly.

"Of course. It's not what either of us wants. But it is what we must do, for now." She sipped her tea and closed her eyes, savoring the warmth. "Are you worried about the project?"

"I am," he admitted. "I won't be working on it alone, but I've been given leadership of my part."

Saskia smiled at him. "That's wonderful, Alistar. You have the skill to solve any problem."

"I hope so," Alistar replied, smiling in a show of confidence that he didn't feel.

If I fail, I go home in disgrace. I admit that I was wrong, I leave my love of engineering behind, and I set sail. His gaze moved to the lights glowing around the tea house. *If I fail, what happens to Lewarden? The city relies on the mahiy lines. If the web breaks, there won't be a rival company providing magic—there will just be chaos. And these people don't have anywhere else to go.*

As the evening grew late, Alistar and Saskia talked of other things, sipping their teas and listening to the music. Finally,

Alistar walked her home. As he bid her goodnight, he raised Saskia's hand to his lips and bowed.

"I dream of the days when our time will be our own, and I do not have to leave you," he said softly, quoting from "The Dragon's Harvest."

"May that day come on wings swifter than the soaring falcon," she replied. "Good night, Alistar. I hope I will see you soon. At devotions, at the very least."

"Good night, Saskia. I hope so as well."

She opened the door and stepped inside. Alistar dipped one final bow, then turned to call a carriage and return home alone.

CHAPTER 5

Unlike the taxi coaches Alistar was accustomed to, the carriage provided by the Silver Prince was a thing of luxury. The ride was smooth even over the roughest streets and roads. A pair of horse automatons drew the carriage, moving with an even, untiring gait. Inside, the plush, padded seats were spacious enough that a passenger could lie down for a nap without feeling cramped. A side bench held a chiller with a bottle of wine and a tray of candied fruit, lacking only the valet to serve refreshments.

The carriage could have carried six comfortably, but Alistar had only two companions, a pair of elves from His Highness's personal guard. Neither demonstrated an inclination to idle banter. The taller of the two, Dahr, had given their names when escorting Alistar to the carriage, and the other, Voit, had not spoken at all. In the absence of conversation, Alistar began to read the thick packet of information on his seat.

The first few pages provided an overview of Tiyron Onyxflame's known criminal career. The impressive list ranged from burglary to industrial sabotage, with some suspicions of smuggling thrown in. The latter half of the list indicated that his interests had focused primarily on Silverline Power—causing disruptions and stealing magic. Alistar's brow furrowed. Allegations clearly indicated that Onyxflame had successfully stolen magic from the mahiy lines or generators, even noting that he had acknowledged the thefts during his trial, but Alistar found several noteworthy absences in the information.

"How did he actually steal magic? And what in Rechmal's Beard did he *do* with it?" he asked of no one in particular.

Dahr and Voit both shifted uncomfortably. "If you are able to determine the answers to either of those questions, sir, His Highness will be most appreciative," Dahr said.

Alistar started. "Are you saying that even the Silver Prince doesn't know?"

"Onyxflame has been extremely reticent to share any details of his work. When he was discovered, he was working on some manner of device, but succeeded in destroying it before his capture. If he kept notes, they were lost as well."

"So Onyxflame is an artificer as well?" Alistar asked.

"Unknown," Dahr told him. "No records of him receiving formal education, but he could be self-taught."

Alistar shook his head, looking at the summary again. "When did he have *time?*"

"I am afraid that is another matter on which he has been reticent to expound, sir," Dahr said.

Dahr seems well-informed about this situation. I should take advantage of his knowledge while I can. "Is there anything he *is* willing to talk about?" Alistar asked.

"I understand he's quite eloquent on his opinions of His Highness and the nobility as a whole," Dahr said in a flat, even voice.

Well, isn't that encouraging?

The next page provided a physical description of Onyxflame. At five foot nine, he was on the short side for an elf. Brown hair, black eyes, forty-two years old. Alistar skimmed the details until he saw mention of two long scars across Onyxflame's chest. The description sounded like results from a knife fight, but that wasn't what caught Alistar's notice.

"Who provided the description of the scars?" he asked. "Chirrod Prison?"

Both guards shifted uncomfortably at the mention, however obliquely, of the taboo subject of exposed skin. "No sir," Dahr said. "Two years ago, Onyxflame signed on for a brief stint as a sailor on a Narnan merchant ship. His reasons remain unknown, though smuggling is the suspicion. To better fit in, he evidently adopted their obscene standards while aboard. An agent of the Crown observed and provided the description."

Alistar bit his tongue to avoid responding to the "obscene" comment. Many Rillwater privateers went shirtless aboard ship, though they usually put something on once they came to port.

He flipped through the rest of the documents. His attention caught when he saw a reference to his home city of Rillwater, followed by a name he didn't recognize, on official-looking identification papers. He extracted the papers and read them over. They identified one Lord Taslor Aspendark as a resident of Rillwater, owner of several warehouses on the docks. At least whoever had put the papers together had the decency to invent false warehouses as well, rather than attributing existing ones to the persona.

A second set of papers instead identified Aspendark as a commoner employed as a servant, still from Rillwater. Alistar considered the two sets, then looked to Dahr again. "So, Onyxflame is either supposed to be a fellow noble, or my manservant?"

"Yes sir," Dahr responded. "His Highness trusts you to decide which will better suit your task."

Alistar nodded slowly, then put away the papers. "Well, since he's sailed before, he should at least know the jargon well enough to pass for a resident of Rillwater." He gazed out the window as they finally neared their destination.

Chirrod Prison was a grim, looming building of gray stone sitting at the bottom of a ravine three hours outside of Lewarden. The canyon walls were sheer and high, not even home to scrub brush. Birds, reportedly, had trouble finding ledges large enough to nest. The ravine had been carved by a sweep of magic, slicing the gouge into the earth, polishing the sides and ground smooth, then etching a narrow road down one side. If a prisoner managed to somehow escape from their cell, then also from the prison complex, they still faced those smooth walls, with barely a shadow to hide in and only the single road leading out, and relentless hounds on their heels. Even if they had natural talent as a channeler, magic dampeners were locked around each prisoner's neck, wrists, and ankles, preventing them from drawing power from the mahiy lines. Supposedly, dampeners even limited how well devices powered by magic would respond to them. A prisoner had to somehow find a means of getting past all of those barriers without being caught.

So far as Alistar knew, no one had succeeded.

He gazed at the prison through the carriage window, preferring to look at the structure instead of the long drop that awaited if the carriage slipped off the narrow road. Alistar breathed a silent sigh of relief when they finally attained level ground. The carriage rolled up to the prison gates, and the driver conferred with the guards there. Alistar sat nervously. He had never approached Chirrod Prison before, and had never thought he would have need to do so. Already he felt the oppressive air around the place.

Dahr looked at Alistar. "Is your protective ward in place, sir? You should activate it."

The guards had provided Alistar with a ward, and Dahr's words reminded him of it. Alistar nodded quickly and fumbled for the talisman. It was a simple pendant on a silver chain—one of the more basic channeling devices. Alistar whispered the activation phrase, and immediately, the sense of oppression eased. He could still sense it, but it was distant, and he could breathe easily once more.

"Chirrod Prison maintains many layers of protection, sir," Dahr said. "The aura is one of them."

Alistar nodded. "Thank you."

The guard simply nodded, as if Alistar should already have known what he said. Perhaps he should have; auras of suppression made sense at a prison, especially a prison meant to hold the worst criminals of the empire.

The carriage entered the yard, and Alistar caught a glimpse of massive, twelve-foot-tall ogres on either side of the gates. The aura of suppression might be one of the protections against prisoners escaping, but it certainly was not the only one. More ogres patrolled the yard, carrying axes and spiked maces casually over their shoulders, though the weapons were large enough that a man could hardly have lifted one with both hands, much less actually wielded it.

The carriage halted. Both Dahr and Voit sat at attention, eyes on the door. The driver opened it, and both elves stepped out ahead of Alistar. Voit turned to Alistar and gave a brief nod, indicating that he should follow. It was one of the few things Dahr had impressed on Alistar as they left the city—they were here to protect him, and as such, he should allow them to do their duty and check for dangers. Alistar normally disliked feeling as if he was being coddled and overprotected, but in this place, he had no objections to the guards taking whatever precautions they thought necessary.

When Alistar stepped from the coach, a short, stocky human man waited for him. The man wore a suit coat over a rumpled, stained white shirt—an attempt at class and refinement in a line of work that offered neither. He had probably pulled on the suit coat specially for greeting his visitors; Alistar couldn't imagine it practical for daily wear at the prison. He had a thick head of black hair and a short beard.

"Warden Mon'serrat," Dahr said. "This is Alistar De'seneth, representative of the Silver Prince."

"Mi'lord De'seneth." The warden bowed slightly. Dahr cleared his throat pointedly, and the warden gave a deeper bow, then glanced nervously at the elf. The second attempt was enough to satisfy Dahr, and he didn't insist on the warden making a third.

"Warden Mon'serrat. Thank you for granting me leave to come here," Alistar said. He inclined his head in a polite nod and held out his right hand, displaying the Silver Prince's badge.

"Of course, Mi'lord. Without His Highness's contributions and support, Chirrod Prison would not be what it is today." The warden sounded proud of the grim place. "Now, you are here to speak with the prisoner Tiyron Onyxflame." He said the name with distaste.

"Yes," Alistar agreed.

"The prisoner is being prepared and will be brought to an interview chamber, sir. When you are ready, I will show you there."

"Now will be fine, Warden Mon'serrat," Alistar told him more confidently than he felt. Twists of anxiety settled in the pit of his stomach in spite of his efforts to remain calm and collected. *I pray that all the Reyker will watch over me in this place.*

The warden led them inside. The halls of the prison were as stark and colorless as the exterior. Alistar wondered how the prison guards tolerated the monotonous blankness. His footsteps echoed on the stone, and he shivered, feeling a chill radiating from the walls even with his protective ward in place. It felt like an eternity before Warden Mon'serrat stopped and opened a door. The room beyond the door was not extravagant, but the walls were painted a light shade of blue, and several chairs sat against the walls. The burst of color and comfort jarred Alistar.

Warden Mon'serrat indicated a second door at the other end of the room. "If you enter that hall, sir, it will take you to the interview chamber. Your guards may wait here."

Alistar glanced at the elves to see if either of them appeared surprised or displeased that they were not expected to be present for his conversation with Onyxflame, but neither did. Alistar himself felt mixed reactions. While he was not certain he wanted them listening to his interview with the criminal, he couldn't help but feel uneasy about being alone in a room with Tiyron Onyxflame.

Enough of this! It's embarrassing for an As'enel to quaver about questioning a prisoner.

Perhaps his face showed his doubts, because the warden continued, "The prisoner will be restrained, sir, both physically and magically. Should he make any attempt to assault or harm you, the restraints will stop him in an instant." The warden paused, listening to something in the air, then he nodded to Alistar. "The prisoner is in place, sir. Whenever you wish to speak to him, he awaits you."

"Thank you." Alistar nodded.

The warden left the room, leaving Alistar and the pair of guards alone. Alistar looked at the far door, but didn't move toward it immediately.

Voit settled on one of the chairs with a grunt of irritation. Alistar cast him a questioning look.

"The chairs are uncomfortable, poorly made, and flimsy as straw," Dahr said. "This is not a place we are overly fond of."

"Are you here often?" Alistar asked.

"Not usually more than once every year or two. But it doesn't get any better between visits."

Voit nodded in agreement.

"How long is a prisoner usually kept waiting in situations like this?" Alistar asked them, having no other source to consult.

"Long enough to imply that you're in no great hurry or need to see them," Dahr answered. "Not so long that they lose interest. If you walk slowly down the hall, your timing should be acceptable."

Alistar took a deep breath to steady himself, then opened the far door. The hall was also painted, rather than a return to the gray stone, which he had dreaded. Alistar walked slowly down the hall, hearing his steps and trying to keep them even and steady. He reached the far end and opened the door into the interview chamber.

The room was plain, the walls pale tan. The only real features of the room were a square wooden table bolted to the floor and two chairs. One was already occupied.

The lanky figure unfolded from his chair, standing as Alistar entered. Black eyes studied Alistar from an angular face, like a hawk waiting for an opportunity to dive down on prey. His prison stripes were shapeless, with the collar of the shirt snug to his throat and the sleeves of the shirt ending at his wrists, covering most of his skin in the elven fashion. He was pale from lack of sun, but even in a cell, in chains, he had not fallen prey to lethargy, judging from what Alistar could tell of his frame.

The prisoner tossed his head, shaking brown hair back from long, pointed ears. One hand started to rise to push the offending locks aside, but his wrists were chained to the table. "How unusual. I was given to understand that I would not be allowed visitors. Perhaps I was misinformed, and my former associates don't care for my company as much as they claimed. Or does the lack of visitors simply mean that our glorious ruler's efforts to keep my arrest and imprisonment a secret were unusually effective?" He studied Alistar. "You have the look of a Silverline lackey. What does Prince Cero want badly enough to drag me out of my cell?"

Alistar raised an eyebrow as he pulled out the free chair and sat across the table from the prisoner. Oddly, Onyxflame's greeting put him more at ease. He was accustomed to dealing with contempt and airs of superiority from elves. "Tiyron Onyxflame, I presume? I am Alistar De'seneth of Silverline Power," he said.

"Of course I am, and of course you are," Onyxflame cut in. "Do you mistake this for afternoon tea? Is there a point to polite trivialities, or do you have a reason for being here?"

"Why? Am I keeping you from something of pressing importance?" Alistar asked.

"I *was* perusing a volume of the history of Calarand, but I suppose the conquest of the western mountainlands and its people can wait, if you insist."

"How very generous of you," Alistar said dryly.

Onyxflame settled onto his chair with a rattle of chains, as composed as a king holding court. He had the air of a man confident in his control of the situation—an attitude that unsettled Alistar, especially when he did not share the elf's confidence even though he was the one free to leave. Onyxflame's eyes met Alistar's and the elf waited for Alistar to speak.

Alistar considered his words briefly, then began, "Recently, someone has been sabotaging and stealing powers from the mahiy lines."

Onyxflame's back stiffened slightly. "And the Silver Prince believes that I am somehow responsible for it, from within these walls? Either he has little faith in the defenses of Chirrod Prison, or a terribly high estimation of my ability to scheme."

Alistar paused momentarily. He hadn't gotten the impression that Prince Cero thought Onyxflame had a direct part in the attacks, but the Silver Prince quite likely had not told Alistar everything that he suspected, either. "You are something of an expert in the area of attacks on the mahiy lines and the theft of power."

Onyxflame's expression darkened. "If I had the ability to do either right now, I would not be sitting here and we would not be having this conversation. You can tell the Silver Prince to shove his suspicions—"

Alistar's eyes narrowed as he cut in. "I recommend that you not finish that thought aloud."

"In that case, kindly provide parchment. I'll draw a diagram, in case he can't find his posterior," Onyxflame said coolly. "If he's looking for saboteurs, he should be looking somewhere closer to home than Chirrod Prison."

"Like where?" Alistar asked, trying to keep his voice bland and not betray the sudden interest that rose in his chest.

"Like everyone else who has reason to dislike him or his stranglehold on the energy that feeds the mahiy lines," Onyxflame said. He snorted. "Do you want me just to tell you that it must be this person or that one? There are far too many people who would love to see the Silver Prince fall—making a list would take all day. No, he'll have to launch an extensive investigation, eliminate suspects one by one..." He trailed off, then looked at Alistar sharply. "Which is exactly what you're doing, isn't it? Eliminating the least likely suspects to narrow down the search."

"Not entirely," Alistar answered. "There is slightly more to my visit than just the elimination of you as a suspect. Which I would not say has been done conclusively yet."

Onyxflame sat back in his chair, wary. "What else brings you here, De'seneth?"

"Your talents," Alistar said. "Your knowledge and experience regarding means of siphoning magic from mahiy lines. You know ways that someone could do so, and what they might be doing with the magic they steal."

Onyxflame barked a laugh. "You want me to *help* your prince and his precious company? What *possible* reason would I have to do that?"

"Your current sentence calls for what?" Alistar inquired with false courtesy.

A scowl. "Twenty years served in Chirrod Prison, followed by five in the Skelocs."

Five years in the Skelocs Mines was a death sentence. Most prisoners didn't last a year in the harsh conditions. "And what restrictions are you under currently?"

Onyxflame gazed at him suspiciously. "High-security cell, with communal meals and several hours of labor each day. Access to the prison library."

"Only a few hours of labor?" Alistar asked. "If you have so much free time for reading, the warden should consider putting you to work."

Onyxflame snorted. "You want me to believe that a Silverline lackey has any authority to threaten me?"

Alistar drew the Silver Prince's token from under his shirt and held it for Onyxflame to see. "Yes, I do."

Onyxflame jerked back as if burned. "You're no underling. What has a human done to earn the favor of the Silver Prince? Who are you, Alistar De'seneth?"

"I'm a human not originally from Lewarden, and I've not gotten involved in capital politics. My employer required someone who he thought could be a neutral judge."

"Neutral?" Onyxflame laughed sharply and gestured at the token. "*That* is anything but *neutral.*"

"Neutral regarding the rest of the noble houses in court," Alistar said. "For that reason, His Highness has given me the authority to requisition whatever resources I need."

"And I am one of those 'resources'?" Onyxflame asked.

"This investigation would benefit from someone with your unique skills and knowledge," Alistar said.

"What do I get in return?" Onyxflame rested his elbows on the table and leaned forward. "Tracking magic isn't a simple matter, De'seneth, and it isn't something that can simply be taught in a day. You are right; with the right tools, I can find where your power is going. But not from here. I must have access to the sites of these incidents."

"You expect me to let you loose on Lewarden? No," Alistar said sharply.

"Do you want to find out what is happening or not, De'seneth?" Onyxflame snapped. The acoustics of the room gave his voice an odd pitch, higher than Alistar expected. "What did you expect, that I would meekly hand you everything? *You* want answers. *I* want out of these walls! I want out of them badly enough to make a deal with the Silver Bastard's ambassador rather than telling you to rot in your own filth! Of course you're not going to 'set me loose' on the city. Even if you agree, I am trading my jailers here for a new one—but at least being shackled to *you*, I won't see the same walls every moment and wonder when they'll crash closed around me."

Alistar tucked the token back into his breast pocket as he stood. "And *that* is what you want as payment for your work?"

"No. As payment, for success in this, I want freedom. Charges dropped, sentence commuted. *That* is what I want."

Alistar turned and walked to the door, feeling Onyxflame's eyes boring into his back. "I'll think about it."

"You don't have *time* to 'think about it', De'seneth!" Onyxflame said, voice rising again. "You know that!"

Alistar didn't turn, and he made his voice hard. "I am also pondering whether it would be more effective to consider the alternative—the punishments you could receive for *not* assisting me. As you indicated, the Silver Prince has great interest in my success. I doubt that he would be pleased if I was not receiving all the assistance that I need. Would you care to visit the Skelocs early?"

Onyxflame sharply jerked the chains against the table. "You wouldn't. You need me."

"Do I?" Alistar asked. "Are you sure of that? You have yet to convince me."

Onyxflame shoved to his feet, the chair scraping across the floor. "You came to me, foot-licking, half-bred *lackey*, and you expect *me* to convince *you* that you need my help? Why don't you go back to the Silver Bastard and tell him that you need someone to hold your hand next time? Or are you just going to run off like a coward?"

Alistar didn't respond to the taunts. He opened the door and walked back up the hall. As the door swung shut, Onyxflame's voice rose, spitting curses at his back.

You're right that I don't have the time to waste. But that doesn't mean I'm simply going to accept your terms without argument. I refuse to allow you to control my success or failure. Return to your cell and stew.

CHAPTER 6

When Alistar entered the waiting room, Dahr and Voit both rose. "Sir?"

"I left Onyxflame to fume while I think about a few things," Alistar said. He sank into one of the chairs and grimaced. "You are right—these *are* uncomfortable."

"What is there to consider, sir?" Dahr asked. "Does the prisoner have the knowledge you need?"

"He might. And he wants something in exchange for his knowledge." Alistar sat back, considering. He shifted, futilely attempting to find a position that didn't dig into his spine or tailbone.

"He should be satisfied with not being beaten within a step of his life," Dahr growled.

"Maybe so, but he would prefer release with his charges dropped," Alistar told the guard.

Voit grunted and rose to walk around the room. Dahr nodded, understanding something from his partner that eluded Alistar. "You can grant him that," Dahr said. "His Highness has given you that authority, even to release prisoners." His frown deepened. "I think doing so a bad idea. Onyxflame is dangerous."

"I know. But that doesn't change the fact that I could make good use of his skills." Alistar rested his chin on steepled fingers.

"You also have the authority to extend his imprisonment for obstruction," Dahr said. "Or have him relocated. Perhaps to the Skelocs."

Alistar almost winced. "I did make the threat. I left him cursing at my back for it."

Both elves gave him an appraising look.

Alistar shifted uncomfortably. "What?"

"We had a wager over whether you would actually make threats, but doubted that you would do so unprompted. I am impressed," Dahr commented.

You're impressed that I threatened a man imprisoned and in chains? I'm not.

"Would you send him to the Skelocs?" Dahr asked.

Alistar gave the question long thought. "No. My choice would be a mine on the island of Hollow Wind, near Rillwater. Miserable conditions, harsh work, but he's more likely to survive long enough to have a change of heart about assisting me."

"Most can survive a *few* days in the Skelocs," Dahr said.

That was true, but the Skelocs were also owned solely by the royal family, while Alistar's family held the controlling interest in the Hollow Wind mine. So if he was going to direct penal labor anywhere, he would choose a location that benefited his family. Although his father likely would not approve. And Onyxflame did not seem the sort of man who would take well to an offer than contained threat only.

He stood. "I need to speak to the warden. Where will I find him?"

"Warden Mon'serrat should be overseeing the return of the prisoner to his cell. A guard will be waiting outside this room to take you anywhere you need to go within the prison, sir," Dahr answered.

When Alistar opened the door, he saw the promised man

standing in the hall. The large human had the expression of someone more inclined to rely on strength than wits. The guard saluted quickly to Alistar.

"I need to speak with Warden Mon'serrat," Alistar said.

"Yes sir! I'll take you to him, sir!" the guard said quickly. Apparently the idea that Alistar was Someone Important had been firmly impressed on him. He strode down the hall with a swift step, and Alistar followed, the pair of elven guards keeping pace behind him.

They were moving down yet another trackless hallway when the lights flickered. Alistar looked at the glimmering ghost lights in alarm. His guide stopped in his tracks, expression bordering on panic.

"I'm sorry sir! This… this should only last a moment, I assure you!" He looked around quickly, then opened a door that Alistar hadn't noticed. "If you will just wait here, sir?"

Alistar saw another waiting room much like the one he had left, except that it had a tiny window high up the wall. Relieved that he would not be caught in total darkness, Alistar stepped inside. Moments later, the lights dimmed to the faintest glimmer, but they did not completely extinguish.

He looked to the shadowed shape of the guard. "Does this happen often?" Outages in the city were one thing, but if they extended so far as Chirrod Prison, an entirely new element of concern entered the matter. *Could someone use the disruption of magic as an opportunity to escape, or to break someone free?* He recalled Onyxflame's assertion that he was not involved in the disruptions, and wondered.

"No sir!" the man assured him quickly. "I've only seen it happen once. We never completely lose magic, of course, thanks to His Highness and the backup he provided. Too many dangerous people here to risk a complete loss of magic."

"That's why the lights are still glowing?" Alistar asked.

"Yes sir! They run low in areas where there are not many

people, but in the guards' and prisoners' areas, most of them wouldn't know much more than some flickering. The high-security cells are sealed, of course. As a precaution."

"Sealed how?" Alistar asked.

"Each of those cells is surrounded with stone barriers suspended by magic," Dahr answered. His voice betrayed no concerns about the situation. "If power to the prison fails, those barriers fall, creating a seal around each cell. No light, little air. A prisoner will not suffocate within, but will have, at best, only twenty minutes of consciousness before the air grows too thin. Once power is restored, the guards must reset the spells to raise the barrier again. There is little danger of any prisoner escaping from those cells."

"Exactly, sir, yes," agreed the prison guard.

Alistar turned toward Dahr's voice, recalling Onyxflame's statement about the walls closing around him. *So that wasn't just a turn of phrase.*

The lights remained dim for less than five minutes before returning to full illumination, as best Alistar could guess. The guard breathed a sigh of relief. Alistar glanced at his elven companions and noticed that neither of them appeared concerned by the event.

This seems... unusually convenient. Why should it fail now? I find it hard to believe that this is simply coincidence. Is this incident by order of the Silver Prince? Would he risk the chance that a prisoner could escape just to make a point and attempt to force Onyxflame to comply?

Alistar thought to the man he had met the previous day, and the determination in the Silver Prince. *Yes. Yes, that is a man who would take such a risk.*

They walked for at least another five minutes. Alistar's guide looked both nervous and relieved when they found Warden Mon'serrat standing amid a group of guards. The warden saw Alistar and immediately began to apologize.

"Mi'lord, I am appalled that you had to witness this incident. I assure you, such things do not happen at Chirrod Prison, and even when they do, there is no danger of prisoners breaking free!"

Alistar raised a hand to cut him off. "I don't doubt you, Warden. Your concern for my person is unnecessary. I am certain that His Highness has provided you with all the tools you need to maintain order even in such an unfortunate situation as just took place."

The warden relaxed visibly. "Thank you, sir. Now please, what can I do for you?"

"Onyxflame was returned to his cell before this occurred?" Alistar asked.

"Indeed, sir." Warden Mon'serrat indicated the hall ahead of him. "The high-security cells lie down here, sir. We were about to begin the process of raising the barriers again."

"Good. If it is possible, I would like those on Onyxflame's cell raised before he passes out," Alistar told him.

"Of course, sir. We always endeavor to raise the barriers before a prisoner loses consciousness." His tone implied, however, that the warden did not rush to raise them before the prisoners were *close* to passing out from the thin air. "You wish to speak with him again?"

"Yes."

"Kliment, show Lord De'seneth to the appropriate cell," Warden Mon'serrat ordered.

Alistar's guide nodded quickly. "Yes sir. This way please, sir."

The hall felt uncomfortably narrow and closed in. To either side of Alistar, massive blocks of stone towered. "These are the barriers?" he asked Kliment.

"Yes sir!" Kliment said, proud. "No prisoner has escaped from this area during a loss of power, sir."

"I believe it," Alistar murmured. As he passed, one block of stone, easily three feet thick, began to rise in a laborious climb, where a web of magic would hold it in place.

They stopped as another slab of stone rose. Alistar felt the rush of air from inside the cell, followed by the sound of someone gasping and coughing. Once the stone was firmly settled in place, Alistar approached the barred cell door.

Tiyron Onyxflame lay curled on the stone floor of the stark cell, panting for breath, eyes squeezed shut. Alistar waited until the elf regained some degree of control over his body's instinctual reactions, then cleared his throat loudly.

Onyxflame's eyes snapped open and found the door. It took him a moment to identify Alistar, but when he did, he pushed upright on shaky arms. "Either you are far more ruthless than I judged you, De'seneth, or that was a most… convenient coincidence," he panted.

"It was not my doing," Alistar said. "More than that, I cannot say."

"Of course not. That's why you have underlings." Onyxflame shut his eyes for a moment, wavering dizzily. "Suffocating is a very unpleasant experience that I dislike repeating, De'seneth. What terms will *you* find acceptable to let me out of here?"

Here is an open invitation to make whatever demands I want. Right now, he's willing to agree to almost anything, so long as he doesn't have to be here the next time the walls crash closed.

"Provided that you do provide the knowledge and skills I require for my task, I will agree that if the assignment is complete to the satisfaction of both myself and His Highness, your charges will be dropped," Alistar said. The words came more easily than he expected, but he felt confident in them. That promise was the one thing he was certain would hold with the elf even after he recovered.

He sensed the surge of disapproval from Dahr. Onyxflame gazed at Alistar in disbelief. "I will be released?"

"*If* my task is successful, and *if* you contribute to that success," Alistar said. "However, know that if at any point you attempt to escape, or impede my investigation, the offer is immediately rescinded and you will go directly to the mines."

Onyxflame sat on the floor, expression cautious. "If I *do* contribute, and do not attempt to escape, I want it on record that I will *never* be sent to the Skelocs, now or in the future."

"If you do your part, it shouldn't come up as an issue," Alistar said.

"And if I am arrested again? I have my future to consider, De'seneth."

That gave Alistar pause, reminding him again that he was promising freedom to a criminal. Yet Onyxflame's request was not a condition to which he could find objection. The Skelocs were a hellish series of mine caverns where convicts labored under vile conditions, often not seeing the sun or sky again. Few lived to see the end of their sentence.

"Agreed," Alistar told the elf. "It will be on record."

"You are certain of this, sir?" Dahr asked in disapproval behind him.

"Yes, I am," Alistar said. He turned to face the guard. "Carrots and cart-whips, Dahr."

The guard's brow creased in a puzzled frown. "Pardon?"

"Never mind. It's a human expression."

Dahr still frowned, but nodded and walked back to Warden Mon'serrat. Alistar glanced at the silent Voit, who remained with him. The guard studied Onyxflame through the bars of the cell as if seeing a particularly noxious insect. He gave a short grunt of disdain.

Men dressed in the uniforms of prison guards approached. "Begging your pardon, sir," one said to Alistar.

He moved aside, and the men entered Onyxflame's cell. Alistar walked back and joined Dahr and the warden.

Warden Mon'serrat gave him a small bow. "I understand that I am to release Onyxflame into your custody, sir."

"That is correct," Alistar agreed.

"If you will come with me, sir, I must have you sign the appropriate release forms, and will provide you with the needed restraining and containment wards."

Warden Mon'serrat's office was cluttered, and the shelves were stuffed with files in an order known only to the gods and, hopefully, the one who filed them. The warden seemed able to navigate easily enough, pulling files from the shelves and stacking them on his desk, then rummaging through his drawers and producing a stack of forms. Warden Mon'serrat set a quill in the inkwell and spoke an incantation. The pen rose and began to fill out the forms, pausing only when the warden needed to supply specific details such as names and dates. Alistar sat at the warden's invitation and waited.

The warden checked over the papers, then offered them to Alistar. He scanned them. He had never dealt with prisoner release forms—had never expected to need such things before, so he had no way of knowing whether these were standard, or if there were particular versions used in cases where the Silver Prince bestowed authority on someone. He didn't find anything that he objected to, though he didn't relish being held responsible for damages or other complaints resulting from Onyxflame being placed in his custody. He *was* assuming responsibility for the prisoner. Alistar signed the papers where indicated, though doing so sent a shiver of apprehension up his spine.

"Are you familiar with restraining wards and spells, sir?" Warden Mon'serrat asked. His tone implied that he expected that Alistar *ought* to be if he expected to be responsible for a prisoner.

"I would appreciate a refresh of the specifics of those you employ here," Alistar answered, sidling around the question.

The warden nodded. "Of course, sir. Our restraint measures are more specialized than those commonly available. Each prisoner wears dampeners, limiting their ability to use magic. The restraining wards are linked to those dampeners." He offered Alistar a sheet of parchment. "The key words specify which manner of ward activates. They are divided according to the length of time they will last, from an hour to a week. You can, of course, cancel the ward early if you need to. Those in the left column prevent the prisoner from moving outside a certain range —for example, a room. Those in the right column serve the purpose of eldritch shackles. They will not hinder the movement of anyone but the prisoner, but can be used to restrain his limbs or chain him to a desired location. For example, this key word could be used to bind Onyxflame's wrists to my desk with a one foot length of chain."

Alistar studied the list, nodding. "I see. Thank you, warden."

"We employ another precaution when releasing a convict into the custody of someone outside Chirrod Prison, sir," Warden Mon'serrat continued. He handed Alistar a pendant on a chain. Alistar examined the pendant, finding a small amber disk etched with symbols. "Onyxflame will wear a collar marked with runes identical to those you see here, sir, and it will activate as soon as he sets foot outside the walls of Chirrod Prison. While the spell is active, any time that Onyxflame is farther than fifty yards from that pendant, he will be immediately placed under a compulsion to return to it. This compulsion can be canceled only if he is already within any of the other wards. So if you have personal business to attend to, I strongly suggest placing him within wards first, or he may follow you."

"Can he break this compulsion?" Alistar asked. "I have heard that some people of particularly strong will are able to resist such things."

"With the addition of the magical inhibitors, there is little danger of him resisting the compulsion, sir." Warden Mon'serrat spoke stiffly. "This is the result of many years of study and experimentation by His Majesty's Royal Academy of Magical Sciences. Additionally, Onyxflame will be unable to touch the linked pendant. Any attempt to do so will cause immediate paralysis. He will not be able to take it from you, nor even pick it up should you drop it."

"That is most reassuring," Alistar told him, wishing to soothe ruffled feathers over any implication of doubt in the warden's abilities or the tools he provided to Alistar.

"Tiyron Onyxflame is a dangerous criminal, sir. While I am certain that His Highness would not entrust you with his blessing unless you were worthy of it, I will also take every precaution to ensure your safety while in the company of this criminal, sir." The warden stood. "Your charge should be prepared now, Master De'seneth. All the forms appear to be in order. If you are ready…?"

I doubt that I am, but it is too late to change my mind now. "Thank you for all your assistance, Warden Mon'serrat." Alistar rose. He rolled the sheet of key words and tucked them into his inner coat pocket, then slid the pendant chain over his neck and tucked it under his shirt.

Stepping out of the building and into the inner courtyard was a relief to Alistar. Even though the walls of Chirrod Prison still rose around them, simply being outside relieved some of the oppression. Dahr and Voit waited for him, and between them stood Tiyron Onyxflame. The prisoner was dressed in plain brown workman's clothes, no longer wearing the prison stripes. His sleeves were long, and the collar of his shirt sat high around his neck, the elven style conveniently concealing the inhibitors he undoubtedly wore. Alistar glimpsed a hint of amber at the dip of the shirt collar, the ring around Onyxflame's neck. Onyxflame tried to appear nonchalant, but his eyes held doubt still—doubt that he would actually be permitted beyond the gates of the prison.

The carriage awaited outside. Alistar nodded to the three elves. "We have work to do." Turning, he walked to the prison gates.

They followed. As they crossed the threshold, Alistar heard

someone stumble. He turned and saw Onyxflame picking himself up off the ground with a wince.

"Problem?" Alistar asked.

"No, no problem. Only a pointed reminder that I am not a free man yet," Onyxflame answered, rubbing at his neck. "Lead on, De'seneth. I am here to serve."

CHAPTER 7

Both Dahr and Voit watched Onyxflame suspiciously, as if they expected him to lunge for the carriage door at any moment. Onyxflame lounged back on the padded seat, eyes half closed and lips twitching in amusement at the guards' attention. He did not look out the window as the carriage climbed the steep slope and the view overlooked Chirrod Prison.

When they reached the top, Alistar let out a soft breath of relief, glad to be leaving the prison behind. On the open road, the driver gave the horse automatons rein, and the tireless creations sped to a smooth gallop. Frost-capped fields and bare trees flashed by the windows.

Alistar opened the folder of information he'd reviewed on the way to the prison. He didn't miss the perk of attention from Onyxflame or the elf's surreptitious efforts to see the pages. Sorting through to the two sets of identification papers, Alistar considered the options. It was very tempting to relegate Onyxflame to the role of a servant, except for a few details. One of those was that servants had far more influence over their masters' reputations than most people admitted. A rumor started at an inconvenient place and time could tarnish a noble's name for years.

Alistar selected one set of papers and held them to Onyxflame. "You'll be playing the role of a lesser nobleman named Taslor Aspendark."

Onyxflame raised an eyebrow and accepted the profile. "Nobility? Not 'Chief Bootlicker and Errand Boy'?"

Alistar tugged up the other set of papers. "I could still change my mind."

"No, no," Onyxflame said with equanimity. "I'm sure there are others more qualified for the bootlicker position than I."

Dahr scowled at him, then looked to Alistar. "You're sure, sir?"

Alistar leaned back. "Should this investigation take us into noble circles, I'm afraid it will be necessary. Given the nature of his restrictions, Onyxflame must remain within a certain proximity. There are a number of situations where a nobleman insisting on his manservant's presence is akin to having his nanny at his side."

Onyxflame snorted. "The way some act, they could use a nanny to mind them." He scanned the papers, then gave all three of them a dubious look. "Rillwater? Really? I'm supposed to be a pirate?"

Alistar gave him a hard look. "Onyxflame, if you wish to keep all your teeth intact, do not refer to the privateers of Rillwater as pirates to their faces. Sailors throw excellent punches."

"Pirates, privateers, what's the difference?" Onyxflame scoffed. "I doubt I'm in too much danger of encountering one here."

"You're sharing this carriage with one," Alistar said coolly.

Onyxflame stiffened. He looked at the two impassive guards, then back to Alistar. "Ah." He considered in silence, then said, "I presume that is why Rillwater was chosen as Aspendark's residence?"

"I presume so," Alistar agreed. "As well as your relatively recent experiences as a sailor."

"My wha—" Onyxflame caught himself. "Ah. The Silver Prince really *does* have spies everywhere, it seems."

Onyxflame lapsed into silence for a time, studying Aspendark's papers. Alistar poured himself a glass of wine and read through his information again. *We need to start the investigation as soon as possible. Shale Lane is the most recent site, so the best place to begin. If those responsible left any clues, we have to find them.*

Onyxflame appeared to nap, leaning against the carriage wall. He roused when they entered Lewarden, watching the city through the window. Eventually the carriage pulled to a stop before Alistar's house. He stepped out, nodding for Onyxflame to follow. The elf looked around with interest. "I thought that employees of Silverline Power had their own housing. You don't live there?"

"No," Alistar said simply, offering no further explanation.

"Do you wish us to remain, sir?" Dahr asked from the carriage.

Onyxflame tensed at the question. Alistar considered inviting the guards inside just to nettle the convict. But he shook his head. "Not at the moment, thank you."

"Very well, sir." Dahr's tone said that he did not entirely agree with Alistar's decision. "If you have need of us, make use of this speech stone." He handed Alistar a polished black stone inscribed with a sword and two rippling lines that symbolized a river. " 'Lord' Aspendark's personal effects will arrive tomorrow."

Alistar accepted the stone. "I will use this as needed. Good evening, gentlemen. Thank you once again." He unlocked the door and walked inside.

"Good day, Mr. De'seneth," Mrs. Ke'lyn greeted, descending the stairs with a feather duster in hand. "Ah, your guest is here." She did look askance at Onyxflame's plain clothes and his lack of baggage.

The lingering scorn vanished from Onyxflame's expression the instant that the housekeeper came into sight. He bowed. "Good evening, madam. Taslor Aspendark at your service."

Alistar caught himself quickly, startled by the sudden change in Onyxflame's demeanor. "Aspendark, this is my housekeeper, Mrs. Ke'lyn."

Onyxflame nodded. "A pleasure to meet you. Pardon my intrusion, please."

"It is no intrusion, Mr. Aspendark," she said, smiling pleasantly. "Mr. De'seneth told me that you need a place to stay while you are in Lewarden on business."

"Ah, yes," Onyxflame agreed. "And I do appreciate De'seneth's generosity." Somehow, he said the words without evident sarcasm.

"The guest room is clean, and I've placed out fresh linens," Mrs. Ke'lyn told them. "I prepared dinner for two; it's in the oven, Mr. De'seneth. The dining room is set."

"You are, as ever, a rare gem, Mrs. Ke'lyn," Alistar told her.

"And you are a flatterer as always, Mr. De'seneth," she replied with a laugh. "Is there anything else you need before I leave for the day?"

"No, I don't think so," he told her. "Have a good evening."

"I wish you gentlemen the same," she said.

As she pulled on her coat, Alistar climbed the stairs, followed by Onyxflame. Alistar opened the guest room door. "You'll be staying here."

Alistar hosted few guests, and had never focused on trying to impress those he did receive. The bed had fresh linens, as Mrs. Ke'lyn had promised. She had dusted and polished the dressing table, desk, and wardrobe, and tucked the chamber pot discreetly in a corner beside the bed. An antique oil lamp sat on the desk, but held no oil, serving only as decoration.

Onyxflame walked to the wardrobe and opened it. "Ah... I don't suppose you have anything but human styles?"

Clothing. Alistar had not given that matter any thought, but dressed as he was, Onyxflame couldn't have passed as a nobleman's servant, much less an actual nobleman. Alistar would not have expected the criminal to be a traditionalist in dress, but the custom seemed so integrated into elven culture that even rebels didn't deviate far from it. *Although he evidently isn't so tied to them that he couldn't let them lapse while aboard the Narnan ship.*

"Nothing suitable for daily wear." He had several suits cut to elven fashion for formal occasions, but those were unlikely to fit Onyxflame, even if Alistar *did* feel willing to volunteer their use. Which he did not.

Onyxflame nodded, unsurprised. "Chirrod Prison's provision will serve for now, though I will have to appeal to your generosity for something more suitable."

"You'll have the clothing you need," Alistar said, reminding himself that Dahr had promised some manner of "personal effects" for Onyxflame. "Dinner is hot in the oven."

Onyxflame followed him to the kitchen, looking all around the house as he did. He didn't speak any critique, but Alistar sensed disdain. Alistar found a matching pair of plates and utensils, setting places at the small kitchen table. He knew Mrs. Ke'lyn had prepared the dining room for company, but Alistar was not interested in impressing Onyxflame. The elf didn't comment until Alistar pulled a large meat pie from the oven.

"No noodles and chopsticks? I thought it was human tradition to embarrass elven guests by handing them a pair of sticks and expecting them to use them to eat one of the most impossible foods ever devised."

"I'm sure that if you really want them, I can find chopsticks for your meat pie," Alistar responded. "Do you want water or tea to drink?"

"If your tea is that bitter, noxious brew that humans prefer, then water."

"Our tea is more drinkable than the hot sugar-water that elves like," Alistar countered, filling two glasses with cold water. "Have a seat."

"My thanks." Onyxflame settled into a chair, waited for Alistar to sit, and served himself a generous helping of pie. "You have no idea how marvelous this smells."

"Mrs. Ke'lyn is an excellent cook," Alistar said, scooping a helping onto his plate.

"I have no doubt she is, but I admit, my perspective is skewed. Chirrod Prison is not known for its fine cuisine."

"No, it's known for housing criminals who generally don't get a chance to leave unless it's to be sent somewhere worse," Alistar commented dryly.

"Ah… is that a suggestion that I should shut up and eat?" Onyxflame asked.

"Take it however you choose," Alistar told him, picking up his fork and spearing a chunk of meat. "But the longer you talk, the colder your dinner grows." And he had no intention of letting his food get cold.

Onyxflame, thankfully, stopped talking and dug into the meal with relish. For a time, the only sounds were those of two hungry men finally given food. Alistar realized belatedly that he hadn't eaten lunch, and his breakfast had been little more than a pastry and a cup of tea.

"You are correct—your housekeeper is an exceptional cook," Onyxflame announced once he'd cleaned his plate after a second helping. He gulped down the last of his water. "So, now that we are here, and the Silver Prince has strong-armed me into his service, tell me what we face, De'seneth."

"So far, we've seen a total of seven blackouts in Lewarden, primarily in the poor areas. They don't hold to the pattern of natural mahiy line fluctuations. Instead, there is a sudden drain that causes a loss of power to all the mahiy lines within a several-block radius," Alistar began.

"Seven. Is that including the one today, or not?" Onyxflame cut in.

"Not counting today," Alistar clarified. *Because neither you nor I think that was the doing of anyone but His Highness.*

"Very well. Continue, please."

"His Highness suspects that one of the other noble houses is responsible, and that this is an effort to destabilize Silverline Power, creating enough public restlessness and mistrust to cause them to insist on change. He wants to know who is responsible and put an end to their efforts," Alistar said.

Onyxflame frowned, considering. "You doubt your prince's theory, De'seneth."

"I'm not writing it off—it is possible he's right. However, I'm remaining open to other possibilities. If someone wanted to stir up outcry and protest against Silverline Power, they should be arranging for the nobility to lose power, rather than the commoners," Alistar told him.

"Perhaps. Or perhaps the nobles are still to come. How effective would it be, do you think, if the nobles began to suffer these incidents, and complained, only to learn that this has been an ongoing problem, and Silverline Power has been covering it up rather than addressing the problem? It is about timing—timing is everything, De'seneth, especially in politics." Onyxflame smiled. "A ruthless game."

"Just because I don't play the game, it doesn't mean I don't know the rules," Alistar said. "A political force could be driving this, building up to create a case against Silverline Power and Prince Cero. But to do so, they are stealing a huge amount of power, and they must do something with it. They would be foolish to just waste it."

"And that, of course, is why you had to have me," Onyxflame said. "Because I *did* steal vast amounts of power from your company."

"Certain people would still like to know what you did with it," Alistar said.

"I'm sure they do. Magic *can* be stored, De'seneth, although that is difficult and you always lose some in the storage process. It will leak over time, as well. That was one of the errors that led to my capture. If your thief's goal is to store the magic and then begin supplying it in limited amounts after breaking Silverline Power's stranglehold, I know several means of finding those stores, assuming it's being kept in raw form. If they want to have it on hand when the mahiy lines fall—if such is their plan—that would be how they need to keep it. They could be condensing and refining it, however. Doing so assumes that they want it for another purpose, and not to have a 'backup' supply of magic."

"Condense magic?" Alistar asked. "How do you 'condense' raw power?"

"Very carefully," Onyxflame replied. "The process is dangerous and it creates hazardous waste products. But refined magic… now *that* is power in its purest form. It is power transformed into a physical object, and a person could hold all the magic they could ever wish for in the palm of their hand. Of course, *using* it in that form presents challenges. All of the channeling devices in Lewarden are designed to draw on the power that runs through the mahiy lines."

"Of course," Alistar agreed. "And unregistered devices either will not properly draw from the mahiy lines, or are excessively expensive to make."

"They are nearly *impossible* to make," Onyxflame corrected. "Not completely so, but the time and effort required to find parts to suit your needs that do not have the Silverline Power tracer spells embedded within them are extreme." He paused. "Did you know, I believe I missed a single switch in my device? A single switch that slipped by me with a tracer spell."

"If you expect sympathy from me over that, you'll be disappointed," Alistar told him.

"It seemed worth the attempt," Onyxflame responded evenly. "But the point I was making is that the devices in Lewarden are crafted to use the power of the mahiy lines, or possibly to accept the power of a channeler. They are *not* designed to function under the power of pure, refined magic. Most would likely erupt in flames if they attempted to do so, or possibly explode."

"So if someone is refining magic into a solid form, we don't know what they would be doing with that power," Alistar concluded.

"Exactly," Onyxflame agreed. "But if that *is* what is taking place, we need to use different tracking methods."

"Which you also know," Alistar said.

"Yes…" Onyxflame trailed off.

"But?" Alistar prompted when he didn't continue.

"But Chirrod Prison's dampeners severely restrict my ability to employ those methods."

Alistar's eyes narrowed. "No. The restraints will not be removed until *after* this task is complete."

"Very well, De'seneth, but if that is the manner of tracking we need to employ, this will hamper our efforts," Onyxflame said.

"No." Alistar rose. "The matter is not open for debate, Onyxflame. Now, if you do not mind, I think it is time you retired to your room for the evening."

The elf's eyes flashed with anger and irritation for a moment, but he stood and dipped his head in a slight bow. "As you wish. I bid you good night then, De'seneth."

Alistar followed him to the guest room. Onyxflame shot him a glower before entering the room and shutting the door. Alistar pulled the list of key words from his pocket and selected a twelve-hour ward to prevent Onyxflame from leaving the room.

He heard a hiss of pain and a curse from the other side of the door. "That's quite unnecessary, De'seneth," Onyxflame said.

"If you expect me to trust the word of an acknowledged and convicted criminal on the first day he's placed in my keeping, you must truly think me a fool, Onyxflame. Good evening."

Alistar turned and walked back down the stairs, once again leaving the elf muttering curses at his back. Many thoughts tumbled through his mind, but one pressed more persistently than the rest.

Too much politics involved. Word about this will get home one way or another. Better if I face it now.

Alistar entered his study and sank down at the desk. He wished that he could put off the task, but delaying would make it no easier. He opened a wooden box adorned with a carving of a whale and withdrew the sea-blue polished speaking stone. He needed to speak to his father.

CHAPTER 8

Alistar cupped the speaking stone in his hands until it grew warm and a soft blue glow leaked between his fingers. He settled the stone into a recess on the lid of its box and waited, running a finger over the carving of the whale. His uncle had made the case for him as a gift long before Alistar became an engineer, when he'd still thought he would be a sea captain like his parents. Briefly, Alistar entertained the hope that his father had, for once, retired to bed early. Then the stone's glow brightened, taking on an emerald hue, and a deep male voice spoke.

"Alistar. This is unexpected."

He envisioned his father leaning back in his chair, a glass of brandy in one hand. His hair and beard, once as black as Alistar's, sported salt and pepper gray. His voice was deep, and a lifetime on the sea made him apt to bellow when he raised his voice. When Alistar had been a child, he'd been in awe of the strength in his father's hands, and the arms that could lift a growing boy with ease, tossing him into the air as if Alistar could fly.

"I'm sorry to call so late," Alistar apologized. "I hope I didn't catch you at a bad time."

"Not at all, not at all," his father answered. "Just clearing up some reports. All is well?"

Speaking stones offered great convenience, but they carried only sound, and no other hints as to whether the person at the other side was alone or not. "I'm well enough." Meaning, he was alone. "How are things at home?"

His father chuckled. "Your sister has been keeping me busy! Three shipments of eastern cigars this month alone. Roddek's going to have to work harder if he's going to keep up with her."

Alistar smiled. His younger siblings had a friendly rivalry, each of them captains of their own ships. At times, he missed being on the sea with them, though he did not miss the other pressures that had accompanied those days. "That's good to hear. The cigars are becoming quite fashionable in Lewarden. At least among the people who can afford them."

"Well, if you need a case or two, I think we can spare a few from the official final count," his father offered jovially.

"I don't think—" Alistar paused. "Actually, that might not be a bad idea after all."

The long moment of silence from his father dragged palpably. "Either you're developing expensive habits or expensive friends."

Alistar shifted uncomfortably. "I've received a special assignment that may require me to rub elbows with the court. Bribes might be useful."

His father's voice grew stern. "What sort of assignment requires court politics of an engineer?"

"Sabotage to the mahiy lines, Admiral." The honorific came automatically when his father took that tone. "The Silver Prince believes political rivals are responsible, and chose me for the task because, in addition to other qualifications, I *have* remained out of capital politics. As such, I'm the closest thing to a neutral party available to him."

"Sabotage? Like that business with the factory fire?" His father fell silent for long moments. "Blood and sand. This assignment came directly from the Silver Prince?"

"Personally," Alistar said. "Someone's stealing magic, and he wants to know who and why, by whatever means necessary."

"Ahhh." Alistar could all but see his father nodding. "The royal family *does* have a history of turning to us when 'whatever means necessary' enters the matter. Royal politics brought us where we are now." He heaved a sigh. "Very well, as our duty to the crown, I cannot forbid it. What does he expect you to do?"

"I intend to start by studying the sites of the thefts and locating any evidence there. I'll use anything from that to narrow my suspects. After that... as necessary, he expects me to enter the court openly as your heir."

"Nothing like chumming the waters for the sharks. So, you'll use our name to open doors and gain access a De'seneth wouldn't have."

"I'll make no promises and no alliances without your approval," Alistar said.

"I trust you, Alistar. You're my son; you can handle a pack of cutthroats no matter what clothes they wear. If your tutor didn't teach you how to hint and imply without actually agreeing to anything, I'll toss him in the bay."

Alistar chuckled. "I think he did well enough in teaching discourse and speech. If you recall, I *did* argue you into letting me serve as Mother's cabin boy when I was nine." *Which turned out to be one of the worst decisions I ever made, but that's not my tutor's fault.*

A guffaw answered him. "I do remember. Ah..." Alistar heard papers shuffle. "Since you're going to be dallying in the court anyway, I'll send you some names to look into. Not for the prince, for the Family."

Alistar straightened. "Thank you."

"Mind you, Alistar, I'm in no way approving of all this. But the matter is Silverline business, and the prince has his eye on you. Do the Family well, and remind the court why they prefer that we

As'enel stay out of their business. I'll send three boxes of cigars. Open them before you share them with the leeches."

"Yes, Admiral." Alistar's curiosity was piqued as to what private communications would be stashed into the cigar boxes.

"This is *your* ship, Alistar; you're her captain. Sail her well and mind the reefs. For each one you see, there are seven you don't." A pause, then Alistar heard the smile in his father's voice. "Just make sure you take enough loot and plunder to show up your siblings. If you can't manage *that* in the imperial court, I'll be extremely disappointed."

Alistar laughed softly. "Yes sir."

"So, aside from pretending that you're in the court by my wishes if anyone asks, what other support can the Family give you? Does the Silver Prince want your brother and sister to make an appearance as well?"

"Winds guard us, I hope not!" Alistar said quickly. "They'd scandalize the court."

"That's usually the expected outcome to inviting privateers into noble circles. But they have skills as well. Are you working this task alone?" his father asked.

"I have an assistant," Alistar answered. "An expert in certain fields related to the thefts—"

"You have an assistant who's a criminal, presumably coerced into working with you," his father clarified.

"With a promise of a pardon if he complies, and a threat of the Skelocs if he doesn't," Alistar agreed. "According to the provided papers, he's Lord Taslor Aspendark of Rillwater. Owns several warehouses in the stretch between Midora's Dock and the Fathomdeep."

"Huh. Well, that strip is owned by the Crown, so they can say whatever they want about it. It's still empty. So. Tell me more about Aspendark."

"Minor noble, elf, obviously. Unmarried, only child," Alistar said.

His father snorted. "Standard imperial-supplied identity. Give him a bastard sister and have her running his business while he's gallivanting about the capital. He took some risky ventures that didn't pay out, so he's in the capital in the hopes of finding business partners to offset his debts. Possibly a marriage if he can manage it, though he's unlikely to find worthwhile prospects."

"The sister—a Wave or a Tide?" Alistar asked. The two were the most common surnames given to bastards around Rillwater.

"Tide, I think. Rozika Tide, managing her brother's business." Another pause. "Aspendark must have sailed with you, putting in his ship time. That would explain why he approached you to enter the court. Yes, that should do."

Alistar admired the ease with which his father spun a history for Taslor Aspendark. "Thank you. I'll coach him on the details."

"If you start digging deep enough, someone will try to verify your story, and his with it. I'll see to it that the tale holds, Alistar. Have Aspendark write letters home now and then with instructions and updates on his work in Lewarden. For that matter, write a few yourself. Your mother has usually retired by the time you call, when you do, and I'm not risking the Leviathan's wrath by waking her. But she misses hearing from you."

I'd write more often if she didn't start every conversation by asking whether I've had my fill of playing at engineering yet and am ready to take my proper place and don the captain's hat. "I will," Alistar promised.

His voice must have carried some of his thoughts, because his father added, "Since your last promotion, she seems to have resigned herself to the idea that you're not about to jump ship and swim back to home port. Secure yourself another one, and she's likely only to bring it up at High Festivals."

"Meaning, only the times when I'm most likely to be coming home for a visit?" Alistar asked dryly.

His father coughed. "Well, yes, I suppose there is that. Give your fiancée our greetings. Unlike you, she's been quite faithful in sending at least a note every month."

Alistar smiled wryly. "I will. Give my love to everyone. Winds guide your sails, Father."

"And may the storms always take you home," his father answered. The glow of the stone faded, and it fell silent.

CHAPTER 9

Alistar knocked on the guest room door. "Good morning. I'll be making breakfast shortly if you're interested."

He heard shuffling movement, grumbling, then finally, "Still black as Slee's Pits out there. What time is it?"

"A little after six thirty," Alistar answered. "High time to be awake."

Onyxflame's reply was less than gracious.

"As I said, breakfast will be ready soon," Alistar said. "Come to the kitchen if you're hungry."

"Is the door going to bite me again?" Onyxflame said. "That was quite unpleasant."

"I've released the ward on your room. You can, in fact, open the door," Alistar told him. "Though if you are truly concerned, I can open it for you."

"No need," Onyxflame said hastily. Steps approached, paused, then the knob turned. Onyxflame opened the door cautiously, then nodded in brief greeting to Alistar, raking fingers through his brown hair. "I will have to trouble you for a looking glass, a comb, and a visit to the bath. Preferably before I have to appear in public." His rumpled clothing indicated that he hadn't undressed before sleep, as if determined to wear his only set of clothing as long as possible.

"I'm sure I can arrange something," Alistar replied. "Later. We're not appearing in public before breakfast."

Onyxflame followed him down to the kitchen and sat at the table as Alistar took eggs and slices of pork from the cold chest. The pork was a poor substitute for smoked eel, but he made do with what he could get in the capital. He should have asked his father to send fish with the cigars.

Alistar cracked eggs into a pan. "You'll be pleased to learn that overnight, Lord Aspendark has acquired a bastard sister, Rozika Tide. She's managing his business while he's in Lewarden."

Onyxflame stared at him for a long moment. "I… see. I don't believe that information was included in his profile."

"It wasn't," Alistar agreed. "Neither was the massive debt he's trying to keep concealed while he searches for business partners in Lewarden."

Onyxflame raised an eyebrow. "So we're allowed to tailor his identity to complement my skills? That's oddly refreshing."

"You'll be expected to write to your sister now and then with updates on your efforts and to give probably terrible instructions regarding your business and warehouses. We can assume she will ignore the latter," Alistar continued.

"Really? And am I expected to acknowledge our relationship in these letters?" Onyxflame asked.

"Oh, certainly not! Refer to her as 'cousin.' It's the surname that gives it away."

"How lovely. And what happens when someone looks into this tale and asks questions about Aspendark, his sister, and his business in Rillwater?"

Alistar raised an eyebrow. "What do you mean? No one is likely to actually *go* to Rillwater. If anything, they will send an inquiry."

"Exactly," Onyxflame said. "Someone, sometime, *will* send an inquiry."

"And your sister will send them a politely scathing confirmation that Aspendark is indeed who he claims to be," Alistar said. "A few of those, and word should spread that Aspendark is a verified presence with a harpy of a business manager."

Onyxflame just looked at Alistar before finally saying, "How is this supposed bastard sister going to accomplish this?"

Alistar met his gaze evenly. "It's under control, Onyxflame. Just don't do anything stupid enough to make her disown you."

"Since when do bastards get to disown their legitimate family?" Onyxflame said with a faint laugh.

"Aspendark left her in charge in his absence," Alistar said with a shrug. He flipped the eggs, then split them onto two plates, adding a slice of pork to each. He set one plate in front of Onyxflame and added, "You don't want to be cut adrift in the court, Onyxflame. Believe me on that. You have support and legitimacy from Rillwater. For now."

Onyxflame met his gaze, then dipped his head in a sarcastic bow. "My handler has spoken. Far be it from me to argue." He picked up his fork and began to eat.

Alistar bit back a retort, sitting and eating his breakfast. He had finished his eggs and just taken his first bite of meat when he heard the echo of the knocker rapping soundly against his front door. He frowned, surprised, and rose. "Stay here."

"As you wish," Onyxflame agreed, barely pausing his meal to respond.

Alistar descended to the entrance and opened the door. Dahr stood on his front steps. Alistar looked for the carriage but saw none, leaving him to wonder whether the guard had walked or employed a public taxi—or perhaps left the carriage parked out of sight. The guard's face was impassive as he presented a large garment bag to Alistar. "Lord Aspendark's luggage has arrived."

Alistar accepted the heavy bag and stepped aside, allowing Dahr to drag the accompanying trunk inside. "Come in."

As soon as the door closed, the guard let his stiffly formal stance fall. "Where is he?"

"Onyxflame is upstairs in the kitchen," Alistar answered.

"You are certain?" Dahr asked.

"Such little faith you have in me," Onyxflame called down from upstairs. "Yes, I am indeed still sitting here, eating the food that Mr. De'seneth so graciously prepared."

"I have no reason to have faith in you," Dahr retorted. "How many times did you test the wards?"

"Once was quite enough," Onyxflame called back. "Might I be excused from the table yet?"

Alistar ground his teeth in annoyance at the tone, mimicking a child's request to a parent. Rather than answer, he offered a hand to Dahr. "Can I help you carry that upstairs?"

Dahr waved for him to drape the garment bag over the trunk. "I can manage it, sir, but if you insist."

Alistar took hold of a handle on one end of the trunk, and between them, they hauled it up the two flights of stairs to the guest room. "You brought this yourself?" Alistar asked.

"One of His Highness's coaches brought me most of the way," Dahr told him. "I hauled it the rest of the way." He set the trunk down with a grunt. "This should suffice for the essentials. His Highness would prefer that you not waste time at a tailor's shop that could be better spent elsewhere."

"Thank you. That will save us finding something suitable for him."

The guard nodded curtly. "His Highness wishes me to accompany you and Onyxflame today." His scowl said that he would rather be doing something else. Like scrubbing chamber pots.

Alistar gestured for the guard to follow him to the kitchen. "Can I get you anything to eat, or something to drink?"

"Tea," Dahr said. Then he paused, remembering that he was speaking to a human. "You *do* have sugar, don't you?"

"Of course," Alistar assured him.

Onyxflame still sat at the kitchen table with an air of patience. His plate was empty—and Alistar noticed that his own was as well, the slice of pork long gone. Onyxflame gave Dahr an exaggeratedly pleasant smile. "So good to see you again. His Highness is kind to spare you for such an onerous duty as watching me eat breakfast."

Dahr gave him a long, silent look, heavy with disdain.

Alistar tapped the faucet, and it released a stream of nearly boiling water into the waiting mug. "Tea is here; have your pick."

The guard chose a very mild variety, and Alistar knew that the elf wouldn't steep it for nearly long enough to make what a human considered a proper cup of tea. Then he would drown it in sickeningly sweet doses of sugar before finally drinking it. Alistar brewed his own tea strong and dark, and they both withheld voicing their opinion of the other's drink.

"Tea, if you would," Onyxflame said to Dahr.

Dahr folded his arms across his chest, nearly spilling his mug. "Get it yourself. I am not your servant."

"I would fetch it myself, but Mr. De'seneth's house seems to bear a dislike for me, and I would rather not start my first day here with more burns," Onyxflame said.

"There are no wards preventing you from getting a mug of water," Alistar said, mildly exasperated. "And teas are on the counter. With the sugar."

Onyxflame rose and nodded. "Thank you, De'seneth. You are most generous." He examined the options and chose a stronger variety of tea than Dahr had. He also allowed it to steep longer, and added less sugar. Alistar wasn't certain what he was trying to prove, if anything.

"Lord Aspendark's wardrobe and luggage have arrived, if you want to change clothes," Alistar told him.

"Oh?" Onyxflame perked up. "So that would have been the thumping and dragging I heard earlier." He drained his mug of tea.

Alistar waved a hand. "Go see what you have and if there's anything you still need."

"My thanks, De'seneth." Onyxflame left his mug on the table and left the kitchen. Alistar heard him climb the stairs and enter the guest room.

Dahr frowned. "You are permitting Onyxflame to roam your house unmonitored?"

"I can tell which room he's in from the creaking of the floor. Last night I warded his room, and intend to continue doing so."

"I hope he tested the wards. I've been told those employed by Chirrod Prison are extremely painful when triggered." Dahr settled into the chair Onyxflame had vacated.

Nearly ten minutes later, Onyxflame returned dressed in a suit that fit as if tailored to him. The azure silkweave shirt shimmered slightly as he moved, complemented by a silver jacket. A deep brown cloak hung over his arm, and the image he presented would have been one of refinement, had Onyxflame bothered to tuck in the shirt tails.

Onyxflame shook his head. "*This* is the closest thing I could find to normal daily wear in either the trunk or the bag. Must Aspendark *really* be such a traditionalist that he can't wear a coat?" He shook the cloak on his arm.

Dahr sniffed in derision, ignoring the complaint.

"I expect he's trying too hard to appear fashionable and convey the impression that he is up to date on the current styles of the court," Alistar said.

Onyxflame scowled. "Well damn Aspendark's pride. And it's no wonder he's in debt if he's investing *this* much on his clothing."

Dahr looked between them. "Is there a development I am not aware of?"

"Further clarification of Aspendark's identity and purpose in

Lewarden," Alistar said. "A background that will hold up to someone verifying it in Rillwater."

Dahr stiffed. "De'seneth, this situation demands discretion and confidentiality! His Highness—"

"His Highness put me in charge of this investigation, Dahr. And the person I've spoken to is well aware of the need for discretion." Alistar held the guard's gaze.

"Knowledge of the incidents is not to be revealed to anyone not directly involved," Dahr said, stiff.

"Do you know who I am, Dahr?" Alistar asked in a low voice. He loathed having to pull rank and draw on his family name so soon, but this mattered too much to let it pass.

"Yes sir," Dahr said.

"Has my family ever, to your knowledge, failed to keep the Royal Family's confidences?"

"No sir."

"They're not going to start doing so now," Alistar told him. "My father will not spread this tale."

Dahr's jaw tightened, but he bowed his head. "Very well, sir." His voice was as stiff as his spine.

"Now *I'm* curious as to who your family is," Onyxflame said.

"You'll know when you need to know," Alistar said curtly. "We have work to do. We'll start by visiting the site of the incident here on Shale Lane." He piled dishes in the sink, knowing that Mrs. Ke'lyn would wash and put them away.

Onyxflame eyed Dahr. "Can you act a bit less like an animated statue? You'll stand out like an ogre among sprites."

Dahr scowled indignantly. "Noblemen are entitled to a guard."

"While that's true, most noblemen are *not* entitled to one of the Silver Prince's personal guards," Alistar interrupted. "While I realize this is an abnormal request to make of you, Dahr, can you act… less formal when we're checking the sites of the outages?"

Dahr nodded with evident reluctance. "If it is necessary, sir, then yes."

"My neighbors include a brothel and a religious fanatic, and this is one of the better neighborhoods in which incidents have taken place," Alistar told him dryly. "Yes, it is necessary."

Descending the stairs once more, Alistar pulled on his sealskin coat and turned out the lights, then opened the front door. He winced against the first blow of frigid air. Frost coated the ground and shone on the steps. Alistar looked at the sky as he locked the door. A few clouds hung overhead, but no snow.

Onyxflame and Dahr followed him. Alistar started down the street at an easy pace. One of the bums on the street raised a gloved hand in greeting, and Alistar returned the courtesy. The bum eyed the two elves warily, giving them only a slight nod of the head, to which neither responded. Alistar recalled the blackout and the view he had seen through his window, and turned north. He guessed that the center of the outage should be within two block of his house, estimating by the spread of the drained lines. If an individual was responsible, they would have sought someplace out of immediate sight. He recalled the glimpse he'd seen of light and figures before the darkness.

At a crossing with Grain Street, he paused. Speaking in a low voice, he said, "This would be my best guess as to where the outage originated, if something drained the mahiy lines."

Onyxflame crossed the street to an alley. Dahr followed closely, and Alistar trailed after them. Rotting boards lay piled along one wall and murky water pocketed the chipped cobbles. If someone had come through, there was little evidence.

Onyxflame pulled off his gloves and ran a hand along the wall of one building, then he shook his head. "Damn these. While I'm wearing these cursed dampeners, I can't tell anything from this without tools, De'seneth. I can't feel enough about the mahiy lines to know if this was even the center of your incident, whether your records say so or not."

"This is where the lights I saw would have been," Alistar said. "Somewhere near here." He turned around slowly.

"Who're you? Whadda ya want?" demanded a young voice.

All three men started and turned. A street urchin glowered at them, hands planted on his hips. Alistar guessed him to be around ten years old. He wore a wool coat that was more patches than original cloth and gloves much too large.

Alistar addressed the boy. "My name's Alistar. I live a couple blocks up. These two are with me. Mind if we pass?"

The boy remained wary, but his hostile air eased slightly at Alistar's respect for his claim on the alley. "Whadda ya want?" he repeated.

"We think some people came through here a couple nights ago," Alistar began.

"You lookin' for the shining men?" The new voice was younger and higher pitched. The scrawny, dirty girl could have been anywhere between five and nine. She peered at them from a nest among the rotting boards.

"Hush! Don't you talk to them," the boy said quickly. "And don't be telling that stupid story again neither."

"It's not a story," she said with all the indignation she could muster. She looked to Alistar and his companion. "He thinks I made them up, but I saw the shining men."

Onyxflame gave her a friendly smile, sinking down on his haunches to be eye-level with her. "Tell me more about them. Where were they?"

The girl pointed at the wall. "Up there. Runned right up the wall they did! And then the sky went dark, but they were all glowing."

"The shining men were on the roof?" Onyxflame asked.

She nodded.

"How many did you see?"

She frowned, then held up four fingers. "This many. And they was carrying great big jars, 'cept one of them had a giant crate instead. They was real strong—lifted all that stuff right up! My brother's strong, but he couldn't have picked those jars up." Her eyes gleamed with excitement. "An' they runned up the wall like spiders!"

"They don't care none about your stupid story!" her brother cut in sharply.

"Yes they do!" she said. "And I'm not making it up. One of them gived me candy. See?" She pulled a handful of what looked like dirty rock candy from her pocket and held them out for Onyxflame's inspection.

Onyxflame raised an eyebrow. "That was very generous of your shining men."

She nodded. "I'm gonna save it. Gran said when you get a nice thing, you should save it until the right time, because having a nice thing makes a bad time not so bad, and a good time even better."

"Your Gran was a wise woman," Onyxflame said solemnly. "You should at least save a piece for the Ice Blossom Festival. It's tradition to have candy then."

She considered the candy, then the elf. After a long moment of thought, she said, "You can have a piece if you want. But I'm not sharing none with my brother, because he don't believe me."

"You're very kind. Thank you." Onyxflame took one of the grimy candies from her hand. "I'll save it for a special time too."

She beamed at him and tucked the rest into the pocket of her oversized coat. Her brother watched every movement warily, only relaxing when Onyxflame stepped back.

Onyxflame turned to Alistar. "Well, De'seneth, shall we?"

Alistar looked up the side of the building in unrealistic hope that he would find an easy way to ascend. "After you."

Onyxflame chuckled and moved deeper into the alley until he came around the back side of the building. A rickety iron ladder clung to the side of the building. Onyxflame gestured at it.

"The chimney sweeps have to get up somehow," he remarked.

The ladder creaked ominously when Onyxflame pulled himself up the first rungs. Alistar winced at the sounds, but

Onyxflame appeared unconcerned. He made the ascent in a careful but steady pace and scrambled onto the roof. Alistar looked at Dahr, then steeled himself and took hold of the ladder.

The climb wasn't quite as bad as he had feared. Each rung felt as fragile as a tree branch about to snap under his weight, but none broke. Alistar pulled himself up onto the roof, and was immediately slammed by the wind.

He wavered, then Onyxflame caught his arm and steadied him. "No falling now, De'seneth. It would be a terrible delay on this investigation, and thus on my release."

Alistar caught his balance and nodded, pulling his coat tighter around himself against the sharp, biting wind. "I'm fine. Found anything?"

Onyxflame closed his eyes. "The dampeners are still working against me, but I believe that child was right. A lot of residual magic—the levels that I would expect." He pointed up. "And we are almost directly below the main mahiy line through this district. This would be an ideal location."

"On the roof," Alistar murmured as Onyxflame paced across the roof. Out of immediate sight, with clear access to the mahiy line. "That explains the figures I saw."

Alistar walked slowly across the lightly sloped roof top. The shingles felt solid and sturdy, making good footing, at least in the absence of snow. Alistar crouched when his eye caught a glint of metal. He picked up an engraved ivory button rimmed with gold. No chimney sweep's lost coat button, certainly.

"So, shining men," he commented.

"Natural channelers, I would guess," Onyxflame said. "Probably unregistered, knowing how you people try to keep a tight leash on the registered."

The ability to draw power directly from the mahiy lines without needing the use of a focusing device was rare. While focusing devices could be registered and billed for the magic they used, a channeler could, in theory, pull as much power from the mahiy lines as he or she was capable of holding. The law required all channelers of any significant ability to be registered, and failure to comply resulted in prohibitive levels of punishment; the worst of which was to be Silenced, where a channeler's ability to use magic at all was burned from him. Most who suffered that fate went mad shortly after. Even healers were required to be registered, although the Crown granted them leave to tap into mahiy lines without charge whenever they needed.

"A group of unregistered channelers, draining mahiy lines? That's reckless. If they were caught, they would all be Silenced," Alistar said grimly. "And for what purpose?"

"They must think the reward greater than the risk." Onyxflame gestured around them. "Just look. The city lies before you, the power hangs above you, and no one knows who you are. There is a thrill to such things, De'seneth. A thrill to the confidence that you are invincible. It is an addictive sensation."

"You learned that you aren't invincible," Alistar said. Not that Onyxflame was a channeler, but he spoke as if he understood the thrill of that confidence.

"You have a talent for spoiling a good mood, De'seneth." Onyxflame scowled at him. "Fine. There isn't much more to find here without proper tools. We can leave."

Dahr still waited on the ground. "Anything?" he asked once they were both safely on the cobbles again.

"Someone was up there. Onyxflame got what he could without tools, and I found this." Alistar handed the button to the guard.

"You found what?" Onyxflame asked with sudden interest.

"A gold-rimmed ivory button," Alistar answered. "Cuff sleeve size."

"Really? That could be hard to replace quickly. Someone of money. We'll have to watch for who might be missing a button." Onyxflame smiled.

"I doubt it will be quite *that* easy," Alistar said. "No one with any fashion sense would go in public with a missing button on their coat. However, we have an idea where to look for these activities."

"Where now, sir?" Dahr asked.

"Silverline Power," Alistar said.

Onyxflame's jaw tightened. "Why should we have to go *there*?"

"If we need tools—accurate and legal tools, that is—we go to Silverline Power." Alistar continued north toward Archers' Way.

"Walking?" Onyxflame asked.

"Hiring a coach," Alistar told him. "I am sure that Lord Aspendark would not wish to arrive on foot like a common man."

"Good. I have my doubts that these shoes were intended for any sentient creature who intended to walk farther than out of a door and into a carriage," Onyxflame said, shooting a glower at Dahr.

Dahr scowled back at him. "You climbed a ladder well enough in them."

"Only because I wasn't willing to freeze my feet to the rungs by taking them off!"

"If you don't shut up, I'm hiring the carriage for myself and you can *both* walk," Alistar said. He raised a hand to hail a taxi as they rounded the corner onto Archers' Way.

"Ah… my apologies, De'seneth. If there is any idea I like less than that of walking in these shoes, it is that of running in them." Onyxflame rubbed his neck, a reminder of the warding and the requirement that he remain close to Alistar.

"Good." Alistar gave him barely a glance, then turned to the coach that clattered to a stop before them. "Silverline Power."

The driver answered with a curt nod, his team stamping impatiently as Alistar, Onyxflame, and Dahr climbed inside. The coach door closed, and they rattled into the busy street.

CHAPTER 10

"What tools do you need?" Alistar asked, leaning back on the hard bench.

"Something to measure the strength of the lines, and a meter to read residual power levels. If all the magic was drawn to one location, it will have left a mark." Onyxflame tucked his hands under the cloak. "Perdition, it's cold out here."

"Blood and sand," Alistar corrected.

Onyxflame blinked. "What?"

"Aspendark's from Rillwater. He should swear like it. So, 'blood and sand' should be one of your most used curses," Alistar said. "You can use ones more appropriate to Lewarden in situations where you would have opportunity to think of what to say."

Onyxflame raised an eyebrow. "And I thought I had enough to worry about just trying to curse like a noble. You shall have to teach me how to swear like a pira— privateer, De'seneth."

"Yes, I will," Alistar said. "Later." He wasn't sure he looked forward to providing Onyxflame with an entirely new vocabulary of profanities and insults. "Although whatever curses you picked up from the Narnan sailors should serve in the meantime."

The coach rattled to a halt. Alistar braced for the cold and opened the door, climbing out into the frigid day. Onyxflame pulled his cloak tight, and even Dahr shivered. Alistar paid the driver and walked to the gates of Silverline Power. He eyed the huddled clump of protesters across the street, wondering, not for the first time, how they could afford to idle their time away without working.

Unless this is also part of the plot that His Highness thinks is going on, and they ARE being paid to stand there and rave at us.

Onyxflame eyed the protesters with interest. "Have they been here long?"

"Off and on for several months now," Alistar said. "It was more popular before the weather turned foul. Now just the truly insane or devoted show up."

He easily tuned out the shouts from across the street. The ogre at the gate sniffed him and nodded, but eyed Onyxflame with a threatening scowl. Dahr spoke in Elven, and the ogre shook his head firmly. "No. No entry without a pass. He has no pass. No pass, no entry. Director's orders."

Alistar looked at Dahr, but the guard shook his head, chagrined. "I apologize, sir. I failed to collect one for Lord Aspendark."

"I'll go in and get a guest pass for him," Alistar said. He turned to the ogre. "If that will be acceptable?"

Onyxflame cleared his throat. "De'seneth? That *could* be a bit of a problem." He rubbed his neck.

"You bring him a pass, Associate De'seneth, he can enter," the ogre said.

"And while I obtain a pass, can these two wait in the guard house, out of the wind?" Alistar asked, ignoring Onyxflame's discomfort.

The ogre frowned, considered, then finally answered with a short nod. Alistar walked Onyxflame and Dahr to the building. The guard house sat outside the wall, and offered shelter, though not a great deal of comfort. Three chairs sat around a table littered with pamphlets and handbills strewn about by the protesters.

"I am not certain that Lord Aspendark will appreciate this, De'seneth," Onyxflame said. "And I am *quite* certain that the distance is farther than I am permitted to remain from you."

"I imagine that even if Lord Aspendark is inconvenienced by the oversight, he is not foolish enough to argue with a devoted gate ogre," Alistar said. "And the distance requirement is stayed if you are already held under a ward."

Onyxflame opened his mouth to protest. Alistar fixed a sharp look at him, and the elf bit back his words. Alistar recalled one of the eldritch chain wards, and activated it, locking Onyxflame's wrist to the table by a four-foot invisible chain.

"I'll return shortly. Please wait here. Dahr, if I was misinformed and he attempts to follow me, I will trust you to restrain him before an ogre cleaves him in half."

"Of course, sir." Dahr's tone implied that he would prefer to see the second happen.

Alistar walked through the gates and up the path, patting the gargoyle Morath as he passed. When he entered the lobby, Assistant Torrent sat at the desk. "Associate De'seneth? Director Strey'mend said that you would probably not be in today because of the assignment he has given you."

"Yes…," Alistar said. "Actually, as part of my work on that assignment, I need some tools. However, I am also escorting a guest, and he needs a pass."

She consulted her book. "I do have a message from the director that you might be accompanied by a Lord Taslor Aspendark. Did he not receive his pass already?"

"It doesn't appear so. His baggage encountered some troubles along the way, and I can only guess that if he was issued a pass, it was never picked up," Alistar said. And he was certain that if any such pass had been in the trunk or bag, Onyxflame would have found it.

The sprite checked several record books. "You are correct, De'seneth. A pass was issued, but not delivered. Let me retrieve it for you."

She drew several lines on a sheet of parchment, then hummed an invocation. Sprites drew magic from the mahiy lines, but their methods of channeling were different from those of humans or elves, and seemed unreproduceable by anyone who was not a sprite. With a soft pop of displaced air, a thin metal card dropped onto the desk. Assistant Torrent checked it, nodding as she did so.

"This seems to be in order. Lord Aspendark is granted temporary permission to enter Silverline Power grounds when in the company of you, Associate De'seneth, and otherwise, he is to be turned away, restrained if necessary, but not killed." She considered the name thoughtfully. "I have heard a very similar name—perhaps even the same surname—used before, but I believe it was being used as an alias for a criminal. It must be difficult to have someone abuse one's name in such a way."

Alistar opened his mouth, then closed it again. The sprite gave him a very pointed look that told him without any words: she knew the name was false. She quite possibly knew who was using that alias. "I'm sure that it must be," he agreed finally.

She handed the card up to him. "Associate De'seneth, I wish you good luck in your assignment, and hope that you and the assistant His Highness selected will find what you need."

She not only knows who Onyxflame is, she knows that the Silver Prince is involved. Just how much DO the sprites know?

Clouds had begun to drift in when he walked back up the path to the gate. Alistar shivered and pulled his coat tight around him. In the gate house, the two elves still waited for him, neither looking the worse for wear.

"Any problems?" Alistar asked.

"None, sir," Dahr said. "He was quiet."

Onyxflame thumbed through a pamphlet that lay on the table. "Interesting theories that your protesters hold about mahiy lines and magic. I have to presume that they are incorrect, although the idea that Prince Cero has hunted down and imprisoned pixies and sprites in order to generate magic is… unique. Of course, when a man *is* so secretive about his methods, there are bound to be many theories."

Alistar released the ward and handed Onyxflame the card. "Your pass."

"I am to be allowed to come and go from Silverline Power as I please?" he asked.

"Only if you're with me," Alistar retorted. "Otherwise the guards have full permission to beat you senseless. I wouldn't recommend testing the theory. Come on."

The ogre grunted and continued to eye Onyxflame with suspicion, but allowed them all to pass. Alistar crossed the yard quickly, eager to be out of the cold. Inside, Onyxflame looked around the lobby and nodded in approval.

"Very nice. Far more pleasant than the exterior would lead a man to expect."

"Lord Aspendark, welcome to Silverline Power Cooperative," Assistant Torrent greeted. "I am Assistant Torrent. Can I help you?"

Onyxflame started when he saw the sprite at the desk. "Thank you, Assistant Torrent," he said after a moment. "However, I believe that Associate De'seneth has everything in hand." He looked to Alistar for confirmation.

"Very well, sir. You spoke of needing certain tools for your assignment, Associate De'seneth. Where can I direct you?"

"I need tools to read the strength of the mahiy lines, and to analyze the ambient magic fields," Alistar answered.

"Chief Botanist Riverbed's department, then." The sprite indicated the door on the first floor behind her desk. "I will inform him that you are on your way."

"Thank you, Assistant," Alistar said, stumbling slightly over the words. Chief Botanist Riverbed ruled the generators—he was equal in rank to Director Strey'mend. Alistar had never personally met him.

Followed by Onyxflame and Dahr, Alistar pushed open the double doors that led into the depth of the building and the generator facility. The doors swung shut behind them, and Alistar continued down a hall to the next set of doors, heavy steel portals. They looked as if they should require enormous effort to open, but they swung easily thanks to the enchantments on them. At least, they opened easily to employees of Silverline Power who had business beyond them. Anyone else would be pitting their strength against the weight of massive doors that offered hindrance rather than assistance.

He was immediately hit by the fragrance of thousands of kurowa blossoms. The scent was pungent, though not overpowering, thanks to the movement of air through the generator rooms and the high ceilings. They always reminded Alistar of exotic spices rather than flowers, like a pleasant mixture of cinnamon and cloves with a hint of something sweet and hard to describe.

Onyxflame inhaled deeply. "Kurowa flowers?" he asked. "And why are we going to be speaking to a botanist about mahiy lines, exactly?"

Alistar didn't reply. At least there were *some* things about the mahiy lines that Tiyron Onyxflame did not know. He couldn't see the plants from the entrance—the generator rooms were closed off, with no windows to contaminate them with outside light. Some of the protesters outside claimed that Silverline Power imprisoned magical creatures and drained them of their essence. The truth was far more mundane, and while not completely secret, it wasn't widely known, either. When entering the Silver Prince's employ, all candidates had to sign a contract permitting trade secrets to be erased from their memories when they left the company.

Alistar walked slowly down the hall. To either side, closed doors were labeled with short names and numbers. Red Twenty,

Yellow Fifteen, Green Forty-Six—Low Light. He knew a little about the various designations. Different colors of the flowers produced different levels of magic, and required different amounts of light to flourish. Alistar had rarely been in this area; he didn't often have cause to do so. Ahead of him, the hall widened into a circular room with branching cross halls running from it. A young human man dressed in plain trousers and a long-sleeved shirt stained with sap frowned at Alistar and the two elves.

"Excuse me, sir. Your business?" His tone was not rude, but firmly implied that if they did not have a reason to be here, they should leave. Immediately.

"Associate Third Degree Alistar De'seneth, with Lord Taslor Aspendark, to speak with Chief Botanist Riverbed," Alistar replied.

"Wait here, please," the young man told them, then he vanished down one of the halls.

"Botanists and flowers, De'seneth?" Onyxflame asked. "I thought that we had work to do. I know that the kurowa tend to grow near the mahiy lines, but if you are going to tell me that the prince maintains fields of flowers in the basement of his building simply to make this all somehow 'feel' natural, I am going to say that he's lost his mind."

Footsteps approached, and a stern voice replied, "The kurowa plants do not simply grow near the mahiy lines. Without the kurowa, we would *have* no mahiy lines." A heavy-set middle-aged elf tromped into the room. His clothing was spotted with small green stains, and his hands appeared to be permanently stained brown and green. "Come with me, all of you."

Alistar hurried after the elf, and he heard Onyxflame and Dahr behind him a moment later. The heavy-set elf opened a door and ushered them inside an office. The space bloomed with plants of all sizes and hues, none of them kurowa plants. The desk was home to at least three different varieties of ivy, leaving little room for any paperwork that might need to be done. A climbing rose bloomed on a trellis on the far wall. Ornamental shrubs competed with a collection of flowers around the floor space.

The Chief Botanist shut the door behind them and walked to the desk. "So, Dahr, these must be your charges."

Dahr nodded. "Yes, sir. Associate Alistar De'seneth and—"

"And Tiyron Onyxflame, yes, I know. Presently going by 'Taslor Aspendark', I believe His Highness said?" Chief Botanist Riverbed studied them with narrowed eyes.

"So I have been informed," Onyxflame said. "So delightful to know that I haven't been forgotten."

"I do not forget someone who causes me as much trouble as you have, Onyxflame," Chief Botanist Riverbed said coolly. "I was less than pleased to learn that His Highness intended to use you in this investigation. However, he did point out that you have some uses, and your skill in attempting to rob Silverline Power could be a benefit, if properly contained." His eyes narrowed. "I have been given to believe that you *are* properly contained now, which is the only reason you are permitted entry."

Onyxflame's eyes narrowed. Alistar pointedly cleared his throat. "Chief Botanist, Onyxflame's skills and knowledge will be put to good use. However, I need tools to measure the mahiy lines, their strengths, and the ambient magic. Also, we need to know all the locations where incidents have taken place, and if anyone was able to pinpoint the center of the outages."

"Yes, yes. I've sent my assistant to retrieve the tools you should need. He will return with them shortly," the chief botanist said.

"You said that without the kurowa plants, there would be no mahiy lines," Onyxflame interrupted.

"I did," the chief botanist agreed. "Because it is true. People have often observed the link between mahiy lines and kurowa plants. The theory for years has been that the plants are drawn to the magic of the mahiy lines, and that the stronger the magic, the more plants one will find. That theory is entirely backwards."

Onyxflame's face ran through expressions of puzzlement and confusion before hardening back to an attempt to appear impassive. "Fine then. So what *is* the connection between the plants and the mahiy lines?"

"Kurowa plants generate magic." A simple statement that threw thousands of theories about magic into confusion. The chief botanist continued, "They flower, but they do not seed. That observation was the starting point that led His Highness to discovering the nature of mahiy lines. Kurowa plants do not seed, yet they spread. The question was 'how?' "

Onyxflame shrugged. "Runners. Roots. Plants spread in many ways other than seeds."

"They are small plants, and their roots do not run so deep. They shoot off no observed runners."

"They send seeds over the mahiy lines. I don't know," Onyxflame snapped. "The point?"

"You are almost correct," Chief Botanist Riverbed replied. "The mahiy lines do not carry seeds. They *are* the runners of the kurowa plants."

A frown formed on Onyxflame's brow. "They are... what?"

"They are the runners that the kurowa plants put out," Alistar said. "They link the plants together, and we tap into those runners to draw our magic."

Onyxflame laughed sharply. "And *this* is how Silverline Power generates magic? Flowers? So anyone could simply grow their own generator, if they knew."

"No," Chief Botanist Riverbed cut in. "Our generators are the result of many years of careful breeding for reliable, sustainable, and directable mahiy lines. The magic we spread across Lewarden is stable, attuned to a certain level optimal for the operation of machines and tools. Wild growths do not produce steady power. They fluctuate. They vary. They grow erratically."

"And no one knows any of this? No one in all these years has realized this before?" Onyxflame said. "Perdition, no disgruntled employee of Silverline Power has gone spreading rumors?"

"His Highness has containment measures in place," the chief botanist said simply. "If you *really* want to learn first-hand about those containment measures, I do invite you to attempt to spread rumors, Onyxflame." His gaze was icy.

"When one of the Silver Prince's own guards watches my every move? No thank you. I expect that he would be more than happy enough to remove my head if he thought it necessary. That is enough of a 'containment measure' for my tastes."

A knock sounded on the door, and the young man who had stopped them earlier entered, carrying a sack. "Chief Botanist, the tools you requested."

"Thank you, Nikaze. They are for Associate De'seneth's use."

"Yes sir." The young man set the bag beside Alistar's feet. "Will there be anything else at the moment, sir?"

"Not now. You may go."

The young man nodded and withdrew, closing the door again. Chief Botanist Riverbed rose and opened a desk drawer. He lifted a roll of parchment from the drawer. Looking at the ivy plants, he spoke in the sharp, abrupt Elven tongue. The ivy vines wove themselves into a framework, and Riverbed unrolled the sheet of parchment across them. "Here is a map of the incidents we have recorded so far."

The ivy plants turned the map to face Alistar, Onyxflame, and Dahr. Alistar looked it over carefully, noting the locations.

"You've had incidents at Goldlane, the Diamond Walk, and Dragon Quarter—two noble sections and one high merchant section of the city, and you've managed to keep this *quiet*?" Onyxflame asked.

The Chief Botanist frowned, his expression that of a man who had asked himself the same question. "It seems so, thus far. All three incidents were brief—less than five minutes—and so far it appears that they have taken place on nights and times when the nobles of the house were away at another event."

That doesn't make sense if this is about politics. It would make a far stronger statement to have the affected area be where the party itself was taking place. That way, it causes immediate problems with no easy way to cover up the incident. But if someone is stealing power for another use, then that would be an ideal time. And the magic output to the rich areas of town is higher. If they can only steal a limited amount, then they'll get it faster from the rich section of the city.

"Can I have a copy of this map, Chief Botanist?" Alistar asked.

"Of course. I will send one to Assistant Torrent, and it will be waiting when you are ready to depart. Is there anything else I can do for you, Associate De'seneth? His Highness instructed that I should aid you as needed. Even if that means providing restricted devices and sensitive information to *him.*" He glowered at Onyxflame.

"No, thank you," Alistar said. "Your assistance is appreciated, sir."

"Find out who is trying to kill my mahiy lines, and I will be more than satisfied, De'seneth."

They returned to the lobby, and Alistar climbed the stairs. The two elves followed him, though Dahr looked puzzled.

"Is there something you need here, sir?"

"Yes." Alistar stopped outside the door into the office area. "Ony… Lord Aspendark, please wait here. I need to retrieve something from my desk."

"Go ahead. Don't let me hold you up," Onyxflame said casually.

Alistar entered the room, and some people turned to look at him with surprise. "Where have you been, De'seneth?" one man asked. "Thought you must be sick—you never miss a day."

"I'm on a project," Alistar replied. "Probably going to be away from my desk for quite a while."

"Field work in this weather? Good luck. You wouldn't see *me* out there."

Alistar smiled. "With the right motive, you never know." He ducked over to his desk and pulled several files from the drawer, then locked it again. They were unimportant and unrelated to his task, but they served as an excuse.

He stepped over to Lamorage's desk. The elf smiled warmly. "De'seneth, how is the project going?"

"Looks like it could be a long one," Alistar admitted. "But, I wanted to ask you something."

"Oh? What is it?" Lamorage asked with interest.

"I was hoping you could tell me whether there was a ball or celebration on these evenings." Alistar passed him three dates written down from the map—the three dates that corresponded to the outages in the high-class section of town.

"Hmm…" Lamorage looked at the dates, then nodded. "Sure. The first was Lord Snowfall's first ball for his daughter—her coming of age celebration. Practically everyone who was *anyone* was there. The second was The Court of the New Moon. The third…" He hesitated. "I wouldn't say it was a ball or celebration. But a rather exclusive gathering." Lamorage paused again. "I really can't say much about it, De'seneth. One of those private club sorts of gatherings. A friend introduced me there, invited me in. I'm not supposed to talk about it, though."

Such private clubs were not illegal, but they tended to cater to questionable dealings—especially gambling, a vice that some elves found fiercely addictive. Alistar nodded his understanding, but added, "Be careful that you don't get into something you can't get back out of, Lamorage. Thank you—that was what I needed to know."

Lamorage chuckled wryly. "As long as my father hasn't secretly hired you to keep him apprised of my activities, it's no problem, De'seneth."

"He hasn't," Alistar assured him. "Although I might consider it, if he were to offer me enough."

"He wouldn't," Lamorage responded. "He's a cheap old goat."

"Then you shouldn't have a thing to worry about," Alistar remarked. "When is the next gathering of note?"

To that question, Lamorage did look taken aback. "Four days, at the Proudmoor estate. Why?"

Alistar lowered his voice. "I've gotten word that a couple of noblemen from Rillwater plan to spend some time in the capital, do some mingling, find business connections. I know them, thought I could ease their way a little by giving them some information on the court and events." He hated to lie to his friend, but the truth wasn't something he could easily offer here, with all the listening ears. He was already aware that Lamorage's neighbors were leaning toward them, trying not to be obvious in their eavesdropping.

"Slee's Heart, Alistar!" Lamorage whispered. "Are you serious? Rillwater nobles in Lewarden?"

"I'm afraid so," Alistar agreed. "Don't worry, I promise there will be no open looting and plundering."

To that, Lamorage chuckled slightly. "If you say so. I'll make a list of the notable events I know about, De'seneth, and send it to you by post. That will give me a chance to make sure I'm not missing any important ones. Look for it tomorrow evening."

"Thank you," Alistar said sincerely. "I appreciate it more than you know."

CHAPTER 11

After departing from Silverline Power, they stopped at a modest diner for early lunch. The proprietor recognized Alistar as a Silverline employee and greeted him warmly. Once they ordered, Alistar studied the map of incidents while Onyxflame sampled an assortment of meat hand pies. Dahr confined himself to a bowl of stew and a hot mug of sweetened tea.

"Where next?" Onyxflame asked around his food. "Back to Shale Lane?"

Alistar nodded. "We have the tools for something more focused than 'shining men running up the walls.' While I don't deny that girl's observations were useful, they were anything but precise."

Onyxflame nodded agreeably. In fact, he had been suspiciously pleasant and agreeable since leaving Chief Botanist Riverbed's domain. Alistar was not willing to wager that a hot meal was enough to quell his resentment, and kept a wary eye on the elf.

Dahr gulped down his tea. "We're ready, then?"

"I am dining on His Highness's purse," Onyxflame said mildly.

"I intend to enjoy every moment of it." He took another bite of his meat pie.

"Bring it with you," Alistar said. "You can finish eating in the coach."

Onyxflame raised an eyebrow. "Like any good Rillwater nobleman would?"

"Like any sensible noble of Rillwater with business to attend would," Alistar retorted. He counted out a handful of ivory marks for their meal and set them on the table. Onyxflame took a moment to wrap the rest of his meat pie in a handkerchief and tuck it into his pocket. Without looking back, Alistar said, "And put the tip back on the table."

"Really, De'seneth, do you think I would—" Onyxflame began.

"Yes, I do. Put it back."

"Seems I'm out of practice." Onyxflame returned the chip to the table and followed Alistar out of the diner.

"It was also predictably obvious," Alistar told him as they stepped onto the noisy street. "I expected better."

Onyxflame blinked at him, brow furrowing as he tried to decide whether or not Alistar was encouraging him to be more subtle in his thefts.

"A privateer boasts about the great plunder from his latest victory, not the mountain of slivers he's collected from filching tips off tables," Alistar said blandly. He raised a hand and hailed a taxi coach, glad that Dahr had apparently missed their exchange.

Returning to the alley on Shale Lane, Alistar gave a brief nod of greeting to the street rat and his sister. "Mind if we pass through one more time?"

The boy scowled, but gave permission with a curt, silent nod. Dahr chose to wait at the mouth of the alley as Alistar and Onyxflame ascended the creaking metal ladder again. Had it been a rope ladder secured to deck and mast, Alistar wouldn't have minded it, but the noises this ladder made suggested that it was ready to tear out of the wall at any moment. He rather envied the "shining men" their ability to climb the wall directly.

Onyxflame looked through the bag of tools and drew out what appeared to be a dowsing rod made of iron, ringed with bands of silver. He turned it over, checking the make and mark, then nodded, satisfied. "Abde mahiy lamor."

The dowsing rod glowed, pulses of blue light flickering across the bands of silver. Onyxflame walked slowly around the roof, watching the dowsing rod and frowning. "Hmm."

"Problem?" Alistar asked.

"Not near as much residual as I expected. There is some, but I expected a much higher power bleed. More waste. Whoever did this, they were remarkably efficient." Onyxflame gestured up. "And we are almost directly beneath the primary mahiy line through this area."

Alistar frowned. "You're saying that, whatever means they used, they actually captured and contained the majority of the magic they stole?"

"It seems that way, De'seneth," Onyxflame said. "You have some very skilled thieves on your hands."

Alistar raised an eyebrow, hearing the note of irritation in his voice. "Skilled thieves, and you don't approve?"

Onyxflame tucked the dowsing rod into the bag and cupped his hands over his mouth to warm his fingers. "I don't approve when they aren't me. Per— Blood and sand, this wind is bitter."

Alistar nodded in agreement and held out a hand for the bag of tools. Onyxflame relinquished it with reluctance, then climbed down the ladder to the alley. He moved quickly, dropping down the last few rungs to the ground as Alistar began his descent. The ladder trembled even more than it had on the climb up, and Alistar looked up suspiciously. One of the bolts holding it to the wall shook loose, tumbling down to the ground. Abandoning grace in favor of haste, Alistar half climbed, half slid down, landing feet-first on the icy cobbles hard enough to knock his breath from him. He shook his head to clear it, steadying himself against the wall. Rapid footsteps darted away, farther up the alley. Alistar looked in either direction, and realized that Onyxflame had vanished.

"Rot and reefs," he snarled. *Did he loosen the ladder? Is this his idea of doing "better" than stealing marks off a table? Was that a distraction or an attempt to be rid of me?* Alistar glanced up the side of the building. If the ladder had come loose and fallen straight back, it would have hit the next building, and he would likely have been stuck, but not in severe danger, at least until the ladder listed to one side or the other and fell the rest of the way. His jaw tightened. He didn't see the elf, and the sound of running steps was fading enough that he couldn't be sure which way they'd gone. Gritting his teeth, Alistar hurried back to Dahr.

The guard straightened when Alistar returned alone. "Where is Aspendark, sir?"

"Took off down the alley while I was distracted," Alistar admitted through clenched teeth. "I couldn't tell which way. We need to—"

Dahr raised a hand to stop him. His expression showed irritation rather than concern, and did not seem directed at Alistar. "Come this way, sir." He crossed the street, moving farther from the alley rather than closer. "If you chase him, sir, you increase the chance that you'll remain within his permitted range. The best option to give him the least opportunity for further mischief is to trigger the compulsion for him to return." Dahr walked quickly, and Alistar followed.

"He's attempting to escape on the first day out of my house," Alistar said, as angry at himself as at Onyxflame.

Dahr just nodded. "Yes, sir." He considered Alistar. "I expect Onyxflame to make such attempts, and to continue to do so for so long as he is under your keeping. The fact that he's done so now does not reflect ill on you or your wardenship of him. The wards placed on Onyxflame were chosen for such occasions."

Alistar raised a dubious eyebrow. "So you're saying I should feel better that I didn't anticipate the attempt because he was going to do it anyway?"

Dahr shifted uncomfortably. "I… well, yes, sir."

They walked half a block before Alistar heard a string of curses that were pure Lewarden slums. Spitting breathless obscenities, Onyxflame stumbled from an alley and limped to them, one hand pulling at his shirt collar as if it strangled him. He bit the curses back when he staggered across the street to join Alistar and Dahr.

Alistar raised an eyebrow. "Have a pleasant run?" he asked icily.

"Not particularly," Onyxflame said, wincing. "Even before the sudden stop." He glared at Dahr. "Were these shoes chosen specifically to discourage swift movement?"

Dahr's expression was a mask. "They were fashioned by the court cobbler from the specifications provided by His Highness. There is nothing wrong with your shoes."

"Except that they don't *fit*," Onyxflame muttered. "Too large."

Alistar's jaw tightened. Without a word, he strode down the street and turned into another alley. A quick look showed it to be unoccupied, lacking the piles of debris someone might use for shelter. Onyxflame and Dahr followed him, Onyxflame's face quizzical, Dahr's blank.

Alistar seized Onyxflame by the embroidered jacket and slammed him hard against the wall. "What, exactly, was that stunt you pulled in the alley? You think you can escape if you get me killed? Claim it was an accident if the ladder came off the wall and I fell?"

Onyxflame had started to voice a glib response, but it died on his lips at the accusation. His mouth opened in surprise, then shock. "What? What are you talking about, De'seneth? That ladder was loose when we first climbed it!"

"And it was missing bolts after you went down it," Alistar said, eyes narrowing. Beside Alistar, Dahr's expression grew dark and grim.

Onyxflame blinked, and his surprise seemed genuine. "De'seneth, I don't know what you're talking about. Getting you killed would be one of the stupidest things I could do. Testing the wards is one thing, attempted murder is something entirely different."

"Yes, it is," Alistar said in a low voice.

Onyxflame raised his hands quickly in a gesture of surrender and defense. "The ladder was shaking when I descended, but not by any sabotage at my hands. If bolts were missing, I didn't take them."

"And your word is entirely trustworthy," Dahr said, voice hard.

"I did not attempt to harm or kill my handler," Onyxflame insisted, looking from one to the other. "I swear."

"Pure coincidence, then," Alistar said dryly.

"Bad luck. Chance. The 'shining men' took out a few bolts when they were up there and it took a couple of trips for things to work loose. I don't know, De'seneth!"

The last blurted suggestion actually caught Alistar's attention. Perhaps the "shining men" had taken precautions—though that didn't explain one of them being careless enough to lose a coat button.

"Of course," Dahr scoffed. "Doubtless they first called upon their mastery of divination to determine that you and Associate De'seneth would climb that ladder."

"Rotting Souls of Kessel's Brood, I did not try to murder anyone!" Onyxflame burst out. "Anyone with half their wits could guess *someone* from Silverline would investigate!"

"So you 'just' attempted to escape," Alistar said.

"Yes!" Onyxflame caught himself. "Um, I mean… What difference does it make? The wards dragged me back all the same. Don't we have other sites to inspect?"

"I think fifty yards is overly generous," Alistar said. He stepped back, releasing Onyxflame, and fished a rumpled sheet of parchment from his pocket. Onyxflame shifted uneasily but said nothing as he straightened his clothes. He did rub his left wrist when Alistar triggered an ethereal shackle.

"You're reducing the distance, sir?" Dahr asked.

"Ten feet," Alistar said. "Enough time wasted. The next closest site is Halfmoon Hill, nearly a month ago." He strode from the alley.

Onyxflame trailed him, still massaging his wrist. Dahr took the rear guard. Onyxflame spoke. "If they used a rooftop again, any signs they left behind are probably undisturbed except by birds."

Alistar answered with a curt nod, then shot a look of irritation at Onyxflame. "I'm sure it doesn't actually chafe."

Onyxflame caught himself still rubbing his wrist, and tucked his hands under his cloak. "It's more akin to a shirt cuff buttoned a little too tight, without the means to unbutton it." He cast a look up and down the lane. "We aren't... walking to Halfmoon, are we?"

Alistar's hands sought the depths of his pockets. "It's not much more than a mile. A brisk afternoon stroll to warm the blood. You were eager enough to travel on foot a little while ago."

"A notion these damnable shoes quickly cured," Onyxflame countered. "And is it really suitable for noblemen to be walking in this part of the city?"

That, regrettably, *was* a valid argument. Alistar didn't comment, turning up toward Archers' Way again. He did hear Onyxflame's sigh of relief when he hailed a coach, and Dahr's soft snort of scorn at the other elf. For all the twists around blocks and weaving through traffic the driver did, Alistar suspected that walking would actually have been the faster way to travel.

Halfmoon Hill was a moderately questionable neighborhood, and Alistar appreciated the security offered by Dahr's presence. Onyxflame spent a little time questioning the local urchins, but they regarded him with deep suspicion—too well dressed, in spite of his ability to mirror their street accents, and a stranger with none to vouch for him. Alistar knew his own presence nearby didn't help the matter either, but he wasn't willing to extend Onyxflame's leash. More than once, Onyxflame stopped sharply, finding himself at the end of his ten-foot allowance. He didn't openly voice his complaint, though the looks he gave Alistar spoke them clearly enough.

The dowsing rod led them to a derelict building. Alistar tested the ladder carefully before climbing to the roof, followed by Onyxflame. Dahr waited below, wary and watchful. The sloped roof creaked and groaned, and in more than one spot, the rotting timbers had collapsed, leaving gaping holes. Onyxflame scoured the entire roof with the dowsing rod, and Alistar calibrated the meter to estimate the loss of power.

Onyxflame leaned cautiously over one of the holes, frowning at the dowsing rod. "De'seneth? The residual traces are stronger over here. Perhaps they employed the upper floor rather than the roof itself."

Alistar considered the hole, then the sky. "How clear a view do they need? Or do they need one at all?" Channelers didn't need a clear line of sight on the mahiy lines to channel from them, but in both sites they'd seen so far, the thieves seemed to seek open air.

Onyxflame hesitated, looking up, then into the hole. "I'm not certain, De'seneth. If they are using some manner of mechanical device rather than organic, the evidence suggests they do require line of sight." His expression was wary. "I don't know how much trust I would put in stairs inside this building. And anything they left has likely already been looted by the locals."

Alistar raised a silent eyebrow at the elf. *Now you're advising caution about crawling through deserted buildings?*

Onyxflame's back stiffened as he read the unspoken thought on Alistar's face. He rubbed his wrist. "As things stand, De'seneth, if either one of us falls, I'm the worse off. I don't care to test whether this warding is such that if I fell, I would hang suspended by one arm, nor do I wish to test whether it would allow me to prevent you from falling or, more likely, simply drag me after you. If you insist that we must look within, we obviously will, but I advise against it."

Alistar looked down on the warped and rotting boards inside, and shook his head. "Not today. Come on. We won't find anything else here today, and dinner will be waiting when we return to my house."

Onyxflame nodded, following Alistar back to the ladder. He noticed that they both checked the ladder for all bolts before descending.

"Nothing new there," Alistar told Dahr. "It'll be dark soon. We'll start on the next sites tomorrow."

"Yes sir," Dahr said. "I will return before you set out in the morning." He followed them back to the main street and rode the carriage back to Shale Lane with them, then gave the driver a second destination once Alistar and Onyxflame disembarked and paid. Alistar raised a hand in farewell to the guard and hurried to the refuge of his home.

CHAPTER 12

Alistar briefly greeted Mrs. Ke'lyn as he tossed his coat and hat into the closet, waving off her question about his day and climbing the stairs. Onyxflame called a farewell to the housekeeper as he tailed Alistar. When Alistar opened his bedroom door, Onyxflame cleared his throat uncomfortably.

"De'seneth, if you would be so kind, might I retire to *my* roo—well, to your guest room? Please."

Alistar turned, fixing the elf with a cold stare. "I trust that you will stay there."

"I assume that you intend to be certain I do," Onyxflame answered. "I'll make no attempt to leave the room without your permission."

"Ward-chain cancel and release," Alistar said in a low voice.

Onyxflame rubbed his wrist and stepped back. "Thank you." Alistar watched him walk down the hall to the guest room. There was a definite limp to Onyxflame's gait, though he tried to minimize it. Once Onyxflame was inside and the door closed, Alistar reached toward the sheet of parchment in his pocket. He didn't pull it out. Even if Onyxflame did leave the room, he wouldn't go far, and locking him in right now felt petty.

Alistar entered his room and closed the door. He ran a hand through his hair and let out a long breath. Stripping off the day's clothes, he dressed down for the evening and slipped on a pair of house slippers.

"I was careless," he said, with no listeners but his wardrobe. "I should have stayed alert, and shouldn't have been surprised when he ran. I should have considered traps at the sites of the incidents." Those rankled more than Onyxflame's escape attempt: his failure to expect the attempt, and his failure to anticipate potential sabotage from the criminals he was investigating.

Alistar shook his head. His father had drilled into him many times that a good captain didn't punish those under him for his own failure to predict the enemy. And, escape attempt or not, it wasn't right to punish Onyxflame for crimes he hadn't committed.

He walked downstairs to the kitchen and checked the oven, where a roast waited alongside a dish of garlic potatoes. Alistar inhaled deeply as he pulled the pans out and turned off the oven. He set the kitchen table for two and ascended the stairs.

He knocked on the guest room door. "Dinner's ready downstairs. The door is open."

Inside, the bed creaked as someone sat up. "Dinner? And... am I invited?" Onyxflame asked cautiously.

"I'm not sending you to bed without supper, Onyxflame," Alistar said. "You're invited."

"I'll be down shortly," Onyxflame said. "I need to dress."

Alistar returned to the kitchen and brewed himself a mug of tea. After waiting several minutes, he gave in to the delicious smells and carved a slice from the roast, then loaded his plate with potatoes. He'd taken several bites of the tender, juicy meat before Onyxflame limped into the kitchen.

The elf wore the shapeless worker's clothes from the prison and the matching shoes. He served himself and sat across from Alistar. "My apologies for being late. I expected my banishment to last until morning at the least, and I didn't think it appropriate to come to dinner in my nightshirt."

"From the way you're walking, you'll be paying penance enough for the next few days," Alistar said. "After dinner, you can bathe, then soak your feet. Blisters?"

Onyxflame grimaced. "Blisters." He applied himself to the meal. Only after his plate was clear did he speak again. "I did not sabotage that ladder, De'seneth. I *did* test the wardings, for two reasons."

Alistar's eyebrow rose. "Two reasons?"

"The first, obviously, to test whether they actually existed. Though doubtful in my situation, there is always some question of whether such things are real or a myth told to keep a ward from straying from his handler." Onyxflame rubbed his neck. "Definitively *not* a myth."

"And the second reason?" Alistar asked.

"To learn how you would react."

"A question that has also been answered, I trust," Alistar said dryly.

"Less definitively than the first," Onyxflame answered. "I *thought* it had been answered until you called me down for dinner. You aren't what I expected from a Silverline lackey, De'seneth."

"And have you worked with many 'Silverline lackeys' in the past?" Alistar asked.

"Only in passing," Onyxflame said. "My dealings have more often been with those in the upper ranks, and I can't say those experiences were positive. I assumed they would seek to employ people who matched their mold."

"And you don't think that I do," Alistar said.

"De'seneth, I have no idea *what* to think of you," Onyxflame told him. "A human Rillwater privateer turned engineer turned investigator of criminal activity against the Silver Prince's pet project? No, that does not at all match the mold in my mind of a Silverline lackey."

"Then perhaps it's the base assumption you need to rethink." Alistar sipped his tea and fished a gold-rimmed engraved ivory button from his pocket. "Thinking of assumptions, what assumptions would you make from this?" He set it on the table.

Onyxflame picked up the button and ran his finger over the engraving. "Abstract image, fraught with great symbolic meaning, I'm sure. Good quality. Probably worth a good fifteen marks street value, closer to twenty or thirty actual cost. In short, I assume it's from either a noble's coat or that of someone with pretensions of grandeur and plenty of money. Who was prancing about on a rooftop in the middle of winter, engaging in theft of magic, which lends a certain weight to the idea of a noble conspiracy. Or a young thrill-seeker fallen in with the wrong crowd."

Alistar nodded. "What other evidence did we find?"

"The meter indicated that the mahiy lines were drained, and—"

"What other evidence did we find of the *people*," Alistar interrupted.

Onyxflame stopped, frowning. "The child in the alley who talked about the 'shining men' who gave her candy. If her report is valid, they were strong and able to run up the walls—neither of which are outside the abilities of some channelers."

Alistar nodded. "Such odd tidbits to leave behind. They gave the girl candy, so clearly they knew she saw them."

"They didn't consider her a threat, perhaps. Or they fed her false information? Though there was little in what she said that could be used to help or hinder your investigation." Onyxflame frowned. "You're right, it does seem odd, De'seneth."

"I can't pin down anything more solid yet," Alistar said. "Tomorrow we'll be checking more sites. Bring the shoes you're wearing as well as the others. And wrap your feet well."

"These shoes as well as the others?" Onyxflame repeated. Alistar didn't offer an explanation, and the elf shrugged. "Yes sir."

After dinner, Alistar showed Onyxflame to the bathing room

and left him to run a tub of hot water. He read until he finally heard Onyxflame return to the guest room. Alistar warded the guest room, then found his own bed and slept deeply.

In the morning, Alistar rose, dressed, and washed for the day, then knocked on Onyxflame's door until he received grudging acknowledgment from the elf. He had made breakfast by the time Dahr arrived, though the guard declined to accept more than a mug of tea and a slice of ham. Onyxflame trailed down to the kitchen dressed but barely half awake. He eyed both Alistar and Dahr suspiciously.

"People who like mornings are insane." With no more comment, Onyxflame flopped into a chair and ate the eggs and ham set before him.

Alistar shook his head with a chuckle. "When was the last time you saw the sunrise, Onyxflame?"

"Last time I saw the sun rising, I hadn't gone to *bed* yet," Onyxflame muttered around a bite of ham.

"Where are we bound today, sir?" Dahr asked, ignoring Onyxflame.

"The Hollows," Alistar said. Both Dahr and Onyxflame stiffened. Alistar continued before either could raise objections. "And we will aim to arrive there shortly after ten in the morning, because today is the Day of Prayer for the Successors of Heiset, and anyone who isn't deep in their devotions by then isn't going to be much of a believer, and thus is less likely to take aggressive action against elves. Especially if you both keep your heads down."

"Is it truly necessary to venture into the Hollows, De'seneth?" Onyxflame asked. "I realize one of the incidents happened there, but... really? The absolute heart of fanatics who believe that elves are somehow responsible for the destruction of your people's homeland?"

"I am not comfortable promising that I can fulfill my duty to protect you there, sir," Dahr said. "And relying on them to all be absorbed in their rites is not enough."

"The Day of Prayer is not just *a* holy day for the Successors," Alistar said. "It is *the* holy day. If they are even remotely followers of their faith, they will join the assembly today. The rituals last until the last bell. You can walk the streets of the Hollow and not see anyone. Believe me; I've actually done it before."

Onyxflame shifted uneasily. "Yes, but De'seneth, *you* are not an elf."

"We're going to the Hollows today," Alistar repeated. "And we're making a few stops on the way."

"Yes sir," Dahr said tightly, not hiding his displeasure. "Whenever you are ready."

"Is this payback for yesterday?" Onyxflame asked.

"No, this is taking advantage of the one time in the next seven months when we might be able to get through the Hollows without a fight," Alistar said. "Are you ready?"

Onyxflame sighed heavily. "If you go there, I'm following, like it or not. Allow me to collect the shoes from the room, if you would."

Alistar nodded, and Onyxflame climbed the stairs. Dahr watched him, frowning.

"He is limping. I assumed his complaints about the shoes were exaggeration."

"He spent most of the evening soaking his feet," Alistar said. "If anything, he may have understated the problem."

"And you still wish to enter the Hollows, when he cannot outrun a mob?" Dahr pressed.

"I have a couple of cobblers to visit before we get there," Alistar said.

Onyxflame came downstairs carrying a sack over his shoulder. Alistar carried the bag with their metering tools. They bundled up and ventured into the frigid morning. Alistar hailed the first carriage he saw and directed the driver to Sapphire Square.

The market was awake and alive even in the chill of winter. Old women wrapped in shawls and scarves bartered and argued with vendors, determined to fight for every last sliver to get a bargain. Around them, mothers in sarafans bustled about with children on their heels, making their purchases and lingering over displays of nesting dolls or teapots painted with flowers or elaborate designs. Clumps of men smoked and talked around the heating stones set throughout the market. The stones chased away some of the winter chill—enough that merchants didn't risk frostbite while hawking their wares.

Alistar wove between other shoppers, tuning out the cries of vendors hawking their wares as he made for his target. Before they reached the cobbler's shop, Alistar turned to Dahr. "Could you wait out here? We shouldn't be too long."

"Yes sir." Dahr nodded curtly and began to examine jars of preserves in a nearby stall.

Alistar waved for Onyxflame to follow him. "Which shoes are you wearing?"

"The ones that fit," Onyxflame told him, gesturing at the worker's shoes. "The other damnable set is in the bag."

"Good. When we go in, you're my manservant." Alistar walked to the door. "Hired locally."

"I'm what?" Onyxflame protested. "I hope that means you're paying!"

"Technically, the Silver Prince is paying, but yes," Alistar told him. "I'll be paying the man." He opened the door and stepped inside. Onyxflame hurried after.

The smell of leather filled the air. An elven man sat at a bench, hammering nails into the sole of a boot. He turned to them and rose stiffly. "Mornin' to you, sirs, and welcome. What can I do for you?"

"Good morning, sir," Alistar replied. "I am here to see about new shoes for my attendant. What he currently owns is insufficient for his duties."

The cobbler looked Onyxflame over briefly, gaze settling on his feet. "Aye, come and sit. Let me get your measurements."

Onyxflame settled on a stiff-backed chair and, at the cobbler's instructions, pulled his shoes off. The cobbler considered the wraps around his feet. "You have delicate soles?"

"My other pair of shoes didn't fit right. Thought they was okay, learned too late they wasn't." Onyxflame matched the cobbler's lilt easily. "And milord says these aren't good enough for fancy work."

The cobbler nodded. "Aye, too plain." He crouched and took a measuring cord to Onyxflame's feet, muttering numbers under his breath. He rose and shuffled across the room, picking several sets of shoes from a shelf. "Try the fit on these, tell me which feels the best."

Onyxflame eased on the shoes, trying on each pair. "These, I think."

"You think, or you know?" The cobbler gave him a firm look.

"I'm sure. This pair fits the best." Onyxflame handed the shoes back to the cobbler.

The man nodded again and collected all the shoes, returning them to the shelf. He turned to Alistar. "What crest will you be needing on them, sir? And color?"

"Brown," Alistar said. "And a wave."

"Yes sir." The cobbler vanished into his back room for several minutes. He finally returned with a pair of polished brown shoes, the image of a wave imprinted into the soles. He handed them to Onyxflame, who tried them on. His eyebrows rose in surprise and approval.

"Thank you, sir. They feel like they was meant for my feet."

"As they should," the cobbler said proudly. "You take good care of them."

Alistar paid for the shoes, and Onyxflame wore them out of the shop. Outside, he eyed Alistar. "So what was the purpose of that?"

"The purpose of that was to get you a new pair of shoes. A pair of shoes that *don't* announce themselves as accessories to a noble-man's wardrobe," Alistar answered.

"And the purpose of telling me the story moments before entering the shop?" Onyxflame asked.

Alistar waved for Dahr to join them, and ignored Onyxflame's question.

"You have what you need, sir?" Dahr asked.

"Almost," Alistar said, weaving between stalls to the more expensive end of the market. "Aspendark, you'll need the other shoes in the next shop."

Onyxflame cast him a bemused look. "The ones I just replaced?"

"No, the ones you haven't worn today," Alistar answered. "And yes, you do need to wear them."

"I still don't know what game we're playing, De'seneth, but it's too damned cold for this." Onyxflame found a seat at a tea stall and hastily swapped footwear.

Alistar handed him a purse. "Lord Aspendark needs proper shoes as well." He nodded to another cobbler's shop.

The purse vanished into Onyxflame's sleeve. "And what's Aspendark's explanation for his lack?"

"I'll leave that to Aspendark to provide," Alistar told him.

Onyxflame shot him a glower and entered the shop, trailed by Alistar and Dahr. Alistar listened to the elf spin a tale of lost luggage and loaned shoes. The cobbler, a young human man, listened with equanimity, and responded with glowing praises of his fine products, fit for lords and ladies, as he measured Onyxflame's feet. He offered test pairs in a wider variety than those the other cobbler had provided. Onyxflame probed a little in search of names of other noble clients, but the man would not answer beyond vague and general hints. For his clients' sakes, of course, and not because he was exaggerating or possibly outright lying.

A nobleman's shoes could not be simply pulled from a shelf in back and sold as they were. Onyxflame placed an order for several pairs, styled to match the ones he wore in colors that, presumably, would match his wardrobe. With the cobbler's promise to have them done within a week, and a pair of unornamented shoes to wear in the meantime, Onyxflame paid a generous pile of marks, and they left the shop.

Onyxflame glowered at Alistar and, using the noise of the market as cover, demanded in a low voice, "What's your game, De'seneth?"

"I've heard that you're a good actor, adaptable to many roles. I wanted to see how well you could improvise," Alistar told him, holding out his hand for the purse.

Onyxflame scowled and relinquished it. "Satisfied?"

"Yes," Alistar said. "It gives me more confidence that, should the need arise, you actually can play the part of a Rillwater nobleman in court."

"You *would* have a halfway reasonable answer," Onyxflame muttered.

"And you have new shoes. So let's be on our way," Alistar said.

They took a carriage part of the way to the Hollows, then walked the rest. Both elves kept their hoods up and heads down, easily justified by the bitter wind. The wind whipped down the streets, flinging a scattering of snowflakes in its wake. Graffiti marked walls and buildings, at first sporadic, but growing thicker the closer they came to the Hollows, calling for an end to elven oppression and the downfall of those who aided them. The nearer the Hollows they approached, the less subtle the messages became.

Few people braved the weather, encouraging Alistar that they might actually get in and out without being questioned. Silverline Power employees were almost as unwelcome in the Hollows as elves were. The Successors of Heiset were not the only radical group intent on driving the division between humans and elves, but they were one of the largest and best known of the human-driven groups. They had taken control of a neighborhood known as the Hollows. Initially the authorities had tried to drive them out, but the Successors had proven both well-entrenched and ready to defend their territory. Lewarden leaders had eventually decided it best to leave them alone, so long as they, in turn, kept their activities confined to the Hollows. It was an uneasy arrangement at best.

"You seem to know your way around this area well," Onyxflame remarked a little too casually.

"Family business has brought me into the area a few times in the past," Alistar said.

"Your family does business with the Successors?" Dahr growled.

"Family business unfortunately does sometimes require working with unsavory people," Alistar replied. "But no, I've not had to work directly with any Successors. Even if there was business to be done with them, a Silverline 'lackey' would not be the best person for the task."

Onyxflame stopped suddenly, cocking his head to one side. "I thought you said the fanatics would all be busy with their holy day, De'seneth."

"They should be," Alistar said. "I know this is the right day. What's wrong?"

Onyxflame turned to Dahr. "You do hear that too, don't you?"

Dahr frowned, face growing grave. "I do. And it has the sound of rabble-rousing."

Alistar listened, and heard the echo of a raised voice within the Hollows, then the rumble of a crowd in response. He looked at Dahr, and the guard gazed back at him, grim. "We need to get closer, don't we?"

"Our patrols do not enter the Hollows, De'seneth. If trouble brews within, this may well be our only opportunity to learn of it," Dahr said.

Alistar nodded, though he would rather Dahr have recommended they leave immediately. "All right. Let's... get a little closer." He turned toward the sound of the gathering and, against his better judgment, started walking.

CHAPTER 13

"Mighty Rechmal blesses our gathering!"

Alistar could finally understand the raised voice, and frowned at the invocation of the Lord of Magic. Rechmal was not considered one of the Prime Gods of the pantheon by most Successors of Heiset, too often associated with the Crown's control of the mahiy lines. However, the crowd roared in approval, leaving Alistar wondering what the orator did to demonstrate the god's favor. He stood in an alley off the main street with his two elven companions, close enough to hear but not to see. He cursed under his breath.

"Sounds like they're practically under the site of the outage," he hissed. "If the crowd's as large as it sounds, people are probably packed into the buildings and roofs, if they can."

"The elves pervert Rechmal's gifts to us, his people. They would deny it to us! They claim it comes from *them*, and that we must sacrifice our food, our clothing to pay them for the privilege of access to *our god's gift to us*! You have seen it, every one of you! When we raised our voices and cried out that we would not endure it, they cast us into darkness and cold. They thought we would bend once again, bow down to them and accept their oppression. Did we?"

"No!" The crowd roared.

"What's he talking about?" Alistar growled. "Silverline knows that people in the Hollows won't pay their bills. The company writes off the expense every time as not worth the bad blood of cutting the lines. No one would shut off their access to the mahiy lines in the middle of winter. Not even to these fanatics."

"You *did* say this gathering is centered under the site of the incident, didn't you?" Onyxflame asked in a low voice.

"Venom's Shoals," Alistar cursed. "Of course the outage in the Hollows probably lasted longer than most. The nearest generators are some blocks away, and no one wants the job of going *into* the Hollows to look for a problem. These people could have been in the cold and dark for hours."

The speaker continued, and Alistar missed the beginning in the ongoing shouts of the crowd. "You've seen Rechmal's gifts, his blessings upon us! The elves think to make us weak, but Rechmal has shown us that we do not need them! We shall cast off the chains our persecutors would lay upon us, and we shall be free."

Alistar frowned, looking to the sky. The faint glow of purple told him that the mahiy lines did indeed power this section of the city, making the man's rant seem nonsensical. But the people cheered and shouted in agreement, praising Rechmal and decrying Silverline Power.

"In their arrogance, our oppressors claim that *they* are doing Rechmal's will. That *they*, who neither follow nor respect our gods, follow his guidance. Yet they pervert his very symbol, mixing the essence of frost's breath, one of the last remnants of our homeland, and breeding it into their creations!"

Alistar jerked as if someone had poured ice down his back. His mouth opened and closed, but words failed him.

Onyxflame cast a long look at Alistar. "Judging from your face, he either said something that was incredibly wrong, or incredibly right."

Alistar opened his mouth, closed it, and finally sputtered, "That is *incredibly* confidential information. How in Venom's Shoals does this rabble-rouser know *any* of this?"

Onyxflame shrugged slightly. "Doesn't mean anything to me. Might if I knew what frost's breath is."

"A plant of Heiset origin," Alistar said. "If you enter a human house of worship, you'll see a spray of eight jagged leaves marking Rechmal's altar."

Onyxflame nodded. "I've seen it." He cocked his head to one side. "And the Silver Prince is cross-breeding it into his kurowa plants to make all this, I presume?" He waved up at the glowing violet lines in the sky.

Alistar nodded, though he gave Onyxflame a curious look, wondering when the elf had been inside a human sanctuary.

"And no one outside of Silverline is supposed to know this," Onyxflame finished.

Alistar nodded again. "Only those above certain levels *in* Silverline know it." He stepped from the mouth of the alley.

Dahr grabbed his arm and jerked him back. Alistar pulled to free his arm, but the guard did not release him. "De'seneth, I cannot allow you to risk the life of both you and your ward by getting closer to these madmen."

Alistar bristled. "You heard him! You don't think His Highness will want to know who's responsible for spreading secrets he's taken extraordinary methods to protect?"

Dahr forcibly drew him farther into the alley. "His Highness will wish to know, of course. And if we are murdered by a mob, he will receive no information at all, rather than learning that someone has released information they should not."

"Never thought I'd say this, but I'm in agreement with our esteemed guard. I don't care to linger here," Onyxflame said. "We can't go poking around the site of the outage, clearly. You said the sites that feed this area are some ways off. I propose that we visit them instead. Perhaps the attendants will have some insights?" He spoke quickly, casting an uneasy look over his shoulder.

The orator continued. "Mighty Rechmal does not forget the insults the elves hurl in his face. He will unleash blight upon them and upon the unbelievers who follow them like sheep. Pestilence spreads through the unpure! He will cleanse this land and purge those who dare call themselves our 'leaders' while they bow and scrape to the oppressors!"

"Blight?" Alistar stopped trying to free his arm from Dahr's steel grip. *Is he talking about Rat's Disease, or something else? Is it related? Who is this man and what exactly does he know?*

"So not only is Rechmal the lord of magic, he's now taking over Kalyp's domain?" Onyxflame asked. "I'd think the Blightbringer might object." He tried to sound casual, but edged farther down the alley, away from the street.

Dahr used Alistar's distraction to pull him back the way they'd come, following Onyxflame. "Sensationalist ravings," he scoffed. "The gods can handle their own matters. We have ours to care for."

Alistar capitulated to the elves, much as it rankled to leave without knowing the orator's identity. Taking the lead, he retraced their route through the narrow alleys. Most of the streets in the Hollows weren't much wider, but they were better maintained and more traveled. The alley stones were slick with frost and a skiff of snow, disturbed only by their feet.

As they reached the end of the alley, Alistar paused, taking his bearings. The street was empty when he looked up, then down it. He turned left down the street, then right and right again.

"Are we going the right way, De'seneth?" Dahr asked in a low, worried voice. "The Hollows twist too many directions."

"We're going the right way," Alistar promised with slightly more confidence than he felt.

His concerns eased when they entered a courtyard. At a small fountain in the center, ice ran from the mouth of a roaring bear, and icicles extended its claws to nightmarish length.

Alistar nodded at the fountain. "We're a couple blocks from the official edge of the Hollows." Now that they were on their way out, he admitted that Dahr had been right to insist they leave, and that he had been as tense and worried as the elves.

He jumped when a woman spoke. "I don't recognize you. You fellows aren't from around here."

Alistar spun quickly and saw a woman probably a few years older than him, bundled in a coat that didn't hide the pregnant bulge of her stomach. She looked at all three of them with a dark, suspicious glare.

"It's the Day of Prayer," Alistar began, adopting his best Lower City drawl. "I thought—"

"You thought you and your fellow hooligans could come in and harass honest folks. Interrupt our worship with your faithless mocking." The woman's glare hardened. "I s'pose you didn't count on Zhrets Vonn gatherin' the faithful in the square, hmm?"

"Zhrets" was a title given to the most respected human leaders in the faith. Vonn wasn't a name that he recognized. Alistar scowled at the woman. "I *thought* we might listen to the service," he told her. "Wasn't looking for trouble, but clear enough we aren't wanted here." He gave her a scowl.

She didn't back down. "That's right, you're not. Get back where you came from. And if you heard anything of the service, best you think about what you heard. Rechmal's judgment is coming on you and all the rest of the faithless."

"Clear enough that you 'faithful' sorts don't want to share your coming paradise with the rest of us," Alistar sneered. "Or you'd be welcoming folks that came to hear more."

Dahr took his arm and firmly began pulling Alistar past the fountain. "We are not wanted here, and we wish no further trouble," he said into Alistar's ear.

The woman watched them go, her eyes narrow. She didn't call

anything after them, nor did she raise a hue and cry. But Alistar felt her eyes on them, even after she was well out of sight. Her words hung with him.

Rechmal's judgment. What does that mean? These people believe that something is coming, something tied to magic. Something disastrous.

CHAPTER 14

Despite the better shoes, Onyxflame was limping. He voiced no complaint as they moved farther from the Hollows, lagging only slightly despite their pace. Alistar slowed once they had put some blocks between themselves and the den of fanatics. The inflammatory graffiti lessened in frequency and fervor, but neither elf looked comfortable with the change of their pace.

Alistar caught his breath, filling his lungs with frigid winter air. "Redpine's the nearest generator. About six more blocks." He turned to Onyxflame. "Can you manage?"

Onyxflame blinked, surprised to be asked, then found his rakish smile. "Certainly, I'll be fine. Although expect me to flagrantly waste your soaking salts tonight."

Alistar nodded. "Dahr?"

"There is no need for concern on my behalf, sir. We should make haste." Dahr waited for him to take the lead once more.

Redpine Generator was a cramped station tucked in barely enough space between a cliff face and a factory building, making it one of the smallest generator plants in Lewarden. A single pair of gargoyles stood guard on the path to the door, evidently the only security at Redpine. The generator relied on anonymity more than force for protection. Alistar pulled off a glove and patted one of the grimacing stone figures. It blinked listlessly, then it stuck its tongue out at him. Pulling his glove back on, Alistar told it, "These two are with me."

He strode to the sturdy wood door unchallenged. It was locked and lacked a knocker. He banged his fist against the door, paused, listened for steps, and banged again.

The door opened a crack. "I'm sorry, but we aren't interest—"

"Associate De'seneth, Third Degree," Alistar interrupted.

"Third deg— We aren't scheduled for an inspection!" The technician's voice rose in alarm.

"This isn't an inspection," Alistar said. "However, it's bitter cold out here."

The woman hesitated, then opened the door enough to peer out. After another moment, she stepped aside to let them enter. Her gaze lingered on Dahr, then Onyxflame, as they removed their hats. She pursed her lips. Tone carefully neutral, she said, "Don't see many elves in this area."

Rather than respond, Alistar peeled off his gloves and rapidly rubbed his hands together. The office space was pleasantly warm and bright, heated by residual from the greenhouse. A kettle sat atop a small iron stove in one corner, and the table beside the stove held four mugs and a compact tea chest. The office only had three desks with no dividing walls between them.

The technician wore thick denim overalls stained by dirt, pollen, and tea. The knees were patched several times over. Once the door was closed, she rolled up her sleeves. Her black hair was chopped short and her skin was a rich brown, whether naturally or as a result of the constant exposure to the grow lights, Alistar didn't know. She watched all three of them warily, waiting for someone to reveal their reason for intruding into this domain.

"Your name?" Alistar prompted.

"Technician Bar'rege," she answered, sitting on one of the desks.

"I'm Associate De'seneth," he said. "Aspendark there is my assistant, and Dahr Lakewatch is a member of the Prince's Guard. I'm investigating the recent outages."

Bar'rege stiffened. "We filed a report on our incident, Associate. Whatever happened, it wasn't the result of any mismanagement on *our* end."

Her sharp defensive reaction startled Alistar. "I agree, Technician. Were you present when the incident occurred?"

Her eyes narrowed. "What, you want me to believe this isn't a ghost hunt to throw the blame on us?"

"It's not," Alistar promised. "I want to know what occurred here, with the goal of finding ways to prevent it from happening again, here or elsewhere in the city. Mind if we sit?"

Bar'rege considered that in silence for several moments, then slowly said, "You can sit. Yeah, I was here. Happened right on the tail of my shift. Everything had been pretty quiet, then the instruments went wild. Errors everywhere." A wide gesture seemed to encompass the entire building.

Alistar perked up slightly. "You still have the records of the incident? I'd like to see them later." He pulled a chair from a desk and sat.

Her head jerked in a quick, nervous nod. "I'm… sure we can find them if you need them, Associate."

"Not just yet. Please, continue." Alistar waved her on. She was uneasy, but he couldn't be sure of the cause yet. "You began to see errors."

"Yes, Associate. The readings indicated that all power to the Hollows and surrounding area was just gone. Vanished. We couldn't make any sense of it. My partner, Technician En'ard, ran to check the greenhouse, but nothing had gone obviously wrong there. That didn't show up until later. We focused on amplifying the generation and directing the magic into the affected areas. Around the Hollows, we got proper readings quickly."

"What about inside the Hollows?" Alistar asked. "And what issues showed up later?"

"Inside the Hollows, it didn't seem to matter how much we directed the mahiy lines. It just kept disappearing, like something was… drinking it. We didn't know what the Successors might be doing. If they had some crazy plan in motion, we didn't want to keep feeding power to it. So…"

"You cut off the Hollows," Alistar said.

She shifted, looking down at her hands and nodded.

"Was this in your report?" Alistar asked.

"The ineffectiveness of sending magic to the Hollows was, sir. I… we didn't outright say that we did so, but it was implied." Bar'rege toyed with a quill pen. "We filled in the other shift when they came in, and told them what we'd seen. Proper procedure would be to test the lines every hour or so, and call someone to check the lines for problems. We didn't do the second part— would have been suicidal to send anyone from Silverline into the Hollows in that kind of mess."

"So when were the lines into the Hollows reactivated?" Alistar asked.

She continued to turn the quill in her fingers. "After I came back on shift, sir. So, near on thirteen hours."

"What!" Alistar stiffened. "In the dead of winter?"

"The magic wasn't *getting* to them, sir! If they're left alone to a trickle, the mahiy lines will fix themselves if they suffer damage, but not when something's sucking them dry. What else were we supposed to do? Pardon me for saying it, sir, but this is the blight boil of all assignments. *No one* gets sent *here* unless someone's being vindictive. We already *knew* we wouldn't get assistance from headquarters if we asked for it." She pushed to her feet, glowering at Alistar.

"So you didn't ask," Alistar said. "And didn't report the problem."

Her scowl deepened. "No one *cares* about a generator like

Redpine, sir. You're the first, outside of the annual inspections, to even stop here. Doubt anyone even read our report."

"If no one had read it, I wouldn't have known about the outage and wouldn't be here," Alistar told her. "And if Redpine is having troubles getting the assistance it needs, I'll see to it that the matter is brought to the attention of those who can do something about it."

She eyed him dubiously. "I'm sure."

Alistar reached under his shirt and drew out the Silver Prince's emblem. "What is it you need?"

Her eyes grew wide as saucers and she stumbled back, catching herself against the desk. "Wha—You— Who are you?"

"I'm the engineer assigned to investigate these outages," Alistar said. "And I need to know whatever you can tell me."

Bar'rege swallowed hard. "Um, look, could we talk in private, sir? Without them?" Her eyes shifted to Dahr and Onyxflame.

"All right," Alistar agreed with caution. He stood, motioning for the elves to stay where they were, and tucked the emblem back into his shirt.

Bar'rege opened the inner door leading to the greenhouse. The air was thick with the scent of kurowa flowers. Bar'rege turned into a side room and ran a hand through her short hair. She didn't turn to face him. "Sir, I'm sure you can guess that this close to the Hollows, there are problems."

"I'd be surprised if there weren't," Alistar said.

"A lot of folks don't care for Silverline Power or the elves, and we're the easiest targets." She laced her fingers together, drew a deep breath, and turned to face him. "Can you get us assigned somewhere else? All four of us. I don't care if we aren't all together, just as long as we aren't working *here*." She paused again. "And… can you promise that my family will be safe? I've got a husband and a little boy."

A chill ran down Alistar's spine. "They live near here?"

She shook her head quickly. "No, no. But if someone finds them…"

"Someone's threatened you," Alistar said.

"There's a man in the Hollows. The people call him Zhrets Vonn and say he's a holy man, preaching Rechmal's will. I don't think I believe that, but…" Her voice dropped low. "He's terrifying."

"You've met him? Personally?" Alistar asked. "When?"

She shivered. "Day before the incident. So… a couple weeks ago, now. I don't know if it was really him. He said that's who he was, but he was wearing a mask. Wasn't dressed like any starving Successor, though. Good clothes, rich stuff. More than *I* can afford. Something one of your sort would wear." She laughed faintly. "Except his coat sleeve was missing a button—isn't that the strangest thing to notice when someone's threatening to hunt down your family and murder you? That stupid missing button."

"Technician Bar'rege, what threats did he make, and what did he want?" Alistar asked.

She gulped. "Said he'd kill me and my family if I didn't do what he said. Said he'd reward me if I did, give me opportunity and power I'd never imagined." A thin laugh. "Still waiting to see *that*. But he knew we would react certain ways to the loss of magic. He… wanted to make sure we kept the power flowing into the Hollows for a certain amount of time, and then, when we cut it off… to leave it off until the next day." She looked aside. "So I didn't tell the other group to test the health of the lines like I was supposed to. And the Hollows stayed dark." Bar'rege closed her eyes. "People could have died because of me. Frozen to death."

"I don't think they did," Alistar said. "I think that Zhrets Vonn, whoever he is, used that as an opportunity to sway the Successors, convince them somehow that he really could call on Rechmal's power. If people had died, there would be riots, and, unfortunately, you and your companions here would be the first to know of that."

She didn't look appeased, and Alistar could understand why. He shifted the subject. "You mentioned other problems that came up."

She sucked in a breath and nodded. "I'll show you."

Leading the way to the greenhouse, Bar'rege pointed through the observation windows. "The middle row. Those are the plants that feed directly into the Hollows."

Alistar wiped a sheen of precipitation from the glass and looked inside. Tri-pointed kurowa flowers bloomed in rows, sending their violet tendrils of magic into the ceiling. His brow furrowed. The central row, where Bar'rege had indicated, the flowers drooped. Not enough to be wilting, but clearly unhealthy. Their colors were off, too sharp and vivid compared to their neighbors. The long petals curled in on themselves at the edges. And the light rising from them seemed more azure than violet.

Alistar turned to Bar'rege quickly. "Have you reported this to anyone?"

She shook her head. "They'd blame us. Say we messed up something, are responsible for the damage to the Silver Prince's property."

"No," Alistar said. "No one is going to accuse you of that. A botanist needs to see this. I'm no expert, but I've never seen kurowa do this before. Have you? Has this happened before?" *Have you been accused of damaging the kurowa before?*

"Just rumors," she said. "From a long time ago. I never saw anything like this." She shifted uneasily. "But a botanist coming *here*?"

"Not all of them are elves," Alistar assured her. "I'll make sure it happens." He gave her a long look. "Do your coworkers here know about the threats or your actions?"

"Technician En'ard might. He hasn't said anything directly, but I think he suspects," she answered. "At least he doesn't have a family to worry about."

"Your family will be safe," Alistar told her firmly. "However, I may need you to report all this directly. Can you do that? If possible, I'll do what I can to protect you. It'll be better overall if you report this blackmail and threat yourself."

"I did." She looked Alistar in the eyes. "I told you. You've got the Silver Prince's favor—what more do you *need*?"

Alistar paused, then nodded slowly. She was right. "I'll do what I can," he promised. "Please be careful. Write down everything you remember about the man. Everything, no matter how inconsequential it seems. Even coat buttons." He recalled a fine ivory button found on the roof. "Anything at all. Put it with the records from the incident."

She nodded, jaw tight. "Yes sir."

Alistar returned to the outer room, thoughts spinning. Onyxflame and Dahr waited, both acting as if they hadn't followed to listen in on the conversation, though he was sure they had. "Let's go."

CHAPTER 15

Heavy clouds blanketed the sky, stealing the thin remains of daylight. Delicate snowflakes drifted from above. Alistar pulled his hat farther down, grateful that the wind at least had died away. Onyxflame had wrapped his cloak tightly around himself, trudging after Alistar. Dahr brought up the rear, and Alistar couldn't tell if the guard was as chilled as the rest of them.

Alistar hailed the first taxi coach to rumble by. The driver grunted and nodded at the coach door. "Where to?"

"Shale Lane," Alistar answered. He caught a frown from Dahr, but none of them had energy for conversation in the cold. Alistar climbed into the coach, followed by the elves.

As they rumbled down the street, Dahr spoke. "Sir, the information you've gathered today must be reported."

"Yes, it must," Alistar agreed. "You both heard the technician at Redpine? I assume you were listening when she asked to speak to me in private."

Both elves nodded.

"She's been threatened and blackmailed. Her family has been threatened. And it appears that the person who's done so has intimate knowledge of Silverline Power and its operations. And its confidential information." His face darkened. "Dahr, I need you to ensure that she and her family are moved to a safe location."

"Tonight, sir?" Dahr asked. His voice didn't imply that the request was outrageous or impossible, only that he wanted a time frame.

"Tonight, soon," Alistar said. "And have someone keeping an eye on them until they are relocated, as a precaution. First thing tomorrow, I will—" He paused. He'd been about to say he would speak to Director Strey'mend, but he knew that wasn't who he really should report to. Alistar drew breath and lowered his voice. "Tomorrow, I need to speak to His Highness."

Onyxflame stiffened sharply, mouth opening with protests on his lips.

Alistar turned to him. "I can leave you in the guest room if you prefer."

Onyxflame laughed sharply. "Yes, I'm sure it will look good if I act like a petulant child and refuse to attend. Very encouraging that I'm doing my part in your work."

"Petulant child? No, I would rate you at least as a sullen adolescent," Alistar said. He looked out the window slats. They had returned to the crowds of Lewarden, and the driver navigated between horses and coaches, snapping curses at other drivers, which they returned in kind.

"Then both you and Onyxflame will attend the meeting with His Highness?" Dahr asked.

"Unless something changes by tomorrow morning, yes," Alistar told him. "I'll defer making any additional plans for the day until after that." He sighed. "Ideally, I'll have a chance to attend evening devotions." He wanted to hear prayers to Rechmal that didn't call for death, plague, and judgment. He wanted to worship in peace. And he wanted to have the rest of that evening to spend with Saskia without the worries of his assignment looming overhead. He shot a look at Onyxflame. "And if I do go, I am leaving you in the guest room."

"De'seneth, I'm hurt. I assure you, I would be entirely respectful in a sanctuary of the gods," Onyxflame said.

"That's beside the point, Onyxflame," Alistar said. "And it's not open for debate."

The carriage rattled over a series of bone-jarring bumps, then clattered to a halt. The driver opened the door. "Shale Lane. Two marks."

"T—" Alistar grimaced, digging into his pocket and pulling out the payment. It was practically highway robbery, but they were back in familiar territory, only a few blocks from his home. The driver took the marks with a grunt and clambered back into his seat, rattling back on his way.

Dahr took his bearings and turned to go. "I will arrange the watch you requested, sir. And I will return tomorrow morning to escort you to His Highness."

"Thank you, Dahr." Alistar strode up the street, Onyxflame limping after him.

Street lights reflected off the falling snow, giving the evening an ethereal glow. The few people still out hurried toward their homes, or in some cases, toward the warmth and comfort of Madame Faybel's brothel. A sigh of relief escaped Alistar when he opened his door and a wave of warm air rushed over him.

Mrs. Ke'lyn had already gone home, leaving a note in the foyer bidding him a good evening and a pot of hearty stew on the stove. Alistar could smell it as he hung his coat and hat. Both he and Onyxflame retired to their rooms to change for dinner, reconvening in the kitchen. Onyxflame, dressed in the workman's clothes once again, sank into a chair while Alistar ladled stew into bowls.

Onyxflame sighed in relief to be sitting. "I had no idea that working as an engineer for the Silver Prince involved so much walking. I suffered under the impression that it was primarily a desk job."

"Special assignments require unusual activities," Alistar said.

"Such as leaving the desk from time to time." He set the bowls on the table and sat. His feet ached and stiffness crept through his calves.

Onyxflame ate with relish, scraping his bowl clean and taking a second serving before Alistar had finished his first. The elf gazed at him, growing serious. "De'seneth, I truly won't cause any sort of scene in a sanctuary of the Reyker. I prefer your human gods to ours. More egalitarian, less smite-happy."

"I said it's not open for argument, Onyxflame," Alistar said, irritated.

Onyxflame leaned forward, propping his elbows on the table. "Believe me or don't, but I attended services to the Reyker faithfully in Chirrod Prison, and as I was able before my arrest. It is a practice I wish to continue. I'm not asking this on idle whim and fancy. And under my current restrictions, the only way I *can* attend services is by joining you."

Alistar let out a long breath. He'd not thought Onyxflame religious, much less a convert to the Reyker. "It's not just about the services. This is also one of the few opportunities I'm likely to have during this assignment to spend time with my fiancée."

Onyxflame straightened, eyebrows flying up. "Fiancée? Ah, I see. That could make my presence a bit awkward, I acknowledge. Still, the allowed distance is plenty inside the sanctuary. I tend to stay in the back to avoid distracting others. And if you and your lady have plans afterward, you can employ the wardings to confine me within the sanctuary."

"Leave you unattended in public?" Alistar eyed him dubiously, then sighed. Onyxflame seemed sincere in his plea. "I'll consider it."

"I appreciate it, De'seneth." Onyxflame cleaned the last of the stew from his bowl.

"And the entire matter might be beside the point, depending on the Silver Prince," Alistar added.

Onyxflame's expression soured. "I was trying to ignore that

part." He slouched. "So you're going to tell him about information leaks, blackmail, fanatics, and coat buttons?"

Alistar frowned. "To be honest, the button bothers me."

Onyxflame started to laugh, then caught himself when he saw Alistar's serious expression. "All right, compared to the *rest*, why in perdition does a *coat button* bother you? The rabble-rouser lost one. We... well, you found one."

"I found it at the site of the Shale Lane outage," Alistar said. "That happened just a few days ago. The outage at the Hollows took place weeks before that. And he was missing his button when he spoke to Technician Bar'rege."

Onyxflame's brow furrowed. "Assuming it *is* his button, that timeline doesn't work at all."

"Exactly." Alistar toyed with his spoon. "Unless it was left intentionally."

"And whoever left it didn't think we would notice the time gap?" Onyxflame asked. "I realize that a certain minority of Lewarden residents have opinions on the intelligence of Silverline Power lackeys, but even *I* wouldn't assume an investigator would be *that* stupid."

Alistar didn't bother responding to the barb. "It implies that someone wants our attention aimed at Zhrets Vonn and his actions in the Hollows. Which implies that they want our attention aimed *away* from something or someone else. Unfortunately, we can't ignore Zhrets Vonn either. He seems to have a connection to the outages, and he knows more than he ought to about Silverline Power."

Onyxflame raised a finger. "More than he ought to as a layman. I would not overlook the possibility that he knows what he does because he is, or was, involved in Silverline Power. It was implied by the botanist that former employees have some magically enforced restrictions against revealing company secrets. Do current employees have the same?"

"We're under sworn contract," Alistar said. "That shouldn't be easy to break. Not impossible, I'm sure, but not easy."

Onyxflame nodded slowly. "Contracts can be broken… too true. Even the best have loopholes somewhere. So, what *do* you intend to tell Prince Cero? And what role am I to play tomorrow?"

"Yourself," Alistar said. Then he amended the thought. "A version of yourself that can hold his tongue long enough to avoid insulting the Silver Prince to his face."

"That's more challenging than you make it sound, De'seneth. But I will do my best. What do you plan to tell him?"

"He needs to know about the leak of information. And the threats against his employees at Redpine. I need to arrange for the technicians there to transfer to other sites, and get a botanist out to Redpine to find out what's happening with their greenhouse. I should have taken a sample. Too late to do anything about that now."

"Send an engineer as well," Onyxflame suggested. "Check the fluctuations and frequencies of the affected lines. I would think questions like that might interest the Silver Prince enough that his workers there might avoid his displeasure."

"Whatever happened there is not their fault," Alistar said firmly.

Onyxflame shrugged. "I'm not the one you need to convince, De'seneth."

"I know." Alistar cleared the table. "Blood and sand, I want to know who is doing this and *why!*"

If Onyxflame had any answer, he kept it to himself. He helped Alistar clean the kitchen, then they each retired to their rooms.

A thudding roused Alistar from sleep. Groggy, he sat up and fumbled for a light. The thudding persisted, a repeating pattern. He shook his head, and finally identified it as the sound of someone at his front door. Rubbing away sleep, he pulled on a heavy dressing robe and descended the stairs. "Who's there?"

"Associate De'seneth?" The voice wasn't familiar. Female, he thought, and stern. "Dahr Lakewatch sent me to fetch you with all haste."

Alistar blinked, confused, and opened the door a crack. The woman outside wore the uniform of a member of the Silver Prince's personal guard. A coach waited on the street behind her, its tracks clear in the fresh snow. "What's going on?" Alistar asked. "Who are you?"

"I am Star, in the service of His Highness, sir. Guard Lakewatch told me to bring you at once. The matter involves a Silverline Power technician whose home you asked to have watched." She stood at attention.

Sleep clouded Alistar's thoughts, but he collected his wits as best he could. "Can you verify your identity?"

Taking no apparent offense at his request, she produced a pendant with the Silver Prince's seal. "By this mark, I swear that I am in the service of His Highness, Prince Cero." In response, the pendant glowed, outlining the prince's seal.

Alistar opened the door. "Come inside. Let me get dressed."

"Yes sir." She stepped inside. "I apologize for waking you."

Alistar shook his head. "I'm sure Dahr has good reason. I'll be... just a moment."

He took the stairs two at a time, then paused in the hall outside the guest room. "Onyxflame, if you're awake, get dressed."

"Perdition, sand, blood, and pestilence, this is *not* morning," came a mumbled response.

"No, it's not," Alistar agreed. "If you're not dressed and ready in five minutes, I'll leave you here and you can go back to sleep."

A groan answered, then a thump as if Onyxflame had rolled out of bed to the floor. "Coming, coming..."

Alistar wasted no more time, returning to his room and grabbing sturdy, warm clothes as worry gnawed at him.

What's happened?

CHAPTER 16

Alistar wrapped his hands around a steaming mug. The tea was too sweet, but it was hot, and he was still muddled from interrupted sleep. Onyxflame, wrapped in his cloak and an additional lap blanket, leaned against the carriage wall. He'd managed to dress within the five-minute window Alistar allowed, too tired to voice more than token complaints as the guard had rushed them into the waiting carriage.

"Where are we bound?" Alistar asked. He gulped down a swallow of the overly sweet tea and grimaced. "Technician Bar'rege's residence?"

"Yes sir," Star said. Unlike her charges, she sat alert and at attention as the carriage raced down the streets of Lewarden. "Guard Lakewatch personally escorted the technician to her residence at the conclusion of her shift. He is there now, with another of His Highness's Guard."

Alistar blinked. "Does Dahr *sleep*?"

An actual hint of a smile twitched on the woman's stern face. "We have trained in special techniques that allow us to sleep less than most people, sir."

"Why am I not surprised?" Onyxflame muttered, proving that he was at least nominally awake.

"The safety and well-being of the royal family depend on our ability to remain alert and aware of all dangers, Lord Aspendark," she said. "This aspect of our training is only one of many such methods of ensuring their safety."

Onyxflame mumbled something incomprehensible and pulled his cloak tighter around himself.

Alistar gulped down the last of his tea when the carriage finally halted. He had no good sense of where they were in the city. When the guard opened the door and stepped out, he saw streets shrouded in falling snow. Alistar climbed from the carriage, shivering, and looked down a row of apartment buildings crowded close enough that the falling snow barely dusted the alleys. Most of the residences were dark, only the street lamps casting their ghostly light onto the night. Alistar knew technicians earned less than engineers, but the sight of the drab residences squeezed tightly together reminded him starkly of the disparity.

His guide made for a set of worn stairs, climbing to the third level, where amber glowed in the windows of a residence. Alistar started after, then paused to be sure Onyxflame followed. The elf dragged himself out of the carriage, blinked muzzily, and followed Alistar without a word. The wooden planks groaned underfoot as they ascended the stairs.

"Where are we and why are we here?" Onyxflame asked. "Are you sure this is really one of the Silver Prince's guards?"

"She verified her identity as one of the Silver Prince's guards," Alistar said. "Why and where we are… I'm less sure." Doubt nibbled at his thoughts like a persistent rat. He paused at the doorway, debating the wisdom of entering against the want to be out of the cold.

Dahr stepped into view. "Sir, thank you. I apologize for the hour." He looked past Alistar and raised an eyebrow. "And you dragged Aspendark from bed as well."

Somewhat reassured, Alistar stepped into the room, Onyxflame on his heels. "What happened, Dahr? I assume you wouldn't send for me without good reason." He glanced around. The apartment was cramped, its outer room barely large enough to hold the current occupants. In addition to Alistar, Onyxflame, Dahr, and the guard who'd brought them, another elf in uniform stood near a closed door. The room held three chairs, one of them sized for a child, a scattering of needlework and knitting in baskets around the room, and several days' worth of news rags and broadsheets.

Dahr nodded. "I escorted Technician Bar'rege here this evening, sir. When we arrived, she requested that we immediately relocate her husband and child; however, she declined to leave with them. They have been moved to a secure location."

An unpleasant lump sat in Alistar's stomach. "And Technician Bar'rege?" He glanced at the closed door.

"We kept watch on the residence, sir, and saw no one enter or leave. However, approximately an hour ago, we heard shouting from inside. When we entered, we found no one but the technician, ranting and shouting. Some of what she shouted related to the Hollows and the leader there, so I sent Star to bring you, and another of the patrol to fetch a healer." His face was grave. "The healer has not arrived yet, and Technician Bar'rege has grown very quiet in the last quarter of an hour. We confined her in the other room, as she was growing violent."

The chill in Alistar's spine grew. "Let me speak to her."

To his surprise, Dahr didn't protest. "Yes sir."

The guard at the door opened it and stepped aside. Lamps lit the room, allowing Alistar to see Technician Bar'rege sitting on the edge of the bed. She appeared calm and collected, as if waiting for him. Her sharp gaze followed him.

"Technician Bar'rege. Pardon me for entering your home uninvited," Alistar said.

"Bar'rege? You are mistaken, sir." Her voice was calm and even. "But you are forgiven, for I am lenient."

Alistar blinked. "I... beg your pardon again, then. You are?"

A sniff of disdain. "Peasant. I am called Ziana of the Restless Wind."

Alistar bit back his first response, that "Ziana of the Restless Wind" was a fictional character from a series of popular half-chip novels. He looked at the technician again, and saw a sheen of sweat on her skin. Her hands were folded tightly in her lap. Spots stained her shirt, as if a nosebleed had escaped her efforts to contain it. "I am Alistar De'seneth of Silverline Power."

Her gaze softened slightly, and she nodded. "Yes. There are words for you, words that have been sent to you, of magic and treachery and grave danger."

"The reports we discussed earlier?" Alistar asked.

She nodded. "Words written twice and again. Sent to you. Sent with my beloved. Buried in the dirt." Her face showed lines of strain as she tried to remain focused. "Words of flowers and coat buttons, and gifts... gifts..." She doubled over with a gasp and fell to the floor.

Alistar ran to her side. "Technician Bar'rege, what's wrong? What is it?" He remembered a man who'd shouted that he was a legendary hero as convulsions took him in Doctor Tan'shyo's office. Like that man, blood now trickled from the corners of Bar'rege's mouth, and she shook. Alistar looked over his shoulder. "Dahr! Is that healer here yet?"

"Not ye— yes, sir, she's just arrived."

Footsteps sounded up the stairs, then across the floor. Alistar relinquished his spot to a petite elven woman in pale green robes. The healer grimaced and eyed her surroundings with open disdain. She cast a scowl over her shoulder, then rested a hand on the writhing technician.

Is this Rat's Disease? Alistar watched, praying that a healer might be able to succeed where a doctor had not. Violet light streamed through the ceiling to the healer as she channeled.

"I... am... Ziana... of the Restless... Wind," Bar'rege gasped. One hand rose, fingers curled to grasp at something. "I will never... be... defeated. I will fly... to the stars..."

Her fingers stiffened like claws, and her entire body jerked. She shrieked, then fell still. The healer pulled back, wiping her hands on her robes as if to clean off something clinging and disgusting. "What sort of filthy disease did this human bring with her?" The look she cast at Bar'rege was the sort Alistar might give to a pile of rotting fish guts stinking up a dock.

"This was a disease?" Alistar asked, tightly reining in his desire to snap at the healer for her obvious disdain. "Could it have been a poison?"

She looked at him, eyes narrowing. Her voice dripped with scorn as her mouth twisted in a sneer. "If you paid for this woman's services, I would suggest you get yourself to one of your human *doctors* for treatment."

"Associate De'seneth has been assigned by His Highness to investigate certain matters," Dahr said icily. "The woman who just died under your tending was a valuable witness."

"Pah." The healer stood. "I say it was some filthy human pauper's disease that killed her. Who would care to poison *this*?"

Alistar drew a deep breath, eyes hard. "Someone who does not want His Highness to learn what this woman knew. Are you so casual with *all* your patients' lives, or only those who have the misfortune of being born human?" He tugged the Silver Prince's emblem from under his shirt and held it up. "Please, do tell me."

The healer eyed the emblem, then Alistar with no sign of contrition. "If the Silver Prince is reduced to working with *your* sort, we truly *are* in dire straits." She strode from the room without a second glance. Walking to the front door, she curtly announced, "There is nothing I can do here. Return me to my home at once."

"It's so *good* to know that Lewarden's healers care deeply about the citizens who actually keep the city functioning." Onyxflame's voice was dry.

She whirled on him, eyes smoldering, but bit back her first retort when she identified him as an elf. Her gaze swept him up and down. "I would not expect a provincial to grasp the fineries of such matters."

"Dahr, get her out of here before I say or do something I might not regret later," Alistar growled, voice low.

Dahr raised a hand in a curt signal, and one of his companions hurried the healer outside. Dahr's face was thunderous with outrage. The door had barely closed before he spoke. "I said to bring a skilled healer. At what point did you think that meant fetching one who thinks that *speaking* to a human is beneath her, much less healing one?!"

The other guards shifted uncomfortably, looking at the floor. The newcomer, who must have brought the healer, began, "Lady Vineworth has never objected to healing one of us. I thought—"

"This woman is *dead*," Dahr said. "Dead because Vineworth could not even bother to arrive in a timely manner."

Onyxflame slipped into the bedroom and crouched beside Alistar. "De'seneth?"

Alistar gazed at Bar'rege's bloodstained face. "Would it be considered overly cruel punishment for the prisoners if I asked for that woman to be transferred to serve in Chirrod Prison?" His hands clenched. "Bring me the wash basin."

Onyxflame poured fresh water into the basin and handed it to Alistar. Alistar used a cloth to wash the technician's face and close her eyes, praying softly. Onyxflame murmured the words with him. "Lord Starbinder, have mercy upon this woman, and grant her soul peace in death. Carry her to your hallowed halls, where she shall dwell forevermore. May it ever be."

Alistar washed his hands in the basin. Onyxflame drew the blanket over the still form on the floor, then washed as well. The room was silent; Dahr had cut his tirade short and stood at attention with his fellow guards. Alistar closed his eyes. "Someone needs to come here and purify this residence of disease—someone whose solution will not involve burning down the building to cleanse it. Someone who can learn any and every detail of this disease. We need to know what it is, how it spreads"

Star spoke. "It will be done, sir."

"Her family needs to be told." Alistar's throat tightened, choking off the end of the sentence. "I should—"

"Sir, allow me to do so," Dahr said. "Her death took place on my watch, and I failed to prevent it. I will bear the news to her husband and son."

I feel like a coward, but this task, I am relieved to give to Dahr. Alistar nodded. "Tell them that I'll find whoever is responsible for her death. I know justice won't bring her back to them, but maybe it will be… a little comfort."

"Whoever is responsible, sir?" Dahr repeated.

Alistar raised his head, meeting the guard's eyes. "This was no accident, no coincidence. She was struck by this disease the day she spoke to me? And after the calls for plague and pestilence we heard in the Hollows? This wasn't coincidence. This was murder."

The guards all stiffened, then nodded, not arguing. Alistar looked down at the shrouded body once more. *I'm sorry, Technician Bar'rege. You warned me that someone would strike at you, and I didn't do enough. We'll keep your family safe; I promise you that. May you fly to the stars, and there find peace.*

"Sir, allow us to see you and Aspendark to a healer, to be sure you have not been exposed to this disease as well," Dahr said.

"I'm fine," Onyxflame said quickly. "I didn't touch anything, and I'm no more exposed than the rest of you. Less, I expect."

"No more healers yet. Dahr, if Technician Bar'rege's husband does not object, have a doctor conduct an autopsy," Alistar said.

All the elves stiffened and paled. "Sir! That is—" Dahr fumbled for words.

"That is an acceptable request among humans, Dahr. And they won't expect you to remain present while they do so. Also, ask Lower City doctors and healers if they've seen any similar symptoms in patients. This looks similar to something I've heard of there. I don't know if it's related to what some are calling 'Rat's Disease,' and I don't know whether to hope that it is or isn't." He washed his hands again and rubbed his eyes with the back of his hand.

"Rat's Disease? I've not heard of this, sir." Dahr's brows wrinkled in a frown. "We will see to it, and report whatever we find to you directly." He turned. "Star, see Associate De'seneth and Aspendark back. De'seneth, I will reschedule the meeting with His Highness until late morning."

Alistar frowned for a moment, then realized that Dahr was offering the delay so that they could try to reclaim some of their interrupted sleep. Not that he expected sleep would come easily now. "Thank you."

Star bowed and led them back to the carriage. Alistar cast a final look over his shoulder at the tiny residence, and wondered again what he could have done.

CHAPTER 17

Once the carriage started moving, Star cleared her throat. "Sir, if the technician was struck by a disease, you should see a healer with all haste."

Alistar raised his head wearily and turned toward her, but didn't answer.

She pressed on. "If you have been exposed to a sickness so virulent, you could contribute to its spread. And if you are to meet with His Highness, I must insist that your health be confirmed first."

"I don't suppose it's too much to ask that you find one who *doesn't* hate humans, is it?" Onyxflame cut in.

Star's expression was grave. "That is a perfectly reasonable expectation, Lord Aspendark, and one that will be met. Although given this evening's events, I understand your desire to specify it."

Can't this just be a bad dream? Let me go to sleep, so I can wake up and be out of this madness.

Onyxflame nudged him with an elbow. "De'seneth."

They were waiting for him to answer. "You know of another healer who will be awake at whatever forsaken hour this is?" Alistar finally asked.

"Yes, sir. A human healer. He is who I would have sought to attend Technician Bar'rege, had that assignment fallen to me. With your leave, sir, I will direct the carriage to his offices."

Alistar nodded. "Very well."

Star rose and opened a small panel in the wall and manipulated the controls to alter the carriage's course. During the day, when the vehicle had to contend with other traffic, a driver assisted in the navigation, but the automatons that drew the carriage really only needed a destination. Alistar closed his eyes, leaning his head against the side of the carriage, resting while he could.

He roused when the carriage stopped. Star got out first, and Alistar shivered in the rush of cold air. He peered outside to see that the carriage stood parked directly in front of a modest brick house. Ghostlights hung from the gable, washing over the carriage and casting long shadows across the still street. Star pulled a cord to the side of the door. Alistar didn't hear any chimes, but a moment later, the door opened.

He climbed from the carriage, followed by Onyxflame. Two steps through the snow brought them under the shelter of the gable, and Star waved them inside. A short man waited in the front room, and studied them as they entered.

"How may I be of assistance to His Highness this night?" He spoke with the rasp of a lifelong smoker.

"Good evening, sir. Earlier this evening, we were exposed to an unknown illness," Star answered.

The man raised an eyebrow, but nodded. "You're concerned that you contracted this illness? What level of exposure? Did any of you have contact with the blood of someone who might have been infected?"

Alistar thought back quickly. "Possibly," he allowed. "I cleaned the victim, though I washed my hands thoroughly afterwards."

"I didn't touch anything," Onyxflame said, hanging back slightly as if he thought the man might pounce on him.

"Victim?" The man's bushy eyebrows rose. "Tell me what you can. I am Serhiy Paj'ari, a healer, as I hope you already know."

"Alistar De'seneth, engineer with Silverline Power." Alistar shook off as much weariness as he could. "Have you heard of Rat's Disease?"

Paj'ari grew still. "Only by rumor, from a colleague in the Lower City. I had hoped that the symptoms he described came from an isolated incident. Is it spreading?"

"The victim who fell this night was a technician living in the Lower City," Star said. "I have heard of no other incidents. Do you know enough of the illness to determine if Mr. De'seneth has contracted it?"

Paj'ari studied Alistar. "With your leave, sir." He raised one hand, and tendrils of violet light flowed from the ceiling and gathered around his fingers. Alistar nodded, and the healer rested his hand on Alistar's arm. The magic tingled across his skin.

After several minutes, the glow faded and Paj'ari withdrew his hand. "I find nothing abnormal. No sign of infection or sickness, no indication of damage to your organs. From all that I can determine, sir, you are in excellent health. Which, in my line of work, is a refreshing change from my usual patient." He turned to Onyxflame. "Did you also have contact with the victim?"

Onyxflame raised a hand to ward the man off. "Less than De'seneth did. If he's not affected, there's no reason I would be. And His Highness's devout guard likely had more contact than either of us. Shouldn't you check her first?"

Alistar eyed Onyxflame with a frown, surprised by the unsubtle avoidance and attempted redirection. Paj'ari took no apparent offense, turning instead to Star and raising an eyebrow in question. She nodded, holding out her hands. The healer cupped his hands around hers, drawing magic again from the mahiy lines. Alistar waited, a knot of worry in his stomach as he considered that, like her, Dahr and the other guards had also been exposed longer than he or Onyxflame.

"I find no indication of disease or infection," Paj'ari announced, releasing her hands. He considered Onyxflame, then inclined his head. "Given the lack of symptoms in your companions, I will not insist, although I still recommend that you remain overly alert to any changes. Should any of you begin to exhibit symptoms of any sort, find the nearest healer or doctor at once. If this Rat's Disease is as vicious as I've been led to believe, immediate treatment may be the only recourse."

Alistar let out his breath. "If you hear of any additional cases of Rat's Disease, please inform His Highness's guards at once."

Paj'ari bowed. "I am always at His Highness's service."

"Thank you." Star bowed in return. "We will be on our way."

She ushered her charges back out to the carriage before Alistar could do more than offer a swift farewell. "What about payment?" Alistar asked as they climbed into the carriage.

"Healer Paj'ari will be paid for his services by His Highness's Guard," Star answered. "He is familiar with the process for compensation." She triggered the controls, and the carriage began moving. "Thank you for agreeing to this, sir. I will have you back to your home with all haste."

"You were right to insist," Alistar admitted.

She accepted that, and they rode without conversation the rest of the way to Shale Lane. Alistar dozed off and on until they arrived. The sky was still black with night when the carriage stopped at his doorstep. Star waited until he and Onyxflame were safely inside before departing. Alistar nodded farewell to her and closed the door.

"It's still too early to be awake, isn't it?" Onyxflame asked.

Alistar fumbled his watch from his pocket. "Yes. Nearly four in the morning is too early to be awake. And I will not be getting up at six thirty today."

"Good to hear. I'm going to bed." Onyxflame started up the stairs.

Alistar shed his coat and followed. He knew he needed to give thought to Technician Bar'rege's death and the circumstances around it, but without sleep, he might as well be trying to navigate with torn sails and a broken rudder. He activated the wardings once Onyxflame entered his room, then sought his own bed. Sleep claimed him at once.

Morning came too soon, but Alistar was up and moving not long after the weak winter sun reached his windows. He allowed himself more time than usual to dress and groom, pulling out clothes from his infrequently used formal wear. The ebony brocade on his lavender shirt matched the lace frill, though both were nearly hidden under the heavy silver-gray waistcoat. In court, he might reasonably leave the coat open, but with winter's chill gripping Lewarden, Alistar welcomed additional layers.

He knocked on Onyxflame's door and canceled the wards before descending to the kitchen and brewing a pot of strong black tea. He couldn't muster interest in breakfast, but the tea was hot and helped him shake off the dregs of sleep. The formal clothes hung tight across his shoulders, and the ruffle down the front of his shirt was a constant distraction seen in the corner of his eye. He toyed with it as an alternative to running his hands through his hair and smearing his fingers with styling grease.

Eventually, Onyxflame came downstairs. Like Alistar, he had dressed up, and was tugging on a pair of silkweave gloves. In true elven fashion, the stiff collar of his gray shirt rose halfway up his neck, minimizing exposed skin. The sea green waistcoat and embroidered chestnut vest complemented Onyxflame's complexion. Or Onyxflame had applied cosmetics to help his complexion match the clothes. Alistar decided the second was more likely, given the absence of shadows or lines of weariness even as Onyxflame yawned and rubbed his eyes.

"Tea for breakfast?" Onyxflame asked.

"I'm not hungry," Alistar said. "Help yourself."

Onyxflame perused the teas until he found one he liked. "If you're trying to look awake, you're failing."

"I'll be fine," Alistar told him.

"While I would never question my handler's self-assessment, if you're interested, whoever packed Lord Aspendark's trunk included enough makeup to make a stage actor jealous. I have no idea what the current conventions are, but I could practically apply it with a trowel and still have excess."

Alistar chuckled softly. "I'll wait until after I'm done with my tea. I have a bad habit of smearing any cosmetics I wear onto everything else I touch."

"Smearing?" Onyxflame frowned. "Nothing should be smearing after you apply it unless your cosmetics are grease-based."

Alistar raised an eyebrow. "There's another kind?"

"Reyker help us!" Onyxflame shook his head. "I had the impression you were a nobleman, someone of means, De'seneth!"

"From Rillwater," Alistar said. "Where grease and fish oil are quite common in cosmetics."

Onyxflame shook his head again. "And you've never looked at what's used in Lewarden?"

"I've had little need to do so," Alistar replied.

With his mug of tea in hand, Onyxflame climbed back up the stairs. He returned with a pair of cosmetic jars and a hand mirror. Setting them on the table in front of Alistar, he said, "At the *very* least, cover up the circles around your eyes. Just wet your finger, dip it in the powder, and apply it. It dries quickly."

Alistar opened the jars dubiously and considered the fine powder. He licked a finger and brushed it over one of the jars of powder. Taking up the mirror, he wiped his finger under one eye, leaving a streak of makeup almost the same shade as his skin. Applying enough to hide the shadows required several coats, but once the face paint dried, it didn't flake off or smear when he touched it, and it didn't have the heavy, greasy feel of the cosmetics he was accustomed to.

As he applied the makeup, Alistar said, "You didn't want the healer checking you last night."

Onyxflame started at the comment, then shifted uneasily. "I am not comfortable with healers."

Alistar looked up at him in surprise. "Oh?"

"The very nature of what they do invades a person's body, De'seneth!" Onyxflame shuddered.

"What about doctors?"

Another shudder. "Even worse."

Onyxflame was not someone he would have thought to be phobic of healers. "If you need care, will this be a problem?" Alistar asked.

"If I need care, I am perfectly capable of bandaging myself," Onyxflame said firmly. "I've done so before and I can do so again."

No doctors or healers? No wonder he has noticeable scars on his chest. Alistar decided not to press the matter, especially regarding a theoretical crisis. He smoothed the face paint, blending it against his skin until even he could barely tell what was the natural color and what was not. "Thank you."

"Looks better," Onyxflame said. "So, what are you planning to tell the Silver Prince about all this?"

"He needs to know of the situation in the Hollows, and of last night's events. Also, a summary of what we've found at the sites." Alistar poured the last of his pot of tea into his mug and gulped it down. He started to say more, but was interrupted by a humming and faint vibration in his coat pocket. Alistar pulled out a black stone inscribed with a sword and rippling lines—the speaking stone Dahr had given him. He cupped his hands around it, then opened them. "Yes?"

Dahr's voice came through the stone. "Sir, His Highness is

flying his wyverns this morning, and bids you and Aspendark to join him at your convenience. I apologize for not offering you more time, but I saw that the lights were on in your house, and presumed that you were awake."

Alistar rose. "You're here?" He walked to the window and looked down on the snow-covered street. A carriage stood parked on the street, and while it didn't bear the Silver Prince's emblem, it was clearly of higher quality than most vehicles seen on Shale Lane.

"Yes, sir," Dahr answered. "However, His Highness is aware that you were called out for an emergency last night, and does not expect you to arrive until you are prepared."

Alistar glanced at Onyxflame, then back to the stone. "We're ready, and will be out shortly."

Onyxflame grimaced. "Well, this will be fun. The last time I saw the Silver Prince was... oh, yes, at my trial, where I do believe he said I would 'never walk free again.' I think we are both going to enjoy seeing each other *so* much."

"Just mind your tongue," Alistar said. "Consider it practice. Try to convince the Silver Prince that you are, in fact, Lord Aspendark of Rillwater rather than Tiyron Onyxflame."

Onyxflame's mouth curled in a slight smile. "He knows better."

"No one takes a challenge because it's *easy*, Onyxflame. Show me what you can do, and if I'm satisfied, we'll revisit that matter of you accompanying me to devotions." Alistar set his mug on the counter beside the sink.

Dahr awaited them outside. The carriage tracks in the snow indicated that he hadn't been there long. Alistar wondered what his neighbors thought of his recent comings and goings. His breath misted into a cloud as he hurried into the waiting vehicle. As soon as all three of them were settled, the automatons sprang into motion. Alistar leaned back and tried to relax, but couldn't. He was too aware that lives hung in his hands. Technician Bar'rege had proven that.

This is more than politics. People are dying because someone is concealing something, and I don't know who or what. I have to figure this out before more people die.

CHAPTER 18

"How are Technician Bar'rege's husband and child?" Alistar asked, breaking the silence in the carriage.

Dahr's eyes were weary, though he carried himself with his typical stiff attention. "As well as can be expected, under the circumstances. The technician's husband was at first in shock, and afterwards nearly silent. He requested privacy, so I did not stay long. Their son was asleep when I was there."

"Did you get any rest?" Alistar asked.

"As much as I needed, sir," Dahr answered. "What of you and Aspendark?"

"I could have used a few more hours, but I slept," Alistar said. "I've had longer nights aboard ship."

"One night of short sleep isn't likely to kill me," Onyxflame put in. He leaned forward and pulled back one of the window curtains. "We're not bound for the palace?"

"His Highness decided to take advantage of the weather to bring his wyverns out to hunt," Dahr said.

"Wyverns?" Onyxflame raised an eyebrow. "We aren't talking about the ten-foot-tall flying lizards, are we?"

"Dwarf wyverns," Alistar answered. He held his hands about

two feet apart. "Head to tail, about this long. They're trained for hunting small game, and certain breeds are partial to cold weather."

"Ah. So, falconry for those who are too disgustingly rich to pursue the hobbies of lesser nobles." Onyxflame shook his head.

"It is a sport of the elite," Dahr said stiffly. "I doubt you could appreciate it, Onyxflame."

"And you could?" Onyxflame countered. "Do correct me if I'm wrong, but your blood is hardly more noble than mine."

Alistar cleared his throat sharply, giving Onyxflame a pointed look. Dahr chose to ignore the comment entirely.

The carriage turned down a street lined with statues of elven heroes, approaching the thick wall that surrounded Lewarden's royal hunting preserve. Once it had been at the edge of the city, but as Lewarden grew, it had crept around the edges of the preserve, though few people were foolish enough to try climbing the wall and entering without permission.

The gates opened without a sound, admitting the carriage and its occupants. Alistar peered out the window and saw the gates weave themselves shut like tanglevines. The carriage slowed, turning into a large patch of cobblestones swept clean of snow, and stopped.

Dahr opened the door and unfolded the steps. Alistar pulled his coat tight and tugged on his gloves before leaving the carriage. The air was sharp and cold, freezing the hairs in his nose as he drew a breath. Snow blanketed the ground and trees. The sky was clear but for a few thin clouds. A thin sheen of frost gleamed on the cobblestones, disturbed by their feet.

Dahr pointed at a footpath, also swept clean of snow. "His Highness awaits this way."

Alistar and Onyxflame followed him, and Alistar wondered how many groundskeepers worked in the preserve to keep the paths cleared and the grounds maintained. When they passed the first ice sculpture, he stopped to stare at the swan. Its wings were extended in flight, water carved to stream off its feathers, and around its feet, curls of ice shaped the waves disturbed by its movement. Dahr paused a moment, waiting for his charges to catch up.

"Please do not stray from the path, sir," he cautioned.

"The Silver Prince actually *pays* someone just to do *this*? Would that make these the work of some of the Grayfeather family?" Onyxflame asked, gesturing toward the next sculpture, a rearing stag with songbirds perched on its antlers.

"The Grayfeather family of artisans has been in the employ of the Crown for five generations," Dahr said. "During the winter, they produce these sculptures. In summer, I understand that they work in other mediums." He strode up the path.

As they passed more ice sculptures, Onyxflame leaned close to Alistar. "Do you have any idea how tempting it is to break off one little piece—say, a leaf off the branch that nymph is waving—and see how long it takes for someone to run and fix it?"

Alistar gave him a sidelong look. "I wouldn't recommend indulging that curiosity, Onyxflame. I suspect that Dahr would break your fingers if you tried."

Dahr didn't even turn. "De'seneth suspects correctly."

"Simply a thought, I assure you," Onyxflame said easily. "No sense of humor."

"Given what you seem to consider amusing, I find very little of it humorous," Dahr replied.

Onyxflame chuckled and smiled innocently. "Mere idle curiosity, I promise."

"You're not helping your case for attending devotions, Onyxflame," Alistar warned in a low voice.

Onyxflame sighed, but shut his mouth and kept his hands tucked under his cloak. They walked for probably a mile before Alistar saw a wyvern darting through the air, pursuing a fat pigeon. The bird fluttered and tried to avoid its pursuer, but the red and black wyvern pulled up and dove, claws extended. It slammed into the pigeon, digging in its claws and taking the bird down. Bird and wyvern both dropped out of sight, but a sharp whistle pierced the air, and was answered by the wyvern's chitter and chirp.

Dahr raised his hand in a gesture of greeting, though Alistar saw no one. The guard stopped a moment, then nodded. "We are expected."

The trees opened and they entered a meadow. The Silver Prince and a young woman stood beside a temporary aviary. Both wore heavy fur coats and hats to ward against the frigid air. Prince Cero fed the red and black wyvern scraps of meat as it curled around his arm, its feet and wing claws gripping the coat sleeve. The pigeon lay at the prince's feet, feathers and blood spattering the snow. The young woman opened a cage and coaxed out another wyvern, this one almost solid indigo. It crawled up her arm and nestled against her hat.

"And who's that?" Onyxflame asked in a voice low enough that it wouldn't carry to Dahr. "The Silver Prince has a pretty young 'personal assistant'? Must be a nice job."

Alistar stiffened and answered just as quietly. "Lady Syri does assist Prince Cero at times, yes. She is, after all, his *daughter*."

"Daughter?" Onyxflame hissed. "Is she even thirty?"

"Approaching forty, I believe," Alistar said. Elves didn't quite live twice as long as humans, but halving an elf's age was close enough to the equivalent human age.

"The Silver Prince is what… a hundred and thirty? A hundred and forty?" Onyxflame blinked. "*How?*"

"Through the normal means, I expect," Alistar said mildly. "His wife isn't yet a hundred."

Onyxflame shook his head. "Maybe those rumors about eating unicorn hearts *are* true."

The wyverns watched them approach with curious eyes, and Prince Cero's hissed, batting its wings before settling and accepting another scrap of meat. The Silver Prince ran a finger down its spine, calming it, before examining his visitors.

Alistar bowed low. "Your Highness, thank you for the audience."

"I told you to request one whenever you felt there was need, De'seneth. I am pleased you have done so." Prince Cero's gaze moved to Onyxflame and stayed there, eyes narrowing. "Aspendark."

"Your Highness. I must thank you for your... generosity." Onyxflame dipped a bow.

Alistar saw Lady Syri raise an eyebrow as the two elves exchanged cool greetings, and guessed that she didn't know Onyxflame's identity. She did nod to Alistar. "Associate De'seneth." Then, before he had more than a moment to wonder which title he should use to address her, she mouthed "Technician."

He gave her a quick smile of thanks. That, at least, put this firmly in the realm of Silverline Power business. "Technician Feyblade."

Onyxflame looked askance at him, but no one else did. Prince Cero nudged his wyvern up to his shoulder and began a leisurely walk across the meadow. "What have you learned thus far, De'seneth?"

Alistar followed, the others coming behind him. "Someone either within Silverline Power or closely associated with the company has spread confidential information, and it's being used to incite unrest in the Hollows." Alistar briefly outlined their foray into the Hollows, highlighting the gathering led by Zhrets Vonn. Prince Cero listened, his face dark. When Alistar described the situation and the blackmail employed at Redpine Generator, the Silver Prince stopped cold.

"This Hollows priest has openly threatened one of my employees?" Prince Cero's eyes narrowed.

"He's done more than threaten," Onyxflame put in. "Unless your technician was cursed with Fortune's disfavor."

Prince Cero turned and fixed a long look at Onyxflame. "Explain. I was informed of the death of an employee last night under questionable circumstances, but the formal report has not arrived yet. Apparently there was a request for an *autopsy*." He said the word like it tasted foul.

"Yes, Your Highness. I requested it," Alistar said. The elves could, and would, cringe at the thought, but he would not apologize for his decision. "Have you received any reports of a sickness called Rat's Disease, sir?"

"No, though by the name I would presume it to be limited to the slums," Prince Cero answered.

"I've heard references made to it, but no description I would trust," Lady Syri added.

Alistar nodded, not entirely surprised. Class divisions held strong even among healers and doctors—and doctors, being almost exclusively human, and almost exclusively treating the lower classes, were given less credence by the nobility of Lewarden. "The illness kills quickly once it sets in, destroying the victim's internal organs. In both the cases I've seen, the victims suffered delusions and became erratic in their behavior, growing more so the closer they came to death. Technician Bar'rege claimed to be Ziana of the Restless Wind, and the male victim I saw declared himself Ardum, Conqueror of the Six Heavens."

"Well, at least they aspired high," Lady Syri said in an undertone.

"You do not believe Technician Bar'rege's death to be coincidence," Prince Cero said.

"I do not," Alistar agreed. "It's too close on the heels of her speaking to me. I suspect that she was murdered either to keep her from telling me more or as punishment for speaking to me in the first place. I don't know *how* she was murdered, though. I hope that the autopsy will reveal the source. Zhrets Vonn claimed that he could call down divine plagues, but if he had that power, I doubt he would waste it on shows in the Hollows."

The Silver Prince pondered, reaching up to stroke the head of his restless wyvern. "It does seem unlikely. However, you have no evidence to support your suspicion yet."

"No, sir," Alistar acknowledged.

"Yet Technician Bar'rege's report indicates that this man is a noble, or able to pass as one well enough to convince her. And if he does have connections to Silverline Power, he most likely is related to someone of station." Prince Cero's boots crunched through the thin layer of ice atop the snow.

A dove cooed, and both wyverns raised their heads sharply to the sky. Prince Cero nodded to his daughter, and she released the indigo. It launched into the sky in search of prey. The Silver Prince watched the wyvern fly. "What of your findings at the sites of the incidents, De'seneth?"

"A girl on Shale Lane claimed that she saw 'shining men' running up the wall, which led us to investigate the roof," Alistar said. "Lord Aspendark's analysis of the ambient magic confirmed that it was most likely the site where the incident occurred. I found a coat button there as well. Technician Bar'rege's description of her visitor included mention that he was missing a coat button, however the timing doesn't line up—she was threatened weeks before the Shale Lane incident, and if the button had been there that long, it would have been lost in the snow."

"Why would it have been there, then?" Lady Syri asked, frowning. She turned to Prince Cero. "There seems to be a pattern of leaving some item or small sign that would point toward the nobility."

"There have been others, Lady?" Onyxflame asked. "I have not heard of this."

Neither have I. Is this why Prince Cero is so certain political sabotage is at work? Alistar shifted, feeling the chill now that they'd stopped moving.

"A cigar stub at one of the first ones, a scrap of a handkerchief at another," Lady Syri answered. "I documented all the items found and where, and provided the list to be included in the information given to the assigned investigator. Did you not receive it, Associate De'seneth?"

"I'm afraid it was not included in the information that I was given," Alistar told her, frowning. He cast a glance to Dahr, who shook his head.

"I do not recall seeing such a list, sir. And such information as was assembled was to remain entirely within the possession of His Highness's Guard until it was given to you." The guard's expression was troubled. "And I say that without bearing any doubt that Lady Syri did exactly as she said."

"Did the guards involved in assembling that information include the one who so inconveniently 'forgot' that the healer he chose to bring to Technician Bar'rege's house loathes humans?" Onyxflame asked.

All three of the other elves stiffened.

"I only ask because I wonder what else he might have 'forgotten' to provide, or tell, or not tell," Onyxflame continued.

Prince Cero's jaw tightened. "Indeed. Look into the matter, Dahr. Technician Feyblade, see to it that Associate De'seneth receives the list and access to the items of interest."

"Yes sir." Lady Syri bowed.

In a flutter of wings, a dove rose from the shelter of the trees. The indigo wyvern soared up above it, and descended with a screech. The dove turned sharply at the last moment, barely avoiding the wyvern's claws and darting back into cover. The wyvern shrieked in frustration, wings pumping angry beats to lift it back into the sky.

"Associate De'seneth, two evenings from now, Lord Proudmoor is holding a banquet. I expect you and Aspendark to attend. Arrangements will be made for you to receive an invitation,"

Prince Cero said. "I trust that you will make good use of the opportunity."

Alistar's friend Lamorage had mentioned the gathering as well, when Alistar had asked him if anything noteworthy was coming up. "We will be there, Your Highness." The dismissal was clear.

"If you will come to the offices tomorrow, Associate De'seneth, I'll provide you with the list personally," Lady Syri said. "I apologize that you did not have it before." She bowed to him, then inclined her head in a polite nod to Onyxflame. "Lord Aspendark, was it? Thank you for your assistance in this matter."

Onyxflame bowed in return. "I am in His Highness's service, Lady." He managed to say the words without evident sarcasm. "Until such time as we meet again."

"Well, if you are assisting Associate De'seneth, I believe that would be tomorrow." Lady Syri's mouth quirked in a smile. She turned to the sky and whistled sharply. The indigo wyvern reluctantly circled down, and she held out her arm for it to alight.

Prince Cero eyed Onyxflame, then nodded curtly. "Your service will be remembered."

"I'm sure it will be," Onyxflame muttered under his breath as he followed Alistar. "And I hope you choke on it."

CHAPTER 19

The carriage returned them to Alistar's house. Dahr lingered after his passengers climbed out. "Do you need anything else, sir? Will you need a carriage?"

Alistar considered. The hour was near noon, past morning devotions but too early for the evening. "I will be attending services later, but I think a hired carriage would be more suitable." He smiled faintly. "With no offense intended, even without royal markings, His Highness's carriages are… noticeable, and would be even more so at the sanctuary I attend."

"If you wish, sir, I can bring one more suitable to the area," Dahr told him. "Do you intend to leave Onyxflame unattended here in your absence?"

Alistar hesitated and cast a look at Onyxflame. The elf stood at the door, patiently waiting for Alistar to unlock it and acting as if he wasn't keenly interested in the answer. Alistar turned back to Dahr. "That's still under consideration. However, if he does accompany me to devotions, would you be available to keep an eye on him afterwards? I'd like to spend some time with my fiancée."

The guard didn't even blink. "Sir, I am available at your

request. His Highness's orders. What time do you wish me to pick you up?"

"Come at four," Alistar said. "Thank you."

"Of course, sir." Dahr pulled the carriage door closed, and the automatons set off at a smart trot.

Alistar unlocked the door and stepped into the welcome warmth. Onyxflame waited until Alistar had hung up his coat before obliquely broaching the subject of devotions.

"I hope that my day's performance has met your expectations thus far." Onyxflame hung his cloak on a hook by the door. "I did not yield to the temptation to say any of my opinions regarding your esteemed employer."

"You weren't entirely subtle in your dislike of him either," Alistar pointed out. "You did avoid openly antagonizing him or offending Lady Syri. Still, you'll need to do better when we attend the Proudmoor gathering."

"Rest assured, De'seneth, I shall be the perfect gentlemen to those I have no deep, abiding personal grudge against, and I shall avoid interactions with those few nobles who I did actually know. Few of them had enough station to mingle in high nobility's circles in any case."

Alistar nodded in slow consideration. "Do you have clothing that falls somewhere between 'overdressed' and 'day labor'?"

"Whoever packed Aspendark's bags had a far more refined sense of 'leisure wear' than I do, but I can assemble a somewhat suitable outfit," Onyxflame answered. He paused. "Ah, and along such lines, does your housekeeper attend to the laundry as well, and if so, how should I best request that my clothes be washed?"

Alistar raised an eyebrow in surprise, then realized he'd never covered the matter with Onyxflame. "You can launder your own clothes—yes, even the silkweave suits that His Highness provided." He waved for Onyxflame to follow and opened a small side door. The room was little larger than a closet and housed a waist-high metal box with a hinged lid at the top. Lifting the lid revealed a tub. "Whatever clothing you need washed, place inside. Then shut the lid—it won't start if the lid is open—and press this button." He indicated a slightly recessed yellow button. "The machine takes care of the rest."

Onyxflame peered around the back of the machine. "Pipes? For water?"

Alistar nodded. "This is an older model, so it doesn't dry as well as some of the newest styles, and isn't as fast, but it won't damage your clothes like a public laundry might."

"Should I decry a luxury such as having clean clothing without leaving this house simply because it could work faster?" Onyxflame asked. "De'seneth, despite the fact that something like this undoubtedly puts hundreds of poor washer women out of work, I see no reason to complain about the improvement."

"Actually, I think many of the former washer women have now been trained on the repair and maintenance of these machines," Alistar said. "And from all I've heard, few of them complained about it either. If you have clothes you want washed, you should have time enough to put them through the machine before we leave for devotions."

"We?" Onyxflame stopped and turned to him. "You'll allow me to attend, then?"

"Unless you manage to do something in the next few hours to make me change my mind, yes," Alistar answered. "Don't make me regret this."

"I will not." Onyxflame's tone held neither scorn nor jest. "Thank you."

Onyxflame washed a load of laundry, enamored with the machine though there was nothing noteworthy to see while it operated. Alistar changed into comfortable clothes and wrote several brief reports during the afternoon, and also made a complete list of every document included in his packet about the incidents, in case additional information was missing. As the afternoon grew later, he called Onyxflame to get ready, and dressed for devotions. Both of them stood ready at the door when Dahr arrived at four.

The carriage, to Alistar's relief, looked like a well-maintained hired coach rather than a vehicle that a nobleman would use. Dahr sat on the driver's bench, dressed in plain, heavy clothes that didn't proclaim his occupation. Alistar suspected he found them nearly as unnatural as Alistar did his court dress.

"Are you familiar with the midcity sanctuaries, Dahr?" Alistar asked.

"I reviewed their locations this afternoon, sir," Dahr answered. "Which is our destination?"

"Night's Eve," Alistar told him, opening the carriage door. It was far from the largest sanctuary in Lewarden, but it was where Saskia and her family attended, and the priests there were always welcoming and pleasant.

Onyxflame climbed into the carriage after them, and Dahr set the team of horses into motion with a snap of the reins. The streets of Lewarden were as busy as ever as Dahr steered them into the rush of traffic. As a driver, he was more direct than the average hired driver, directing the team with the expectation that other drivers would yield to him. By in large they did, though not without a certain amount of cursing.

Onyxflame cleared his throat after a particularly virulent string of obscenities flew after their carriage. "Perhaps I am mistaken and overthinking the matter, but it seems to me that our driver should confine himself to vehicles that lend themselves to the respect his attitude assumes."

Alistar stifled a snort, though he doubted Dahr could hear them. "He *does* rather seem to be an aggressive driver."

"Ah, yes, that's the term," Onyxflame agreed. "I was sure there had to be one more diplomatic than 'raging maniac.'"

Alistar looked out the window. "On the other hand, we're

arriving a good ten minutes earlier than I normally would taking a public taxi."

"Assuming we get there alive," Onyxflame said.

The carriage turned into the carriage house across from the sanctuary, and Dahr paid the attendant. Alistar had no idea what they charged, but he always saw a number of coaches and horses stabled when he attended services, and this day was no exception.

Dahr opened the door and unfolded the steps for them. Alistar climbed out and asked, "Will you attend the services, or would you prefer to use the time for other purposes?"

Dahr glanced over his shoulder toward the sanctuary and shifted uncomfortably. "If you do not mind, sir, I have a few other matters I can attend to in this area of the city. What time do the services conclude?"

"This time of year, they are usually done by six or six-thirty," Alistar said. "I won't leave until you're back." Dahr's response was one he was accustomed to seeing from elves invited to worship the Reyker, which made Onyxflame's desire to attend all the more unusual.

"I will return by six, sir." Dahr eyed Onyxflame. "Though if you require my presence earlier to resolve any disruptions, please do not hesitate to contact me."

Onyxflame wisely held his tongue, though Alistar could see him biting back a response. Dahr strode down the street while Alistar and Onyxflame crossed to Night's Eve Sanctuary. Compared to the looming elven temples, full of sharp angles and fraught with symbolic images and patterns, human sanctuaries were subtle structures of graceful design. Even a sanctuary like Night's Eve, rising four or five stories, didn't strive to dominate the surrounding structures, but seemed to draw the gaze naturally. A trickle of people entered the sanctuary, reminding Alistar that he was arriving earlier than usual. He joined them, nodding and smiling to familiar faces. Onyxflame followed as unobtrusively as possible, slipping into the shadows toward the back of the sanctuary once they were inside. Alistar looked over his shoulder and searched for the elf. Onyxflame raised a hand in acknowledgment and sat on a bench. Somewhat to Alistar's surprise, Onyxflame wasn't the only elf taking refuge in the rear of the sanctuary. He wondered why he'd never noticed the four others before.

Because they sit there to avoid notice, he reminded himself. *Clearly, the effort is successful.*

Leaving Onyxflame unmonitored made Alistar uneasy, but demanding that the elf sit where he could see him would place Onyxflame under the open scrutiny of the human worshipers. That would be disruptive to the service in far too many ways. Keeping his qualms under check, he sought his usual seat, toward the middle of the sanctuary. Saskia and Doctor Tan'shyo had not yet arrived. Alistar quietly studied the murals, depictions of the gods based on woodcuts in books brought by refugees from Heiset when they came through the portal.

When someone slid onto the bench beside him, Alistar turned with a smile. Saskia smiled in return. "You're early."

Alistar rose and helped her take off her fur coat. Her strawberry blond curls were tied back in a loose tail, and she wore a teal and black brocade dress. Alistar waited for her to sit before resuming his seat. "I managed to catch the most insane driver I've ever ridden with. Not sure that he understood the concept of sharing the road with other drivers, but he *did* get here fast." He looked behind them toward the rear of the sanctuary, looking for Doctor Tan'shyo, and checking that Onyxflame remained where he'd been. The elf sat at the back, not appearing engaged in conversation with the others. Of Doctor Tan'shyo, though, Alistar saw no sign. "Is your father here?"

Saskia shook her head. "No, I'm afraid not. He was called in to perform an autopsy on a woman who died last night." She lowered her voice. "Possibly Rat's Disease. He didn't want me to join him, for risk of contagion."

Alistar stopped. "He's performing the autopsy?"

Saskia nodded. "I didn't hear much of the explanation; the messenger was very insistent that the matter be kept confidential." She smiled faintly. "So I can't tell you more than that, I'm afraid."

"I understand," Alistar said softly. *Does Doctor Tan'shyo regularly perform work for the Royal Guards, like the healer we visited last night? Or was he chosen because someone knows his connection to me?* He squeezed Saskia's hand, torn between the need for confidentiality and the desire to tell her that the autopsy had been his request.

"Do you have a little time after the services?" Saskia asked. "Or do you need to return to your work?"

"I have time," Alistar promised. "What would you like to do? Dinner? Go to a show?"

She considered. "A show does sound nice. Though I haven't had dinner yet either."

"A walk at the park?" Alistar suggested. It would be cold, but the wind was barely a whisper, and the park offered many shelters to combat the chill.

Saskia brightened. "With a visit to the tea stand, I assume. Let's do that."

The priests filed in through the sanctuary, and Alistar and Saskia, with the rest of the assembly, bowed their heads for the invocations. They murmured the chants of devotion and sang. Alistar loved listening to Saskia's rich alto. He let himself become lost in the familiar chants and songs, reiterating their worship and dedication to the pantheon of human gods, vowing to serve their will and honor their laws. The priests each read a portion of the Divine Creed, repeating the words of the god they served. Alistar closed his eyes and listened, the words finally driving back the miasma that had clung to his mind since the Hollows.

Mighty Rechmal, guide me as I walk this path. Help me expose those who pervert your name and worship and who murder your followers.

When the service drew to a close, Alistar drew back to himself. Saskia gave him a smile and squeezed his hand. "Better?"

"Better," Alistar agreed. He let out a long breath. "Yes, better."

"Father asked me to pass on a couple of messages." Saskia stood and reluctantly released Alistar's hand. "I'll meet you at the back?"

Alistar nodded. "I'll wait for you." He stood. "I'll take your coat."

"Thank you." Saskia passed it to him and slipped into the crowd of worshipers.

Alistar worked his way to the back of the sanctuary. Of the elves, only Onyxflame remained. He greeted Alistar with a polite nod and moved back into a more shadowed corner to avoid drawing notice. Alistar joined him, ostensibly to stay out of the way while waiting for Saskia.

"I trust no one will have reason to complain about you?" Alistar said in a low voice.

"As I promised, De'seneth, I will not disrupt the worship of the gods." Onyxflame spoke without jest, even when he added, "And if I had considered it, I was told under no uncertain terms that my benchmates would silence any distractions immediately. A sentiment that I assured them I shared."

"Ah." That made a great deal of sense, and eased Alistar's concerns a certain degree.

A man approached Alistar. "Excuse me, Mr. De'seneth? There's an elf outside who says he's looking for you." His tone was hesitant, asking whether Alistar wanted him to offer an excuse and send the elf on his way.

Alistar smiled. "Thank you. I'll be right out."

The man nodded quickly, relieved, and hurried back outside.

Onyxflame stifled a sigh. "The changing of the guard, I take it."

"I expect I don't have to tell you to mind yourself with Dahr," Alistar said.

"No need at all, De'seneth," Onyxflame promised. "He will have no cause to complain about my behavior."

Alistar raised an eyebrow dubiously, but accepted the statement. "Let's go."

Dahr stood to one side at the gate to Night's Eve, failing to be inconspicuous. Alistar walked over to him and nodded in greeting. "I hope you haven't been waiting too long."

"No, sir, not long," Dahr answered.

Alistar glanced over his shoulder to Onyxflame. "I'm putting you on a ten foot leash to Dahr."

Onyxflame grimaced, but accepted without argument. Dahr scowled at Onyxflame, then turned to Alistar. "Restrictions, sir?"

"Just keep him out of trouble," Alistar said. "Six hours should be more than long enough. Don't worry about giving me a ride home—I can handle that myself." He fished into his pocket for the spare key, which he handed to Dahr. "I expect I'll be home by ten if not before, but if you come by earlier, let yourself in."

Dahr accepted the key with a grave nod. "Yes sir."

"My fiancée and I plan to get some food and take a walk. Feel free to take dinner, see a show, or whatever." Alistar pulled out his purse.

Dahr waved the marks away. "Any expenses I incur will be covered as part of your assignment, sir."

"Are they?" Onyxflame asked. "Then can I pick the eatery?"

"No." Dahr shot him a scowl. "And wherever we eat, braised dragon liver will not be on the menu."

Alistar chuckled softly as Dahr named the dish currently rumored to be the most expensive, exotic, and desired meal among the nobility. He murmured the key words to activate the wards, leashing Onyxflame to Dahr for the next few hours. "I'll see you later."

He hurried back inside just as Saskia came to find him. She cocked her head with a look of concern. "Someone said you went outside to speak to an elf. Is there a problem? Something come up at work?"

Alistar waved a hand, giving her a reassuring smile. "Nothing so serious that it can't wait. Are you ready? All messages delivered?"

"They are." Saskia retrieved her coat from Alistar and pulled it on. She linked her arm with his and they left the sanctuary.

Dahr and Onyxflame were already gone when they stepped outside. Alistar couldn't entirely put them out of his mind, but he let his concerns occupy a back part of his thoughts. Dahr and Onyxflame didn't like one another, but Dahr would do his duty, and Onyxflame should have the sense not to antagonize his guard too much. Alistar cast a look around once more out of habit, noting the vagrants begging outside the sanctuary gates and the groups of people milling and walking down the cobbled streets, but seeing nothing that struck him as a threat.

Arm in arm, Alistar and Saskia walked the few blocks from Night's Eve Sanctuary to Wintertide Park. Named after the king who established it, the park offered a welcome respite from the crowds and buildings. Spruce and pine trees offered an illusion of separation from Lewarden, and vehicles were forbidden on the park's paths, though horses were allowed, so long as their riders minded pedestrians. Enterprising vendors set up booths along the common walkways. Attendants ensured the walkways remained free of snow and ice both day and night. Alistar looked toward the open-air stage—an unofficial addition that stories claimed had been set up within the first month of the park's establishment— but the only performers on it were a handful of children running back and forth pelting each other with snowballs.

Alistar let out a long breath, and the mist hung in the air before him. "It feels like it's been ages since I saw you last."

Saskia laughed. "Barely a week, Alistar. Hardly *that* long."

"Is that all?" he murmured. "It feels longer."

"Your assignment?" Saskia asked.

Alistar nodded.

"Is it not going well?" she asked in concern. "Running into barriers?"

"Not the ones I expected," Alistar answered. "And it keeps growing more complicated and twisted. I went into it knowing that it wouldn't be simple, but the politics are going to be a gnarled mess to sort out." He glanced around and brightened, pointing. "Ah, there's the Crimson Spice tea stand."

"I hope they have some ginger or juniper hot tea," Saskia said, smiling. They'd discovered the tea stand during one of their walks through the park, and tried to find it every time they visited. The task wasn't always simple—vendors kept their booths mobile and frequently moved to different areas of the park to capture new customers.

When they approached, the proprietor beamed at them. A plump human man at least five years younger than Alistar, he kept his hair dyed a vivid shade of red that matched the banner fluttering over his stand. Alistar had never seen him wear a hat, even on the coldest days. He'd also never seen the man be anything less than cheerful, greeting his customers like they were long-lost friends.

"Ah, sir, madam, it's good to see you again! What can I get you? The tea is hot, and my lovely sister has just delivered a fresh batch of pies and pastries, still steaming from the oven." The proprietor waved at a warming pan.

They ordered tea and an assortment of hand pies, with an apple pastry each for desert. The meat in the pies was mostly pheasant or rabbit cooked with a mix of winter vegetables. Alistar and Saskia walked slowly as they ate, and when they reached one of the heated benches that was open, they claimed it immediately. A bubble of warmth surrounded them, activated when they sat. Saskia made a pleased sound as she sipped her ginger tea.

"This is perfect. I'm glad we could do this today."

Alistar nodded in agreement, savoring both the food and the warmth. In winter, the enchantments on the benches not only offered respite to visitors, but heat and shelter to vagabonds, and so long as they caused no trouble and moved on in the morning, the guards left them alone.

If the mahiy lines fail, people will freeze to death here. The sobering thought sent a shiver down his spine. Alistar glanced up to the faint shimmer of violet lines overhead.

"You're wandering, Alistar," Saskia said.

"Sorry." He gave her a small smile. "And after I told you that work could wait, too."

Saskia looked up as well. "I'm as guilty of that as you right now, worrying about Father."

Alistar glanced around for anyone who might be close enough to hear him. Wintertide Park constantly attracted visitors, even on the short, chill winter days, but none stood close enough to eavesdrop easily. "Saskia, the woman he's performing the autopsy on. Was her name Bar'rege?"

Saskia started, breath catching. "What? Did you know her?"

"Not well," Alistar said. "She worked at Silverline Power, but I just met her..." He paused. "Yesterday."

Saskia's mouth formed a silent "Oh."

Alistar looked down at his mug of tea. "I should apologize to your father. I requested the autopsy. The timing and circumstances of her death so soon after she spoke to me were... suspicious."

"But it appeared that she died of Rat's Disease," Saskia said, frowning. "Do you think she was intentionally infected?"

"I don't know," Alistar admitted. "I was hoping that an autopsy might reveal something. I wouldn't know where to begin."

"I'll talk to Father," Saskia said. "He can send you a full report, or, if you'd rather, he can send a runner and you can come down to the clinic to talk to him directly." Lines of worry pinched her face, and she lowered her voice. "We still aren't sure how it spreads, but it's spreading. I know of another five cases in the last week, not including this one. If it continues, they might quarantine the Lower City. And if they do that so close to the Ice

Blossom Festival, resentment is going to flare. It could turn bad fast. Doesn't help that we've had Successors stirring things up in the poorer quarters."

"The Successors are preaching outside the Hollows?" Alistar sat up straighter.

"Well, it's what I've heard," Saskia told him. "I haven't heard them myself, so it's all second and third hand reports." She cocked her head at Alistar. "That must mean something to you that it doesn't to me."

"It… might be related to my project," Alistar answered. "Maybe. Or it may be nothing at all."

Saskia set her tea mug on the bench and rested her hand on his shoulder. "Are you trying to do everything on your own, Alistar? What sort of project *is* this?"

"A very sensitive one," Alistar answered. "But no, I'm not completely on my own. I have an assistant with expertise in the subject, and I have resources available." *More resources than I know how to responsibly use, at that.* "The situation is still daunting."

"I didn't think privateer captains were daunted by anything," Saskia said, her eyes twinkling.

"Oh, there are a few things," Alistar replied. "Especially when he's venturing into unfamiliar waters and hasn't yet gotten a feel for the mettle of his crew."

"You won't let anyone down," Saskia said with confidence.

He smiled, cheered by her conviction. "Not if I can help it," he agreed.

They stood, reluctantly leaving the warm bench to return their mugs to the tea stand. Alistar shivered as the cold settled around him again. Another couple claimed the seat as soon as it was free.

"I'm sorry to be putting this on you, Saskia," Alistar said. "Especially when I can tell you so little about what I'm doing, even though your father is now involved."

She shook her head. "Don't be. All I will ask is that if you do learn something about Rat's Disease or how it spreads, tell us. It's a horrible way for anyone to die."

"I will," he promised. "Anything I can."

They walked in silence for a time, the specter of Rat's Disease hanging over them. Finally, Saskia broached a topic that seemed safer. "You said you have an assistant for this project. What are they like?"

Saskia was the last person he wanted to lie to. "I can't tell you all the details." If he'd been speaking to a member of his family, they would understand that to mean that everything he was about to say related to the public persona of the individual in question, and might not be strictly accurate. But his family had, through the generations, developed an intricately complex system of second meanings, coded phrases, and subtexts that he'd only barely begun to teach Saskia.

From her small frown, she recognized that he'd used one of those phrases, but wasn't certain of the meaning. "Tell me what you can."

"He's Taslor Aspendark, from Rillwater. He's in Lewarden for business, and while he's here, he's staying with me."

Saskia cocked her head. "I don't believe I've heard the name before."

"You wouldn't have," Alistar assured her. "He owns several warehouses between Midora's Dock and the Fathomdeep Tavern —you remember that area, don't you?"

Saskia had visited Rillwater with Alistar several times. Her brow furrowed. "I think so. But isn't that..." She trailed off, glanced around, and mouthed, "Empty land?"

Alistar nodded. "His sister is his business manager, and she's handling things there while he's in Lewarden. And he has some specific talents that relate to my assignment, so he's agreed to help me."

"And he's staying with you? Was that your choice?" she asked.

Alistar made a face. "More that it was the best option." He

lowered his voice. "He doesn't have a lot of disposable income at the moment, and his options are limited."

"Mmm." Saskia nodded. "And his limitations limit your options as well?"

"Not as much as they might," Alistar told her. "It's just expected that he'll accompany me most of the time."

"Not here, I hope," Saskia said, mouth quirking in a smile.

"No, no, not tonight," he assured her quickly. He considered how best to describe Onyxflame to her. "Overall, he's got a sharp wit and holds some unpopular opinions, but he *is* good at what he does, and he's motivated to see the assignment through. He's educated and can debate. Tends to respond with sarcasm to people and situations that irritate him."

"He sounds like an interesting man. I hope I can meet him sometime," Saskia said. "If the opportunity comes up."

"Well, if I come by the clinic to speak to your father, he'll be with me." Alistar paused. "Although he does have a fear of both healers and doctors, so he may not be at his best."

"That phobia is not uncommon among elves," Saskia said. "Don't worry; I'm used to it. You can assure him that we aren't going to lay hands on him without his permission."

"He'll be on his best behavior, I'm sure," Alistar said. *Or rather, I will make sure that he will be.*

Saskia just laughed softly. "I'm not worried about that, Alistar."

You would be if I could tell you who he really is. Alistar forced a smile in spite of his thoughts. He started to reply when the clock tower began to chime.

They both turned toward it, counting the peals. "Is it really nine already?" Alistar asked. It hadn't felt that long at all, and the lamps in the park had kept him from noticing just how dark the night had grown.

Saskia sighed, but nodded. "I guess it is. I should start home. Father ought to be getting back soon, and I'll be minding the clinic tomorrow unless he's completed the report, which isn't likely."

They walked together to the edge of the park. Taxi coaches still drove the streets, and they each hailed one. Alistar bid his fiancée good night with a long kiss and a promise to see her at devotions if not before, helped her into her coach, then took his own for his solitary ride back to Shale Lane.

CHAPTER 20

No lights were on when Alistar arrived home, so he assumed that Dahr and Onyxflame hadn't yet returned. Snow dusted the street and walkways, and he paused to sweep off his steps before going inside.

The house was quiet, and he enjoyed the window of solitude. Somehow, the air about the place was different when Onyxflame was present, even if the elf was in the guest room. Alistar dressed down for the evening and brewed a pot of tea. It had just finished steeping when he heard the front door open, then close. No conversation, though. Cautious, Alistar stepped out of the kitchen and looked down the stairs.

Onyxflame hung his cloak on a hook beside the closet. Dahr stood beside the door, watching his charge like a bloodhound, radiating displeasure. Onyxflame turned toward the stairs and looked up, giving Alistar his first glimpse of the bruise darkening the elf's jaw. "Ah, hello, De'seneth. I trust your evening was pleasant."

"What happened?" Alistar looked from Onyxflame to Dahr and tromped down the stairs.

"Lord Aspendark learned that not everyone shares his idea of humor," Dahr answered, voice flat. "I was able to remove him from the situation before further injuries resulted."

"Nothing some makeup won't cover," Onyxflame promised breezily.

Onyxflame's flippant response set Alistar's teeth on edge. If any member of his father's crew had dared speak in such a manner to his captain after a fight, that sailor would have been lucky to sail with any Rillwater vessel again. "What. Happened." Alistar repeated, giving each word hard emphasis.

"We visited a game hall. I was speaking with a few men and read my audience wrong," Onyxflame said. "A drunk fellow took offense and started swinging. I avoided him well enough until his buddies got involved, though. If they hadn't started shoving, I doubt he would ever have connected."

Alistar glanced at Dahr for confirmation. The guard nodded with a scowl. "The situation and circumstances were such that I could not immediately remove him, sir. I apologize."

"No brawls, no property damage, and no missing teeth," Onyxflame added, as if that covered the sum total of potential offenses.

Alistar's jaw tightened. "Go get ice in the kitchen."

Onyxflame stepped toward the stairs, then stopped, rubbing his wrist. "I would be delighted to do so, but I doubt Dahr wishes to accompany me."

"If De'seneth deems it necessary to keep you out of further mischief, I will do so," Dahr said, though he clearly did not relish the idea.

Alistar almost accepted the reluctant offer, but he wasn't certain whether his intent would be to punish Onyxflame for getting into the situation, or Dahr for not preventing it. He canceled the warding that bound Onyxflame to the guard. Both elves breathed soft sighs of relief. Onyxflame climbed the stairs and entered the kitchen. Dahr bowed to Alistar.

"Unless you need me further, I will take my leave, sir." The guard paused. "I apologize for my lapse tonight, De'seneth. I should not have allowed the situation to occur. Do you wish me here tomorrow?"

"We'll be going to Silverline's offices first thing in the morning to collect Technician Feyblade's report," Alistar told him. "You can meet us there."

"Very well, sir." Dahr bowed again and left. Only after Alistar locked the door did he remember that Dahr still had his spare key. He debated calling the guard back, but decided he could wait until tomorrow.

When Alistar returned to the kitchen, Onyxflame sat at the table holding a towel full of ice to his jaw. Alistar sat and poured his tea. He fixed Onyxflame with a long, hard look. "So, an entire day of good behavior is apparently too much to expect from you."

"I made an error in judgment," Onyxflame said. He lowered the towel and gingerly touched the bruise, then resumed icing it.

"It seems that I did as well. One I don't intend to make again," Alistar said.

"It won't happen again," Onyxflame said quickly.

"No, it won't." There was a certain tone that Alistar's father took, a calm, icy tone that could chill a room and make seasoned sailors quail. Alistar was gratified to see that it had the same effect on Onyxflame. "You seem to think this an insignificant, trivial matter. You think that starting a fight in public—a fight that necessitated a member of the *Silver Prince's personal guard* to remove you—is inconsequential?"

Onyxflame shifted uncomfortably, not meeting his eyes. "I was not announcing my identity or Dahr's, and he's out of uniform. I don't think that it would've been obvious."

Alistar's eyebrows rose. His voice remained even. "And you know with complete certainty that not one single person present would ever have had dealings with Dahr or recognize him? You are sure that none of them were attendants to nobles, who might remember and recognize Aspendark in court? Nobles might not see past the costumes of the court, but servants are better than most think about recalling where they've seen a face before." His eyes narrowed. "To say *nothing* of the absolute *stupidity* of doing exactly what I told you not to do, then acting as if you expect it to have no consequences. Were you *trying* to ensure I confine you to your room next time I go out?"

"I made a mistake!" Onyxflame snapped. "I was tired of hearing Dahr criticize every single thing I did, I sought company I thought would be more pleasant, and an exchange of words turned into someone taking a swing at me. *That* is what happened." His voice rose in pitch as he spoke, higher than seemed to fit him.

"I specifically told you to mind yourself while with Dahr." Alistar didn't let his expression shift, keeping in the back of his mind an image of his father reprimanding a crew member. "Was that directive not clear enough, Onyxflame? Did I need to spell it out in specifics for you?"

"No." Onyxflame took a sullen tone, voice sinking back to the lower range.

And not a hint or the slightest indication that he thinks he did anything wrong, or that he could have endangered everything I'm doing. Alistar gave Onyxflame a hard, unblinking stare. "People are dying, Onyxflame. They are dying in one of the most horrific ways I've ever seen. Someone is stealing magic from the mahiy lines, leaving portions of Lewarden cold and dark in the middle of winter. The people who depend on the magic could very well begin to freeze to death unless we uncover who is responsible and why. This is a subject on which your expertise could be the difference between success and failure. Life and death for hundreds of people. Yet you are going into gaming halls and picking fights because you're annoyed to have a handler? And then you are surprised that I harbor serious doubts as to your judgment or reliability?"

"I'm not getting anyone killed by having one scrap in a bar!"

Onyxflame argued. "It wasn't even a fight. Who will even remember it in a few days? Other than you, apparently."

"Do you recall a nobleman by the name of Keylos Greenroad?" Alistar asked. "A few years back."

Onyxflame's brow wrinkled as he tried to follow the apparent shift in topic. "Was he the one who got into a brawl with a dock worker? Over some girl, maybe a prostitute?"

"Three years ago," Alistar said. "That incident happened three years ago, yet you still remember it. The name. The scandal." His eyes narrowed. "*That* is who will remember, Onyxflame. *That* is what happens when a handful of people push something that could have gone unnoticed into a scandal. I doubt Greenroad thought he would be recognized any more than you do."

Onyxflame started to speak, stopped, and pressed his lips together in a thin line. Alistar refilled his mug with tea and walked to the window. Snow was falling again, tiny delicate flakes that glittered when the light caught them. A carriage rumbled down the street, tossing flakes up in clouds like a ship's wake. The driver was running his team faster than the conditions of the streets would recommend, but seemed to maintain control, even when the vehicle whipped around the corner and vanished.

"What do you want to hear, De'seneth?" Onyxflame pushed away from the table. "Shall I offer a trite apology that neither of us will believe? Promise it will never happen again?"

Alistar turned and faced the elf. "I want to hear *some* hint that you comprehend how serious this is, Onyxflame. Neither you nor Dahr were seriously injured, but you could have been. You don't think that anyone will remember you, but they might. In two nights, we will be rubbing elbows with the upper nobility of Lewarden. One stupid mistake could irreparably damage our chance of identifying suspects. One tavern scuffle tonight could become tomorrow's gossip. Do you know what would happen if Aspendark's reputation had that sort of a stain before he even *sees* the court? You'd be useless there, a distraction. And lest you think that would be an improvement, what that would mean in practice is that I'd ask Dahr to have someone watch the house, then I'd leave you confined in the guest room."

Onyxflame's jaw tightened. "That will not be necessary, De'seneth."

"Yes, it *will* be, if you get Aspendark's persona tangled up in brawls and common scuffles," Alistar said icily. "For your safety as well as for the success of this assignment. I don't throw bleeding sailors to the sharks, even when their own foolishness caused the wound."

Onyxflame didn't believe him. The elf's angry eyes and tight mouth proclaimed that without a word spoken. Alistar waited, daring him to argue. In silence, Onyxflame strode to the sink and wrung out his towel, then added fresh ice from the coldbox. "Good night, De'seneth," he said curtly.

"Good night, Onyxflame," Alistar replied as tersely. He listened to the elf tromp up the stairs and into the guest room. The door shut firmly, not quite a slam.

Alistar let out a long breath of frustration. He'd wanted a quiet, restful end to the evening, a peaceful conclusion to the hours spent with Saskia. Instead, he'd learned why he shouldn't have ignored his unease about giving Onyxflame more liberty. *Was one day really so much to ask?* He dumped the last of his tea, now tepid, into the sink. *If this assignment is my ship, and my crew consists of Onyxflame and Dahr, I'm not sure we're going to clear the shoals.* He grimaced. Dahr's first loyalty was to Prince Cero; Alistar was only borrowing him. And if Onyxflame held loyalty to anyone other than himself, he hid it well. *Maybe I can count Saskia and Doctor Tan'shyo in my crew as well. At least then I know I have someone I can depend on. And I have inadvertently drawn Doctor Tan'shyo into the matter. I think I owe it to him to count him in my crew. Even if I can't tell him or Saskia the full situation.*

He climbed the stairs to his office and gazed at the papers stacked on his desk. He felt no enthusiasm toward sorting through them right now, but his mind was still too active for sleep. He paced the office, then finally shut off the light and retired to his room. His pocket watch read nearly midnight.

Alistar was pulling his night clothes from the wardrobe when urgent knocking echoed from his front door. He jumped, and a chill ran down his spine. Checking that Dahr's speaking stone was still in his pocket and hadn't activated, Alistar rushed down the stairs.

Has someone else died? Was Technician Bar'rege's family attacked? Caution made him slow as he approached the door, and his fingers itched to grip the hilt of the long knife he wore on his thigh when at home in Rillwater, though he'd stopped carrying it in the capital.

The knock paused, then came again, rapid. Alistar stood at the door. "Who's there?"

"De'seneth? Are you there? Please, are you there? It's Lamorage."

Alistar blinked, then unlocked the door. Opening it slightly, he positioned his body to block the door from being forced open farther and looked outside. Veril Lamorage stood on his stoop, arms wrapped tightly around himself and shivering. He lacked both coat and hat, and his rumpled clothes were suited for an evening out on the town, not wandering the streets.

Alistar stared at him. "Lamorage? What are you doing here? It's late, and you must be freezing. Come inside."

Alistar's fellow engineer shook his head quickly. "No, no, I can't. I just... I need... I..." He looked desperately at Alistar. "De'seneth, I need to borrow some marks. I'll pay you back, I swear! I just need... It's..." He swallowed hard and cast a quick look over his shoulder. His eyes were wild and his pupils dilated.

A chill that had nothing to do with the cold crept down Alistar's spine. He spoke in a low voice. "Lamorage, are you in trouble? What's going on?"

"I'll pay you back, De'seneth, I swear on the lights of my father's house." Lamorage was flushed, breathing rapidly.

"How much are we talking, Lamorage?" Alistar asked warily.

Lamorage's eyes dropped to the ground. His lips moved, but it took him several tries to form the words audibly. "Five hundred marks."

"Five…" Nearly two months' pay. "Five hundred," Alistar repeated. Why would Lamorage even think he *had* five hundred worth of ivory marks on hand? Then he stopped, realizing the answer. "I'm saving that money for my *marriage*, Lamorage."

"I know." Lamorage's voice was barely a whisper. "I'm sorry, De'seneth. Please…" He raised his head, fixing a desperate gaze on Alistar.

He's in debt. He owes someone. Five hundred marks may not even be a payment, just an offering to get more time. Alistar was aware of the Silver Prince's purse in his pocket—marks he could not in good faith loan out. Alistar opened the door a little wider. "Come inside, Lamorage."

Again the elf shook his head. "I can't, I can't." He wrapped his arms more tightly around himself.

And if he doesn't get the money, what happens? How badly do they hurt him? Alistar let out a breath. "Don't leave, Lamorage," he said, then closed the door. He climbed the stairs back to his office and unlocked the bottom drawer. Human marriage tradition called for the groom to have money in hand rather than in a bank, to offer proof to his bride's family that he could provide for her. Alistar counted out ten fifty-mark pieces—most of his marriage savings.

I might never see it again. He might never be able to pay this back, no matter what he swears now. But blood and sand, I'd rather lose a small fortune than learn later that because I did not help a friend, he's in a hospital bed somewhere with broken arms and legs because the lenders got impatient.

Lamorage had barely moved from the spot when Alistar opened the door again. A sheen of snow dusted the elf's brown hair. He almost wept in relief when Alistar handed him the marks. "Thank you. Thank you, De'seneth. I'll repay you, I promise. Whatever I have to do."

Alistar caught his wrist. "You can tell me what this is about."

A flash of panic crossed Lamorage's face. "I… I can't. Not… not yet." He twisted free of Alistar and scrambled down the steps, then down the street. Alistar watched him go until Lamorage ducked out of sight.

He closed and locked the door again, double-guessing his decision. From the top of the stairs, Onyxflame spoke. "You know giving him money means you're marked by whoever he owes, right?"

Alistar looked up. Onyxflame leaned over the railing, studying the door. "What are you doing out here?"

"Well, you hadn't locked my door yet, so… I stepped out to see what the ruckus was about," Onyxflame answered. He gestured to a window in the hall. "While you were in your office, there were a couple of toughs outside. Looked like they had stern words for your friend. Next time, they might break his legs before dragging him to your door to beg for another loan." Onyxflame's expression darkened. "I may not know *court* politics, but I do know *street* politics, and there was absolutely nothing of the court in what just happened."

"And you don't believe one payment will satisfy them," Alistar said.

"Do *you*, De'seneth?" Onyxflame asked.

"No," Alistar acknowledged, much as he didn't want to. He climbed the stairs once again. "And that is entirely the sort of thing that the court pounces on. Weakness. Debt. Gambling issues." He looked hard at Onyxflame. "He didn't come here just because he knew I'd been saving for my wedding. He also trusts that I'm not going to release this into the rumor mills. Something like this can ruin someone in a heartbeat."

"Faster than not being able to make a payment and having bones broken?" Onyxflame asked.

"Let's say they are about equal in how quickly they destroy someone's life," Alistar said, grim. *Just what sort of trouble are you in, Lamorage? Gambling? How much do you really owe?*

"And now the people he owes money to know where you live. Isn't that a lovely thought to sleep on?" Onyxflame said. "Good night, De'seneth."

The elf returned to the guest room. Alistar waited for the door to close, then activated the wards to confine Onyxflame before retiring to his bedroom.

CHAPTER 21

Alistar did not rest well. The few times he slept deeply enough to dream, they were disjointed and filled with unsettling images. When the clock chimed the start of a new day, he climbed out of bed and completed his morning rituals. When he knocked on Onyxflame's door, the elf answered, to his surprise.

"I'm up, I'm up," Onyxflame called in a tone of weary resignation. Alistar heard movement on the other side of the door. "What should I dress for?"

"We're starting at Silverline Power's offices," Alistar said. "Collecting the information that was 'misplaced' before being given to me."

A sigh. "Right. Meeting with the Silver Prince's daughter."

"Meeting with Technician Feyblade," Alistar corrected. "Within the realm of company business, she expects to be treated according to her rank, not her station outside Silverline."

"It's too early, De'seneth. What exactly does that mean?" Onyxflame groaned.

"It means that you don't wear court dress to speak to a technician, Onyxflame. Wear something suitable for work. I'll be in the kitchen." Alistar descended the stairs.

When Onyxflame joined him, Alistar noticed a little swelling on his jaw, but no noticeable bruise. Apparently he'd been correct when he claimed that cosmetics could conceal it. At least it wasn't a black eye. Hiding that from sharp gazes would have been challenging even with makeup. He'd dressed in his freshly washed daily wear, accented by an embroidered red vest. They ate breakfast without conversation.

Onyxflame looked at the clock, frowned, and finally asked, "Dahr isn't joining us today?"

"I suggested that he meet us at Silverline's offices," Alistar said. "Perhaps separating the two of you for a little while will be an improvement."

"Ah." Onyxflame turned back to his tea. "I apologize for my actions in the gaming hall, De'seneth, and for my words to you afterwards."

Alistar folded his arms. "My cynical side wonders if you're saying that because it occurred to you last night that I might not be willing to take you to devotions again without some sign of contrition."

"Your cynical side has a valid point," Onyxflame said. "However, to appeal to that very aspect, I would add also my recognition that your opinion carries weight over my fate in matters far larger than just attendance at worship. You have the Silver Prince's ear, De'seneth. If you give your blessings at the end of this investigation, he will reluctantly release me. If you elevate issues with my actions to him, he will take great satisfaction in consigning me to the darkest, foulest pit in the land for the rest of my days." He waved a hand vaguely in the air. "So, I've remembered that it is far more in my best interests to comply with your instructions and expectations."

Alistar raised an eyebrow at the frank assessment. "I see."

"Our bargain was for my freedom," Onyxflame said. "Looking

strictly at that, I have more to lose than you. And I do not like to lose. So, I apologize because I did not follow your instructions for yesterday."

Onyxflame had carefully chosen not to mention the fact that his skills *were* needed for the investigation—a noteworthy omission. "If that means it won't continue happening, your apology is accepted." Alistar let out a breath. "And we can revisit the matter of devotions next week."

Onyxflame simply nodded. "That's fair."

Alistar bit back the urge to say *So glad you think so*. He stood. "Let's go. I prefer to arrive at the office before most of the protesters. You have your pass?"

Onyxflame checked his pockets quickly and nodded. "It's here." The elf set his mug in the sink and followed Alistar downstairs.

Donning coats, hats, and gloves, they ventured into the chill morning. As usual, Shale Lane was still quiet, and they had to walk several blocks to Archers' Way before hailing a carriage. Alistar cast a look down the alley that Lamorage had ducked into the previous night, but anything that had been there was now hidden under a thin layer of snow.

Once they were safely ensconced in the hired carriage, Onyxflame cleared his throat. "A question, if I might."

"Go ahead," Alistar invited.

"Doesn't it seem strange to you that in Silverline Power, you have rank above the Silver Prince's daughter?"

Alistar shrugged. "Not particularly. She's his heir, and she's learning the company by each step through its ranks. Lady Syri doesn't have the experience yet to be an engineer."

Onyxflame shook his head. "Let me rephrase. She is the daughter and heir of Prince Cero. Regardless of her official rank in the company, her birthright says that one day she will be your employer. Can you *really* treat her like 'any other' technician, knowing that?"

"A lot of the engineers and other employees can't, despite it being her stated wish," Alistar said. "I think it must be part of the culture of the court in Lewarden. Aboard a ship, on the other hand, it doesn't matter if you're the son of the commander of the fleet, or the daughter of the stable-mucker—if you're a deckhand, you're a deckhand, and you aren't getting out of swabbing the decks no matter who your parents are."

Onyxflame snorted. "What, nepotism doesn't exist in Rillwater?"

"Oh, it exists," Alistar said. "The son of the commander of the fleet, unless he is utterly incompetent, will become captain and possibly more, as long as he survives. The stable-mucker's daughter may become a sailor, or may go back home when she's served her season. If she wants to make captain, she's got a lot more to do to prove she's worthy of what another got by virtue of birth and blood. But while they're both deckhands, that's all irrelevant." He leaned forward. "Lady Syri is a technician. Like my hypothetical deckhands, she has a job and responsibilities, and not allowing her to perform them helps no one. So, in answer, yes, I can treat her like other technicians, the same way the crew on my mother's ship treated me as any other deckhand."

Onyxflame leaned back, digesting that information. "You may well be the only person in Lewarden who thinks that, De'seneth."

"If so, their loss. People who become too focused on kissing the asses of those they think are above them forget to look up now and then." Alistar shook his head.

The carriage brought them to the gates of Silverline Power. A handful of people huddled across the street, glowering at the ogres guarding the gates. None of them roused enough enthusiasm to shout at Alistar and Onyxflame, though they bowed their heads together and muttered. The gate ogres sniffed Alistar, eyed Onyxflame with suspicion, and permitted them both to pass. Alistar pulled off one glove as he walked past the line of gargoyles.

He patted the winged cat, and it turned away, head raised in a gesture of disdain.

Alistar gave it a thin smile. "Sorry Morath. I've been out of the office lately."

Morath's snub did not relent. Alistar gave it one more pat, then shoved his hand into his pocket. Onyxflame watched the exchange in bemused silence. "The gargoyles are a second line of defense," Alistar said. "They are supposed to recognize Silverline employees, but we're also strongly encouraged to reinforce that connection."

Onyxflame eyed the snarling statues. "Should I be doing the same?"

"You're carrying a guest pass. As long as you have that and are with me, you shouldn't have issues," Alistar told him. "Just don't try to enter without both."

"Of course not," Onyxflame agreed quickly.

Inside Silverline Power, Assistant Goldleaf sat at the main desk. "Good morning, Associate De'seneth. Lord Aspendark." She consulted the list on her desk. "Technician Feyblade told me to expect you. She's at her workstation, and asked me to pass on that she is available at your convenience."

"Thank you, Assistant," Alistar told her. He hung up his coat and waved for Onyxflame to follow. They climbed the stairs and walked down the long hall. Alistar glanced into the room where his desk sat, but it was still dark.

They walked down to the section of the building that housed workstations for the technicians who weren't assigned to a generator. The fact that Lady Syri did not yet have an assignment was, to Alistar, another sign that Prince Cero intended for her to move through the ranks like any other employee, since stations were given based primarily on seniority. Even an undesirable assignment like Redpine Station near the Hollows was generally considered a step up from being in the office, even though it also meant longer hours.

Lady Syri sat at her desk. Several other technicians were also at their stations, but the majority wouldn't arrive for another hour. Alistar cleared his throat, and heads jerked up, eyes snapping toward him. Lady Syri stood, collecting a packet of papers from her desk.

"Associate De'seneth. I have the information you requested."

"Thank you, Technician Feyblade."

She motioned for him to follow, and led them to a conference room. Alistar and Onyxflame entered, then Lady Syri closed the door. "Thank you for coming, Associate De'seneth, Lord Aspendark." She turned to Onyxflame. "I understand that you are serving as Associate De'seneth's assistant in this investigation, sir. While I realize our previous meeting may not have been entirely clear, given the circumstances, I would like to clarify that in court, I am Prince Cero's daughter and heir. Here, however, and in matters related to Silverline business, I am a technician, and prefer that my parentage be left out of consideration."

"De'seneth told me much the same on the trip here, Lady," Onyxflame said. At her pointed look, he corrected himself, "Technician."

"Thank you." Lady Syri pulled sheets of paper from her folder and laid them out on the table. "Associate, I believe that this is the information you're missing."

Alistar pulled out his own list. "If you wouldn't mind double-checking against the information that was supposed to be given to me, this is a list of what I received."

Lady Syri scanned over the list of documents. Alistar had lumped all of Onyxflame's information under "Aspendark's paperwork." Lady Syri frowned. "I believe there was also supposed to be information regarding Tiyron Onyxflame, as the methodology of the incidents bore similarities to some of his crimes. I'll retrieve copies of those files as well."

"I did receive those," Alistar assured her. "They've proven useful."

"Is Tiyron Onyxflame a suspect?" Onyxflame asked.

"Very low on the list," Lady Syri answered. "He was arrested and sentenced before these incidents began." Her voice gave no indication that she believed Onyxflame to be anywhere else, which told Alistar that Prince Cero still had not felt the need to inform her of the true identity of "Lord Aspendark." He'd harbored some concerns on that matter after the meeting with the Silver Prince.

Lady Syri turned to the papers on the table. "This is the missing packet of information. I admit that I'm concerned about it not reaching you, Associate."

"And also concerned about who *does* have it if De'seneth does not?" Onyxflame asked.

She nodded. "Indeed. During the initial inspections of the first few sites, we received reports of items left behind. At a glance, they would seem the sorts of small things that could be dropped by mistake, but the consistency of the occurrence begins to imply intent rather than accident." She unfolded a map of the city above the neat row of pages. "Cigar butts in several places. A crumpled napkin with the imprint of The Topaz Shield. A silkweave hand-kerchief." She touched sites on the map, indicating locations in the Lower District. A single meal at The Topaz Shield could cost two months' worth of Alistar's wages. It was probably closer to a year's wages for someone in the Lower District.

"Someone has expensive tastes." Alistar picked up one of the sheets, reading the description of the cigar butt. "From the Berr Islands. Supposed to be one of the finest varieties."

Onyxflame raised an eyebrow. "You are a connoisseur of cigars, De'seneth?"

"It comes from being in the import business," Alistar said. "A captain should know the value of his cargo when he acquires it. Is the other butt the same variety?"

Lady Syri shook her head. "A similar cost, but from the Tonner Coast. They might not have been left by the same person."

"Given the expense and difficulty of getting either, I would expect a smoker to secure at least a case of one brand only, and not change varieties." Alistar frowned.

"So, either someone has the funds to purchase expensive cigars and dine in the best of restaurants, or they have a job, or a connection who has a job, at The Topaz Shield," Onyxflame mused.

Both Alistar and Lady Syri looked at him in surprise.

Onyxflame blinked. "What? A worker at The Topaz Shield would have easy access to the linens, and someone has to clean the ash trays. Handkerchiefs without identifying monograms get lost all the time. If all you need are the dregs and leavings of a noble, it's just a matter of placing yourself in a position to pick them up when the nobles toss them away."

Is that the voice of experience? I somewhat suspect that it is.

Lady Syri's expression grew thoughtful. "And after all, who watches the servants, the guards, the attendants? Is that what you are saying, Lord Aspendark?"

"I'm saying that it's easier to do than many people think," Onyxflame told her. "Though it would still require a great deal of planning and the opportunity to get someone into the necessary position. Bribes or blackmail might help grease those axles, though."

"Unfortunately, rather than narrowing our possible suspects, it expands them," Alistar said. "And if it's not a noble, the motivation becomes less clear. Nor does it explain how they are causing the outages or what they are actually doing with the magic once they steal it."

"I hope that these reports will offer you a little more insight into all three questions, Associate," Lady Syri said. "Please take them with you—these are all copies. The originals are stored elsewhere."

"Thank you." Alistar stacked the pages again, folded the map, and tucked everything into a portfolio. "I appreciate your help, Technician."

"It is my pleasure, Associate. I'll let you return to your investigation. Associate De'seneth, Lord Aspendark." She nodded to each of them before leaving the conference room and returning to her desk.

"I would have thought the Silver Prince would have no qualms about informing his heir of my presence," Onyxflame remarked. "Curious."

"Or he, perhaps rightly, decided that if Technician Feyblade knew who you really were, she would be less inclined to offer assistance," Alistar said. "Remember that her word holds weight in the court, and a positive mention from her could prove very valuable to Aspendark. Come on. I need to recruit a botanist to send to the Redpine Generator to check their plants."

Onyxflame on his heels, Alistar walked back to the stairs. The room where his office sat was lit now, and he saw engineers standing in clumps talking urgently. Lamorage's desk still sat empty. One of the men noticed Alistar and waved him in.

"De'seneth! How early did you get in? Have you seen the broadsheets this morning?"

"I haven't. What happened?" Alistar asked, worry twinging in his gut.

Someone shoved a folded broadsheet into his hands. In heavy, bold text, the headline shouted "Carriage Smashes Through Gathering!" Beneath it was a picture of what looked like a Dockside street strewn with people. Alistar stared at the write-up.

"Last night, a gathering of factory workers from all corners of Lewarden met in Dockside in answer to a call for a forum for peaceful discourse regarding working conditions. Shortly before eleven o'clock, a carriage driven at full speed burst down the street. Witnesses report that the vehicle showed no effort to slow or avoid the crowd."

His breath caught as he read the next line. "Scores were injured, and at least fifteen are confirmed dead."

Alistar looked up to his coworkers. "Who was responsible?"

The man who called him over shook his head. "That's the worst part. No one knows. Gods only know how, the driver kept control and managed to push the team all the way through the crowd without stopping. No one even got a good look at them, although a few reports claim there were multiple people on the driver's bench."

"Was a damned fancy carriage, too," someone else added. "And heavy, to get through all those people." He looked away, shaking his head. "A lot of people didn't make it in today, going down to help at Dockside, or find out if someone they know was there… was hurt."

The room fell silent. Finally someone said, "I guess… we should get to it." Engineers slowly dispersed back to their desks. Alistar left the room, chilled to the bone.

Who could do such a thing? And why? Why murder and maim innocent people?

Onyxflame watched Alistar's face. The elf had read the broadsheet over Alistar's shoulder. He offered no wisecracks as they returned to the lobby.

Assistant Goldleaf had a copy of a broadsheet spread open in front of her. Several more stood in a neat pile on the floor. She looked up when Alistar and Onyxflame approached. "Have you heard the morning's news, Associate?" she asked.

"I just heard," Alistar answered. "A carriage in Dockside. Is there anything new? A suspect?"

"Not in the reports I have received," she answered, shaking her head. "But I am reviewing all the information to assemble a report and, we can only hope, determine a starting point for locating the responsible parties. Is there something else I can do for you, Associate?"

Alistar's thoughts went blank for a moment. Onyxflame prompted, "Botanist?"

Alistar nodded. "Yes. Yes, I need to speak to Chief Botanist Riverbed. Is he available, or someone else in his department? I need a botanist to inspect the kurowa at one of the generator plants."

Assistant Goldleaf lifted the broadsheet and checked a list underneath it. "Chief Botanist Riverbed hasn't arrived yet this morning, however his aide is in. Go ahead."

"Thank you."

The scent of kurowa flowers filled the air as soon as they entered the botany department. Alistar walked down the hall, and almost immediately was met by a human in sap-stained coat and work scrubs. He recognized the young man as the same one who had stopped them the first time they came to speak to the Chief Botanist. This time, however, the botanist inclined his head politely.

"Associate De'seneth, can I help you?" His tone was professionally neutral.

"Assistant Goldleaf told me that Chief Botanist Riverbed is currently unavailable, but that his aide might be able to assist me," Alistar said.

"I will do so as I can, Associate," the botanist answered. "I am Nikaze Tur'sah, aide to Chief Botanist Riverbed. The Chief Botanist instructed that we should support your investigation." He seemed to put particular emphasis on Alistar's title, as if to emphasize that he outranked Alistar, and that his cooperation was strictly a result of his superior's instructions. Tur'sah motioned for Alistar and Onyxflame to follow him, and led them to a small office, the available space made all the more cramped by the collection of tools that occupied much of the floor. "What can the botany department do for you, Associate?"

The engineering department and the botany department occasionally suffered low-level rivalries and territorial spats, but

Tur'sah projected an air that said he considered his upstairs coworkers to be lesser creatures, as if they had only become engineers because they could not comprehend the more pure art of botany. Alistar had little patience for such attitudes on the best of days, and after the news from Dockside, this was far from the best of days. Ignoring the implied disdain, he answered. "Redpine Generator requires the attention of a botanist. Following the recent outage, some of their plants are exhibiting abnormal growth and color patterns."

"Redpine." Tur'sah made a sour face. "What did they screw up this time?"

Alistar's eyes narrowed. "Botanist Tur'sah, based on the evidence I've seen so far, some person or persons outside of the generator drained the magic from the mahiy lines for an extended period of time. They could possibly have also used the mahiy lines to transfer some manner of blight or alteration back to the affected plants. Without a botanist's experienced analysis, unforeseen mutations could take root at Redpine Generator, then spread through the mahiy lines to other generator stations." He leaned forward. "And the technicians assigned to monitor the station did not report it precisely *because* of an attitude such as yours—a belief that they would be blamed for matters entirely outside of their control."

Tur'sah's brow furrowed. "We *have* had incidents where careless actions by technicians or others working at Redpine Generator have led to failures in the system. My opinion is not without justification. However, if you believe that another factor is at work, please do explain."

Onyxflame raised an eyebrow. "You mean De'seneth's theory that the parties responsible for the outages are trying to corrupt the mahiy lines isn't enough for you? I would hope you don't suspect that the technicians at Redpine are responsible, through some sort of carelessness, for the *other* incidents in Lewarden."

Tur'sah blinked. "Of course not. However, Redpine has a

history of failure to follow proper procedure and repeated failures of inspections."

Alistar gritted his teeth and spoke in a slow, clear voice. "I need a botanist to examine the greenhouse in Redpine Generator, as part of my investigation, and I need this completed with all possible haste. Include an engineer with the team as well. One technician from Redpine is dead of questionable causes."

Tur'sah blanched. "Associate, I hope you are not implying that the kurowa are responsible! Our plants have been bred for generations to ensure they are safe even for those who interact with them daily."

The thought that the kurowa themselves might have played a part in the technician's death hadn't occurred to Alistar, but now that it had been introduced, he couldn't dismiss it out of hand. "All the more reason to investigate the nature of the affected greenhouse. Wouldn't you agree, Botanist Tur'sah?"

Tur'sah let out a long breath and nodded. "I will dispatch a botanist and a flock… team of analysts today. Depending on what they learn, the report will be ready for you tonight or tomorrow morning."

Onyxflame looked at Alistar. "A 'flock'?"

"Of course," Tur'sah said stiffly. "The attendant sprites are extremely sensitive to shifts in kurowa physiology."

"Hmm." Onyxflame crossed his arms with a thoughtful expression. "I did wonder where the protesters got the idea that Silverline Power keeps pixies imprisoned to generate magic. Such interesting theories those people come up with."

"Thank you, Botanist." Alistar inclined his head in a polite nod to draw the conversation back before Onyxflame sent it too far afield. "I appreciate your assistance."

Tur'sah nodded stiffly in return and showed them out of his office. As they walked back up the hall to the lobby, Onyxflame murmured, "And I thought Riverbed was unpleasant. Does the Silver Prince hire his botanists based on arrogance and unsociability?"

"No. That's just what gets them promoted," Alistar muttered in response. "And you didn't hear that from me."

"Didn't hear a thing," Onyxflame agreed.

In the lobby, engineers, technicians, and botanists milled about in clumps, sharing copies of the broadsheets and talking about the news in hushed voices. Alistar listened, hoping for new information, but everything was still speculation and rumor. Someone claimed that the Royal Guard was inspecting every stable in the city, even those of the noble houses, in search of a carriage that matched the description given. Someone else claimed that she had it from a reliable source that the attack was carried out by agents from another country, though *which* country was left to speculation.

"Every clinic, hospital, healer, and doctor in the Lower City is getting called in to help," one technician said. "It's total chaos. I could barely get to work this morning. Even the taxis are under suspicion!"

Saskia. It must be pandemonium there. And if the clinic is still getting victims of Rat's Disease coming in... I hope that Doctor Tan'shyo has completed the autopsy. They'll need every skilled doctor they can find.

"Associate De'seneth," Assistant Goldleaf called. "Dahr Lakewatch has arrived and awaits you." She pointed her quill toward a far corner of the lobby, where Dahr stood quietly at parade rest.

"Thank you," Alistar said. He started toward Dahr, then stopped and turned back to the sprite. "Has Associate Lamorage arrived yet today?"

"Not yet, sir. I've not received word from him, but if he's not arrived yet, he likely will not be in. Director Strey'mend has already decreed that late arrivals or absences today will not be counted against any employee, given last night's event."

That news was a comfort to Alistar, and a kindness on the part of the director, but it did not assuage his worries regarding

Lamorage. And if not for the Dockside attack, Lamorage's absence would have earned him another black mark on a record already spattered with late arrivals. *Is he safe? Or is he beaten and lying in an alley somewhere?*

Dahr nodded to Alistar, eyed Onyxflame, and said, "Sir. You've heard the news?"

"We have," Alistar said. "I think it will be hard not to hear about it today." They collected their coats and ventured into the cold day. "Do you know anything more than is in the papers?"

"The responsible parties have not been identified yet," Dahr said, shaking his head. "Beyond that, I cannot share. Where are we bound today, sir? Under the circumstances, I recommend that we avoid the lower sections of the city if possible."

"I've asked for a botanist to inspect the Redpine Generator. I don't need to accompany the team; I'd only be in the way. I do want to honor Technician Bar'rege's request that the technicians be transferred to other stations, also."

Dahr frowned. "Before you put the transfers through, sir, I would recommend that you wait for the botanist's report. If one of the employees does have a connection to the events in the greenhouse, they should not be set loose on a higher priority generator."

Alistar let out a long breath. Dahr's precaution was reasonable, and the other technicians at the generator didn't have any reason to expect transfers at the moment. A few more days' wait shouldn't make much difference to them. "Any word from the autopsy?"

Dahr and Onyxflame both flinched slightly. Dahr cleared his throat. "I have not received any word about it yet, sir. If you wish, we can attempt to locate the doctor. He runs a clinic in—"

"Dahr, I know who Doctor Tan'shyo is and the location of his clinic," Alistar cut in.

Dahr straightened, mouth opening in surprise. "Sir? How do you know..."

If Doctor Tan'shyo had been selected for the task because of his connection to Alistar, that decision had obviously not been made by Dahr. Alistar smiled faintly. "I'm engaged to his daughter."

Dahr's mouth opened, but no words came out. Onyxflame looked on with interest. "I did not think it was possible to render our esteemed guard speechless. Congratulations, De'seneth."

Dahr cleared his throat. "I… beg your pardon, sir. I was not aware that you were acquainted with Doctor Tan'shyo, much less that you had a personal connection to him."

Alistar's mouth twitched into a smile. "It did make for some interesting conversation yesterday while my fiancée and I talked around confidential matters until determining that the autopsy he was called in to perform and the one that I requested were one and the same. I realize that the Coiled Dragon Clinic has probably been called into service tending to the injured, but if we can get there, I would appreciate the chance to discuss the results of the autopsy directly with Doctor Tan'shyo."

Onyxflame shifted uncomfortably. "A discussion that can be done in private, I hope?"

"The doctor and my fiancée are entirely respectful of elven sensibilities, Onyxflame. No one is going to drag you off and perform an examination against your will. Especially not if they are tending to injured from Dockside," Alistar told him.

"I would still rather not hear a detailed description of the dissection of a body, De'seneth," Onyxflame said.

"I will keep watch on Onyxflame while you speak with the doctor," Dahr said. Alistar thought him quick to pounce on the opportunity to excuse himself from the coming conversation. "I'll call a carriage."

"A taxi," Alistar said firmly. "We'll take a taxi carriage. After last night, noble carriages in the middle or lower sections of town are not likely to be a welcome sight."

"I can drive, sir," Dahr started, but Alistar shook his head.

"It will take longer for you to get a carriage, and the hired drivers know the best routes through the streets. This makes more sense."

Dahr sighed, acquiescing that point. Alistar noticed that the protesters had dwindled to four. He wondered if the absence of the rest was related to the Dockside events. At least for the moment, they weren't blaming Silverline for that. A few hired carriages ran by Silverline Power, and they hailed one without difficulty.

When Alistar stated their destination, the driver nodded grimly. "Aye, sirs. I can get you down there. Been runnin' a lotta folk to the clinics an' hospitals this morning. Wishin' the best to whoever you're there to see. You know they're at Coiled Dragon, or looking for them? I can wait and take you on to the next."

"I know it's the Coiled Dragon," Alistar told him. "Thank you."

"Bad business all around," the driver said, grim. "Bad business."

The carriage took mostly side and back streets to reach the clinic, and the driver kept his team no faster than a quick walk, slowing whenever pedestrians were near. Little conversation stirred within the carriage. Alistar began reading the information that Lady Syri had provided, to distract him from worries about Saskia or the people injured on Dockside. His heart wasn't in the study, though, and little of the information stuck.

"Anything highly confidential, De'seneth, or can I see these lists as well?" Onyxflame asked.

"Go ahead," Alistar invited. "There's something to your theory about these items being acquired by a person in position to pick up a noble's leavings."

"It's worked for me in the past," Onyxflame said. He scanned one of the pages Alistar had finished, and frowned. "In fact, if I didn't know better, I'd say that a few of these *are* items I've lifted in the past."

"High-quality cigars and the like are commonly associated with rich nobility," Alistar observed.

Onyxflame shook his head. "No, De'seneth, I mean that I'd swear I once lifted *this* silkweave handkerchief with silver embroidery off some fop."

Alistar raised an eyebrow. "And what did you do with it once you stole it?"

"Tucked it away in a stash of items I'd collected to make a convincing disguise. Tell me if you find a pocket watch somewhere in the list as well."

"Not yet," Alistar answered, not sure if he should be amused or concerned by the similarity that Onyxflame mentioned.

"I've not heard any reports of watches found at sites," Dahr put in. "Such a find would be significant—and traceable."

"If the watch were to be the one that I stole, it wouldn't be so traceable as you would hope," Onyxflame told him. "It wasn't a local product. Very expensive. Probably illegally imported. Also, very hard to report as stolen without admitting to the possession of restricted goods. Which added to the appeal of acquiring it from the previous owner."

"Too unique for our criminals to be leaving at a site," Alistar said firmly. "They've shown themselves smarter than that so far. They want us guessing who's responsible, which is why nothing so far is immediately identifiable, aside from the coat button." A coat button that had gone missing, apparently, long before it was found at Shale Lane. A coat button that implied someone wanted the investigation's focus to narrow onto the Successors and their leader.

The carriage drew to a halt. Onyxflame returned the pages and Alistar tucked them back into the portfolio. He paid the driver and assured the man again that they would not need a ride to another hospital. Outside the clinic, two young women, one with a baby and the other trailed by a young girl, huddled and talked in low voices. Alistar caught enough of their words to know they were debating which clinic to check next and how to get there. The women looked like they might have pooled their funds just to get this far. Alistar glanced back at their carriage and driver, then motioned to the man and handed him ten marks.

"Can you give those women a ride until they find who they're looking for?"

The driver looked shocked at the sum Alistar offered. "Sir, this is too much—" he began.

"Whatever's left over, give to someone who needs it," Alistar said. "Or count it toward someone else's ride."

The driver touched his hat in acknowledgment. "Aye, sir. I will." He walked to the women and spoke to them as Alistar, Onyxflame, and Dahr entered the clinic.

The air smelled of chemicals and blood. In the waiting room, men and women hunched in chairs or sat on the floor. Many of them sported bandages or slings, but all the injured Alistar saw appeared to have received at least some care, and no one looked to be in dire straits, though people were clearly in pain. Heads turned when Alistar and his companions entered, hoping for the arrival of a familiar face. Onyxflame glanced around the room like a nervous cat ready to bolt and finding no suitable cover.

A woman with a bandage wrapped around her head and covering one eye sat near the front desk. She reached up from her chair and rang the bell on the desk. Turning to Alistar she said, "If you don't see who you're looking for, wait just a minute and the doctor will be out." She said the words as if she'd repeated them frequently through the morning.

"Thank you," Alistar told her.

Doctor Tan'shyo opened the inner door and stepped into the waiting room. His face was lined and his eyes dark with shadows. "New patient, or looking for someone?" he asked wearily. His gaze found Alistar, and he smiled faintly. "Ah. Come in." He held the door open.

Alistar nodded his thanks and followed the doctor farther into the clinic, Onyxflame and Dahr trailing him. Doctor Tan'shyo led them into his office. "Your pardon, De'seneth. This day has been… chaotic." He sank down in his chair with a tired sigh.

"I understand," Alistar assured him. "Can I do anything to help?"

The doctor shook his head. "I'm sure you have more important things to do than roll bandages or sterilize tools. In fact, I'm guessing you want the results of the autopsy."

Dahr glanced at Onyxflame. "Sir, Aspendark and I can assist while you speak with the doctor." He looked to Doctor Tan'shyo. "I assume that these tasks do not require contact with your patients."

"They do not," the doctor said. "Thank you…?" He gave Dahr a quizzical look.

Alistar cleared his throat. "My apologies. Doctor Tan'shyo, this is Dahr Lakewatch, from His Highness's guard, and Taslor Aspendark, my assistant in my current assignment."

Doctor Tan'shyo nodded to both elves. "Again, thank you for your offer of assistance. If you go down the hall and through the third door on the right, you'll be in the prep room. My daughter can give you tasks."

Onyxflame glanced between Dahr and Alistar, shifted uncomfortably, and finally decided that he'd rather accompany Dahr than hear the details of an autopsy. Alistar knew that the distance was still within Onyxflame's allowed range, saving him the need to alter the wards or explain any particulars to his future father-in-law.

Once the elves had left, Alistar sat in the chair across from Doctor Tan'shyo. "I'm sorry to pull you away from your patients."

Doctor Tan'shyo shook his head. "At this point, all the critical cases are either going to live or going to die, Alistar. I've done all I can, and the rest I must leave in the hands of the Starbinder." Lord Starbinder, god of death, was the only deity that the elven and human pantheons shared. "I expected to be writing up the results of Bar'rege's autopsy today, to send to the offices of the Silver

Prince to deliver to whomever requested it. I had no idea that person was you until Saskia told me yesterday after she returned."

"And I had no idea that you had been called on for the task, though if you'll pardon my saying it, I'm glad you were," Alistar said. He let out a long breath. "Was it Rat's Disease?"

"My official conclusion: yes. The victim's internal organs showed much the same decay as I've seen in other cases. However, her case was peculiar in that the disease seemed…" Doctor Tan'shyo searched for the right word. "Targeted."

"Targeted how?" Alistar asked. "How can a disease be targeted?"

"That's what I find puzzling," Doctor Tan'shyo said. "In other cases, as I told you before, the victim's internal organs were destroyed. I also found damage and decay on their skeletal structures. In Bar'rege's case, I found none of that. The organ damage was consistent with Rat's Disease, but she did not suffer the other effects. That is what I mean by 'targeted'."

Alistar's brow furrowed. "Did you find anything else unusual? Residue, or unusual levels of magic, or… I don't know, really."

"Bar'rege did have an elevated level of magical residue; however, I expected that, given that she worked at a generator." Doctor Tan'shyo rubbed his eyes. "If you are looking for specific answers, Alistar, it would help if I knew the questions."

"It would help if I knew them as well," Alistar admitted. "I think that Technician Bar'rege was murdered for passing certain information on to me regarding matters of threats and blackmail. I hoped an autopsy might show how she was infected, or if it really was Rat's Disease or something that mimicked the effects. In your professional opinion, Doctor Tan'shyo, do you think that she could have been deliberately infected, and if so, do you have any idea how it could be done?"

Doctor Tan'shyo gave him a thin smile. "Do I think it's possible? Certainly. But that answer is based on the fact that I still don't understand how Rat's Disease spreads in the first place. It doesn't appear to transfer through contact between skin or by bodily fluids. Humors are inconclusive. If it were an effect of overexposure to the mahiy lines, I would expect to see it cropping up in Silverline employees first, not in vagrants and homeless beggars. A contaminant in the water, perhaps. Some manner of contamination that I simply do not recognize. For all I know, it might not be a disease at all, but a horrible side effect of a drug. And if *that* were the case, then yes, someone could have administered it to your victim by many different methods."

"A drug?" Alistar repeated. "But why would anyone produce a drug that would cause the horrible, painful death of those who take it? And once they realized it had such an effect, why would they continue to provide it?"

"I have only theories, Alistar," Doctor Tan'shyo said. "I wish that I had more to offer." He stood, and wavered.

Alistar jumped to his feet and steadied the doctor. "You're exhausted, and I've interrupted your work in the midst of a crisis. You need to get some rest."

"No, I need to get some of that bitter drink from the tropics that's rumored to rejuvenate energy," Doctor Tan'shyo said. "Forgotten what it's called now. Too bad it runs two marks a cup. Perhaps your father could arrange a bag of that for a wedding gift, hmm?"

Alistar chuckled. "I'll ask him next time we talk."

Doctor Tan'shyo straightened. "I'll keep your questions in mind, and I'll send you word if I discover any answers. I'll get the official report written up later and file it with all the appropriate parties."

"If I might ask a potentially delicate question… are you properly compensated when you're called on for tasks like this autopsy?" Alistar asked.

"I'm compensated quite well, Alistar, don't worry. The Crown pays generously, especially when dealing with matters that any respectable elf simply would not talk about. I hope that I've been some help to you." Doctor Tan'shyo let out a long breath. "Now I'll let you rescue those two elves. Aspendark particularly looked ready to jump out of his skin. A phobia of doctors, I assume."

"Doctors and healers both," Alistar said.

"I'm sure Saskia has found some innocuous task for him. Gods know we have enough of those that haven't been getting done last night and this morning." Doctor Tan'shyo rested a hand on Alistar's shoulder. "Don't worry about us, Alistar. We'll get through this, and do all we can for the injured."

"Of course I'm going to worry," Alistar told him. "What sort of future son-in-law would I be if I wasn't concerned for you and Saskia at a time like this?"

"Be one who trusts that we each do our parts," Doctor Tan'shyo answered. "Whatever those parts might be."

"That I do," Alistar promised.

They found Dahr sterilizing medical tools while Onyxflame folded linens. Alistar picked up a strip of freshly washed bandage and began rolling it. He was pleased, though not surprised, to see that Dahr had not allowed Onyxflame to perform the task that gave him access to potential weapons.

Onyxflame cast several glances at Alistar, waiting for hints that they would be leaving soon. Dahr finished the tray of instruments. "Do you need further information from Doctor Tan'shyo, sir?"

"Not at the moment," Alistar said. "Thank you for helping out while you waited."

"Of course, sir." Dahr nodded. "Are you ready?"

He wanted to stay and offer what assistance he could to Saskia and her father. But it was clear that both Dahr and Onyxflame would rather not stay, though Dahr hid it better. "We can go. I'll meet you out front."

Dahr gave him a puzzled look. "Is there something you need, sir?"

Onyxflame rolled his eyes and finished piling the linens neatly.

"He wants to greet his fiancée without a couple of awkward tagalongs."

"Oh. Of course. My apologies, sir," Dahr said quickly. The two elves made their way back to the waiting room as Alistar checked in patient rooms for Saskia.

He met her leaving a room and on her way to another. Her eyes held the same weary shadows as her father's, but she greeted Alistar with a smile. "I hoped I would see you before you had to go."

"I couldn't leave without at least seeing you," Alistar told her. "I hope Dahr and Aspendark were some help."

"They were," she assured him. "They were no trouble at all, though I see what you mean about Aspendark being uncomfortable around medics." She set aside the tray she carried and embraced Alistar. "So glad to see you. Last night was utter chaos. Father was trying to finish up his reports, and I was closing down the clinic when everything started. I caught a ride down to Dockside as soon as they called for doctors." Saskia shuddered. "I've seen accidents, but this was utterly horrific, Alistar. I'm just glad that it was late, and children were already in bed. I don't want to consider how much worse it could have been with young ones there as well."

Alistar nodded. Saskia had seen more blood and death than he probably ever would, and she knew how to handle it. Knowing that this had rattled her, he was all the more glad he hadn't seen the immediate aftermath.

"I was there until we finally had sufficient medics, and enough patients manageably stable to be transported. Coiled Dragon is far enough from Dockside that most of our patients were people with less life-threatening injuries at first. A lot of crushed bones, though. We had to perform some amputations—not even a healer could have saved those limbs. As other options filled up, some of the more critical patients were brought here as well." She let out a long breath. "Every doctor and healer in the Lower City has patients, and there's not really anyone left to call in. I haven't heard complaints, though. We had to give people spaces in the waiting room, but they've been satisfied simply to be getting treatment at all."

"No one seemed overly surprised when we arrived. Have many people been coming in search of family or friends?" Alistar asked.

"A lot. When people were being sent for care, they focused primarily on numbers—how many could go to each location—and somehow, someone didn't think to record names. So people are going from place to place, trying to find their loved ones, and hoping desperately that their final destination isn't the graveyard. I understand that now there's some effort to list the names of patients and begin circulating that information," Saskia told him. She was warm against him, and Alistar wrapped an arm around her shoulder. "But even that requires someone who can read and write."

Such academic skills were not widely known in this area of Lewarden or among this class of people. Which placed the burden of making those lists on the medics who were busy trying to save lives and had little time to spare. "Can I do anything to help?" Alistar asked.

"Convince some of the higher-ranking and more prosperous healers to lend a hand?" she suggested. "And no, Alistar, I don't expect you to actually do that. We'll do what we can, and if any of our patients remember details that might help identify the culprits, we'll pass that information on."

Alistar gave her a tight smile, embraced her, and let her go. "You are amazing, you know."

Saskia laughed softly. "If you say so, Alistar. Right now I'm just exhausted. But, I also have patients I need to check on."

"I know." He held her hand in his until she slipped it free and picked up her tray again. "I'll see you again as soon as I can."

Saskia nodded. She cast a look over her shoulder at him when she entered the next room, and Alistar raised his hand in farewell before returning to the waiting room. Not seeing Onyxflame or Dahr there, he continued outside, and found the two elves standing along the wall of the building, wrapped in their respective winter wear.

"Where to next, De'seneth?" Onyxflame asked.

"Dahr, do you know of any plans to encourage doctors and healers not in the Lower District to assist in the care of the injured?" Alistar asked. *I know I can't save everyone, but perhaps I can send some help all the same.*

"I am not aware of any at this time, sir," Dahr answered. "However, I will mention it. If not healers, it would appear that clinics such as this could also be helped by those willing to assist in the tasks of cleaning and preparation so that the doctors can continue to treat their patients."

Onyxflame shook his head. "While I respect the work that your human doctors do, I wouldn't be able to work in such a place. I'm afraid the list of people whose blood I am willing to mop up is extremely short." He shuddered and wiped his gloved hands on his cloak.

"I'm not going to volunteer you," Alistar assured him. "I do appreciate you helping for a time."

"Your fiancée, assuming she is the lady who pointed us to tasks, was quite polite about it," Onyxflame admitted. "But I don't care to make a habit of it."

"As long as no one starts making a habit of smashing a carriage through crowds, let's hope you won't need to," Alistar said. He buttoned his coat and started up the block at a walk. A carriage rumbled past and stopped in front of the clinic, disgorging an older man and woman. The couple looked around anxiously before opening the clinic door and stepping through.

"Where next?" Onyxflame repeated.

"I'm not sure," Alistar said finally. They walked a couple blocks up from the clinic. Traffic moved slowly, everyone more careful and more aware of those around them. It was past noon, but he wasn't hungry. What he truly wanted to do was go back to his house and relax in solitude, but he'd already taken most of a day off from his task for services yesterday, and the trails grew no warmer while he waited. "Dahr, were any incidents in this area?"

Dahr frowned. "I don't believe so, sir, but Thornguard Generator lies about five blocks east of us, and it was affected by an incident, if you would like to compare their status with that of Redpine."

"Good." Alistar oriented himself to the east and set off at a respectable pace.

Alistar had visited Thornguard previously, but only as part of a brief tour to new Silverline engineers. Unlike Redpine, Thornguard boasted a gate with a guard as well as a pair of gargoyles. When Alistar knocked, a technician answered promptly, inviting them inside. Alistar introduced himself and his companions, and was met with polite greetings from all four technicians on duty. Polite greetings and hints of confusion and concern at an unannounced visit from a Silverline engineer.

"I've been assigned to investigate the outages that have been affecting the mahiy lines," Alistar told them. "I understand that Thornguard was subject to one of these outages. Can you describe for me what you saw?"

The technicians leapt forward with descriptions and answers with an alacrity that suggested they thought he would blame them for the event. Standard procedures were outlined and documentation produced to demonstrate that they had followed policy. Alistar listened, mentally comparing their description of events to the one he'd heard at Redpine. Aside from the absence of a blackmailer and the length of the outage, the incidents bore many similarities.

The technician's stance relaxed. "No problems then, Associate?"

"None that I am aware of," Alistar answered. "I appreciate your time and your answers to my questions."

"Of course, sir. This isn't... an official inspection, is it? We aren't going to get docked points for not having the desks cleaned up and the floors swept?"

Alistar chuckled. "No, not an official inspection of the facility. An investigation of the incidents only."

The technician looked more relieved than Alistar expected, and he raised a questioning eyebrow. "Is there some problem?"

The technician shook his head quickly, flushing. "No, no sir, nothing at all."

"Something at your desk that you shouldn't have there? Something you shouldn't have at work?" Alistar pressed a little.

"Just a gift. From a friend! I didn't mean to leave it here; I'll take it home when I leave tonight," the technician said quickly. Realizing from Alistar's expression that he'd said too much not to sound suspicious, and not enough to identify the contraband, his shoulders slumped. "A, um, stimulant, sir," he mumbled. "I swear I haven't tried it, Associate. I'd never do something like that while at my station. But a friend swears that it's given him amazing energy and vitality and... other things. I didn't ask for it, he just gave a few pieces of it to me. Called it Ambrosia."

Drugs in the Lower City were an ongoing problem. Silverline employees signed a contract that they would not partake in recreational use of drugs, but the farther from the headquarters one went, the more loosely those restrictions were enforced. Alistar gazed, unblinking, at the technician. "You've been keeping drugs at your work desk?"

"Just since yesterday," the technician blurted. "I forgot to take them home last night. I'm sorry, sir. It won't happen again." He swallowed hard. "Please don't tell the Director."

"I cannot leave here knowing that such things are on Silverline property," Alistar said, growing stern. "You say you haven't used these stimulants thus far, and I am willing to believe you, but—"

He started to say that the drugs needed to be turned over to someone, but the technician cut in, voice rushed. "I won't use them! I swear! I should never have let him give them to me in the first place, Associate! Take them away, throw them in the river or something. I don't want them!" The realization that his career and livelihood lay at stake decided the matter for the man. "Please don't tell the Director."

I could do far worse than simply telling Director Strey'mend, Alistar thought. His jaw tightened. "Once," he said. "I will believe you on this *once*. I'll dispose of this 'Ambrosia,' and I will record your possession of it with a statement that this instance has been excused. If it *ever* happens again, don't expect lenience to be repeated."

The technician swallowed hard. "No sir, of course not. I understand. Thank you, sir. Thank you."

The technician fidgeted nervously on the way back to the office area, and quickly led Alistar to his desk. Onyxflame was engaging the other technicians in conversation, and Dahr listened, offering rare contributions to the discussion. Alistar felt Onyxflame watching him from the corner of his eye. The technician cast an anxious glance around the room before unlocking a drawer, pulling out a small leather pouch, and pressing it into Alistar's hand.

"I swear, sir, it won't happen again."

Alistar nodded gravely. "Good. The last thing any of us should want is to be impaired if a situation arose." He tucked the pouch into his pocket.

The technician gulped, nodding quickly. "Yes sir."

Alistar joined his companions, added a few thoughts to the discussion of the local ice-puck teams, now that the river was frozen enough to support games, and declared his business at Thornguard Generator concluded. With thanks given to the technicians for their assistance, they returned to the chill afternoon. The lingering moisture in Alistar's clothes froze almost immediately and flaked off as he moved.

"So, De'seneth, find anything interesting?" Onyxflame asked as they walked.

"The kurowa appear to be healthy and producing properly," Alistar answered.

"Mmhmm." Onyxflame watched him, waiting for more. When Alistar didn't immediately continue, the elf said, "I do have to assume, based on what I know of you thus far, that your guide was not, in fact, slipping you a bribe."

"No, he was not attempting to bribe me," Alistar said. "I was confiscating contraband materials that he inadvertently revealed to have in his possession. At his work desk. Because he somehow forgot to take it home with him."

Dahr's eyes narrowed. "Sir, possession of illicit drugs is a prosecutable offense."

"I know," Alistar said. "A fact that he realized. He surrendered the material voluntarily. I'll make a record of it, including my decision not to pursue disciplinary action unless there is a second offense."

"So what did he have?" Onyxflame asked curiously. "That pouch looked small for most of the drugs I know."

"The person who gave it to him called it Ambrosia," Alistar answered. "Heard of it? Supposed to be some sort of stimulant."

Onyxflame frowned and shook his head. "Either it's new, or someone's given an old drug a new name."

Alistar paused in the shelter between two buildings and pulled the pouch from his pocket. He opened it and tilted the pouch to see inside. "Looks like bits of crystal." Alistar considered, then chuckled softly. "Actually, looks somewhat like rock candy. Smear some dirt and grime on it, and these would practically look identical to that piece of candy the girl on Shale Lane gave you."

Onyxflame's brow furrowed, then he drew a sharp breath. "The girl who saw the 'shining men,' you mean."

A chill ran up Alistar's spine, freezing his moment of humor. They had wondered why the men gave treats to a potential witness. "That might not have been candy that they gave her."

Onyxflame let out a breath in a cloud of steam. "Gods, now I truly hope she saved them all for the Ice Blossom Festival." He looked to Alistar. "Do you think she would believe us if we told her not to eat it? Maybe if we offered her some fresh candy in trade?" He paused. "Do you think that we can even find her again?"

"If they live in that alley or nearby, we should be able to find her," Alistar said. "Though we don't know that anything actually *is* wrong with her candy." Other than it being absolutely filthy and coated in grime. "But there's little harm in trying. At worst, she receives more candy and we end up with some bits of crystallized sugar." He closed the pouch and stuffed it back into his pocket.

"There is the possibility that what you have in your possession is nothing more than rock candy itself," Dahr pointed out. "Whoever supplied it could easily have lied."

"True," Alistar acknowledged. "However, even if that is the case, the technician believed that he possessed a drug, and that drug strongly resembles something that may connect to our investigation. It bears looking into."

"And when you began all this, you never thought your work would require you to patronize a confectioner's shop, did you?" Onyxflame quipped.

Alistar chuckled softly, but he saw that Onyxflame's eyes were serious, in spite of the flippant tone.

They hailed a carriage to take them to the market at Sapphire Square. Onyxflame paid a visit to the cobbler commissioned to provide him with shoes suitable for the court, and left the shop with three new pairs of fine leather footwear. Alistar located a confectioner's shop and ventured inside. The air radiated sugar and honey, and his teeth ached just looking at the bright, garish displays of candies in all shapes, sizes, and colors. Even the gingerbread sported colorful icing and sugar glazes. The proprietor greeted him quickly, engaged in an effort to satisfy three loud, whining children and their overly doting nanny. Alistar found a package of rock candy tied with a silver ribbon—one of the traditional gifts for children during the Ice Blossom Festival. He paid for it and escaped the store as quickly as he could with any dignity. One of the children started to wail "But I wanted *that* one!" as he shut the door behind him.

Dahr and Onyxflame had wisely opted to wait for him outside the shop. Dahr shuddered. "I'll face any enemy in service to His Highness, but I will never voluntarily enter a confectioner's shop. I have no fondness for children throwing tantrums, and little liking for that degree of sugar. My taste for sweets runs no further than dried fruit."

"What, you don't care for children?" Onyxflame asked in mock disbelief. "Not a family man?"

"Other peoples' children, so long as they are behaved, I like well enough. And I can hand them back to their parents or caretakers when they start to scream," Dahr said. "The Guard is my family."

"Any siblings?" Alistar asked him as they walked through the market. "I have both a younger brother and a younger sister."

"One sister, so far as I know," Dahr answered. "She and I were in the same orphanage, and now we are both members of His Highness's Guard. If we have other siblings, I do not know of them."

An orphan? The Guard truly is all the family Dahr has, then.

"You didn't miss much," Onyxflame said. "The whole 'idyllic family life' looks lovely in paintings of smiling parents and children around a table with a beautiful roast and as much food as anyone wants to celebrate the festivals. Kindly skips over the part where that is the family's food for a week, and don't you *dare* hint that you are sick of yet another round of mutton disguised as… anything else. All because your parents were determined to put on a show of that 'happy' family. They didn't approve of a child who failed to appropriately appreciate such sacrifices as not eating during the days leading up to the event." Onyxflame drew a deep breath, then plastered a smile on his face. His voice was forcibly pleasant. "But since no one in polite company wants to hear how I spent several years looking for ways to get myself put *into* an orphanage, what sort of quaint and lovely tales of familial bliss should Aspendark have at the ready, De'seneth?"

"You did not want to be in Lewarden's orphanages for the poor," Dahr cut in coolly.

Onyxflame's smile vanished as if it had never been. He met Dahr's gaze evenly. "Yes, I actually did. I heard they fed you at least once a day there."

"That depends on what you define as 'food'." Dahr scowled.

"Back then, I would have defined it as my plate not being empty, and not having to scavenge from our neighbors' leavings. Yes, I very much would have preferred the orphanage." Onyxflame's voice was flat.

Alistar cleared his throat. "This is not the best place for this conversation." He wasn't willing to say there was any *good* place for such a conversation, but the middle of a busy market, where anyone could overhear, was certainly not that place. He looked at both elves, made sure he had their attention, and headed back to the street to flag down a carriage.

Dahr and Onyxflame followed without a word. The ride back to Shale Lane passed in uncomfortable silence. Dusk was falling when they arrived, and Alistar directed the driver to his townhouse.

"We'll look for that girl tomorrow," he said firmly. He waited for someone to argue the need to find her immediately, but received no response from either elf. "Dahr, do you want to stay for dinner?"

"No sir, thank you," Dahr said, finally breaking his silence. "I will return tomorrow morning." He offered a curt nod to Alistar, none to Onyxflame, and strode up the street.

Onyxflame chose to ignore the guard. When Alistar opened the door, the elf headed straight to the guest room.

Alistar went to his own bedroom and changed into evening leisure wear, then checked the kitchen to see what Mrs. Ke'lyn had made for dinner. He found a large pot of stew simmering on the stove, and when he lifted the lid, he smelled barley and beef. A loaf of bread was wrapped in a towel, and beside it rested a wedge of soft cheese.

When Onyxflame didn't come back downstairs, Alistar knocked on the door. "Dinner's ready. You're not confined to your room."

After a few moments of silence, Onyxflame answered. "My apologies, De'seneth, but I don't think I'll be down. I'm poor company at the moment."

Alistar raised an eyebrow, but didn't argue. "All right. Come down if you change your mind."

"My thanks." Onyxflame sounded exhausted.

Alistar ate in the kitchen, gazing out the window and watching the snow dance in the winter wind. *Tomorrow night, His Highness expects us to attend the party at Lord Proudmoor's estate. I don't know if Onyxflame is ready. Blood and sand, I don't know if I am ready. Most of my news of the court comes from Lamorage, and he's not moving in the inner circles.*

The sight of a carriage stopping in front of his house interrupted his thoughts. The woman who jumped out, portfolio tucked under one arm, wasn't familiar. Alistar hurried down the stairs, opening the door at the first knock. "Yes?"

"Associate De'seneth?"

"I am," he agreed cautiously.

"Botanist La'sel, sir." She stuck out a gloved hand. "Botanist Tur'sah instructed me to bring you the Redpine Sanctuary report at the earliest possibly opportunity. I apologize for the hour, but I just completed the report."

Alistar opened the door to her. "Come in."

She stepped inside. "Only for a moment, sir. I also need to deliver a copy to Chief Botanist Riverbed. However, your copy is… well… thicker." She held the portfolio to him.

"Thicker?" Alistar repeated, accepting it. *You're withholding information from the Chief Botanist?*

"Yes sir. In addition to my report, we found a sealed packet, presumably containing files, addressed to you." La'sel paused. "Buried among the afflicted plants, sir. I didn't break the seal. The symbols indicate confidential information."

Sealed, confidential information addressed to me, then buried in the greenhouse? Why? Who—Technician Bar'rege. She must have hidden them. She said she would send me her report, but I never received it. When she was ranting, didn't she say something about "words written twice and again?" I thought she was raving, but perhaps she was trying to tell me where she'd hidden the report.

"Is anyone else aware of this packet?" Alistar asked.

"Only the sprite flock that assisted me, sir," she said. "Not even the Silverline engineer who accompanied us saw it."

"Good. I would prefer it stay that way until I've had a chance to review the contents," Alistar told her.

"Of course, sir." La'sel nodded quickly. "If that's everything, I should be on my way. Good night, Associate De'seneth." She opened the door and stepped outside.

"Good night." Alistar closed and locked the door behind her. He slowly walked back to the kitchen and opened the portfolio.

The first page of La'sel's report opened with a simple, chilling recommendation. "The kurowa flowers feeding the mahiy lines into the Hollows are afflicted with blight of unclear origin. Botanist recommendation: complete and immediate purge of the greenhouse."

Alistar sat down heavily. Complete purge. That meant

destroying every plant in the generator and completely regrowing the mahiy lines. Not just those into the Hollows, but every line that Redpine Generator fed.

The pages that followed detailed erratic fluctuations in the magic, and predicted the instabilities that would follow if the kurowa were left untreated. Alistar swore softly. The botanist's report broke down possibly consequences and timelines until complete corruption of the mahiy network across Lewarden.

Eventually, she ventured into conjecture, hypothesizing about the source of the blight. Alistar was gratified to see that she clearly indicated that she did not believe the technicians at the generator were at fault. The botanist instead focused on comparisons to other known blights. Alistar found himself most drawn to the similarities to instances early in the establishment of the mahiy network, when uncultivated kurowa plants had interjected into the network, feeding wild magic into the lines. In those instances, the effects had been minor, causing only small disruptions.

However, these analyses determined that the affected kurowa plants in the generator had been permanently altered by the introduction of an outside source of magic. Botanist La'sel suggested that some manner of feedback in the lines during or immediately after the extended outage affected the plants at Redpine. Alistar frowned.

What other power source could have been affecting the lines, though? Redpine is the only generator that feeds into the Hollows, and if someone in the Hollows has their own rogue farm of kurowa plants, we should have seen other disruptions from that source. Zhrets Vonn spoke as if the gods intervened. Just what happened in the Hollows during that outage?

He turned to the sealed documents marked with his name. Alistar considered, then broke the seal. He half expected to find a letter along the lines of "If you are reading this, I must be dead," but Technician Bar'rege hadn't engaged in such melodrama. Her personal message was short, a description of Zhrets Vonn and his missing coat button, and the threats and promises he made to her. The rest was her report on the outage.

Alistar frowned as he studied the charts and graphs. He easily found the beginning of the outage, then the point where the technicians cut off the power flow to the mahiy lines. No further activity should have been evident on the mahiy lines until restoration of power. Instead, he saw blips—small but present—on the lines.

What are those? How? What's the source, and is it the source of the blight that's hit Redpine?

Upstairs, the guest room door opened, then closed. Alistar tucked the reports back into the portfolio. Onyxflame, dressed in his workman's clothes, paused in the kitchen doorway.

Alistar waved him in. "There's food if you want."

Onyxflame walked to the counter, but didn't take a plate, nor did he ask about the portfolio. "I apologize for my outburst earlier, De'seneth. It was uncalled for."

"It's excused," Alistar said. "Family can be a treacherous reef to navigate."

Onyxflame snorted. "A treacherous reef. Yes, that is one way of putting it. A polite way of putting it. Nicer than most of the descriptions I could think of." He flopped down in a chair. "So what *would* Aspendark's family have been like? What's a nice, normal, Rillwater family home look like?"

Alistar gazed at him. "Is this a serious question, or a preamble to something sarcastic and biting?"

Onyxflame sighed. "A serious question, De'seneth. I don't need to belabor the utter failings of my youth."

"I don't imagine Aspendark's home was altogether idyllic," Alistar said. "Not with the little complication of his bastard sister. Probably some tense times when that matter came out. But a typical noble family? Lots of nautical-related items around the house, even if the family doesn't generally sail. Houses are built of stone, mostly. Wood rots too quickly. We celebrate the official festivals, and there's usually a big party thrown after a successful venture by the fleet. Those are held in either the town square, if the weather's good, or the shiphouse."

"The what?" Onyxflame asked.

Didn't he learn even the most basic nautical terms when he sailed? "The shiphouse. It's where the ships are stored for repairs or when they're on dry dock. Not the most creative, elegant name, but that's what we call it. Lots of food, mostly fish. I haven't had a good fish stew or shrimp cake since last time I was home. Steamed clams." Alistar smiled in memory. "As for home life, Aspendark probably didn't have to worry about meals too often, although we've had some lean years. His family runs some warehouses, dependent on the ships to bring home goods so they have something to store and sell. He ought to have learned accounting, but that doesn't mean he's any good at it, and no one's likely to ask you to demonstrate such an unglamorous skill in public. Throw in some nautical language from your venture aboard ship if you need to, but please, try to use terms correctly."

"And no one will be overly surprised that they know nothing of Aspendark, because no one in Lewarden pays attention to who any of the provincial lords are," Onyxflame added.

"Believe me, I've noticed," Alistar said dryly. He let out a sigh. "Hopefully when I'm in court dress, the majority of my coworkers won't immediately recognize me."

"They ought to at least remember your name, De'seneth," Onyxflame said, amused.

Alistar shook his head. "De'seneth is my matronym. I'll be using my father's name in court."

Onyxflame's brow furrowed. "Why did you bother? You just agreed that Lewarden doesn't know the nobles outside its walls. Unless your family name is As'enel and you're a son of the Pirate King—er, sorry, the head of the Rillwater privateers, I mean—no one would recognize it."

"Admiral is the word you're looking for, Onyxflame. And yes, I do know that As'enel is the only Rillwater family name anyone in Lewarden is liable to recognize. Thus, my use of my mother's name."

Onyxflame continued to frown, then understanding dawned. His mouth opened, closed, opened again. Finally, he managed a simple "Oh." Then: "And no one you work with is aware of this?"

"The Director is. And the Silver Prince, of course. Possibly the administrative sprites. Other than them, no one as far as I'm aware. Well, perhaps Lady Syri, as the Silver Prince's daughter."

"And a son of the Admiral of the Rillwater fleet is in Lewarden as an engineer?" Onyxflame asked.

A question far more weighty than Onyxflame imagined. Alistar debated whether to give the full answer, but instead chose the briefer, safer route of answering only the question asked, not the one implied. "Yes. My brother and sister don't mind. From their perspective, if I'm not sailing and not looking to be a captain, I can take charge of the administrative responsibilities of being the family heir while they get to be part of building the family fortune." Alistar shrugged. "It works for all of us."

"For you and your siblings, at least. Does it work for your parents?" Onyxflame asked.

"Are you planning to start gossip that my presence in Lewarden comes without Family blessing, Onyxflame?" Alistar asked. "Because I would warn you against doing so. Weakening my standing won't gain you anything, and won't gain me the contacts this investigation may require."

"So… it doesn't work for your parents," Onyxflame said.

"My father supported my decision to study engineering. My mother remains convinced that it's simply a passing fancy."

Onyxflame raised an eyebrow. "But you're using her family name for your career in Lewarden? I'm sure that must thrill her to no end."

"Her parents were pleased when I asked their permission," Alistar said. "They were honored that I would use their name."

And... yes, Mother was displeased. Strongly displeased. Which was why I didn't tell her until after I was in Lewarden.

"So, at the party, you'll be the focus of attention," Onyxflame said, bringing the conversation back to its origin. "Perhaps I won't have any reason to worry about what people will attempt to speak to me about. They'll be too busy trying to speak to you."

"Oh, they'll talk to you. They'll be trying to get information from you that will help them make contact with me, but they'll come to you," Alistar told him. "Which is when Aspendark should turn on his charm and start trying to collect investors."

"If they hand me money on the spot, can I keep it?" Onyxflame asked innocently.

"If anyone's trying to hand you money on the spot, don't accept it," Alistar warned. "Taking it could be considered accepting a binding agreement, and chances are you haven't heard all the terms of that agreement yet. Those terms will not be favorable to you."

Onyxflame considered that in silence. Finally he said, "So, you are the heir to the most powerful family in Rillwater, and you're marrying a doctor's daughter? Does her family have rank and standing?"

"Doctor Tan'shyo is not nobility, no. I realize that's practically heresy in the capital—"

"Depending on your reading of the Tenants and the Path, it's *literally* heresy to wed outside your station," Onyxflame interrupted.

Alistar continued, not commenting on the tenants of elven faith. "However, Rillwater is less strict. There's too much independence, too much belief that anyone can rise no matter their bloodline. Saskia will officially become a lady by marrying me, and I wouldn't be surprised if my father offers Doctor Tan'shyo a small holding in Rillwater, giving him an official title as well. That's what he offered my sister's father-in-law, at least."

"Now this, De'seneth. This is why I say I prefer the egalitarian nature of your human gods. Within the elven pantheon and teachings, the very idea of a noble marrying a commoner is at best scandal, and at worst cause for divine punishment for breaking the natural order and the proper station of every person. Will the ceremony be held in Rillwater?" Onyxflame asked.

"No, we'll be wed here in Lewarden," Alistar answered, surprised by the elf's genuine interest. "We aren't planning to move away anytime soon."

"Have you set a date yet?" Onyxflame asked.

"Not yet," Alistar answered. "I've been saving for it." Savings that he had lent to Lamorage last night. His stomach tightened at the thought of his friend and the question of Lamorage's safety. "Once this assignment is complete, I expect we'll begin planning in earnest. I expect to have a small ceremony, perhaps at Night's Eve Sanctuary, without an overly bloated guest list. Family and friends."

Onyxflame nodded. "I've seen a few human weddings. They tend to be cheerful affairs, from what I can tell. Happiness among most people, except for those parents who are certain that their child could have done better. Will I be invited?"

Alistar gave him a dubious look. "Do you expect to still be in Lewarden… or even in the country by then?"

"I could make a special trip just for the occasion, De'seneth," Onyxflame said.

Alistar sighed. "You would show up if not invited, simply *because* you were not invited. Fine then, consider yourself invited to my wedding."

Onyxflame smirked. "De'seneth, just because I would show up if uninvited doesn't mean I'll be so contrary as to *not* come if I *am* invited. Now, you're making a wise decision by inviting me."

"Oh really? Do explain," Alistar said, curious in spite of himself.

"One of the greatest worries of a wedding is how the guests will behave. However, another is the matter of gifts. There is always one that is horrible. The packaging is hideous and gaudy, and the gifter seems to wish to steal all the attention away from the happy couple and toward their monstrosity. But now, you and your future bride need not worry about who will be the one to give that gift. I promise you, De'seneth, I will bring the most hideous, garish, gaudy, blindingly ugly gift to your wedding, and in comparison, even the worst of the rest will seem mild and perhaps even attractive."

"Onyxflame, I can honestly say that is a concern that had never entered my mind," Alistar said.

"Not yours, perhaps, but I am certain that if you ask her, you will discover that your fiancée has felt a moment of fear wondering if that most hideous gift will come from someone dear to her. Tell her to rest assured, it need not be a concern any longer," Onyxflame said grandly.

Alistar chuckled. "I'll keep that in mind."

Onyxflame's earlier outburst might never have happened, for all the signs the elf showed, but Alistar didn't believe it was so quickly gone and forgotten. *He's a good actor. He can show the right face, read the cues.* Alistar shook his head. "You might do better at playing the court than I will, Onyxflame."

The nonsequitor didn't appear to surprise the elf. "Perhaps. I fully intend to blame any awkward situations on differences between Rillwater and Lewarden culture."

Alistar cleared the table. "It's getting late, and I've had enough nights of short sleep the last few days."

Onyxflame accepted the hint and climbed the stairs back to the guest room. "Good night, De'seneth."

"Good night, Onyxflame." Alistar warded the room and went to bed.

CHAPTER 23

Alistar slept soundly and woke with his alarm. He moved through his morning rituals with the ease of habit. When he knocked on Onyxflame's door, he got only a weary groan in answer, followed by the thump of the elf rolling out of bed.

Alistar prepared porridge for breakfast, adding bits of sausage and the leftover cheese. Onyxflame eventually came downstairs, fully dressed in fresh, pressed clothes, yet somehow still managing to look rumpled. Cosmetics concealed the shadows around his eyes, but didn't hide the bags.

"Didn't sleep well?" Alistar asked.

Onyxflame shook his head. "About as well as I did in prison. Which is to say, horribly." He considered the porridge, stirred the thick mush, and scooped some into a bowl. He spent more time poking it with a spoon than eating it. Alistar's attempts to draw him into conversation were met with monosyllabic responses.

Alistar had finished his breakfast when Dahr arrived, and Onyxflame had moved on to nursing a mug of tea. Dahr eyed Onyxflame, then addressed Alistar. "Good morning, sir. What's the plan for today?"

"The plan for today is to prepare for tonight," Alistar said. "Do you know the status of our invitations to the Proudmoor party?"

"I will pick them up later this morning, sir," Dahr answered. "Everything should be in order for you and Aspendark to attend." He eyed Onyxflame again. "Although perhaps Lord Aspendark should be reminded of the virtues of moderation."

Onyxflame glared daggers at the guard. "I didn't sleep well."

"Why don't you pick them up now," Alistar told Dahr.

"Sir, I was told they would be ready at ten," Dahr said.

Alistar fixed a pointed look at him. "Dahr, why don't you go pick the invitations up now." He could handle Onyxflame in a foul mood this morning, but not Onyxflame and Dahr sniping at one another. Since sending Onyxflame away was not an option, removing Dahr from the situation would suffice.

Dahr blinked, then inclined his head in a nod. "Yes sir. I will contact you when they are ready."

"Thank you." Alistar walked the guard to the door without further comment.

When he returned to the kitchen, Onyxflame raised his head. "I am *not* hung over."

"You didn't smell like booze when you came down this morning, so I didn't think you were," Alistar answered. "And if you were hung over, I'd be far more interested in how you managed to acquire the drink and smuggle it inside."

Onyxflame waved a hand. "Oh, that wouldn't be so hard. Lifting a flask just takes a few seconds when someone's not looking. About as easy as picking pockets. Easier, maybe. People notice a missing purse sooner than a missing flask unless they like to take a nip while they walk about." He rubbed his forehead. "Damn, my head's throbbing."

Alistar's eyes narrowed. "Did you take anything else last night? Sample that bit of candy the girl gave you?"

"Hematic perdition, no!" Onyxflame said quickly. "I wouldn't trust anything that came from her 'shining men' enough to consume it. Just a poor night's sleep and some singularly unpleasant dreams."

"Maybe a walk will help clear your head," Alistar said. "Let's find that girl, if we can."

"I knew there was a reason I crawled out of bed." Onyxflame stood and rubbed his eyes. "At your convenience, De'seneth."

Alistar wrote a note to Mrs. Ke'lyn that she didn't need to prepare dinner and left it on the front table. Checking that the packet of rock candy was still in his coat pocket, he bundled for the chill morning. Hopefully it would be a sufficient bribe.

Frigid air hit Alistar when he opened the door and stepped outside. His breath rose in clouds. Tiny flakes of snow drifted down, either from the clouds or from the roofs. The street was dusted with snow, and it was too light to stick to anything for long except when the wind stilled. Onyxflame hunched in the cold and followed Alistar.

Shale Lane was quiet, only a few people out and a handful of carriages. Alistar picked his path back to the site of the outage, casting looks into the alleys and shadows as they passed. When they reached the site, Alistar moved down the alley toward the back of the building. The rude shelters remained, but he didn't see anyone inside, nor did he hear movement. The snow hadn't collected enough to show footprints, if there were any to see. He walked slowly through the alley again, looking and listening.

"De'seneth," Onyxflame called.

Alistar strode to the elf, and found Onyxflame crouched beside a scorched tangle of debris. He didn't remember seeing that on their first visit to the alley.

"This doesn't look like an intentional fire. Not one lit for heat. More like just a sudden blast. See? The scorch marks don't go very deep," Onyxflame said, voice low. He turned over a board, showing Alistar the unburned bottom side.

Something shifted and thumped. Both men froze, searching for the source.

Someone sniffled. "Oww…"

"Hello?" Alistar asked gently.

Another sniffle. "My hands hurt."

Alistar moved toward the small voice. It sounded like a child, though he couldn't tell if it was a boy or a girl. "Can I help?"

More shifting, and he finally saw the little figure wrapped in a dull brown wool blanket. One small hand wormed free from under the blanket, the skin red and blistered with burns. "It hurts."

Alistar winced. From the size of the figure, he guessed it was the girl rather than her brother. He crouched beside her and cupped her little hand between his gloves. "It must," he agreed. "What happened?"

"I ate the fire, but it was too hot, and I had to get it out." A pair of eyes fixed solemnly on Alistar from the depths of the blanket.

"You… ate the fire?" Alistar repeated uncertainly.

The blanket bobbed in a nod. "But it was too hot. It crawled all around inside. I had to make it get out! But it didn't like when I pushed, an' made my hands hurt."

"How did you eat the fire in the first place?" Onyxflame asked, matching his accent to hers.

She turned to Onyxflame and gave a little sound of happiness. "I 'member you! You was here before!"

"I was," Onyxflame agreed. "You gave me a piece of your candy."

The blanket bobbed vigorously. "I saved most of it like you said. Had a little bitty bit." Her eyes were big. "I didn't know candy could be fire!"

"You mean that the fire you ate was that piece of candy?" Onyxflame asked.

"I *told* you that!" she said in a tone that implied that adults clearly lost much of their wits when they grew up, because why else would she have to keep repeating herself?

"How did you let the fire out?" Onyxflame asked.

She hesitated. "My brother said I shouldn't tell no one."

"Was there purple light?" Onyxflame asked.

She nodded.

"And did the fire feel like it ran down to the tips of your fingers, and then pop out?" Onyxflame continued.

Another nod.

Channeling. She was channeling. Alistar blinked. She couldn't be older than six, if that. Most channelers didn't wake to their power until puberty. Sometimes earlier, but rarely as young as this girl. *How could a piece of candy—or a drug, if that's what it was—trigger an early awakening of the ability to channel?*

"Ey! What you doin'? Get 'way from her!" Her brother rushed up the alley, a stick in his grip.

The blanket shuddered. "Now I feel all funny and weird inside," she said, as if her brother hadn't spoken. "And the fire burned my hands."

Alistar turned to the boy. "We're not going to hurt her."

"What's she say? It's all nonsense! She's sick. Real sick. You better stay 'way from her."

"If she's sick, there's a clinic not far from here," Alistar said. "They won't charge you if you take her there."

The boy's mouth curled in a sneer. "Hah! That's what they *want* us to think. Go there and they take kids off an' never see 'em again." He edged closer, trying to make Alistar back away.

The girl turned toward her brother. "I didn't tell them that I made fire in my hands," she said. "Like you said not to."

The boy jerked, and his eyes snapped to Alistar and Onyxflame. "It's nonsense, all of it!"

"It is not!" she protested. "You said the shining men were nonsense too! But they gave me candy."

"It *is* nonsense!" the boy repeated urgently. "It's nonsense and no one's gonna take you away."

Oh. Of course. That's what he's afraid of. Alistar looked at the boy. "I can help you get care for your sister, and people who will help her learn how to control the fire, and I promise that they won't separate you."

The boy's lip curled in a sneer. "Hah. You think I'm dumb? That ain't how things work. They'll take her away and toss me out on my ear."

"Not easy for a street rat to survive as a channeler," Onyxflame said in a low voice, for Alistar's ears rather than the children's. "Still, sounds better than losing the only family you have to rely on."

Alistar held the boy's gaze. "I won't let them toss you out." He unbuttoned his coat and pulled the Silver Prince's emblem out from under his shirt. "Do you know what this is?"

The boy peered at the emblem. "A flower with fire?" he said dubiously. "Um... Well it kind of looks like them pictures on those banners around the places that make the magic lines in the sky."

"It's the emblem of the Silver Prince," Alistar said, trusting that even street rats would know who *that* was.

The boy's mouth formed a silent "Oh."

"If I take you to someone who can help your sister, and I show them this and tell them not to separate the two of you, they will do what I say," Alistar promised.

The boy hesitated. He looked at the blanket lump that concealed his sister, then Alistar and the badge. His eyes narrowed with suspicion. "Why you wanna do somethin' like that, huh? What do you care?"

"Your sister saw the shining men," Alistar said. "I think that the 'candy' they gave her was something bad, something that made her sick. The shining men have hurt other people, and I want to stop them from hurting you or your sister."

The girl stirred. "Did you see the shining men? They were so pretty. They glowed."

The boy still hesitated. "You mean... they did this? This happened because of them?"

"Yes." Onyxflame's firm answer saved Alistar from having to decide how to respond to the question.

The boy's gaze flickered to Onyxflame, then back to Alistar. "And you promise they won't take her away an' toss me out?"

"I swear it by my father's name," Alistar said solemnly.

"All right…" the boy said slowly. He held out a grubby hand. Alistar grasped it, and they shook.

Alistar stood. "Keep an eye on them," he told Onyxflame.

"Sure. Not going anywhere," Onyxflame said rather too lightly. Alistar gave him a sharp look, which the elf met evenly.

Alistar walked a little way down the alley, but not so far that he was out of sight of Onyxflame or the children. He pulled Dahr's black speaking stone from his pocket and activated it.

Dahr responded promptly. "Sir. The invitations are not yet ready. They will likely be another hour."

"I apologize for sending you out of the house so sharply, Dahr," Alistar said.

"There is nothing to apologize for, sir. What do you need?"

"A carriage and a destination where I can find both a healer and someone able to take in a newly awakened channeler," Alistar answered. "We're at the site of the Shale Lane incident. Do you remember the two street children we met there?"

"I do, sir," Dahr told him.

"The girl has awakened as a channeler. Burned her hands pretty badly in the process. I promised her brother that they wouldn't be separated."

Dahr was silent for a moment. "She is very young for that, isn't she?"

"Very," Alistar said. "Too young. She needs care and training before she really loses control and lights a city block on fire." He wished it were a joke or hyperbole. Unfortunately, fire was one of the most volatile and challenging magics to harness, and accidents were far too easy. "This is higher priority than picking up the invitations."

"Yes sir. I'll prepare a carriage and be there with all reasonable haste."

"We'll be here," Alistar said. He deactivated the stone and put it back in his pocket.

Seeing the shift in Alistar's stance and concluding that the conversation was complete, Onyxflame walked over to him, tucking something into his pocket. "I convinced the girl to give up the rest of her 'candy.' Her brother was more than happy to help persuade her. Assistance has been summoned, I take it?"

"Yes, Dahr will bring a carriage," Alistar said, relieved to know that the suspect crystals were safely out of the child's hands. Although having them in Onyxflame's hands might not be a vast improvement. "So, based on your response, I'm finding it hard to tell—is this agreement or disagreement with my decision?"

"You offer treatment for her burns, care and training, and a promise not to split apart siblings. What's to disagree with?"

"I don't know," Alistar answered. "That's why I'm asking you."

"Hmm, perhaps it's the use of the Silver Prince's name and authority. Or the thought that by using it, you're practically promising them into his service without so much as a by-your-leave," Onyxflame said.

"And should I instead leave them here, freezing and starving on the streets?" Alistar asked. His eyes narrowed. "What do you really object to, Onyxflame?"

"I object to making them beholden to people who would just as happily have tossed them in the gutter if not for the girl being useful to them," Onyxflame retorted.

"If you were free, would you have taken them in?" Alistar asked. "Or would you have walked away without a second thought?"

Onyxflame didn't answer.

Alistar lowered his voice. "Onyxflame, is this about these children, or is it about you?"

Onyxflame sucked in a sharp breath, then let it out. His lips curled in a tight smile. "Well, I certainly never had anyone offer to whisk me off to a finer life because I burned my hands. Maybe I should have tried it." He shook his head and walked back to the siblings.

The boy scurried around the alley, collecting bits and baubles, hiding some away, packing others into a bag. He handed a threadbare, tattered doll to his sister, and she clutched it tight. He kept his own treasures concealed, constantly glancing at Alistar and Onyxflame as if they might attempt to confiscate his few belongings.

"What's your name?" Alistar asked. "I'm Alistar De'seneth, and he's Taslor Aspendark."

At the question, the boy stopped. He blinked at Alistar. "You gots two names. We just gots one."

"Some people have one name, some have two." Alistar lowered his voice in a conspiratorial whisper. "Some nobles have even more than that."

"Really?" The boy sniffed. "Guess they gots to have lots to say about *everything*, huh?" He pondered. "My gran called me Kaz."

"She called me Tatya," the girl added. She sighed. "I miss Gran."

Kaz nodded quickly. "Gran got sick," he told Alistar. "She went to one of them clinics, and we never saw her again." He fixed his gaze on Alistar. "You better not be lying."

"I'm not," Alistar promised.

It felt like hours before Dahr arrived, but Alistar's watch promised that it was little more than forty minutes. Given that the guard had needed to first get a carriage before driving it to them, Alistar estimated that Dahr had probably violated all of the minor and at least three major traffic laws to make that time. The carriage rolled to a stop at the mouth of the alley and the guard climbed down from the driver's box. Alistar walked out to him.

"Sir." Dahr nodded to him. "I solicited recommendations, and received several strong suggestions to bring the children to the Silver Watch for care."

"The Silver Watch?" Alistar repeated. "Did the people you asked understand that these are two street children? You want to take them into the heart of the nobility?"

"I made their current station clear, sir," Dahr said. "The recommendations stood when I repeated the question. I believe that, given the girl's youth, they wish to ensure she is placed with capable teachers."

That, at least, Alistar agreed with. The Silver Watch's reputation for producing the elite channelers in Lewarden testified to the skill of their trainers. "What about the cost? They have *nothing*, Dahr, and I do not want them trapped in debt-bound servitude for the rest of their lives."

"Payment for their schooling has already been arranged," Dahr promised. "They will not bear any debts."

Arranged by who? And with what expectations? Alistar let out a long breath. *My choices are limited, and the children need help.*

He returned to the siblings. "Tatya, can you walk, or would you like someone to carry you?"

"Can walk," she said. Her brother helped her up, and the two children shuffled toward the carriage.

Kaz eyed Dahr with the same wary caution he'd given Alistar and Onyxflame. When they reached the carriage, though, he gaped. Dahr unfolded the steps and held the door open for them, as if the siblings were young nobles. Tatya jumped, trying to reach the first step. Dahr picked her up and set her on the step, letting her climb the rest of the way on her own. Kaz pulled himself onto the steps without assistance. Alistar waited until the children were inside and settled before climbing in. Onyxflame followed, and Dahr closed the carriage door.

Kaz and Tatya crawled onto a bench and pushed the curtain open. Tatya squeaked in surprise, then delight as the carriage began moving. Alistar smiled at her excitement over things he took for granted. She gaped openly when they moved onto a busier street and were surrounded by horses and carriages. Kaz folded his hands in his lap, occasionally glancing out the window, but trying to project an air of indifference. Perhaps mindful of his young passengers, Dahr drove at a reasonable speed, limiting his hair-raising weaving between the other traffic to a minimum.

When they moved into the Upper City, Kaz forgot his world-weary aloof attitude, pressing his face to the window alongside his sister. Alistar couldn't understand half of Tatya's chatter, but her brother matched her street dialect to offer what were probably wildly inaccurate answers to her questions. As the carriage continued deeper into the heart of Lewarden, the siblings fell quiet, too busy gaping to ask questions.

Dahr turned the carriage toward a pair of silver-plated gates. They opened before him, and the carriage rumbled onto a smooth, paved drive. They stopped before a massive manor house hung with strings of enchanted everbloom blossoms. The flowers glowed faintly, barely visible in the winter daylight.

The front door opened as they were climbing from the carriage. An elven woman with long silver hair stepped out to greet them. "Welcome to Silver Watch. We received word to expect you." She looked to Alistar. "You are De'seneth, sir?" She spoke with authority and grace.

"I am Associate De'seneth," Alistar answered.

"And you are guardian of these children?" She canted her head and looked to Tatya and Kaz.

"I'm guardian of my sister!" Kaz declared firmly, clearly trying not to be cowed by the woman. "Gran said so."

"As the young man says," Alistar agreed. "Though I will be their advocate. The girl, Tatya burned her hands, possibly more, when something woke her channeling."

"I am Lady Emberstone, Keeper of the House of the Silver Guard. Come inside."

Kaz cast a questioning look to Alistar, who nodded. They all followed Lady Emberstone into the manor. The foyer was nearly as large as that of Silverline Power, and at a glance, the furnishings cost enough to build and outfit a warship. The colors of the Silver Guard appeared to be silver, emerald, and amber.

A young human woman in an emerald healer's robe emerged from a side door. She dipped a bow to the visitors, but focused on Tatya. Tatya was too busy staring in awe to notice the attention fixed on her.

Lady Emberstone spoke. "Your name is Tatya, child?"

Tatya nodded.

"This is Healer Ra'shel. She will tend to you. Go with her."

Ra'shel smiled kindly and held a hand out to Tatya. "Right this way."

Kaz shifted anxiously. "I'm going too!"

"It's not proper for young men and young women to—" Lady Emberstone began, her tone gently chiding.

"You can't take my sister away!" he cried.

"Lady Emberstone, they are siblings," Alistar said. "Would you allow Kaz to accompany Tatya for now?"

Tatya stopped, looking between the healer and her brother, suddenly anxious. She scrambled to Kaz, clinging to him. "Not gonna go," she said firmly.

"My lady, it is no trouble," Ra'shel murmured.

Lady Emberstone relented. "Very well. Healer Ra'shel will tend to both of you, this time."

Ra'shel held out her hand again. Hesitantly, Kaz took it, and she led the siblings into the side room.

"Thank you, Lady Emberstone," Alistar said.

"It is quite improper," Lady Emberstone said. "However, I will grant this concession, for now. What do you know of them, De'seneth?"

"I know that they have no known family other than one another. Their grandmother presumably died some time back. The boy, Kaz, said that she was ill, and went to one of the clinics but never returned. He is quite afraid of that happening again. I promised him that if he agreed to come here, he and his sister would not be separated, nor would he be isolated or tossed out for failing to channel."

"Those are strong promises to make to a child," Lady Emberstone said, her voice revealing nothing.

Alistar drew Prince Cero's emblem from under his shirt. "I appreciate your cooperation in making certain those promises are not broken."

She straightened. "These children have the Crown's sponsorship?"

"They do," Dahr said. "You will receive the paperwork shortly."

Alistar looked at the guard in surprise and some shock. *Dahr wouldn't lie about something like that, would he? He wouldn't dare! But does that mean that when he consulted "sources" about the best place to bring Kaz and Tatya, he asked the Silver Prince directly? No wonder the cost of their stay here is covered.*

Lady Emberstone nodded slowly. "Very well, sir. Both children will be tended here. What do you know of Tatya's awakening?"

"She said that she 'swallowed fire, but it was too hot and she had to let it out,'" Alistar answered. "I believe that she may have been exposed to a drug of some sort. Whether that was the trigger to her awakening, or an incidental coincidence, I do not know."

"A drug." Lady Emberstone's mouth curled in distaste.

"She is also a witness in an ongoing investigation," Alistar said, lowering his voice. "At the moment, one of the few surviving direct witnesses I have." *The only one I have.* "I suspect the criminals gave her the drug in an attempt to silence her without drawing suspicion to themselves. If she speaks to you or any of your staff about the 'shining men', I request that you record what she says of them."

"Of course, Associate De'seneth," Lady Emberstone replied, her eyes serious. "In regard to keeping them together, at times during her training, her brother will be unable to join, for his own safety, but so much as possible, we will not restrict contact between them. Tatya is quite young. If, as your observations suggest, she is drawn toward channeling fire, a familiar and trusted companion may help ease her anxiety. Fire is a volatile element, but with direction, a powerful one."

Alistar nodded, biting back a response that magical theory, including channeling, was a required course of study for any Silverline engineer. He did not claim to be an expert in the matter, but he knew more than the average citizen.

"I wouldn't think that should be a surprise to anyone," Onyxflame drawled, the first he'd spoken since their arrival.

"It would seem obvious, yes," Lady Emberstone said. "Yet surprisingly, many seem not to understand the nature of magic. Come, gentlemen. Join me for tea."

They followed her into a parlor. An attendant brought a tray and served tea and refreshments. Alistar practiced polite courtly conversation on Lady Emberstone until Healer Ra'shel entered.

"Pardon me, lady, sirs. Kaz and Tatya are off to the bath now."

Lady Emberstone motioned for the healer to enter. "Your assessment?"

Ra'shel sat uncomfortably on the edge of an overstuffed chair. "Tatya's burns are in keeping with a sudden channeled flare. They were painful, but mostly superficial, and responded well to healing. However..." She glanced at Alistar. "However, I had to exercise caution when healing her. She already had an abnormally high concentration of magic in her body, and it could easily have reached a toxic level. I suspect that her ability was awakened in an instinctual effort to shed some of it—an effort which I believe was successful."

That was another aspect of magic theory covered in an engineer's studies: the dangers of too much concentration of magic in a living being. If it reached a toxic level, it could kill a person. Alistar nodded slowly. "They lived directly under one of the mahiy lines. Do you believe that affected her?" He didn't think the location of the mahiy lines had anything to do with Tatya's condition, but he wanted to hear the healer's thoughts before tainting them with his own suspicions.

Ra'shel shook her head in a quick jerk. "No, this was far too intense a concentration, and if the mahiy lines were responsible, I would have seen signs in Kaz as well. Tatya kept telling me that she had eaten fire, something given to her by shining men?"

Alistar nodded. "She witnessed an event, and the men who caused it gave her what looked like pieces of rock candy. Earlier, she told me that she'd eaten a small piece, and that was the 'fire' she'd swallowed. I have been operating under the assumption that it's some sort of drug. Did you find anything else?"

Ra'shel fidgeted with the sleeve of her robe. "I... do not know if it is related, but I did find, and heal, small spots of damage to her organs. I do not know if they would have spread, and I could not determine the source, but they reminded me unpleasantly of a sickness rumored to be spreading through the Lower City."

Rat's Disease. Alistar straightened. "But you were able to stop the damage?"

"Yes sir. The damage was minor. And I found no sign of it in Kaz. He is undernourished, but otherwise a healthy child."

Lady Emberstone considered. "You are implying, then, that the drug given to that girl caused this damage, and possibly is also related to the excess of magic in her body, thus her awakening as a channeler?"

Ra'shel looked at the floor as if she thought she might be scolded for expressing her opinion. "My lady, I don't have enough evidence to make such a claim. But based on the information I have at this point, I believe some relation exists between these elements."

Onyxflame was shifting uncomfortably at the talk of healers and internal organs, but he did add a question. "You noted that the damage resembled the descriptions you've heard of what's being colloquially called 'Rat's Disease' in the Lower City. If that is the case, how likely do you think it that the other cases of Rat's Disease might have a similar cause?"

Ra'shel looked like she wanted to wilt into the chair. "I... don't have enough information to say, sir."

"Thank you, Healer Ra'shel," Lady Emberstone said. "You are excused."

Ra'shel fled the room with barely a bow to the guests.

"Do pardon her," Lady Emberstone said. "She is excellent when dealing with children, but less so with adults." She turned her gaze on Alistar. "The evidence so far appears to support your hypothesis, Associate. In your opinion, do you believe that Tatya will be in active danger? Will someone make an attempt on her life?"

"Here? I doubt it, Lady Emberstone," Alistar answered. "Those responsible for giving her the toxin have no reason to believe she survived. And I don't think anyone would have reason to look for a street child in the Silver Watch."

Lady Emberstone raised an eyebrow. "You are mistaken, sir. Quite a few young channelers come here for training and education, many of them orphans or street children. Though you believe her assailants will not look for Tatya here, I will keep a watch for any with particular interest in her or her brother. We take pride in providing training and guidance to those who are challenging cases. Those awakened too young—or too old. Those with particular needs that cannot be met by other teachers."

"And here, you can conveniently also teach them to be loyal followers to the Crown and the proper order of things," Onyxflame said. He spoke so evenly that it took Alistar a moment to realize that the words were laced with irony and spite.

Lady Emberstone did not hear the subtext. She inclined her head toward Onyxflame. "That is true as well. It is unfortunate that so many among the less fortunate and favored see their service to the Crown as a burden rather than a blessing. Here, we can teach them the Tenants and the Path."

The Tenants and the Path were staples of the elven faith.

Alistar didn't know them well, but he knew that they emphasized how each person was given a place and a role in life by the gods, and that how well one fulfilled that role influenced the reward or punishment one received in the afterlife.

"What do you teach the human children?" Alistar asked. "About the Reyker, that is?"

Lady Emberstone stopped. The intense care she gave to choosing the right words told Alistar far more than her actual response. "We make the principles of the Reyker available to them, of course. I do not force anyone to choose between the faith of their ancestors or that of their neighbor."

He wasn't surprised. She was an elf, and a follower of the Tenants and the Path. She would naturally point her wards to follow her lead. "I'm glad to hear it, Lady. I hope you will pardon the question; I was simply recalling the furor last summer over that mid-city human-run orphanage. The one that had so many up in a fury that the elven children as well as the human ones were learning and following the teachings of the Reyker."

Lady Emberstone's smile was tight. "I remember the incident, Associate. You need not worry about such a thing happening here."

Because you don't think that anyone will hear about it? Or you don't think that humans will riot like the elves did?

Her expression shifted, relaxing. "I do understand your concern, Associate De'seneth. I acknowledge that I place greater focus on the Tenants and the Path, but many of our human staff, such as Ra'shel, follow your gods, and we encourage our students to ask questions. Even those questions that might lead an elf toward the human gods, or a human toward the elven ones."

"I'm pleased to hear it." Alistar stood. She seemed to sincerely believe what she said. Perhaps the principles she espoused were even followed in practice as well as philosophy. "I think we have occupied too much of your time, Lady Emberstone. Thank you for your hospitality and for your care of your charges. I hope that I can visit Tatya and Kaz regularly."

"Of course, by all means, Associate," Lady Emberstone said. She didn't sound overly enthused by the idea. "If possible, please send word in advance, to minimize disruptions in lessons."

Alistar checked his pocket and found the bundle of store-bought candy. He handed it to Lady Emberstone. "I will try to do so. Because of the nature of my work, I'm not certain I will be able to visit before the festival. Would you please give this to them if I do not? Rock candy, and I can vouch for the source."

"Of course, Associate." Lady Emberstone set the package on a side table. "I look forward to your next visit, as I am sure the children will." She walked them to the door and, with a polite farewell, sent them from her domain.

CHAPTER 24

Alistar was deep in thought as they walked back to the carriage. Dahr said something, but it wasn't until Onyxflame elbowed him that Alistar realized it was addressed to him. "Pardon?"

"What is our next destination, sir?" Dahr repeated. "The invitations should be available now, if you wish."

"That would be fine," Alistar agreed. He climbed into the carriage and settled on the bench, falling back into thought.

Onyxflame let the silence stand for a time as the carriage rumbled down the cobbled streets. Finally he asked, "Have you solved the ills of the world yet, De'seneth?"

"Not yet." Alistar gazed at the window. "What sort of drug would devour its user's insides, and why would anyone take it?"

Onyxflame shrugged. "If it makes them feel good, they might not care what it's doing to their gut until too late. And what sort of drug? There are dozens, probably more, that can do so, depending on the dosage, the concentration, and the impurities. One batch of a drug could be nearly safe, the next could contain so many additive poisons that it could kill a dragon."

"Wonderful," Alistar muttered. "You'd say that no matter how consistent the evidence?"

"I would," Onyxflame said. "Our evidence is biased, De'seneth. We're only seeing the people who die from it. For every one who dies, there could be a hundred who indulge with no ill effects."

Alistar grimaced. "True. So, we know that people are dying, but not what percentage of those who take this drug suffer fatal side effects." He pondered. "However, it appears to me that its creators may have some idea of how dangerous it can be. Both Tatya and Technician Bar'rege showed symptoms of Rat's Disease. Both of them witnessed people and events of importance to this investigation. Which implies that those responsible have some degree of control over the making of it and at least know if a particular batch is toxic." He looked at Onyxflame. "What do you know of making drugs?"

"Not a field I ever dabbled in, De'seneth," Onyxflame said quickly. "I've heard things, but have no personal experience in the drug trade."

Of all the times to wish that Onyxflame's criminal activities were more extensive than they were. Alistar sighed. "And still no closer to knowing who's involved or responsible."

"Someone with enough time and equipment to brew up foul concoctions, and the means to sell them through the slums," Onyxflame said. "Or someone with agents and underlings to take care of that messy aspect while keeping their own hands clean."

"But what's the connection to the theft of magic from the mahiy lines?" Alistar asked. "It would be easier and less suspicious to connect to the lines and draw from them like any other machine or device if they need the power to brew their drug. Unless for some reason, the creation of the drug requires a sudden, intense burst of power to trigger a reaction." He shook his head. "Pieces are still missing from this puzzle, Onyxflame."

"I have to agree," Onyxflame said. "Some of them we probably don't even know are missing yet."

"That worries me," Alistar said. "Not yet knowing what I don't know."

The carriage stopped and Dahr climbed down from the driver's seat. Rather than open the door, though, he said, "If you would like, sir, you can wait here while I pick up the invitations."

"Please do," Alistar answered.

As the sound of Dahr's steps on stone faded, Onyxflame said, "Was it my imagination, or did he actually manage to stay at a reasonable speed, without breakneck turns or weaving through traffic on this trip? Did I just not notice? I'd hate to think I was growing immune to Dahr's driving so quickly."

"I didn't notice either, so I think you're right, and he was driving sensibly just now," Alistar answered.

"May miracles never cease," Onyxflame said under his breath.

Measured steps returned to the carriage. Dahr opened the door and handed Alistar a sealed envelope. "Invitations for Lord As'enel and Lord Aspendark to attend a gathering at Lord Proudmoor's home at seven, sir. Dinner will begin promptly at seven-thirty. I will be your driver to the Proudmoor Estate tonight."

"Thank you, Dahr." Alistar accepted the envelope. "Does Lord Proudmoor know we've been added to the invitees?"

"I believe that a rumor came to his ears mentioning that the heir to the As'enel family was in Lewarden, looking to become more familiar with the affairs of the court. He responded appropriately to the news," Dahr said.

"Meaning, he contacted everyone he knew in an attempt to verify the rumor, then issued an invitation on the chance that it was true?" Alistar asked.

"Something to that effect, yes sir. Where are you bound next?"

Alistar checked his pocket watch. "Lunch. Then back to my house. Has there been any new information regarding the Dockside attack?"

"I wish there was, sir," Dahr said, growing grim. "Thus far, no suspects have been identified. Searches for the carriage have been fruitless. Some suspect that the attackers destroyed the vehicle to prevent it from being tied to them."

"I would probably do the same, in their place," Alistar said. "And the doctors and healers in the Lower City?"

"I do not know, sir, though I heard some talk of midcity healers making rounds in those locations that do not have ready access to a healer."

"Well, that's good to hear, at least," Alistar said.

"Not as good as if the upper ranks actually helped," Onyxflame muttered. "Do they have any idea how little it would take to push the disaffected of the Lower City into outright rebellion?"

"They know that the situation is delicate, and that it needs to be resolved quickly," Dahr said. "Thus the intense search for the culprit. Sadly, even the king's investigators cannot conjure genuine evidence out of thin air."

"And how long before they start manufacturing it if they can't find it?" Onyxflame said under his breath.

"With so many dead and injured, and people so tense? Not nearly long enough," Alistar murmured.

They ate at a small diner set solidly in the middle-class area of the city. The food was acceptable, but nothing exceptional. Dahr drove them back to Alistar's house.

As he climbed from the carriage, Alistar said, "Tonight, I assume we will have a vehicle suited to the heir of the As'enel House?"

"Of course, sir. With a fine pair of automatons, and all the luxuries," Dahr promised.

And very little need for an actual driver, Alistar added silently. "Excellent. Then we will see you at six-thirty?"

Dahr nodded. "Yes sir."

The hours passed more quickly than Alistar expected as he prepared for the evening. He'd frequently disdained the idea of a personal attendant such as many nobles in Lewarden employed, but now that he had to prepared for his first appearance in court as his father's son, he regretted not having assistance on hand. His formal clothes fit perfectly, tailored precisely to his frame and enchanted to account for the inevitable changes in weight and mass. For this occasion, he chose a dark emerald coat in the cut of a naval waistcoat—not that a naval waistcoat would ever be burdened with the embroidery and embellishments found on this one. The added weight alone would ensure that if the wearer fell overboard, they would sink like a stone.

He trimmed his beard and styled his hair, then considered the tray of cosmetics that he'd brought from Rillwater. The thought of smearing the oily stuff over his face sent a shudder down his spine, but he knew cosmetics would be expected.

Finally accepting the inevitable, Alistar walked to the guest room and knocked on the door.

"A moment, if you would," Onyxflame said. "I am... less than fully decent."

"I'll wait," Alistar told him. "I hoped to borrow use of your cosmetics again."

"Oh? Oh, if that's all, I'll bring the tray downstairs once I'm dressed. If you don't mind my saying so, I think it would be better if I applied it for you."

"If you're implying that I'm inexperienced in that area, I won't argue with you, Onyxflame," Alistar said. "Come downstairs whenever you're ready."

Onyxflame came downstairs dressed in a high-necked blue taffeta coat with heavy bronze embroidery down the front and around the cuffs. He'd paired the coat with black trousers. His shoes were polished to a shine, and a pair of silkweave gloves hung from the coat pocket. He set a large tray of cosmetic pots on the kitchen table and looked Alistar over.

"Well, you look almost ready, De'seneth," he remarked. "Shall I add the finishing touches?"

"It's a ridiculous tradition," Alistar said, pulling out a chair and sitting.

"Oh, not so much," Onyxflame said. "We can pretend that we aren't actually showing skin when we cover it with makeup. It's all part of putting on the trappings of tradition. One of the histories I read in prison said that before cosmetics became popular, nobles wore elaborate masks at court events." He mixed powders together, took a small brush, and began applying the mix to Alistar's face. "This seems like an improvement, though I've heard some staunch traditionalists still favor bringing that fashion atrocity back."

"Staunch traditionalists also favor trying to send humans 'back where we came from.' I'm sure that as soon as either we or they figure out exactly where the land of Heiset is, they will start making rumblings about how we can leave them to bring the country back to the 'good old days' before progressive ideology entered their perfect society."

Onyxflame snorted. "And would they try to send all the 'progressive' elves with the humans? Or just attempt to beat them into submission with the Tenants and the Path, on the theory that it used to work before?" He dipped the brush in water and dabbed it over Alistar's forehead. "I will say, De'seneth, I've always wondered why your people erased all traces of their origins when they came through the portal."

Alistar snorted softly. "I assure you, Onyxflame, you're not the only one. We humans have been wondering that ourselves for generations. We have theories, some more likely than others, but no facts to prove them one way or another."

"Really?" The elf cocked his head to one side, his gaze curious. "Like what?"

"Are you a scholar of history in your free time, between plotting theft and potential treason?" Alistar asked, raising an eyebrow.

"A dabbler," Onyxflame said easily. "Chirrod Prison allows prisoners not on work assignments to read books from the library, so I took up history as a hobby."

"I wouldn't have thought they had much hope of you bettering yourself," Alistar commented.

"Oh, they held no such hopes. But if I was engaged in a book, I was not engaged in something more dangerous, so they allowed it. However, the available books offered little of the human perspective of our history. What *are* the theories you think least ridiculous?"

Alistar considered. "We know that our people were fleeing from something when we traveled through the portal. One theory runs that whatever we were fleeing was a being or force so powerful that speaking its name draws its attention. Whether it was summoned intentionally or accidentally, it overran our land and destroyed our people. To ensure that no trace of its name remained to draw it to our new home, all traces of it were scoured from our past, and most of our history with it."

"An interesting theory," Onyxflame said thoughtfully. "Some sort of ethereal monster, perhaps. Still, that can't be the only plausible idea. So, what else?"

"Some theorize that our ancestors wiped all traces of the past away so that we would look forward and focus on integrating into our new home rather than on looking into the past at what we left behind." Alistar smiled wryly. "If that theory is true, then it has been singularly unsuccessful."

Onyxflame chuckled. "It would have been better if they had left a dull and uninteresting lie, in that case."

Alistar's face grew serious. "A third theory runs that our ancestors erased the past to hide something that they had done, something that they were ashamed of and wanted to hide forever. Something terrible."

"Ah…" Onyxflame nodded slowly. "I suppose that too is possible." He tilted his head thoughtfully. "Has anyone considered that the loss was not intentional?"

"That the loss was tied to the use of the gate?" Alistar asked. "Yes, it's been suggested. I'm not certain what I think of the idea.

There are just enough hints in the writings left by our ancestors to suggest that they chose to bury the past, rather than it being a side-effect. But not enough to say for certain."

"Hmm." Onyxflame picked a different pot. "Close your eyes a moment, please."

Alistar complied, and felt the brush of soft bristles over his eyelids. "Really? Eye paint is necessary?"

"From what little I've seen of nobles thus far, yes," Onyxflame said. "You didn't notice when we spoke to the Silver Prince?"

"No, Onyxflame. I really pay very little attention to other peoples' makeup," Alistar said.

"If it makes you feel better, you can get by without any lip stain. I can't; I don't have a beard. You can open your eyes again."

Alistar blinked several times. He could feel a faint something on his eyelids, but not the heavy, greasy feel he'd dreaded. Onyxflame wiped brushes clean on a cloth and put lids on all the pots. He offered the hand mirror to Alistar. "Satisfactory?"

Alistar tilted the mirror to examine his face. The cosmetics smoothed his face, and the eye paint was at least a subtle shade that complemented his coat. "Satisfactory," he allowed. "Thank you."

"A pleasure to be of service, of course." Onyxflame dipped a bow.

"Try to keep the sarcasm contained tonight," Alistar told him.

"Of course." Onyxflame flashed a pleasant smile. "Lord Aspendark is here to swindle investors into supporting his latest venture, which will undoubtedly reap rich rewards to all who pledge their support, and their money, to him. But I will accept no money until we have a proper contract written up. For the safety of my investors, of course."

"Of course," Alistar said dryly. "Also, don't accept any marriage proposals. Please."

Onyxflame blinked. "Proposals of marriage? At a first meeting? De'seneth, I want to get as far away from the nobility of Lewarden, and the Crown, as possible when this task is complete and I'm free. The *last* thing I want is to be intimately *tied* to them."

"Good." Alistar checked his watch. "Dahr should be arriving any time."

"I appreciated how neatly you inquired about our transportation and our driver earlier," Onyxflame said.

"Drivers like Dahr make me wonder why no one's yet required a permit to drive a carriage. Hired coaches need one; it would just be an expansion of the idea," Alistar said. "And include mandatory training in traffic laws, with a driving test before they receive the permit." He sighed. "But then I think that unduly harsh on those drivers who aren't lunatics." *And no permits or tests would have made a difference in the attack at Dockside.*

The bell at the door chimed. Alistar walked downstairs and opened it. Dahr stood outside, dressed in formal uniform. Behind him waited a carriage drawn by a team of horse-shaped automatons, one silver, one black. Dahr bowed formally. "Lord As'enel, Lord Aspendark, your carriage awaits." His tone was entirely serious, and Alistar realized that Dahr did, in fact, loosen up while escorting them around the city. Tonight, he was fully proper and stiff.

"Thank you," Alistar said. He waved Onyxflame to the carriage, locked his door, and followed. Dahr climbed into the driver's box, which had to be freezing, and the team started.

Inside, the carriage was comfortably warm. The seats were plush and soft enough to nap on. A chiller held a bottle of wine and a platter of cheeses. Onyxflame eyed the refreshments.

"Are court events so dull, tedious, or difficult to endure that advance fortification is necessary?" he asked.

"Not generally," Alistar answered. "However, depending on how an evening goes, some might find it necessary for the trip back home."

"Ah, of course." Onyxflame started to slouch, then straightened and sat upright, conscientious of his clothes and of not rumpling them. "If you feel the need to do so, by all means feel free. I will abstain."

Alistar waved a hand. "No need yet, certainly. And in any case, unless it's stronger than most wines, it would take far too much to achieve any palliative effects."

"Are you saying that you drink like a sailor, De'seneth? I've yet to see you imbibe anything stronger than tea."

"I'm saying that I *have* drunk like a sailor, and wine is weak compared to the bosun's moonshine. That is guaranteed to knock your socks off." Alistar smiled, recalling the first time he'd been allowed a taste of the fabled booze. The fumes alone had been enough to render him tipsy. He had no recollection of the taste. His memory had a blank spot between raising the mug to his lips and coming to on the floor, head swimming.

"Is this one of those experiences Aspendark has endured as well?" Onyxflame asked.

"Perhaps, if he cared for it. Not every sailor does, despite what the half-chip novels claim," Alistar said. "And some try it, hate it, and never take another drink of anything brewed aboard a ship."

"Good. I'll bear that in mind."

"The Narnan ships don't have similar initiations for new sailors?"

"Mine didn't." Onyxflame turned to gaze out the window. "So, tonight. Do we have a specific target or goal, or is the purpose primarily to establish ourselves and learn what we can?"

"The second," Alistar told him. "I need a sense of who our potential players are before I can start forming a case as to who might be involved. If any of the nobles really are involved, and this isn't a false lead to pull us in the wrong direction."

"And this is why I like you, De'seneth. Always full of encouragement and optimism!"

Alistar gave Onyxflame a long, wordless look. The elf simply chuckled, leaning back to enjoy the trip.

CHAPTER 25

Lord Proudmoor's estate sat along the banks of a long artificial lake, on a rise overlooking much of Lewarden. Carriages glided in and out of the long drive, down a snow-covered lane lit by ghostlights that illuminated massive ice sculptures. Some shapes were abstract, others precise to the most minute detail. The fountain in front of the house held a one-twentieth scale model of a privateer ship bobbing atop the spouting water, surrounded by a spray of icicles.

Dahr drew the carriage to a halt and opened the door. "Lords, the estate of Lord Proudmoor."

Alistar stepped down and looked the grounds over with a clinical, disinterested gaze. He did let it linger on the ship. Whoever had done the work had an eye for fine detail. Even the rigging was correct. *I wonder, was that piece originally in his plans, or did Proudmoor add it specifically for me?*

Dahr held out his hand. "Sir, allow me to present your invitations at the door."

Alistar relinquished the invitations. Dahr strode to the door, where a pair of footmen checked invitations against names on their list. A brief exchange followed, the footmen rapidly checking their lists before accepting the authenticity of the documents and returning the invitations to Dahr.

"Lord As'enel, Lord Aspendark, they await you. I will attend to the carriage and join the rest of the drivers. When you are ready to depart, the footmen will send word, and I will bring the carriage back around."

"Very well," Alistar said. "Carry on."

Giving Dahr no further notice, Alistar strode to the front door, drawing up all his presence and the air of a victorious sea captain. He cast an impatient look at the footmen. One of them scrambled to open the door with a rushed apology, which Alistar ignored. Onyxflame followed in his wake.

Inside, a liveried servant jumped to show them to the grand ballroom. The young woman kept sneaking glances at Alistar, as if trying to assess the nature of a privateer from his stance and stride.

The ballroom was a cacophony of colors, bright and dark, as nobles in their finest mingled all about the room. Musicians played on a raised stage, and a section of the room was cleared for formal dancing. Alistar handed their invitations to the herald at the door, who looked at Alistar's name, blinked, stared, then caught himself and schooled his face to blank once again before announcing them. "Lord Alistar As'enel and Lord Taslor Aspendark of Rillwater."

Most entrances drew a few glances, mild interest and curiosity. When Alistar's name was announced, a good half the room turned toward the entrance. His gut tightened for a moment. But it was no different from facing a new crew for the first time. Like a new crew, these nobles were watching him, waiting for his reactions in order to judge him and build the impressions off which their opinions of him would be founded.

His gaze moved over the room, then he swept a deep bow. "Good evening, my friends."

A tall elf in a high-necked green coat and black silkweave

When the technicians concluded, Alistar asked, "Have you observed any changes or variations in the kurowa plants since this event?"

The technicians glanced at one another. "Nothing noteworthy, Associate," one said. "We requested a botanist review the state of our flowers, and received a clean bill of health on them." After a moment's hesitation, the technician added, "Would you like to view the greenhouse, sir?"

"I would, thank you." Alistar followed the young man through the office and into the inner workings of the generator.

They walked past a wall of monitoring devices. Dials in the mechanical boxes twitched as they followed the ebb and flow of magic through the mahiy lines and the draw from all the devices fed by the lines. Soft clicks sounded on occasion, but none of the ominous, loud thunks that Alistar associated with a serious shift in the stability of a line. The temperature rose noticeably as they neared the greenhouse. The technician opened the door, releasing a wave of warm, wet air, and invited Alistar inside.

The air was heady with the scent of the kurowa flowers, and moisture beaded the walls and windows. Alistar walked down the neat, precise rows of flowers, looking for any signs of drooping leaves or changes in color. "Which section feeds into the area that was affected by the outage?" he asked.

"Here, Associate," the technician answered, indicating a section toward the far end of the room. "Row three, box five."

Each long planter box bore a label with row and number, and Alistar easily found his way to the appropriate section. The plants looked healthy enough to his eye, though the lights in the greenhouse cast a slightly green tinted sheen over everything. Alistar picked up a loose petal from the dirt and turned it over in his fingers. Nothing visibly amiss, and the greenhouse had a report of good health from the inspecting botanist. He nodded to the waiting technician.

"Thank you. I don't see anything out of order here."

pants stepped forward. His brown hair was cut short to his scalp. He dipped a small bow. "Lord As'enel. Allow me to welcome you to my home. I am honored that you could attend this evening and join in our festivities."

"Lord Proudmoor, thank you for the gracious invitation. It is my honor and pleasure to be here tonight." Alistar bowed to the lord. He'd never met Lord Proudmoor before, which eliminated much of the concern that he would immediately be recognized.

Lord Proudmoor turned to Onyxflame. "Lord Aspendark. Welcome."

Onyxflame smiled. "My thanks for this opportunity, Lord Proudmoor." Alistar caught the glint of amusement in his eyes at the contrast between the greetings they received.

With a gesture, Lord Proudmoor invited them to follow him. Or at least, he invited Alistar—his attention to Onyxflame was peripheral at best. Alistar endured a series of introductions around the room: names, titles, and faces he had little chance to fix in memory. He wasn't introduced to everyone, of course, only to those Lord Proudmoor wanted to impress. Each person Alistar spoke to was certain they possessed some vital tidbit of information that would be priceless to his father. Calling cards were pressed into his hand at the slightest provocation, and if they couldn't invent a pretense to give them to Alistar, Onyxflame became the recipient. As a newcomer to court and an unknown, Onyxflame was seen as most likely harmless, and possibly a means of access to Alistar.

Alistar smiled, politely accepting words of welcome while vigilantly avoiding saying anything that could be construed as a promise of anything. Onyxflame barely had to do that, and could easily confine himself to simply thanking overeager nobles for their consideration.

As they worked their way around the room, Alistar half-listened to the herald announcing new arrivals. Few caught his attention until he heard "Veril Lamorage of Icefall." He cast a look toward the entrance and saw his friend enter the room. Lamorage received little more than a few nods of greeting, which he returned before making his way toward the table of refreshments. He moved quickly, and carried himself as if uncomfortable and nervous.

"Lord As'enel, how long have you been in Lewarden? I hope that you will be staying through the winter." The speaker was a heavyset elf by the name of Lord Oremeld, a family that made their fortune through ownership of a number of rich mines around the country, providing the raw metals that fed the factories. Lord Oremeld's tailors were masters, fitting their patron's clothing such that it flattered his figure in spite of a bulk that was excessive even among the idle of the nobility. Lord Oremeld even managed by virtue of size and presence to finally dislodge Proudmoor from Alistar's side.

"The length of my stay will depend entirely upon the business I am conducting, Lord Oremeld. As you can imagine, my esteemed father is keenly interested in certain matters of value to our family." That was a straight lie—his father currently had no active investigations that he needed Alistar's assistance with, and his agents in Lewarden were perfectly capable of gathering any information that the Family needed.

However, Lord Oremeld nodded, his eyes crinkling and his smile knowing. "Ah, yes, of course. I understand completely. Delicate matters, these things. I can see why he would choose now to become more directly involved. I am always ready and willing to be of service. Your family has been an ally of mine many times, and I would be honored to return the favor."

"I will of course keep that in mind, sir. Thank you." Alistar nodded. He knew Lord Oremeld's reputation, and strongly doubted that his father would agree with the noble's self-assessment of his relationship with the Family. Still, his response implied that he believed something was happening in the court to warrant Alistar's presence.

Or he's playing it up just as much as I am, trawling for information to figure out why I'm here and what's important enough to draw the Family into Lewarden's court. And then once he knows that, he wants to see how he can use it. After all, it isn't like either of us have been specific about what "matter" I am here to address.

"I heard that you recently acquired a tin mine to the far north," Alistar said. "It seems the area is often overlooked because of the difficult logistics and the challenge of finding workers willing to go to such a remote location."

Lord Oremeld brightened. "Ah, yes. Truly, it is a beautiful site, rich with tin and ready for the picks. I have spoken with the Crown regarding the issue of workers, and we are testing options at the moment. Two shafts, both showing equal potential. One we are staffing with hired labor, paid nearly double the standard rate. The other is worked by convicts serving their sentence. We will track the output of both shafts and determine which method proves more profitable in the long term."

Onyxflame, beside Alistar, grew very still. "Convict labor?" he repeated. "Do you maintain the same conditions between the two crews otherwise? I have heard that often, the convicts are forced to make do with less food, worse tools and clothing, less sleep, and a blat— a tendency to overlook certain safety precautions."

Lord Oremeld shook his head. "Not at all, sir. If I am to compare the efficiency of one group to the other, the conditions should be as close to identical as possible. It is true that the convicts do not receive the same variety of food as the paid workers, and they are not permitted to leave the mine, but I firmly believe in safeguarding the lives and limbs of my workers." He considered Onyxflame. "If you are considering opportunities for investment, my mines are solid. I believe that cutting corners in the moment can only lead to disaster in the long view."

Alistar could almost have thought him sincere, if he hadn't known the patterns of deaths and injuries through other mines held by the Oremeld family. The first few years always tended to go well, lulling investors into a sense of security. Then safety standards were gradually set aside in favor of profit and expedience. He hated to think how much faster they would degenerate with convicts rather than paid workers.

"The Crown is investing in your mine?" Onyxflame asked.

Lord Oremeld hesitated delicately. "Well, of course, all legal mining operations operate with the blessing of the Crown. However the main funding for this venture comes from investors. There is great opportunity, especially for those who enter the venture from the beginning." He let the words hang a moment, in case his audience wished to lay their marks down on the spot, then continued. "Usually, the bulk of my fellow investors come from among our own ranks. However, for this mine, well over half the funds have come from outside the nobility. The rising industry here in Lewarden is allowing greater wealth to enter the general populace. I know some find it a terrifying thought, but as a man of business, I welcome fresh blood. Why, one of my largest investors is even… Ah, well, I shouldn't tell tales that would identify him. I respect the privacy of those who have trusted me with their money."

"But it sounds like a clever businessman looking for new partners might do well to look outside the insular box of the nobility," Onyxflame said, projecting interest and admiration.

Lord Oremeld beamed at him and leapt on the bait, eager to expound on the ways a clever noble might fleece middle-class investors into supporting a venture. Alistar half listened, nodding and making appropriate noises as he looked around the room.

Lamorage stood off to one side of the room with a small group of elves who wore the colors of lower nobility. He didn't look at ease, barely participating in the conversation and searched the room with the air of a man looking for an excuse to leave his present companions. He toyed with his goblet. One of his companions offered him a pouch. Lamorage accepted it with a thin smile and took a pinch of the contents, sprinkling it into his wine. The others did likewise. One of the women spoke with great enthusiasm, and gestured toward Alistar. Lamorage turned. His gaze fell on Alistar and he froze, wine glass sliding from his fingers to the floor.

It was too much to hope that a change of clothes and scenery would be enough to prevent him from recognizing me. I have to talk to him. He'll likely avoid me if he can, and given the disparity between our ranks, no one would question it. Which means that I have to corner him instead.

Lamorage stared for a long moment, then turned away, finally looking down at the goblet on the floor. A servant rushed over to pick it up and mop up the spilled wine from the tiles. Lamorage quickly turned away from Alistar and waved off the concern of his companions, then excused himself to get a new glass.

Alistar seized a momentary pause in Lord Oremeld's monologue. "Please pardon me a moment, Lord Oremeld. I've not yet had the chance to visit the refreshments our host has so generously provided, and I'm quite parched. The air in Lewarden is far drier than I am accustomed to."

Before Lord Oremeld could do more than offer a slightly puzzled nod, Alistar made his escape. Mentions of "dry air" inevitably confused natives of the capital who had never visited the coast, and Alistar took full advantage of the mystery it offered when needed. Onyxflame shot Alistar a dark look, but accepted his sacrificial role and engaged Lord Oremeld with another question about how he secured investors.

Alistar timed his arrival at the wine bar just as Lamorage ordered a fresh drink. The elf couldn't easily avoid Alistar while waiting for the server to pour. His shoulders tensed when he saw Alistar beside him.

"Lord Lamorage, wasn't it?" Alistar asked politely, presenting the fiction of a first meeting. He held out his hand. "Alistar As'enel."

Lamorage hesitated a heartbeat, but Alistar wasn't giving him any opening to politely extricate himself. He shook Alistar's hand, and Alistar noticed that, in contrast to custom, Lamorage didn't wear gloves. "Just 'sir.' My father is lord. It's… a pleasure to make your acquaintance, Lord As'enel."

"Likewise," Alistar said. He nodded at the staggering variety of bottles on display. "Any recommendations?"

Any observer would likely interpret Lamorage's unease as the natural response to someone of his low station being engaged in conversation by one who outranked him so greatly. "I… do not know your tastes, sir, but I am partial to the icewine." The server presented Lamorage with a goblet of pale blue wine, and he clutched it like a protective talisman.

"A glass of the same," Alistar told the server. His goblet came far more promptly than Lamorage's. Alistar took a sip and nodded in approval.

He stepped away from the bar, motioning for Lamorage to join him, calculating that the social dictates would force Lamorage to follow rather than risk insulting a powerful noble. No place in the room was actually private, but Alistar positioned himself away from those he knew to be among the worst gossips of his coworkers.

Alistar took another sip from his goblet. "The wine is quite good. You should have some."

Lamorage glanced at his glass, still clutched tight. "I…" He licked his lips and spoke in a barely audible voice. "De'seneth?"

Alistar nodded. "My matronym."

"Then you really are—?"

"I am," Alistar told him.

Lamorage swallowed hard. "I'll pay the marks back, I swear."

Alistar looked him in the eyes. "I'm not here to call you out on debts. What's wrong, Lamorage? You've gotten into some trouble —what is it? I want to help." Losing the marks would be a hard blow, but losing his friend would be worse.

"I need to talk to you, but not here," Lamorage said quickly, voice low. "Not here. I… need help."

"What sort of help?" Alistar asked quietly. "I can't afford to make another loan."

"Not money," Lamorage told him in a rush. He swallowed hard. "The sort of help that the As'enel family might be able to give. I can't tell you here. Someone might hear." He glanced around nervously.

Whatever's going on, it's worse than I thought. "But you will tell me," Alistar pressed.

"I will, I swear," Lamorage promised anxiously. He looked past Alistar. "Your friend is looking for you; I should—"

"He's looking for an escape from Lord Oremeld. And he can find me perfectly well," Alistar said, not willing to let Lamorage slip away so easily now that he'd finally cornered him.

Lamorage cast him a pleading look. "De'seneth, *everyone* is going to notice who you speak to tonight. What explanation can *I* possibly offer for getting the attention of the heir to Rillwater?"

"You tell them some of the truth—you made several polite attempts to disengage from the conversation, but I insisted that you stay. Tell them that I was curious about the trade of icewine." Alistar nodded at his goblet. "Besides, you didn't look like you were particularly enjoying your previous company."

"Well, no," Lamorage admitted. "They're a pretty vapid lot, to be honest. But they're good for avoiding… some other people."

Steps approached them. "I am going to pay you back for leaving me stuck listening to that bore," Onyxflame said in a low voice, inserting himself into the conversation. He nodded to Lamorage. "With apologies to you, sir, I escaped under the pretense of 'rescuing' As'enel from the horror of conversing with someone 'beneath his station.' No offense meant to you; I know As'enel initiated."

Lamorage actually smiled slightly. "If I indirectly helped you extricate yourself from Lord Oremeld, I count it no insult. I've seen his victims agree to fund his ventures just to be rid of him."

"He'd already recognized that I'm here to find victims of my own to swindle… I mean convince to invest in my proposals." Onyxflame smiled cheerfully and held out a hand. "Taslor Aspendark."

"Veril Lamorage. A pleasure." Lamorage painted a veneer of courtesy over his anxiety.

"Ah, a westerner." Onyxflame nodded. "I've heard tales of life in the western mountains. I respect anyone who can endure their winters."

Lamorage gave him a thin smile. "Many say that, sir, but in the mountains, it isn't the winters that are to be feared, even with the beasts that dwell in the darkness. Winter is for survival. It's spring, when we tally our dead, that breaks the strongest. Winter is harsh. Spring is cruel."

Lamorage rarely spoke of his home beyond that brief description. Alistar knew he'd lost relatives shortly before coming to the capital, and avoided dark spaces at all costs. "I hope that the capital is less difficult," Alistar said.

"Some times are better than others," Lamorage said, not meeting his eyes.

Before Lamorage could say more, a tall human strode to them. "Lord As'enel, such a pleasure to see you! Come, you must join us. Have you heard the latest about the Dockside incident?"

Lamorage ducked his head, seizing the opportunity to escape. "Pardon me. I'll take my leave, Lord As'enel, Lord Aspendark."

"There's no need—" Alistar started to say, but Lamorage was already retreating. Alistar cursed silently, knowing he couldn't call his friend back without drawing far too many questions. He greeted the newcomer with a nod, biting back his frustration. "I haven't heard anything but rumors about Dockside for a while. Are there new discoveries?"

A clump of nobles enveloped Alistar, leaving Onyxflame to

drift about the ballroom and mingle. Alistar hoped that the elf managed to pick up some useful tidbits, because it rapidly grew obvious that his evening would be subjected to a litany of wild, outrageous, unsubstantiated rumors and conspiracy theories. While he didn't like allowing Onyxflame free rein, he couldn't demand the elf stay at his side without attracting notice. He could only pray that Onyxflame kept his mouth shut on his more objectionable opinions.

As Alistar escaped one cluster of hangers-on and moved toward a group of young nobles, he noticed a tooled leather pouch being passed around their circle, not unlike the one he'd seen circulate through Lamorage's companions. Fragments of crystal glittered in the bottom of wine glasses as they dissolved. The pouch vanished into someone's pocket when the cluster noticed Alistar. He paused and nodded in polite greeting to them. They returned the courtesy and their conversation picked up again.

A human woman spoke in a stage whisper to the group, "I heard the Dockside incident was the work of the Successors."

The man beside her scoffed. "Successors? Those raving lunatics barely have two marks to rub together between the lot of them. Where would they get a noble's carriage and team?"

"Hear me out! They aren't all crazy." She glowered at the man. "At least some of them are pretty clever. They're quietly spreading connections into the noble houses, targeting the youth. There have been grumblings for years about how the human nobles aren't treated as equals by their elven counterparts."

"Not in Lewarden, at least," Alistar put in.

Both the woman and her companion started. The woman flushed and nodded hastily. Perhaps she recognized the bias inherent in her words—the idea that Lewarden's nobles were the only ones that actually mattered. "My apologies, Lord As'enel. I don't know if the situation is different in Rillwater. I... expect that it would be."

"It often is," Alistar told her. "But pardon my interruption. Please, continue. The Successors are trying to recruit disaffected young human nobles?"

She nodded. "Yes. And if they convinced one of them to 'loan' the Successors a carriage and team… well, it keeps the blame away from them even if the officials do identify the carriage and find the owner."

"A very interesting theory," Alistar murmured. "I had no idea that the Successors had gained such a strong following."

"Oh, they want people to *think* they just stay confined to the Hollows, but they're spreading, like rot on an apple." She scowled. "My sister almost got drawn in by some smooth talker who claimed the title of Zhrets. Can't imagine who'd ordain a Successor, but he could talk himself up."

Zhrets Vonn? Or is there more than one Successor claiming that role?

"I may have heard the fellow," a younger man said. "He does talk a good talk, though he's not keen on anyone asking exactly *how* he's going to do all the things he promises."

"You've met him?" Alistar asked.

The young man shifted uncomfortably. "No, not really. I wouldn't listen to someone like that normally. It just… I was with someone, and they wanted to hear him, so I went with them, that's all."

Of course. Most don't want to admit to involvement with a rabble-rouser. Alistar nodded, as if attending seemed perfectly reasonable. "In your place, I would have been curious as well."

The man let out a breath, relieved not to be interrogated on his reasons for attending the assembly. "Yes, yes, I was quite curious. I don't plan to make a habit of it, of course."

"But he has charisma," Alistar prompted.

The young man nodded quickly. "Oh yes, about Rechmal's justice and all the terrible things the elves have supposedly done to offend the gods. He claims the monarchy—not the Royal Family, but the system of monarchy—is an affront that needs to be replaced, so we can return to the oligarchy. Things like that." He flushed. "I apologize, sir. I shouldn't be repeating such base talk."

"I'd heard there was some unrest and disaffection in Lewarden, but I'd not realized that the Successors were involved," Alistar told him. "I appreciate your candor."

The young man cleared his throat and shook his head. "I beg your pardon, Lord As'enel. I... must take my leave." He bowed quickly and withdrew.

The hair on the back of Alistar's neck stood on end. *Someone is watching us, listening in.* That was the explanation that made the most sense. *Someone who doesn't approve of the conversation? Or someone who he recognized as being involved?*

He scanned the room, keeping his air casual and relaxed as he searched for anyone who snagged his attention. Onyxflame was engaged in conversation with a clump of young elven nobles, no doubt doing his part to corrupt the youth of the nation. One of the women had a shrill laugh that set Alistar's teeth on edge.

An awkward pause hung over the group around Alistar until another young man launched a new theory. "Some say that the carriage was driven by the Starbinder himself." His voice was hushed, but drew startled gasps from the others.

"Death doesn't drive a carriage," Alistar corrected. "Rechmal does. And his carriage is always described as plain—a commoner's or taxi coach with live horses, not a nobleman's vehicle. The whole idea is that he can pass unnoticed among us."

Everyone looked at him in surprise. "Are you sure, Lord As'enel?" the young man asked. "I'd swear I heard Lord Starbinder drove a carriage." A few heads bobbed in agreement.

Do none of them read their devotions? "If Lord Starbinder drove a carriage, I can promise you that no sailor would rejoice to see it driving across the waves."

Eyes grew wide. "Across the waves? A carriage?"

Alistar nodded. "It's not often we see it, but when we do, we know our voyage has been blessed by Rechmal."

A woman frowned dubiously. "I've heard that all sorts of odd things can wash in the waves, and sailors claim the flotsam is something else."

Alistar smiled. "That may be, milady, but flotsam doesn't explain why every magical tool aboard our ship lit up like the sun at that sighting. They still glowed when we reached port three days later."

His audience gazed at him in awe. "What about kraken? Have you seen one? Hunted one?" another woman blurted.

Alistar shook his head. "I have not. Wise sailors steer clear of a kraken's nest, and the hunting of such beasts is left to those with more recklessness than sense. The beasts can swallow a ship whole." A small exaggeration—most kraken couldn't swallow anything much larger than a fishing vessel without breaking it up first. "I have hunted whale, though." He offered a brief account of a whaling expedition, glossing over the long stretches of boredom while they searched for quarry. His audience gasped at all the right moments, and he had the sense that his tale quelled the suspicions of some who had doubted his identity.

Alistar politely declined invitations to tell more stories, and excused himself to visit the refreshments. As he perused the selection of baked cheese bites, a short human man with a pale complexion peeled away and joined him. Alistar had noticed him lingering on the edges of the previous group, though not joining the conversation.

"You should try the smoked fish, Lord As'enel. I'm told they came from Lord Proudmoor's personal ponds," the pale man said, indicating a tray with slices of smoked fish and soft cheese on thin rounds of toasted bread.

"Thank you, I will." Alistar took several and added them to his plate. "Lord Proudmoor offers a superb fare." The man had followed him, and Alistar assumed he wished to speak about something other than the food.

"Indeed, I have rarely seen better," the pale man agreed. "Though I admit, the pomp can be stifling." He watched Alistar carefully for reaction.

Agree or disagree, which answer does he want? Alistar chose a neutral answer. "It certainly has more than a similar gathering would in Rillwater. But even pomp has its place, and Lewarden is certainly not Rillwater."

"True," allowed the man. "But look around this room. Elves with elves, humans with humans. High nobility holding themselves aloof from their lesser brethren. Of everyone here, sir, I think that only you have made an effort to speak to those outside your station."

The other's position was becoming clear. "You favor a more egalitarian attitude, I take it?"

The man smiled at Alistar. "Indeed! Sadly, it is rarely found within Lewarden; tradition is firmly entrenched and difficult to break. Not like Rillwater, where the independent spirit lives free."

"Ah, we have our traditions as well," Alistar said diffidently. "I didn't catch your name?"

"I beg your pardon, Lord As'enel. Marus Ko'hut, at your service." He bowed. "I am a member of a growing assembly of nobles and business people, both human and elf, who wish to see change—an end to the divisions between us. We would be honored if you could attend some of our gatherings while you are in Lewarden. I know of no one who could teach us more about the ways of Rillwater." He drew a card from his sleeve, but didn't immediately offer it to Alistar. Casting a look around the room, he added, "I apologize for this, Lord As'enel, but I must ask that, should you join us, you not bring any guests. Certain factions do not approve of us, and as such, we must limit our gathering only to those directly invited."

Exclusive in your inclusivity, I see. That would mean no Onyxflame or Dahr. Alistar nodded slowly. "I understand." He held out his hand for the card.

"I hope to see you there, Lord As'enel." Ko'hut laid the card face-down in Alistar's palm and excused himself.

Alistar turned the card over. Rather than a name, it listed a date two nights hence and location in neat script. Alistar's name had been written on the card by another hand. No other identifying information graced the card.

Well, this is unexpected. I can see the appeal of the idea, except that to make the change they want at the pace they undoubtedly hope for would destabilize the nation. Changes of this magnitude can be quick or *stable, rarely both.* He tucked the card away. *Would they listen if I told them that? I feel like I ought to try. The capital is tense enough without adding another match to the tinder. But is it my responsibility? Do I have time?* He let out a long breath. *I can decide tomorrow, after I've slept on it.*

Alistar steeled himself and resumed mingling. He avoided the dancing—inviting anyone to dance with him would raise far more speculations than he wished to create tonight. He noticed primarily younger couples engaged in the dance, using the music and movement to disguise their whispered conversations. Their elders, on the whole, conversed and plotted without the additional exertion.

Onyxflame was all smiles and pleasantry when he found his way to Alistar, even when he leaned close and whispered, "How much longer do we have to stay here? My face is going numb from smiling and not calling every person I talk to a blithering idiot."

"We can leave soon," Alistar told him. "Have to make a final round first, though, or we'll insult a great many people, including our host."

"Oh, the tragedy," Onyxflame muttered.

"No, 'oh the scandal'," Alistar corrected. "And we are not here to draw *that* sort of attention."

Onyxflame trailed Alistar around the room, murmuring polite platitudes when necessary, but leaving most of the talking to Alistar. Lord Proudmoor gushed with repetitions of his pleasure at Alistar's attendance, offering an open invitation to future events. Alistar ignored the hints the lord dropped about how his daughter was of marriageable age. He managed to shake off the lord as he continued his circuit of the room, and reached the doors with only a few hangers-on trying to catch his attention to pass on information "vital" to the As'enel family.

The herald dispatched a runner to bring their carriage. Alistar shed the last of his followers when he reached the doors. Onyxflame breathed a soft sigh of relief when they stepped outside. The winter night air was frigid, but fresh and clear. Alistar drew a deep breath to clear his lungs of the lingering haze of perfume. He checked his pocket watch. Nearly midnight. It didn't feel so late.

They waited a few minutes for Dahr and the carriage. The footmen at the entrance offered them a space beside the heat stones, which Alistar accepted. A few other guests drifted out— they were neither the first nor the last to take their leave.

I just hope this night was productive, and that we gained something useful from it.

CHAPTER 26

Dahr brought their carriage around to the front door and assisted Alistar and Onyxflame into it with all the stiff formality of a proper driver. Once the carriage started moving, Onyxflame finally relaxed.

"I don't believe I've ever spent that much time smiling and making conversation with people I detest," the elf said. "Are these things always like this?"

"Well, after a few more times, the novelty of having the heir to the As'enel family will wear off," Alistar said.

"That's not what I mean," Onyxflame said. "Would you have called this event and the preparations for it average, or extraordinary?"

Alistar considered. "Above average, but not extraordinary for Lewarden. At least from what I've heard. This is the first I've attended since moving to the capital, though I attended at times when I was younger and visiting Lewarden with my father." He realized after a moment that Onyxflame's experiences with the nobility had never exposed him to this side of their lives, and the sheer decadence it must seem to him. "Events like this are how business is done among the nobility. Alliances are made and broken, wars are quietly waged without open bloodshed."

"And people bankrupt themselves for the 'privilege' of taking part." Onyxflame's mouth twisted with scorn.

"Sometimes," Alistar acknowledged. "Sometimes they decide, as Lamorage must have, that they cannot afford *not* to attend. How many comments did you hear about people who were absent?"

Onyxflame gave that thought. "A fair number. Lady Syri's absence generated quite a bit of speculation. The others weren't names I recognized."

"Lady Syri can weather the speculation because of who she is and the family she's part of. Most nobles aren't so fortunate. They *need* the alliances they build, and to maintain those alliances, they need to be involved. They need to be seen. They need to build the illusion of reliability."

The carriage came to a stop. Alistar frowned, knowing they'd not driven nearly long enough to reach Shale Lane. Dahr opened the carriage door. "Sirs."

"Where are we, Dahr?" Alistar asked in a low voice.

"This is a guest house that the Crown makes available to respected guests, sir. We were being followed, and I could not easily shake them. Go inside. In half an hour, a less remarkable carriage will pick you up at the back entrance and take you back to your residence. I will attempt to identify our tail."

Followed. I didn't expect that. Alistar gave a curt nod. "I understand." He checked that he left nothing in the carriage, then climbed out and walked up to the ornate front door.

Before he could knock, it swung open. A yawning boy in servant's dress rubbed his eyes as he held it open. "Evening, sirs. Th' fire's lit in th' parlor for yous." Weariness emphasized his lower-class lilt.

Dahr gave the boy a stern look. "Be attentive."

"Yessir." The boy rubbed his eyes again. "Guards gotta be awake all'a time."

Dahr glanced at Alistar. "My apologies, sir. The boy is barely a squire in the Guard, but he was available at short notice."

The explanation and Dahr's recognition of the youth eased some of Alistar's concerns. "I understand." He walked into the blessedly warm foyer. "Luck guide you, Dahr. I'll see you later."

"Of course, sir." Dahr closed the door after Onyxflame, and presumably returned to the carriage.

The young squire showed them to the parlor, where a fire burned in the hearth. Alistar settled on one of the chairs and checked his watch. Onyxflame wandered around the room, then stood in front of the fireplace, warming his hands. The squire stood around uncertainly, trying to decide whether he needed to do anything.

"Erm, yous wants som'thin to drink?" the squire finally asked.

"Water," Onyxflame said. "Cold water."

"Yessir!" The boy scampered off.

Alistar half closed his eyes and sighed. "What have you slipped into your pockets, Onyxflame?"

"Here? Nothing," Onyxflame said.

Alistar raised an eyebrow. "And before here?"

"Invitation cards, mostly. I might have acquired a handkerchief or two. A ring. Some older gentleman's little black notebook—I thought he was a little *too* interested in taking notes on any female who was less than half his age. The younger they were, the more notes he made."

"Anything else?" Alistar asked.

Onyxflame reached into his pocket and pulled out a much-folded piece of paper. "Your friend slipped this to me, asking me to give it to you with the message 'Don't trust them.' Of course, he didn't specify *who* he meant, and he took his leave shortly after. He was looking wide-eyed and jumpy. Not sure if he was drunk or something else." He handed the paper to Alistar.

Alistar unfolded the paper. Lamorage had scribbled the note hastily: "In three nights, 8:00, Dockside."

Alistar stiffened. *Dockside? Why in black shoals would he want me to meet him there? Does he know something about the attack?* He let out a slow breath. *Is he caught up with some organized criminal element in Lewarden? Are they be responsible for the attack? If we're dealing with organized crime of that level, he could well be right that he needs the sort of help that the Family can provide.* Alistar folded the note and tucked it into his vest pocket.

The squire returned with two tall glasses of water. "Here yous are, sirs."

"Thank you." Alistar took the glass when it was offered, turning it thoughtfully in his hands. He checked his watch again, disappointed to find they still had another quarter of an hour to wait. He didn't want to discuss anything confidential in front of the boy, who had resumed his restless hovering.

Onyxflame finally settled in a chair near the fire, though he didn't relax any more than Alistar did. After an eternity, a bell chimed from the back of the house. The squire jumped, head jerking up from his sleepy nodding. He looked to Alistar and Onyxflame.

"I think that should be—," he started to say.

"Our new carriage?" Alistar supplied. "I'm glad to hear it." When the boy didn't move, Alistar prompted, "Where's the back door?"

"This way." The boy led them through the house to the servants' entrance.

An unremarkable taxi carriage waited outside. The driver climbed down, pushing back her hood as she stepped into the light. Alistar recognized Star, who had picked them up the night of Technician Bar'rege's death. She nodded politely to him.

"Good evening, sir. If you're ready, I will see you back to your residence."

"We're ready," Alistar said. "Thank you for coming to get us tonight."

"Of course, sir." She opened the carriage door. "Dahr briefed me on the situation. Last we spoke, he had not identified the follower on the carriage. He hopes to have more information in the morning."

"Tell him not to come by too early," Alistar said. "This has been a long night."

Star smiled. "I'll pass the message on, sir, though I'll caution you that he's more likely to find a sheltered place to wait and watch your house for signs of activity."

Alistar groaned and waved Onyxflame into the carriage ahead of him. "In that case, tell him to let himself in. He still has my spare key. He can at least stay warm." He stepped up into the carriage.

Star closed the door and climbed into the driver's seat. Alistar settled onto the bench. The exterior of the carriage looked like an ordinary taxi. The interior, however, held warming stones to drive off the chill, padded benches, lap blankets, and even a small chest with bread and preserves. Alistar ignored the food in favor of pulling a lap blanket over his legs and closing his eyes.

"So, De'seneth, what do we do with tonight's gleanings?" Onyxflame asked.

"I'll go through all the cards tomorrow. Might make Dahr run errands and deliveries." He opened one eye. "We need analyses run on both sets of crystals. Find out if they are the same drug. Find out if they both *are* drugs. What sort of tools would that take?"

Onyxflame raised an eyebrow. "What, Silverline Power doesn't have its own analysis experts?"

"Of course it does. But given how certain important pieces of information have mysteriously disappeared at various points during this investigation, I want a contingency plan." Alistar looked pointedly at the elf. "What tools would you need?"

"I'll make a list of my ideal equipment, and acceptable substitutes," Onyxflame said. "After I've had some sleep." He stretched his jaw in an exaggerated yawn.

"First thing in the morning, so I can send Dahr out to collect them when he delivers samples to Silverline," Alistar told him.

Conversation lapsed. Alistar looked out the window as the dark streets rolled past. He fingered the folded note in his pocket. *How deep in trouble is Lamorage? Can I give him the help he needs? The Family's influence in Lewarden isn't that strong, my presence notwithstanding. And why does he want to meet at Dockside? I'm not going there without backup.*

The carriage rolled to a stop outside his house. Star opened the door. "No sign of anyone following us, sir."

"Thank you." Alistar climbed from the carriage, feeling the weight of weariness in his steps. "Good night, Star. Thank you for bringing us back."

"Of course, sir." She waited until Alistar had unlocked the door and entered his house before she climbed back into the driver's box and turned the team down the street.

Alistar locked the door. Onyxflame headed straight for the guest room with a muttered, "If I never have to wear these clothes again, it'll be too soon."

"No, next time you'll have to wear a different outfit," Alistar said, climbing the stairs after him. "Otherwise, people will notice."

Onyxflame didn't respond to that. Alistar warded the guest room after Onyxflame entered, then retired to his own waiting bed.

In spite of his best efforts, Alistar rose only a little later than usual. He took his time with his morning routine before leaving his room, canceling the wards on Onyxflame's room, and descending the stairs.

Entering the kitchen, he had a heartbeat of alarm, seeing a tall elf sitting at the table, before Dahr jumped to his feet. "Sir! My apologies for intruding."

Alistar relaxed and waved the apology away. "No reason you should wait outside in the cold when you have a key to the house. Please, sit. Would you like tea?"

"Thank you, sir. I would appreciate it." Dahr settled back onto the chair.

Alistar filled two mugs with hot water and brought them with the tea tray to the table. "Any luck identifying last night's followers?"

Dahr selected a mild tea and lowered the infuser into his mug. "The carriage belongs to one Lady Sunward. Despite the surname, she is a human, adopted into an elven household and named as heir. Rumor claims she is in search of a suitable husband, and implies that she is willing to use aggressive tactics to pursue her goal."

"Sunward," Alistar repeated, frowning as he brewed his tea. "I don't remember if I met her last night, though I'd think I would remember a human with an elven surname. I'll watch out for her, especially if she's trying to stalk me."

"I am looking into the matter still, sir, in case this is a false trail," Dahr said. "I do not at this point want to say for certain that the lady is responsible."

Alistar sipped tea and nodded. *We're all growing paranoid, aren't we?* "Dahr, I'd like you to take samples of both the drug we received at Thornguard Generator and Tatya's candy, and have them analyzed at Silverline Power."

"Of course, sir," Dahr said promptly.

"I'll also need you to pick up some tools, depending on what Onyxflame says he needs to do the same here."

Dahr frowned. "Are you sure you want to do that, sir?"

"I want at least two separate analyses of the samples, Dahr. I don't want the results to be 'accidentally' lost somewhere along the way."

The guard nodded grimly. "Understood."

Steps descended the stairs. Onyxflame looked into the kitchen, worn but alert. "It must be another fine morning in Lewarden. Engineers and royal guards are up before the sun."

"It's winter. The sun comes up late," Alistar replied. "Do you have the list of tools?"

"Preferred tools and the alternates that will suffice if necessary." Onyxflame proffered a sheet of parchment to Alistar.

Alistar scanned it, frowning. "Half your 'preferred' tools are illegal."

"I work best with what I know," Onyxflame said breezily. He retrieved a mug and made himself tea. "On the alternates, I noted specific models and years on some items. I will need those precise specifications—those models contain particular features necessary for me to analyze the samples."

Alistar nodded slowly and handed the list to Dahr. "Use the Silver Prince's authority to requisition Onyxflame's tools. And to speed the analysis, if anyone raises a protest about priorities and queues." He pulled the Silver Prince's badge from his pocket. "Will you need this?"

"Not necessary, sir," Dahr told him. "Thank you. If you have the samples, I will accost the analysts at once. I've found it most effective to catch them shortly after they arrive at work. They are more easily intimidated when they're still waking up."

Onyxflame looked at him in surprise. "And I thought His Highness's guards weren't allowed to possess a sense of humor."

Alistar handed a leather pouch to Dahr. "The samples."

Dahr tucked the pouch into his breast pocket. "Do you need anything else at the moment, sir? And do you expect to be home today, or will you be going out?"

"I don't have plans to go out at this point," Alistar told him. "We need to review contacts made last night and see who thought it worth their time to try and get my attention. Thank you, Dahr."

"Of course, sir." Dahr offered a slim metal key. "Your house key."

"Hang onto it," Alistar told him. "It's come in handy once, it might be useful again." He didn't judge Dahr to be a man who would enter another's home on a whim, key or not.

After Dahr left, Alistar and Onyxflame finished their respective mugs of tea. "Bring all the calling cards you received up to my study. I want to review last night."

Onyxflame patted his pocket. "They're here. I'm ready at your convenience."

The elf followed Alistar upstairs. Alistar cleared space on his desk, tucking documents into the drawers and quickly checking that nothing too valuable lay in easy reach of Onyxflame. Onyxflame pulled out the calling cards and dealt them out on the desk like playing cards.

"Most of the names, I don't know," he said. "Which makes their claims of importance suspect. I knew the important houses in Lewarden, and I don't think they would have changed *that* much in a few months. Wasn't interested in fleecing anyone but the best and biggest. It doesn't make as much of a flash to pick easy targets."

Alistar scanned the names. He recognized many from the gossip at work. "A couple of these are coworkers of mine. Seems some people really don't see past different clothes and a different context."

"Or they think the humans of Rillwater are a little *too* closely related and all look alike," Onyxflame said. "I heard a couple of very politely worded implications to that effect last night."

Alistar rolled his eyes. "I wish I was surprised."

"I slightly less politely corrected those allegations, while assuring those who spoke them that I was *sure* they didn't intend to offend the privateers and families of Rillwater who risk their lives to supply us with so many luxuries," Onyxflame added. "That's the first time I've gotten to make nobles gape like fish on land without someone slugging me for it."

Alistar's lips quirked in a smile. He laid out his own collection of cards. Unlike Onyxflame's, his held a mix of upper and lower nobility, with more noteworthy names.

Onyxflame sighed. "De'seneth, if we were competing, you by far won in terms of prominence, though I think I lead in numbers. So, this leads us into the long game—building connections and worming our way into the heart of things. Where to start?" He looked over Alistar's cards, frowned, and picked up the one from Marus Ko'hut. "Well, this looks very mysterious."

"Ah, yes. I was invited to an 'exclusive' gathering of egalitarian-minded individuals who want to bring change. Or so the gentleman claimed," Alistar said. "I'm undecided at this point."

"Change like taking control of the city's power away from the Silver Prince?" Onyxflame suggested.

"I don't know anything more about them yet. Perhaps I should go to this event, at least get a sense of who they are and what their actual goal is." Alistar looked to Onyxflame. "Unfortunately, you weren't included in the invitation."

"Alas, my social life shall suffer terribly for the loss, I'm sure," Onyxflame sighed dramatically. He considered the rest of the cards. "A shame we don't know who among them might be channelers."

Alistar blinked. "I should have thought of that." He pulled Dahr's speaking stone from his pocket and activated it.

Dahr answered promptly. "Yes sir? I haven't yet arrived at Silverline Power." Sounds of traffic echoed in the background.

"Would you pick up a list of all the registered channelers in the city, Dahr? Ideally categorized by class, but at the very least with the nobles called out specifically," Alistar said.

Dahr didn't even hesitate. "Of course, sir. I will have it to you with all possible haste."

"After you've finished the other errands," Alistar told him. "We can progress without it for now."

"Yes sir. Is there anything else?"

"Not at the moment. I'll let you know if that changes," Alistar told him. "Thank you."

"Of course, sir."

Alistar deactivated the stone and returned it to his pocket. Onyxflame gazed at him, expression unreadable. Alistar raised a questioning eyebrow at the elf.

"Silverline Power engineers can request and be given the names of every channeler on record in the city," Onyxflame said, voice flat.

"No, but someone with the Silver Prince's favor can," Alistar answered. "And I wouldn't do so if it wasn't relevant to this investigation. You suggested it, I might add."

"That was an idle wish, not an expectation that we could pry into the private lives of every citizen of the city!" Onyxflame scowled.

"Welcome to the life of an investigator," Alistar said. "Where prying into other people's lives is not just an expectation, but sometimes a requirement. And the list will only tell us who the *registered* channelers are. Those who have kept it hidden won't be included."

"Oh, how encouraging. I'm sure no one would find ways to use that information for ill." Onyxflame continued to scowl.

"I'm sure Prince Cero would be delighted to hear your opinion, Onyxflame. Why don't you take the issue up with him?" Alistar said, irritated.

Onyxflame pressed his lips together in silence.

Neither of them spoke for a few long minutes. The silence was broken by a knock on the front door. Alistar's brow furrowed. "Too soon for Dahr to be back."

Onyxflame followed him out of the office and lingered at the top of the stairs as Alistar descended to the door and opened it. "Yes?"

A gangly young man in the tan uniform of the delivery guild stood outside. "Package for Mr. De'seneth, sir!"

"I'm De'seneth," Alistar told him.

The young man proffered a ledger, and Alistar signed his name to accept the delivery. The young man darted back to his handcart and picked up a hefty wooden crate. Alistar stepped aside and let him set it just inside the door, then offered a pair of chips as a tip.

"Thank you kindly, sir!" The chips vanished into the young man's pocket. He nodded to Alistar and took hold of his cart, heading for his next destination.

CHAPTER 27

Alistar walked slowly inside. Onyxflame lingered on the stairs, gaze curious. Alistar closed the door and waited for snide or sarcastic comment, but Onyxflame offered none. Instead, the elf asked, "Do you know who sent the package? Given the current events, I'd be concerned." His tone offered no levity.

Alistar checked the markings on the crate. "No such worries. It came from home, and it hasn't been tampered with. The seals are unbroken, and are not forged."

"You're certain?" Onyxflame asked.

"Completely," Alistar said. "The Family takes caution and paranoia in sending messages to a level where it could be an art. This package has not been tampered with."

The crate didn't weigh as much as he expected, and though it was a little awkward to carry up the stairs, Alistar managed without Onyxflame's assistance. They returned to the study and Alistar cracked the seals. The straw that lined the crate for packing smelled like home, salty with a lingering smell of fish. The fish odor was explained when he found a large package of salted cod and another of smoked salmon nestled in the straw. Alistar grinned, though Onyxflame's nose wrinkled.

"What *is* that?"

"One of Rillwater's specialties," Alistar told him. "As Aspendark undoubtedly already knows."

"If you say so," Onyxflame said dubiously. He looked into the crate. "And those?"

Alistar removed three cases of cigars. "The finest imports, fresh from the ship."

"You smoke?" Onyxflame asked.

"Rarely." Alistar slid one of the boxes open and extracted a slip of parchment. The smell of cedar and tobacco scented the air as he closed it again.

Onyxflame considered the parchment. "I'm sure there are less expensive ways to send messages."

"The cigars are bribes and gifts as I might need them for making acquaintances. I accepted when my father offered to send some. The messages simply take advantage of a package already bound my way." Alistar drew the pieces of parchment from the other two boxes as well, then set the cigars aside on the desk. He looked down into the crate and ran his fingers through the straw, checking for anything else inside. He encountered cloth, and pulled out a bundle tied with twine. One eyebrow rose when he saw a tag on it with the name "Aspendark." "This one's for you."

"For me?" Onyxflame frowned, accepting the bundle. He picked loose the twine and unfolded an oiled cloak. Nestled inside the cloak lay a shirt and trousers, loose fitted and cut in Rillwater fashion, both a deep blue color. Onyxflame gave the clothes a puzzled look, then unfolded the tag. His brow remained furrowed in confusion as he read, "You left these behind. Rozika."

"Rozika is Aspendark's bastard sister," Alistar reminded him. "And those clothes are what Aspendark would wear on a regular day in Rillwater."

"Aspendark wears *wool*?" Onyxflame examining the underlayer of the cloak, scandalized.

"It doesn't carry the stigma of abject poverty that it does in

Lewarden. Synthetic textiles aren't easy to come by in Rillwater. Wool keeps a person warm even when it's wet—and I assure you, winter in Rillwater is nothing if not wet. Most people can't afford seal or otterskin. And if you judge just by the look, it's difficult to tell that it's not fur."

Onyxflame was silent for a moment, then sighed, "Who do I owe, and how much?"

"How much does Aspendark owe?" Alistar asked.

"No, De'seneth, how much do *I* owe? For this." Onyxflame patted the clothes. "Someone chose to include this in your package."

"It's an investment, not a debt," Alistar told him. "My family has a vested interest in my success, and thus, a vested interest in making sure Aspendark has the support he requires."

"Ah. So it's a reminder that they have an eye on me."

"If you care to interpret it that way," Alistar said. "I didn't think you were in danger of forgetting your circumstances."

"De'seneth, your family has something of a reputation," Onyxflame said. "A pointed reminder that I do not wish to fall out of their good graces is hardly outside that reputation, whether you think it necessary or not." He fingered the cloth of the shirt. "Although there might also be recognition on their part that His Highness is unlikely to have supplied me with clothing suitable for stealth, as this is."

"Are you done overanalyzing a gift?" Alistar asked.

"Oh, no, I'll be overanalyzing it for days. But I'll do so quietly," Onyxflame answered.

"That will have to do," Alistar said. He unfolded one of the parchments from the cigar boxes. At the top of the page, the name "Oremeld" was written in his mother's script. The several paragraphs that followed sounded politely supportive of the lord if one didn't know the Family's code phrases, which painted an entirely different picture.

They'll want to know about his latest venture in the north. Mother suspects that Oremeld is looking for something less innocuous than tin, regardless of what the lord claims they're mining there.

Setting aside the parchment, Alistar grabbed the portfolio from the botanist and extracted the report on the outage at Redpine. "These are the records from the Hollows outage. Thoughts?" He passed the sheets to Onyxflame.

Onyxflame gave them a puzzled look. "What am I looking at, De'seneth?"

Alistar pointed. "The graph shows activity on the mahiy lines and sources. Red line is the power supplied by Redpine. Blue is activity on the lines. Redpine is the only generator connected to the Hollows, though if there were others, they would each be a different color."

"All right," Onyxflame said slowly. "So, where the blue line drops and the red line spikes, that's the outage? And then, where the red line drops off, they shut off power to the Hollows?"

Alistar nodded.

Onyxflame followed the lines. "Then what are these small spikes? Attempts to restore power? But if so, they should be red lines, not blue, shouldn't they?"

"If they originated from the generator, they should be, yes," Alistar agreed.

"But if they didn't originate from the generator, how is there activity on the lines? That would require another source of power." As the words left Onyxflame's mouth, he grew suddenly still, face losing expression.

Alistar watched him. "You know something."

Onyxflame shook his head quickly. "No. I don't, and the more I think on it, the less I can even guess. I don't want to hazard a theory on this, De'seneth. I'm better working with what I know."

"Very well," Alistar said, biting back frustration. "What sort of workspace will you need to examine the samples, Onyxflame?"

"Your housekeeper is liable to object if I take over your dining room table, so really, I just need some space to work and access to magic." Seeing Alistar's eyes narrow, Onyxflame quickly added, "Magic for the tools, that is. A table in the sitting room, perhaps? It certainly doesn't look like you use the room for anything."

"I don't entertain much," Alistar said. "That should work well enough."

"I might need your help with some of the equipment," Onyxflame said. He tapped a wrist. "The prison's dampeners interfere with magic-powered tools to a degree, and I might not be able to get the necessary precision. You'll want to monitor my work anyway." He considered Alistar. "Out of curiosity, what will you do if my results differ from those of the Silverline analysts?"

"A good question," Alistar acknowledged. "On one hand, they are experts, highly trained, while you're a criminal. On the other hand, you've seen someone die from Rat's Disease, and if this drug is the source, I suspect you have more reason than many noble-born to want it gone from the Lower City and slums. To say nothing of the fact that I can actually watch you and see how you get your results."

"So it depends on the divergence, then." Onyxflame shrugged. "All right." He stood. "I'll leave the political machinations to you, De'seneth. I'd like to set up my workspace."

"Staring at calling cards won't give me answers yet." Alistar got to his feet. "I'd rather do something productive."

They moved most of the furniture up against the walls of the sitting room, leaving the center clear. With grunts and curses, Alistar and Onyxflame hauled a sturdy wooden table up from the laundry room. Alistar briefly considered offering the laundry room as an alternate location for the work, but it simply didn't have the space to move around comfortably.

By the time a knock sounded on the front door, they'd arranged the sitting room as a workspace for Onyxflame with table, chairs, and an assortment of glass bottles for mixing and heating samples. As an alchemist's lab, it was unimpressive, but

Onyxflame expressed satisfaction before following Alistar to the stairs.

When Alistar opened the door, Dahr stood outside, a hefty crate beside him. "The equipment Aspendark requested, sir."

"Thank you. We just finished setting up in the sitting room." Alistar held the door for him.

Dahr picked up the crate and grunted thanks. Onyxflame voluntarily helped him carry it up the stairs and into the sitting room. Like a child presented with wrapped gifts, Onyxflame pried open the lid and peered inside. He blinked and looked at Dahr, then Alistar in surprise.

"You said most of the items on my preferred list were illegal, De'seneth!"

"When someone with the Silver Prince's blessings and authority requisitions tools, people are willing to overlook certain inconvenient protocols," Dahr said, voice mild. "I only found it necessary to substitute one item from your secondary list, and that because the preferred item could not be located. Use these tools wisely."

Onyxflame didn't answer, focused on unpacking his new tools and setting them up on the table. Alistar could identify barely half of them. Though he'd recognized the names of the tools on Onyxflame's list, he'd not worked with them, and rarely seen them.

Dahr cleared his throat. "Sir, the list you requested will be available shortly after noon. And the samples you provided for Silverline analysis are being tested as we speak. I have assurances that they have been given highest priority."

"Thank you, Dahr. I appreciate your help," Alistar said.

"It's my duty, sir," Dahr told him quickly. "No need for thanks." He turned to Onyxflame. "Do the tools meet your needs, Onyxflame?"

"Oh, they do indeed," Onyxflame murmured. "I don't suppose I can keep them once this is all done and settled?"

Dahr just gave him a scowl in answer.

"Didn't think so," Onyxflame said. He set up a magnifying scope, adjusting the dials while peering into the eyepiece. "Oh, this is very nice. De'seneth, could I see the samples at your convenience?"

"Which do you want to examine first?" Alistar asked. "Tatya's candy or the technician's stash?"

Onyxflame paused. "The technician's."

Alistar looked over the equipment Onyxflame had set up, and admitted that his sitting room was starting to look far more like an alchemical or arcane laboratory. The magnifying scope occupied one corner of the table, surrounded by small cases holding lenses of different magnification. Onyxflame fitted on the highest magnification, readjusting the focus with care.

A mortar and pestle sat beside a stack of sample jars. A rack beside the jars held small vials of chemicals. Next, Onyxflame had arranged a series of heating rings on stands, each set to a different temperature. The rings were sized to hold and evenly heat the sample jars. Everything Dahr had brought was of the highest quality, if the makers' stamps were any indication.

At the other end of the table stood devices Alistar couldn't readily identify, but judging by shape and design, he assumed the first served to record fluctuations in magic, and possibly changes in temperature as well as other shifts. Such a tool had been on Onyxflame's list, and fell into a gray area in regards to legality—while it was not exactly illegal, few people could successfully justify a need to have access to one outside of Silverline Power. It was normally paired with another device to display the readings, but Onyxflame had neglected to include the display on his list, and appeared unconcerned by the absence.

Alistar fished a small piece from the pouch with his handkerchief and set it in one of the shallow bowls Onyxflame had laid out on the table. Dahr stood back and leaned against the wall, arms folded. Onyxflame picked up the sample with a small pair of metal tongs and set it under the scope. He peered at it intently for several minutes, a frown tugging at the corners of his mouth. Alistar withheld his questions, though he wanted to pepper Onyxflame with them.

After several minutes of intense study, Onyxflame looked over to Alistar. "Are there more samples available, or will this be all I have to work with? I'd like to experiment, but will be limited by the supply, and don't want to risk destroying the sample if this is all I have."

"There are more samples," Alistar told him. "Though kindly refrain from blowing up my house."

"I will do my best to accommodate you, De'seneth," Onyxflame promised cheerfully. "Now, where did I put the mortar and pestle... ah." He put the sliver of crystal into the pestle and ground it to a fine powder. "Interesting consistency. I expected it to be more difficult to crush." He examined the powder under the scope, frowning again, then carefully spooned measured doses of powder into four sample jars. "Starting with the basics, let's see if, and how, it reacts to the humors."

The elf checked and double-checked labels before adding a few drops of liquid into the sample jars. "Phlegm—no reaction. Bile—no reaction. Black bile—no reac... Hmm, maybe something. Blood—perdition!" Onyxflame's arm jerked and he exclaimed sharply in pain, nearly dropping the vial of blood.

"Onyxflame?" Alistar stepped toward him, and Dahr pushed away from the wall.

"Sample—watch the sample!" Onyxflame snapped, voice shrill. He dropped the vial into its rack, then shook his arm and massaged his wrist. "Damned prison wards bit like I was trying to play with magic. Perdition!"

In the sample jar, the powder dissolved rapidly in the drops of blood. The sides of the jar grew hazy, as if covered with a violet film. Alistar glanced quickly at the other jars, where little to no reaction occurred. The powder didn't even dissolve, just floated in the liquid, although it seemed to be very slowly dissolving in the black bile.

"Are you all right, Onyxflame?" Alistar asked once the muttered cursing stopped.

"I'll live," Onyxflame said. "But it felt rather like touching the door after you've warded the room." He shook out his arm again. "And what in Rechmal's Oath is it doing?" He warily studied the sample jar.

"Filling with purple smoke," Dahr said. "What's it supposed to do?"

"Damned if I know," Onyxflame retorted. "The whole point of this is to see how it reacts. Could one of you hand me a stopper?" Alistar found a stopper and offered it to Onyxflame. The elf reached toward the sample jar, then stopped short with another hiss of pain. "Would you be so kind, De'seneth? The wards seem quite opposed to this reaction."

Alistar capped the jar. None of the haze crept out of the sample jar yet, but it was continuing to grow thicker in the bottom of the container. He frowned. "I don't believe the warden said anything about your restraints that would explain them reacting to this."

Onyxflame offered a thin smile. "Believe me, De'seneth, if I knew why they did this, I would be the first to tell you."

"The reaction you describe resembles the manner in which the inhibitors are designed to respond to someone attempting to channel," Dahr said. He eyed Onyxflame. "However, I've seen no indications that you are or have ever been able to channel."

"Even if I could, I'm certainly not stupid enough to try doing so here and now in front of you," Onyxflame said. He wiped his hands on a rag and let out a long breath. "All right, leaving that uncomfortable mystery aside, let's see how Tatya's candy looks in comparison."

Alistar harbored some doubts about the wisdom of proceeding, but gave Onyxflame a small piece of Tatya's grimy treasure.

The elf studied it under the scope as he had the first. Alistar wiped out the mortar and pestle to avoid contamination from the first sample. Onyxflame nodded in thanks and began to grind it down to powder.

"It's not quite the same look or texture," he said. "Similar to the first one, but the dirt from Tatya's pockets isn't enough to explain the variances I saw." He took another four sample jars and measured in scoops of powder. "Um, De'seneth, could I trouble you to add the humors this time? Four drops apiece."

Alistar nodded, understanding Onyxflame's desire to not face another reaction from his wardings. He followed the same order Onyxflame had used. The first three samples didn't react. When he dripped the blood into the final sample jar, thick purple smoke formed immediately, and even several steps back, Onyxflame gave a sharp hiss of discomfort. Alistar grabbed a stopper and capped the jar as the smoke filled it.

"It's darker than the first," Dahr said. Even his face showed worry.

"And more reactive," Alistar said, stepping back from the table. He wasn't sure whether or not he imagined heat radiating from the jar.

Cracks spidered across the sample jar. Alistar raised a hand protectively, but as abruptly as it started, the reaction concluded. The violet smoke swirled inside the jar, but the cracks spread no farther, and the glass did not shatter. Everyone waited several long moments before finally relaxing.

Onyxflame cleared his throat. "It appears that both samples react strongly to blood. Which makes me wonder what it feels like when someone ingests it. It looks like it would be uncomfortable, but people don't generally indulge in drugs to feel like their blood is boiling." He frowned, eyes distant.

Alistar looked at the smoke still swirling inside the jar. "Following our theory that the thefts of magic from the mahiy lines is somehow connected to any of this, the smoke is similar in color to the mahiy lines. Which may or may not mean anything."

Onyxflame's gaze snapped to him sharply, then to the jar. His jaw tightened. "Yes. That does make one wonder." Collecting his wits, he cautiously reached toward the sample jar. "No response from the wards now that the reaction has concluded."

"The act of channeling is the drawing of power from the mahiy lines through a vessel," Alistar mused. "A channeler uses their body as the vessel, while our devices are artificial vessels. The wards interfere with the movement of magic through the vessel. If, perhaps, traces of magic are released when the drug reacts, Onyxflame's wards might have interpreted the sudden presence of loose power as an act of channeling."

Both Onyxflame and Dahr looked at him in speculative surprise.

"Just thinking out loud," Alistar said, waving the thought aside.

"No, please continue," Onyxflame said. "It's a premise worth following." He looked speculatively at the jar. "Raises the question of whether the magic's presence is intentional or accidental. If accidental, I'd like to see their process to find out exactly how they achieved this."

"And if it's intentional?" Alistar asked.

"If it's intentional, we have much larger problems than political intrigue. The only person I know of who could have achieved such results intentionally is dead."

"Dead criminals have an uncanny knack for turning up alive when it's least convenient," Dahr said.

Onyxflame's jaw tightened, and his voice went flat. "There was nothing 'convenient' about that death, Dahr. If they were alive, we would not be having this conversation."

Did Onyxflame have a partner? Rumors always claimed that he worked alone. But it would make sense. He claimed responsibility for plenty of crimes that, while not impossible to do alone, would have been made far easier with a second person. Alistar filed that bit of information into his assessment of Onyxflame. *If there was a partner, they had to be willing to stay completely in the background, never getting any of Onyxflame's accolade or notoriety.*

Onyxflame left the samples and moved to the recording device. He carefully shimmied the right side panel off, exposing the guts of the device. Alistar looked inside, but didn't know enough about what he was seeing to know what Onyxflame sought to learn.

"You could have included a display in your request," Alistar told the elf.

"Never had opportunity to use one, so I wouldn't know what I was looking at if I had one," Onyxflame said. "Normally, I have to work with what's available. When you must, you find creative solutions." He reached into the recorder and put his finger to a small gear, stopping its turn. Other gears spun in response, whirling faster.

"If you break it—" Alistar began.

"I'm doing the same thing a display would do," Onyxflame said. "Triggering the device to announce its readings. And Dahr, this was calibrated when you got it, wasn't it?"

"It was calibrated until you opened it up and stuck your hand inside," Dahr said.

"I'm nowhere close to the calibration dials," Onyxflame said. "But if these readings are accurate, the reactions released far more than 'trace' amounts of magic. Tatya's candy also released noteworthy heat and measurable toxins. Not enough to be dangerous to us once it dissipated in the air, but if the rest of the sample contained the same level of toxins, it could do some harm to a person." Onyxflame frowned. "But neither sample released residue that matches any drugs I've seen."

"Which tells us what?" Alistar asked.

"Which tells us that if this is a drug, it's something completely revolutionary," Onyxflame said. "And that, to me, indicates that it's not easy to produce, or someone would have done so before now. Which leads me to the question of why it's being sold in the slums. They would make *far* better profit marketing it to disaffected nobles, or at least upper-class commoners." He looked to Alistar. "Could be poor marketing strategy, but from what we've seen so far, ignorance and lack of planning or vision do not seem to be among their faults."

Alistar nodded slowly. "They have at least some presence in the middle class, since the technician came into possession of the drug. Perhaps the effects are more appealing to the lower classes? Or they are still working out how to not kill people with it." Neither sounded convincing to him, and from Onyxflame's raised eyebrow, the elf was dubious as well. *But if all this is intentional, part of some larger scheme, what is their goal?*

CHAPTER 28

After the initial excitement, the rest of Onyxflame's tests continued without incident. Alistar observed, though there wasn't much for him to watch. Onyxflame remained pensive. He answered when Alistar or Dahr asked questions, but volunteered little.

Early in the afternoon, Alistar sent Dahr out to pick up lunch for them. A little while after he left, Onyxflame said, "I don't like what I'm seeing, De'seneth."

"Details," Alistar said.

"Tatya's candy is riddled with impurities. Toxic impurities. Might not kill a healthy person immediately, but they could. And a child? Almost certainly." Onyxflame slid one dish of powder toward Alistar. "Our fine, solidly middle-class technician, on the other hand, offers us a sample without those impurities. Clean and refined."

"And you waited until Dahr left to say this, why?" Alistar asked.

"Because anything I say in his hearing *will* reach the ears of the Silver Prince. I trust your discretion." Onyxflame waved Alistar to the scope. "Take a look. Tell me if you see any familiar patterns."

Alistar frowned and looked through the eyepieces at the powder Onyxflame had left on the plate. "Well, it has a solid crystal structure. Interesting shape. Looks similar to sketches I've seen of naturally occurring—" Alistar trailed off, frown growing deeper. He straightened and turned to Onyxflame.

"Naturally occurring…?" Onyxflame prompted.

"Formations of magic crystals," Alistar finished. "Very rarely found around patches of kurowa flowers. Of course, anyone stupid enough to ingest such crystals—and yes, people have tried —poisons themselves on magic, usually manifesting in spontaneous combustion."

"So I've read," Onyxflame said. The elf pointed to the two sealed vials. Purple smoke still swirled within them. "But unless you can tell me what *else* that can be, you have my hypothesis. Magic, somehow distilled and diluted enough to not poison immediately, being used as a blighted *drug* for Reyker only know what purpose."

"What in blood and sand would be the *point* to doing so?" Alistar demanded. "It's ridiculous."

"Let's hear your theory, then," Onyxflame countered.

"No theories until I hear what the Silverline analysts say," Alistar said. He could see, after a fashion, how Onyxflame could interpret his results into his outlandish hypothesis. Alistar was not willing to leap to the same conclusion without some manner of corroboration from experts.

"And when they tell you that you've given them pieces of rock candy, absolutely nothing dangerous or abnormal?" Onyxflame sneered.

"My ship, Onyxflame, not yours," Alistar warned.

"Fine, I'll just go back to mopping the deck then, shall I?"

"Or you could look at what alternative theories might explain some of your findings," Alistar said. "Humor me."

Onyxflame rolled his eyes with a long-suffering sigh. "Fine. But you strong-armed my service because I *am* the expert on criminal use of magic, De'seneth. It might behoove you to at least *consider* the theory said expert offers."

"It will be considered." Alistar's voice was flat.

Onyxflame didn't push the matter further, but the elf's displeasure showed in his movements as he returned to his experiments.

If there is anything to Onyxflame's theory, what does it mean politically? Who benefits from stealing magic from the lower classes, then using that magic to make a drug that kills them? Monetary profit seems unlikely, and murdering your clients doesn't lend itself to repeat sales.

"Waste," Onyxflame said suddenly.

"What?" Alistar turned to him. The elf had said it like an answer rather than a curse.

"Waste," Onyxflame repeated. "That's the difference between the samples. De'seneth, I studied the workings of mines, when I assumed that I was going to be dying in one. Miners dig up ore, but before a chunk of rock can be useful, it has to be refined. Once it's refined, you have the pure product, and you have waste —all the impurities, and a lot of toxins from the refinement process. Did you know that the wastes from refinement processes are the second most common cause of death in a mine, after collapses?" He pointed toward the sample of Tatya's candy. "Whether or not you believe me that this 'drug' is a crystallized form of magic, it's going through a process to filter the dross from the pure. One kills you, one doesn't. One gets sold to the upper classes, the other is sold or given to the people no one's going to miss. How's *that* for a second theory?"

"Disturbingly believable," Alistar said after a long moment. "But they would have to be aware that people *will* notice when the poor start dropping from a mysterious illness. Blackened shoals, people *have* noticed! They've given it a name; it's not going unnoticed."

"But what's anyone with authority *doing* about it, that's the question," Onyxflame shot back. "You want to be the one who orders the entire Lower City put under quarantine right before the Ice Blossom Festival? Especially after the Dockside incident?"

"There's no need for quarantine if the cause is this drug," Alistar said quickly.

"Do you really expect everyone to believe that's the cause?" Onyxflame asked. "Get a few vocal people to stir up a panic, and it doesn't matter what the truth is, because some noblewoman just has to start screaming that without protection from those dirty, foul poor people, her children are going to die horrible deaths from this disease. Who do you placate? The unwashed masses or those of your own class?" Onyxflame paused. "And I don't mean *you*, De'seneth, because I think you would be the sort to grab a shrieker by the ear and drag them down to a clinic to make them actually see the people they're condemning."

"The idea would be high in my mind, yes," Alistar agreed. A bit to his surprise, he appreciated Onyxflame not lumping him with the nobles of Lewarden in uncaring class distinctions. "Onyxflame, it sounds to me as if you have thoughts as to what this is leaning toward."

"Thoughts that I rather hope are incorrect, De'seneth," Onyxflame said. "Because the direction I see this running is straight into chaos and anarchy."

"And that *doesn't* appeal to you?" Alistar asked.

"Oh, I would be overjoyed to see the current system change and witness the downfall of Lewarden's nobility," Onyxflame said. "But I don't want to see it happen by soaking the streets in blood. And *that* is what will happen if people decide they have nothing left to lose and follow some rabble-rouser into revolt. Even if they win, they'll lose. Those who make the promises string along the ones they think are useful, and when they're done and have what they want, they'd far rather make an inconvenient ally disappear than honor their word."

One of Alistar's eyebrows rose. He was learning more about Onyxflame every hour. "What sort of promises?"

"Oh, the usual—equal standing with the nobles, equality between humans and elves, if their target seems the sort who cares about such things, education, and whatever someone claims is an 'honest' wage for a day's work. At least those are the promises they make to rile up a crowd. If they're trying to recruit particular people, the promises get more personalized."

Education. I wonder when and how Onyxflame learned to read and write. Doubt his family could have afforded a tutor, and education in the Lower City is certainly not prioritized by most.

Downstairs, the front door opened, then closed. "Sir, I've brought lunch." Dahr tromped up the stairs and into the kitchen, bringing with him the scent of fresh hand pies.

Onyxflame headed for the kitchen with the haste of one avoiding further questions. Alistar followed. Onyxflame washed his hands twice, making generous use of the soap both times, before heading to the table to eye the tall bag Dahr held. "Smells marvelous. I'm starving."

Dahr ignored the obvious hint. As Alistar washed, the guard said, "Sir, I received word from the Silverline analysts."

"Their analysis is complete?" Alistar asked.

"They said that their results were 'inconclusive' and that they intended to run another set of tests with an expert's guidance." Dahr waited until Alistar sat before depositing the bag on the table and taking a seat. "When I pressed, they said that the results did not match any expectations, and that they wished to verify the results before drawing any conclusions."

"Their results said that the samples look like crystallized magic, and they're not sure what to think of that," Onyxflame offered, carefully not smirking.

Dahr raised an eyebrow. "They did not specify. However, they promised to have some manner of report ready before the end of the day." He eyed Onyxflame. "I presume Onyxflame has just stated his conclusions?"

"One of his conclusions," Alistar said. "The part of his conclusions that I find the least plausible, in fact. I'm not rejecting it at this point, though." He opened the bag, releasing a small cloud of steam, and pulled out two pies, then pushed the bag to Onyxflame.

"So generous of you, De'seneth." Onyxflame took two pies as well, and promptly avoided further conversation by biting into one with obvious relish.

Dahr took the last two pies. Onyxflame made a hopeful check of the bag when he'd finished his. Finding it empty, he helped himself to a mug of tea instead.

Dahr wiped his fingers on a napkin. "And what conclusions did you reach in my absence?"

"No conclusions yet," Alistar said. "However, looked at from a certain point of view, the string of recent events could point toward an effort to cause instability and unrest in Lewarden, possibly even inciting some manner of uprising."

Dahr's face was grave. "The Successors, sir?"

"They may be part of it." Alistar paused. "If Zhrets Vonn is involved, then stirring up the Successors is quite possibly part of it. Also, a call for more equality and a less strict class system."

Dahr stiffened. "That goes against the teachings of the Tenants and the Path! Without divisions of class, we would have—"

"If it's done *well*, we could have something more like the system of governance that the first humans followed when they came here," Alistar interrupted. "Done poorly, however, the result would be chaos, anarchy, and most likely order restored under a dictator—and probably not a benevolent one." *Who would profit from this? Why, whoever gets the power in the end, that's who. And if they are the only one who knows the real end game, they are best equipped to manipulate the pawns into the places that best suit that ultimate goal.*

Dahr nodded slowly. "You believe that some noble or nobles are working toward this end?"

"Might not even be nobles," Alistar said. "Reyker know there are disaffected citizens in all classes. Though they would still need influence, or the means of gaining influence…" He glanced at Onyxflame. "Like, perhaps, supplying a new and unusual drug to those with the money to pay discreetly?"

Onyxflame grimaced. "While selling the waste product in the slums," he finished. "Now there's the way to play both sides. Then just start preaching egalitarian doctrines."

"But only to a select few?" Alistar murmured, the thought catching.

Both Onyxflame and Dahr frowned at him.

"An invitation I received at the party," Alistar said. "A gathering of 'egalitarian-minded individuals of all walks of life,' but only open to those who have been invited. I was invited. Onyxflame was not. Not seen as important enough, I imagine. I hadn't decided if I was going to attend or not, but now I think I should."

"Not alone!" Dahr said immediately, standing. "Surely an attendant or guard would be acceptable."

Alistar shook his head. "Not at the gathering itself. I'll need you and Onyxflame to wait close by, ready to intervene if necessary. The gathering is tomorrow night."

"I do not think it wise, sir," Dahr said.

"I knew I was going to be bait when Prince Cero gave me this assignment, Dahr. And I'm the best bait available to lure in a power-hungry would-be dictator, if that is indeed what awaits." *Bait the hook and chum the waters. Let's see what sharks are really circling this ship.*

CHAPTER 29

"The gathering is at the Da'ness estate." Alistar studied the city map spread across his dining room table, then tapped the location of the estate. "Looks like a modest manor, as such things go."

"Lord Da'ness has been traveling abroad," Dahr said. Alistar wondered if the guard tracked the movements of all the nobles, or just particular families. "In his absence, his daughter has been managing the household."

"Right along the river," Onyxflame remarked. "Perhaps they'll engage in some egalitarian games of ice puck."

"I doubt it," Alistar said. "Egalitarian or not, black eyes and broken noses have yet to make high fashion. The rules may *say* you shouldn't hit other players in the face with the sticks, but I've seen enough games to know it *will* happen." He considered the map, then looked to Dahr. "I wouldn't be surprised if I'm followed when I leave, so we should plan for that."

"This is not a good idea, sir," Dahr said, voice low.

"We can be safe, we can be thorough, or we can be opportunistic, Dahr, but we can't be all three at this point. If someone is inciting unrest in Lewarden, time isn't in our favor. Right now, we don't know if these people are related to any of this, but if I don't look into them, we'll never know. I doubt I'll get a second invitation."

"And if they *are* involved?" Dahr countered. "Do you think they will stand by and permit you to leave with their secrets, sir?"

"That's why I need you and Onyxflame close by and ready," Alistar told him. "I'll have the speaking stone with me to call for assistance if I need it."

"While I can't say I like the idea, I do think De'seneth is right," Onyxflame said. "You and I aren't invited to this 'gathering,' and if they are properly paranoid sorts, they'll have ways of ensuring that only invited guests are allowed. So, where in the surroundings will be warm enough to hide us for a couple of hours?"

Dahr conceded reluctantly. "I will provide heating wards. I would prefer to find a post with proper vantage of the estate. Unless you strongly object, sir, I will request that Star join us for better coverage of the exits."

"No objections," Alistar told him. "Nor for any additional guards, if you trust them."

"I fear few of the Royal Guard will be available that evening, sir. His Majesty has need of them for other tasks," Dahr said. What those "other tasks" might be, Dahr didn't elaborate, and Alistar chose not to ask.

"Hmm. I wonder what other events are scheduled for that evening," Onyxflame mused. Alistar turned to him and raised an eyebrow. "Well, it's easier to avoid attention if enough other events are happening that people are congregated elsewhere. I may be overthinking the matter, though."

A soft buzzing rose from Dahr's pocket. The guard excused himself. Alistar heard the low murmur of voices, and assumed Dahr was speaking to someone via the stone. When Dahr returned, he confirmed the suspicion. "Sir, the report you requested is ready to be picked up. Also, the expert running the second assessment of the samples wishes to speak to you."

Alistar nodded. "All right. Let me dress for Silverline Power." He cast a glance at Onyxflame. "As Lord Aspendark should do as well."

Onyxflame sighed and headed for the stairs. "De'seneth, some days I wish you actually *had* made Aspendark your manservant rather than a noble. Is this 'formal' or 'casually formal'?"

"Casually formal," Alistar said, following him. "Don't forget your access pass."

Onyxflame entered the guest room, and Alistar entered his own. Half an hour later, they rejoined Dahr in the kitchen, dressed to go out. Outside, Alistar saw that the guard had come by carriage, and the vehicle with its two automatons waited in an alley. Alistar and Onyxflame climbed in and Dahr took the driver's seat.

An uneventful, if fast, drive brought them to Silverline Power's gates. Alistar noted that only a bare handful of protesters held vigil, and the clump of people didn't even rouse themselves to shout curses across the street.

The gate ogre greeted Alistar with a grunt of recognition and permitted them inside. The sprite at the front desk, Assistant Torrent, looked at Alistar with surprise. "Good afternoon, Associate De'seneth. I was not expecting you to be in the office today."

"An unplanned visit," Alistar told her. "I need to pick up a couple of things."

She nodded understanding and waved him in. Dahr took the lead up the stairs and down the hall, striding with a purpose that deterred anyone they passed from questioning them. They stopped first at the Archives.

"I will meet you at the testing laboratories, sir," Dahr said, opening the door.

Onyxflame peered in with interest before the door closed, but all sensitive documents were stored in the vault, out of immediate sight or reach.

"So this is the storehouse of all Silverline Power's secrets?" Onyxflame asked with an innocent smile.

Alistar gave him a sidelong look. "Why? Are you planning how to break in?"

"Perish the thought, De'seneth! Simply curious."

"I'm sure," Alistar said dryly. "And no, it's not the storehouse of all secrets. That would require a much larger space than this."

Leaving Dahr at the Archives, they headed to the testing laboratories and into the analysts' domain. Alistar adopted Dahr's purposeful stride, and analysts rushed out of his path as if they feared he would conscript them on the spot. Alistar stopped at the first closed door and knocked.

"Enter—ah, please come in, Associate De'seneth." Lady Syri stood at a workstation not entirely unlike the one Onyxflame had set up in Alistar's sitting room. A pair of protective goggles were pushed up on her forehead, and she wore long gloves and a protective coat. "This is an absolutely fascinating enigma you've provided."

"Technician Feyblade. I didn't know you'd been assigned to this analysis," Alistar said, surprised.

"I wasn't initially," she said. "However, my particular area of research is the natural formation of crystallized magic, so the original analysis team requested my assistance."

"I told you," Onyxflame whispered.

Lady Syri waved them to the worktable as she continued. "These samples bear a surface resemblance to natural crystallizations. However, they are most certainly *not* natural formations, nor are they pure magic. They've been manufactured in some way. The magic has been artificially bonded to a material that naturally forms crystals—in this case, I believe the base is salt." She activated the display and turned it to show a magnified image of crystals. "Because the base material and magic form different types of crystals, the result is slightly unstable, though it holds more strongly to the magic's form."

"Salt?" Onyxflame repeated, frowning. "This is true of both samples?"

"It is. However, one sample is considerably less pure than the other. I'm inclined to call it dross, though I'm not certain of the purpose of either sample." Lady Syri considered Alistar. "Do you believe these are related to the incidents you've been investigating, Associate?"

"I'm rapidly becoming convinced they are," Alistar said.

"When you find those responsible for stealing my family's work and legacy, I would very much like to know how this was accomplished. Do you have any theories about the purpose?"

"From the evidence, I believe it's being sold and distributed as a drug," Alistar said.

Lady Syri stiffened. "What? Is *this* Ambrosia?"

"You know of it?" Alistar asked.

"Talk about Ambrosia moves through the technicians' rumor mill. Supposedly, it's a rare, implausible wonder drug that provides euphoria and heightens senses with none of the detrimental side effects like impaired judgment or addiction. Some even claim they could attend work while using it and no one would notice—which I doubt unless they were naturally overly energetic." She frowned. "Are *both* samples Ambrosia? The impurities in the dross are alarming."

"The sample with the impurities was given to a six-year-old street girl who witnessed one of the incidents," Alistar said. "It nearly killed her."

"She thought it was candy," Onyxflame added.

"And ate it straight?" Lady Syri asked. "Gods above, it's a wonder she survived. Ambrosia is always diluted in wine and taken in small doses, from what I've heard."

"She was very lucky," Alistar said simply. He recalled Lord Proudmoor's gathering and the number of young nobles he'd noticed sharing a pouch and dosing their drinks. *Was that*

Ambrosia as well? How wide-spread is this drug? Whoever is responsible, how many people do they have in their pocket?

Lady Syri handed Alistar a portfolio. "My full report, Associate. Considering the potentially delicate nature of some of the findings, I wanted to personally ensure it reached your hands."

Alistar accepted the report. "Thank you."

"We're all getting paranoid," Onyxflame remarked.

"True enough," Lady Syri agreed. "This investigation has brought to light a number of gaps with our internal policies and containment of information. We've already begun implementing measures to avoid similar problems."

Alistar nodded understanding. "I admit I had concerns about sending these samples and not being present for the testing myself."

Lady Syri smiled slightly. "Sadly, Associate, we have not yet discovered a way to be in two places at once. If you have any further samples that you wish analyzed, Dahr will bring them directly to me."

"Thank you," Alistar said again. "Good day, Technician Feyblade."

"Good luck," she told him. "Don't forget to write up a report sometime soon, Associate De'seneth."

Alistar nodded, accepting the chiding. "Of course."

Dahr met them outside the laboratory. They returned to the carriage, and Dahr handed Alistar the sealed packet from the Archives. "The list you requested, sir."

"Thanks." Alistar climbed into the carriage, followed by Onyxflame.

The carriage rumbled down the street. Alistar considered the two packets of information and opened Lady Syri's first. She provided a thorough, detailed analysis, documenting every step of every test she'd conducted, all neatly transcribed by one of the machines in the lab.

Onyxflame peered over his shoulder and read along. "Ah, good, she tested the humors as well. Similar results, too."

"I would hope so," Alistar said. "And if you'll wait a moment, I'll pass you the pages as I finish them."

"No, this is fine," Onyxflame said cheerfully.

Alistar scowled, but chose not to argue the matter. He continued reading the analysis. "Who would do this?" he murmured. "And *how*? I want to know that as much as anyone else."

Onyxflame shifted uncomfortably on the bench. "I… have heard of a device that was designed to draw magic from the mahiy lines and convert it into a stable form, much like natural magic crystals. It was never completed, though, and according to the rumors, the plans were destroyed when the designer was murdered."

Alistar gave Onyxflame a long, speculative look. "Is that so. Rumor, is it?"

The elf shifted again, gaze fixed on the report. "Probably nothing to it. People have been claiming for centuries that they could perform the impossible. I don't know anything more about it."

Alistar's eyes narrowed. "Don't insult my intelligence with a lie *that* obvious, Onyxflame."

"The device was incomplete, it didn't work, the plans were destroyed, and the designer is dead. It was not reproducible," Onyxflame said quickly. "That's all I can tell you."

Alistar gave him a long, hard look, but Onyxflame sat back, lips pressed together in a thin line of determined silence. *I'm going to find out your secrets, Onyxflame, like it or not.*

CHAPTER 30

Alistar straightened his baldric and brushed a hand down his shirt to smooth a few wrinkles. The evening was chill and overcast, and a dusting of snow drifted from the clouds. Ahead of him, ghostlights and oil lamps glowed along the walking path and lit the Da'ness manor house. The light made every intricate arch and window frame glow against the tan brick walls. Behind Alistar, the carriage rumbled down the street, driven by Star. She'd already dropped Onyxflame and Dahr off at their spy post, Onyxflame leashed to Dahr with a generous allowance on the invisible chain. Alistar had set the ward for six hours; he certainly didn't intend to stay past one in the morning.

He walked through the open wrought iron gates. The entrance to the estate featured one of the newest innovations used on streets: a slightly raised walkway that repelled moisture, allowing visitors to enter without tracking mud and snow with them. When Alistar stepped on it, he noticed that it even pulled off the snow and dirt his shoes had picked up walking from the carriage to the gate.

Ahead of him, a pair of young men, one human and one elf, spoke animatedly as they walked toward the manor. By their dress, Alistar thought them from merchant families rather than nobility. At the entrance to the manor, another clump of people stood around a large warming stone, engrossed in conversation. Alistar heard scraps as he drew closer.

Would-be philosophers, ready to engage in discourse and debate? That would be a welcome change from the normal drivel of bragging, jockeying, and lying. But will they entertain the idea that the equality they think they want will take time? Do they understand that peaceful change, assuming that is what they want, will not take hold immediately?

The animated young men passed the group at the warming stone and entered the manor unchallenged. When Alistar approached, though, a woman peeled from the group.

"Excuse me, sir. Your invitation?"

Alistar proffered the calling card from Marus Ko'hut. The woman took it, checking both sides. For a moment, Alistar glimpsed a purple glow in her hands, then she returned the card. "Thank you. Please be welcome." She gestured to the front door.

"Thank you." Alistar tucked the card away and opened the tall oak doors.

Alistar's gaze swept over the foyer. The tile floor was colored to look like wood, with intricate mosaic patterns in white and blue radiating from the center of the room. A dual staircase ran up either side of the room, meeting at a balcony leading into the second floor. The wooden banisters were gilded. A handful of people stood in front of a full-wall painting of a pair of warriors locked in combat with a dragon. A human in a butler's uniform stood at attention near the door. He nodded to Alistar.

"Good evening, sir, and welcome. I do not believe I have seen you in attendance here before. Can I direct you anywhere?"

They must have regular gatherings and stable membership if a newcomer is noticed so quickly. Alistar nodded to the butler. "Thank you. You are correct. Where is the body of the gathering?"

The butler pointed to the second level. "Upstairs, sir. If you follow the hall, you will find the banquet room to your right. The doors will be open."

"Thank you." Alistar climbed the stairs. Tapestries lined the walls and thick rugs covered the floor. The air smelled of rich spices, and when he paused to look, he found satchels discreetly tucked behind vases and busts. Alistar had heard of the practice before, a trick to cover any potential musty or unpleasant odors.

He had little trouble finding the banquet hall. The intricately embellished doors stood open and the murmur of voices spilled out. Alistar checked his clothes, confirmed that Dahr's speaking stone was secure if he needed it quickly, and drew a deep breath, surprised by the flutter of nerves in his stomach.

When Alistar entered the banquet hall, conversation fell to a hush and gazes turned to him. He felt his shoulders tense at the sudden scrutiny, but he forced a smile. "Good evening."

Somewhere between twenty and thirty people gathered in the banquet hall, humans and elves, men and women, nobles and commoners. Most of them were his age or younger, and they watched him cautiously, casting glances at one another and waiting for someone to claim responsibility for the stranger in their midst.

"Lord As'enel! Welcome!" The short, pale Marus Ko'hut emerged from a clump of people. He smiled warmly at Alistar. "We are honored that you can join us this evening."

"Lord As'enel? From Rillwater?" Caution became astonishment and curiosity that swept the room.

Ko'hut strode to Alistar and raised a hand as if to take Alistar's arm, then thought better of that liberty. "I was not certain if you would choose to attend tonight, or be able to. I can only imagine the many demands you have on your time, Lord As'enel. Please, allow me to introduce you."

"By all means," Alistar agreed.

He followed Ko'hut across the ornate banquet hall. A crystal chandelier lit the room, light gleaming off gilt ornamental panels and scrollwork on the walls and ceiling. The floor was white tile, emphasizing the golds and blues of the patterns set in it. Mahogany tables around the room held refreshments, though Alistar noticed it was light fare, and wondered if the normal practice was for attendees to sup before they arrived.

A chestnut-haired man wearing a pair of dark-tinted spectacles held court by the tall windows at the end of the banquet hall, attended by a woman in a striking dress of red and gold and a man in an elegant evening coat over well-made but unornamented clothes. At a glance, Alistar thought all three human, but as he approached, he began to question whether the spectacled man was human or elf. His ears had some point to their tips, and depending on the fall of the light, his features had a sharp cast, but not so sharp as most elves. The three paused in their conversation as Ko'hut and Alistar joined them.

Ko'hut dipped a small bow. "Lord As'enel, may I present to you Sir Sok'lof," he indicated the man in the evening coat, "Lady Celyn Sunward, and the head of our organization, Cemar." He indicated the man in spectacles.

Alistar nodded to each of them. The only name of the three he recognized was Lady Sunward's. *Cemar. Surname, given name, or pseudonym?* The introduction didn't offer any clarity on the question. "A pleasure."

"No, indeed, sir, it is our honor to have you as a guest among us." Cemar swept a deep bow. "And I must beg your pardon: is it proper to address you as Lord As'enel, or Captain As'enel?"

"Lord is correct," Alistar told him. The question was surprisingly refreshing, a pleasant change from the inane queries that came first from many people. "The title 'Captain As'enel' belongs to my mother. My brother and sister are captains, but at this time, I am not. My present role in the family leaves me primarily landbound." He paused. "If I may ask a somewhat improper question of my own—"

Cemar chuckled. He had an expressive face, even with the

dark spectacles hiding his eyes. "Cemar is my given name. No surname. I presume your question is along such lines, Lord As'enel?"

Alistar smiled wryly. "It is. My apologies."

Cemar waved it away. "The lack of surname is a common occurrence for the mixed-blood in Lewarden, I'm afraid. Neither parent's people wish any claim on us."

Alistar started, then tried to cover his surprise. In spite of the several hundred years of coexistence between elves and humans in Calarand, mixed-blood children remained rare, and tended to be treated as a shameful secret in any family. *Impressive that he's successfully drawn followers, with even his blood against him. Not surprising, though, that someone with such a background would be drawn to an effort to undermine the current system.* "You are the head of this gathering?"

"Indeed. I hope Ko'hut told you a little of our mission," Cemar said. "I have heard that in Rillwater, the division between races and classes is far less strict than it is in Lewarden, and that your family has been instrumental in establishing and maintaining that paradigm."

Lady Sunward cut in, gently chiding. "Cemar, Lord As'enel has not so much as had a chance to get a glass of wine. Do allow him a few minutes to enjoy himself before you ensconce him in political discussion for the rest of the night."

Cemar chuckled. "True enough. I beg your pardon, Lord As'enel. The topic is near to my heart, and if not for the intervention of my friends, I would talk of little else to whomever will listen. Please, do not let me keep you from enjoying our hostess's generosity."

Servants were notably absent from the gathering. Alistar hadn't noticed the lack, but realized that no one circulated to offer drinks to the guests. "It would be my pleasure to discuss Rillwater with you, Cemar, though I warn you I can talk at length on the subject."

"Worry not, Lord As'enel," Sir Sok'lof interjected with a warm smile. "You have an eager and receptive audience here."

Alistar smiled politely and strode to one of the tables of refreshments. He poured himself a glass of white wine and sipped it thoughtfully, looking out the window onto the snow-shrouded grounds. *I wish I had a way to discreetly activate the speaking stone and ask Dahr if he's heard of this Cemar. This room isn't intended for privacy, and stepping out would draw attention.*

He walked back to the trio, collecting his thoughts. Lady Sunward watched him like a cat eyeing prey, and when Alistar rejoined the small group, she said, "Before you gentlemen delve into political theory, might I ask you a question, Lord As'enel?"

"Of course," Alistar said, though in the back of his mind, warning klaxons sounded.

"I have not heard that you are wed. Are you betrothed?"

Both Cemar and Sir Sok'lof laughed softly at the question. Alistar gave Lady Sunward a tight smile. "I am, lady." He hoped the answer would discourage further advances.

"Is it a political match, or personal?" she asked.

Alistar blinked. "Why do you ask?"

She met his gaze frankly. "Lord As'enel, I am in need of a husband, and ideally a husband of standing. I'm not lacking in fortune or political influence. If the match is one of politics, I dare say that a union with the Sunward family is more advantageous. And I have the means and willingness to pay restitution to the bride's family for breaking the engagement."

Alistar raised an eyebrow. "And if the match is, as you say, personal?"

"My Lord As'enel, that simplifies matters by far. If that is the case, there is truly little impediment to a union between our families. Aside from the need to produce a legitimate heir or two, there would be little need for us to disturb each other. There is certainly no reason you would need to set aside your lover. You would have yours, I would have mine, so long as all involved are willing to maintain a certain degree of decorum and discretion."

Alistar blinked at the unflinching proposal, as well as the admission of an existing lover. "Is your lover in agreement with this proposal, lady?"

"Of course," Cemar answered. "We've discussed the matter at some length."

Alistar did stop hard at that. Taking a moment, he collected himself, biting back his first startled refusal. He couldn't afford to turn his hosts against him so early in the evening. "I see. This is… a most unique proposal, Lady Sunward. I… must think about it."

"Please do, Lord As'enel," Lady Sunward said seriously. "All of us who are gathered here dream of days when we are not divided by class, status, or blood, but even if we were to succeed tomorrow, the marriage restrictions my family has laid upon my inheritance will not be so easily set aside."

"I think that any expectations of immediate change within our society are unrealistic," Alistar said, watching the three for reactions. "Though the idea of change is more readily accepted by younger generations, many people in positions of authority remain comfortable in the way things are, or even believe that we have already strayed too far from tradition."

"That stance is only strengthened by the teachings of the Tenants and the Path," Sir Sok'lof added. "The pantheon of the humans is somewhat more flexible, but even the Reyker are restrictive."

Alistar raised an eyebrow. "I hope you are not suggesting we turn our backs to the gods, sir."

"Do we truly owe them anything if they oppress us?" Sir Sok'lof asked. "What do they give us that we cannot provide for ourselves?"

"Is that all you see, sir? Oppression? All that we have is a gift from the gods," Alistar countered.

"Then why do they give some more than others? Why are

some born in poverty? Why do those who have done no wrong die of crippling, painful diseases?" Sok'lof retorted. "No, Lord As'enel, I do not see benevolence in their works. We need no fickle gods, whatever the priests may claim."

"I must disagree with you in this, sir," Alistar said, voice tightly polite, restraining far stronger words. "It seems that you and I have had far different experiences with the gods."

"I heard it told that you have personally witnessed a manifestation of one of the Reyker," Lady Sunward interjected.

"From a distances, yes, some years ago while I was serving my term as a sailor," Alistar answered. He hoped Sok'lof had the sense not to scoff—he did not want to ruin the evening by starting a fist-fight.

To his relief, Cemar spoke first. "Serving your term? Does everyone in Rillwater serve aboard a ship at some point? Do their duties aboard ship vary by their class?"

"Some people aren't fit for life aboard a ship," Alistar said, glad to move from religion to another topic. "But it's expected that, barring such a limitation, a resident who is of age will serve at least one season on the sea." He smiled. "Those who are enamored with the idea of sailing and the supposed romance of the life quickly learn that, as long as things are going smoothly, sailing is, in fact, long stretches of boredom punctuated by moments of frantic activity. Some serve their term and never set foot on a ship again. Some embrace it as their calling. As for duties, if you are serving your first term as a sailor, it doesn't matter what your bloodline or pedigree is. If a wave sweeps you overboard, the sea tries to swallow noble and commoner alike. And certainly no green first-time sailor has any business acting as captain." Alistar sipped his wine. "That doesn't mean everyone's equal on a ship— quite the opposite. A privateer ship is best described as a small dictatorship. Everyone's lives depend on the captain and on following the captain's orders. But it also means that sailors have earned their ranks and their right to be there."

"Are you saying that nepotism plays no part?" Sok'lof asked dubiously.

"I'd be a hypocrite to make such a claim," Alistar said. "If I were to return home right now and say I wanted to captain a ship, I would have one by the end of the day tomorrow." *Sooner, if my mother had any say in it.* "However, I can tell you right now that I know how to be a captain, and a damned good captain. The advantage of rank and family rests in experience, education, and, yes, opportunities offered to me that are not available to everyone in Rillwater. And if I was not fit to be a captain, I would not be allowed a ship, even as the son of Admiral As'enel."

"So it is competence that the people of Rillwater value over bloodlines," Cemar said, nodding. "Now *that* is a lesson that Lewarden could stand to learn."

"Principles that work in smaller groups cannot always be applied evenly to larger ones," Alistar cautioned. *Especially if you're trying to apply privateer principles to the capital of an empire. I'm definitely not going to touch on "your pay is what you loot from enemies." Some people in this room are liable to take that idea much too far.* He was aware that other conversations in the room had stilled, and people listened with keen interest.

"Of course," Cemar agreed. "But there are lessons to be learned. Such as a common ground on which all must meet as novices. What might the equivalent be, though? Mandatory service in the military, perhaps?"

Someone from across the room spoke. "Only if they end the policy of selling commissions to those who can afford them."

Alistar grimaced and nodded. "Agreed. For it to work, it truly must be common ground on which everyone stands as equals. And more than that, it needs to be for more than just Lewarden, but for everyone, wherever they are in the land."

That drew surprised murmurs, as if even in their claims of equality, they'd forgotten that the empire did not end with the city gates.

Cemar chuckled. "My friend, I can see we all have much to learn, and you have much to teach. I am all the more grateful that you accepted the invitation tonight." He adjusted his spectacles. "Ah, but your glass is empty, and it seems mine is as well." He tilted his empty wine glass. "Come, before we talk ourselves hoarse." He strode to a table, waving Alistar to follow.

Cemar refilled both their glasses, then sampled a few appetizers. "Did you dine before you came tonight, As'enel?"

"A light meal," Alistar answered. "The invitation was unfortunately sparse on details."

"My apologies," Cemar said. "I had heard a rumor that you might be attending Lord Proudmoor's event that evening and asked Ko'hut to extend an invitation if he found an opportunity, but I expect he had little chance to offer details. There will be a meal, and the carriages should arrive shortly to take us there."

Alistar paused. "We're not staying here?" *I need to let Dahr know we're moving.* His hand itched to reach for the speaking stone.

"Ah, no. Lady Da'ness has been most gracious to allow us use of her home as our initial gathering point, but because of certain factions that oppose our mission, the true meeting takes place elsewhere." Cemar watched Alistar carefully. "If you are concerned about your driver, rest assured that we will return here at the end of the evening. I would never leave a guest stranded, sir, you have my word."

Alistar forced a smile. "I am… glad to hear it."

He sipped his wine and milled for a little while before asking one of the younger attendees to point him toward the water closet. The young man directed him to the door tucked discreetly in a corner of the room. Alistar slipped inside, checked that no one appeared close enough to eavesdrop, and pulled the speaking stone from his pocket. When he activated it, the stone glowed briefly, then fell dark. Worry twisted in Alistar's gut as he tried again. Again, the stone started to activate, then stopped.

Blood and sand. Some sort of interference. Intentional? It almost has to be. Cemar doesn't talk like an overly paranoid man, but then, I didn't expect to learn we would be leaving here. Alistar tucked the stone away. *I can't plausibly leave now without raising suspicion. I'll just have to hope that Dahr, Onyxflame, and Star can tail us.* He let out a long breath, made use of the facilities, and returned to the banquet hall, hoping he was prepared for whatever came next.

CHAPTER 31

Lady Sunward tapped a jeweled finger against her goblet, making it ring. People turned toward her expectantly. "The carriages will arrive shortly," she announced. "Be courteous to Lady Da'ness and mindful of her generosity, and leave no personal effects behind." She nodded to a well-dressed young woman, who gave an appreciative smile.

The gathering migrated from the banquet hall down to the foyer, where the butler returned coats, hats, and gloves. Aside from Alistar, the attendees apparently gave the shift of venues little concern. Conversations continued easily even as people donned their winter clothing. Alistar joined Cemar, Lady Sunward, and Sir Sok'lof once he had his sealskin coat, his gloves and hat tucked into the pockets.

If we're leaving out the front gate, it should be fairly obvious to anyone watching that the gathering is moving. My backup will follow.

Cemar helped Lady Sunward with her coat, then chuckled as Sok'lof fussed with the sleeve of his evening coat. "Still haven't fixed that cuff, I see."

Sok'lof shot him a look of mixed amusement and annoyance. "The buttons were custom work, Cemar, and the craftsman isn't local. A replacement is expensive, and I spent a mammoth tusk's worth of ivory marks on this coat already. I still think the button will turn up somewhere."

"You've been saying that for how many months now?" Cemar asked with the grin of a man teasing a friend.

A lifetime of practice at controlling his expression served Alistar well, and he kept a mask of polite interest in place, hiding the surge of intense interest that mixed with the chill running down his spine.

"Missing a button is a minor annoyance, and it's far less noticeable than replacing it with one that doesn't match," Sok'lof said. His tone implied that this was not the first time he'd had this conversation.

"Might I see?" Alistar asked. His voice was steady, he was relieved to find. "Sometimes unusual items turn up among the goods that arrive in port. I can keep an eye toward, if not an exact match, something complementary."

Sok'lof raised an eyebrow in surprise. Alistar's pulse beat faster. *Does he suspect? He shouldn't have reason to. Even if he's involved, he doesn't know that I'm investigating the incidents. They all think I've only been in Lewarden a little while now.*

Sok'lof turned his cuff for Alistar's inspection. It clearly should have had two buttons, but only the bottom one remained. A gold-rimmed ivory button, engraved with an abstract image. Alistar recognized the shape. An identical button lay locked in his desk drawer, evidence found on a roof on Shale Lane.

"Beautiful work," Alistar said. "As you say, not easily replicated. I doubt there's its like in Lewarden." *And if there is, what are the chances that someone else not only has identical buttons on their coat, but they are missing one as well?*

Sok'lof preened. "Thank you, Lord As'enel. I've not seen the equal, and I am loath to replace it with something of lesser quality."

Outside, gravel crunched under the wheels of carriages. An

expectant stir ran through the gathering. The butler opened the front doors and a wave of cold air washed over Alistar. He shivered and pulled on his coat. By unspoken accord, the attendees left the house, and Alistar was carried along with them.

The carriages were suitable for the noble quarter, but unremarkable. Horses huffed and snorted clouds of steam. Alistar counted nine vehicles.

Cemar caught his arm. "Come, ride with us, my friend, and enjoy this fine evening."

Alistar had hoped he might slip in with some of the other attendees, then invent an excuse to use Dahr's speaking stone, but courtesy demanded he not reject the host's invitation. "Thank you."

Cemar strode to one of the carriages and held the door for Lady Sunward. Alistar climbed in after her, picking a seat on the bench opposite her and leaving generous room for other passengers. Sok'lof entered, then Cemar. The driver closed the door after him. Alistar felt the carriage shift as the driver settled into the box, then the carriage rumbled into motion.

I feel like a seal in shark-infested waters.

"You devote great effort to secrecy," Alistar observed.

"Unfortunate but necessary," Cemar said with regret. "I wish we could meet openly and without all the concealment, but we've had members arrested on the thinnest of pretexts. For the safety of every one of us, it's proved necessary. Our greatest supporters are among the younger generation, the future of Lewarden. If they are entering that future with a record of conflicts with the established nobility and the Crown, who will listen to them? To succeed, they must conceal their association with this movement."

"Those you've seen tonight are by no means the full extent of our numbers," Lady Sunward added. "Even as the locations alternate, so do the attendees. In fact, it's unusual for all three of us to attend a single event together. We do, however, communicate regularly."

"Ah?" Alistar raised an eyebrow. "You all three share in the leadership of this group, then?"

"We do," Cemar agreed. "I am the 'face' of the group, as it were." He chuckled. "Who better to speak toward an end of the division between elves and humans than a mixed-blood, after all?" He pushed up his dark spectacles in the dimly lit carriage. "But I could not succeed without the assistance and advice of my friends." He gestured to Sok'lof and Lady Sunward.

"Oh, if we weren't here, I'm sure you could find someone to fill the role," Sok'lof said.

"But not nearly so well, my friend," Cemar told him.

Is Sok'lof actually Zhrets Vonn? And if he is, do Cemar and Lady Sunward know? How does rabble-rousing in The Hollows and inciting violence against elves contribute to a mission of equality?

Lady Sunward leaned close to Cemar and whispered in his ear. He grinned and whispered back, taking her hand in his. Alistar turned his gaze out the carriage window, wishing that he shared the ride with Saskia instead of his present company.

He could tell little of their route. The windows were lightly frosted, obscuring the details of the scenery. They rode for at least half an hour, during which Alistar's companions questioned him about Rillwater and its politics. Finally, the carriage slowed and turned. They bounced roughly over several sizable bumps. Alistar braced himself against the side of the carriage.

"Apologies, As'enel," Cemar said. "This drive is unfortunately low on the priorities for maintenance."

"Where are we?" Alistar asked, though it seemed too much to hope for a straight answer.

"Toward the edge of Lewarden, between the noble quarters and the wealthy commoners," Cemar said. "It's an odd little slice of the city that's not quite claimed by either group, and so, it languishes. A number of fine houses that have been forgotten."

"How does one forget a manor house?" Alistar asked dubiously.

"Not forgotten so much as a result of unwise investments," Lady Sunward said. "The investors couldn't afford to keep the estates, but couldn't find anyone to purchase them either. And once that happens a few times, an area gets something of a reputation, and no one wants to live there any longer. Eventually, people forget the origin of the pall that hangs over the neighborhood, but everyone simply *knows* that it's bad luck to live there."

"Thus, there's nearly no one around to see comings and goings," Alistar murmured.

"Precisely," Cemar agreed. "And to help maintain that, the carriages all follow different routes to get here."

Clever. And that makes this area uncomfortably isolated, as well. Gods, I hope the others were able to follow us.

The carriage stopped and the driver opened the door. They were parked at the rear entrance to a manor house, probably once home to a prosperous merchant. A few ghostlights glowed around the exterior. Their power draw from the mahiy lines was negligible, not worth the effort of anyone from Silverline Power coming to disable them. Sok'lof produced a key from his coat pocket and unlocked the house, waving them inside. The room was comfortably warm, and Alistar removed his coat, draping it over his arm. Cemar and Lady Sunward entered confidently and navigated the dark room with familiar ease. Alistar trailed them, straining to see anything more than shadows.

"One moment, Lord As'enel," Lady Sunward said. "I'll get the lights. Cemar?"

A shift of movement, then Cemar answered, "Ready."

Lights flickered on throughout the room. Though the illumination wasn't especially bright to Alistar's eyes, Cemar adjusted his darkened spectacles with a wince.

"Are you well?" Alistar asked, concerned.

"Nothing to worry about, my friend," Cemar assured him. "My eyes are simply more sensitive to light than most. The glasses suffice, but I still need a moment to adjust to changes from dark to light. Please, come." He motioned for Alistar to follow.

They made their way through the plain servants' halls, through a door marked with the symbol of a goblet, into a dining room far less extravagant than their previous gathering place. The long table was set, awaiting only guests. Lights glowed steady, and Alistar smelled the tantalizing aroma of meat pies. The thought of food raised a new question.

"Do people live here?" he asked. "Clearly, someone's been cooking."

"A few members volunteer, alternating tasks like cooking, cleaning, and ensuring that the exterior of the manor shows no sign of habitation," Sok'lof answered.

"And no one notices the draw from the mahiy lines?" Alistar asked dubiously. The exterior lights might not cause notice, but lighting a house, cooking, living in a place would create enough of an anomaly to attract someone's attention, and they were clearly using magic. *Is someone inside Silverline Power concealing this?*

Cemar's face grew grave. "The Crown and the Silver Prince would have us believe that the mahiy lines are the sole source of magic in the world, and that they are the only ones who can grant it to us. Control over the power is how the Crown controls the entire nation." He leaned into his argument, every line of his body proclaiming his intensity. "Control over the magic is *key*, and they claim they hold the only access to it. To enforce that, they actively, deliberately suppress every effort to produce alternatives."

"No one has developed a viable alternative way to access magic," Alistar argued. "Those that have been attempted have proven unstable and unreliable." And he had studied many such attempts.

"Have they?" Cemar countered. "Or are those the only ones that the Crown allows to be revealed, to ensure their hold? As for unreliable..." His voice dropped low. "Are you aware of how many times this winter alone the mahiy lines have failed? Whole neighborhoods left dark and cold for hours—a full night, even! And what does the Silver Prince do? Conceals it! Ensures that the nobles are protected and shielded, while the poor freeze."

He has passion. I can see why he's the spokesman of this group. If I didn't already know there was more to the situation than he's said, I might be swayed.

Cemar studied Alistar's face. "You have reservations—I understand. But so long as we are shackled by dependence on the Silver Prince for magic, the Crown can and will continue to suppress and crush any attempted change that does not favor their goals." The dark spectacles didn't hide his intense gaze. "This is why secrecy is so critical, As'enel. Why we go to such lengths. It is because they are wrong. There *is* another way to harness magic. And we have it."

Alistar's breath stuck in his throat and he was sure his heart skipped a beat. *Impossible.* "How?"

Cemar shook his head. "For now, it is sufficient to say that it exists, and it provides us with the means to use this place without the mahiy lines." He took the coat from Alistar's arm and hung it on a hook on the wall.

If he's telling the truth about another way to harness magic, I need to know it. If Cemar is telling the truth about ANY of this, I need to know. The accusations against Prince Cero stung deep, but in his heart, Alistar asked himself how much came from a realization that they held merit.

Voices came down the hall as members of the group trickled into the dining room. People gravitated toward the table, milling but not taking seats. Someone drew open the drapes covering the stained glass windows overlooking the manor garden, unconcerned about the light that tinted the snow outside.

A door at the back of the room opened. Two young men and two young women entered, pushing carts laden with food. From their dress, Alistar guessed them to be lesser nobility, but they set meals around the table with no indication that they thought serving was beneath them. The streaks of flour and gravy on hands and cuffs of sleeves hinted that they had prepared the food as well.

Cemar greeted them warmly. "Thank you, my friends. You honor us with this welcome."

All four grinned as if they would burst, basking in the words as if no higher praise could be given. "It is we who are honored that you join us this evening. Please be welcome, friends, and dine with us." The statement had ritual formality, but they said it earnestly.

Cemar strode to the head of the table, and invited Alistar to join him with a wave. "Come please, Lord As'enel. Will you sit beside me this evening?"

"Of course," Alistar said. Court manners demanded no less, much as he wanted a little time to talk to the other attendees, find out what they knew about Cemar and their leaders without every word being monitored. "Thank you."

Once Cemar, Alistar, Lady Sunward, and Sir Sok'lof took their seats, the rest followed suit, including the four servers. Alistar waited for someone to say an invocation over the meal, and when no one did, whispered his own before breaking the crust on the meat pie. The pie wasn't as good as those made by his housekeeper, but it was hot and hearty. Sounds of appreciation murmured around the table.

Pushing aside his empty crust, Sir Sok'lof checked his pocket watch and grimaced. "I apologize, Cemar, but I can't stay for the rest of the evening. Another obligation."

Cemar nodded. "I understand. Go ahead."

Sok'lof rose, then nodded to Alistar. "Lord As'enel, it's been a pleasure. I hope to see you next time."

"I hope so as well, if I'm still in Lewarden," Alistar said. *Where is he going? What other obligation? Blood and sand, I wish I could signal someone to follow him!*

Farewells followed Sok'lof from the room, which he returned.

The servers cleared away dishes, then brought out new carts bearing drinks and tea cakes. The assortment of wines would have done any noble proud. Alistar looked over the bottles, and picked up one. "Icewine? I don't often see this in Lewarden."

"Indeed," Cemar agreed. "The bottles we have were a gift from one of our members. He unfortunately isn't here tonight, but I understand you made his acquaintance at Lord Proudmoor's event."

A chill ran down Alistar's spine, but he smiled politely. "Veril Lamorage?"

"The very same," Cemar agreed. "I did hope he would join us tonight, but such is the nature of things; not everyone can make every gathering."

"Ah. He didn't mention anything in regard to this when I spoke to him. That is a shame." *Could this be who Lamorage meant when he sent the message "Don't trust them"? I wish he'd given me more context for that warning!*

"Unfortunately, I can't give everyone the privilege of inviting guests," Cemar said, assuming a different meaning to Alistar's comment. "Would you care for a glass?" He picked up a goblet and poured half a glass of icewine without waiting for Alistar's answer.

Alistar accepted and sipped the wine. *At least I'm not drinking on an empty stomach now.* "So, are these gatherings primarily an occasion to socialize with those of like mind?"

"No, we discuss many matters at our gatherings," Lady Sunward answered, joining them. "Though some of the conversation tonight is subdued by the presence of a guest. We trust one another, but you are still an unknown element to most, Lord As'enel."

"To most?" Alistar asked, raising an eyebrow. "But not to all?" That was less reassuring than she made it sound.

She rested a hand on Cemar's arm. "I trust his instincts. They have not led us wrong yet."

"And I hope never to disappoint you, my dear," Cemar told her. "However, at the moment, my instincts say Lord As'enel still has reservations."

"About the worth of your goals, no," Alistar said. "About the means you will use to attain them, though… Change does not come easily, if history is any indicator."

Cemar shook his head. "The nobles will not accept it easily, I acknowledge. But they are willfully blind if they don't see that change is already here. Lewarden is ripe for a break from the old ways. People are restless, and the oppressed are beginning to recognize that they have options beyond suffering through the life to which they have been born. They see common-born gaining wealth and status with factories and access to magic, and they strive to claim that goal as their own. The people want change, As'enel; what they lack are leaders who can guide that change."

"Leaders such as you?" Alistar asked.

"Such as *us*," Cemar corrected. "Every one of us has the opportunity to shape this into the world we dream of, if we are willing to unite and act. Surely there are things you would change, given the chance. You can—the opportunity lies before you right now."

"And this 'new' means of drawing magic is the key to the change you offer?" Alistar asked. "Will you make it available to all?" *Or will you wield it as a weapon, deigning only to bestow it on a chosen few?*

"I offer freedom from the oppression of the Crown to those who will take it," Cemar said. He looked across the room, then waved over the young woman who had checked Alistar's invitation. "Larisa, would you be so kind as to show Lord As'enel your talent?"

"Of course, Cemar." She dipped her head in a quick bow, swallowed a drink of wine, and set her goblet on the table. "I was tested for the ability to channel several years ago, Lord As'enel, and showed no ability."

Alistar nodded. He was familiar with the testing—an intense, exhausting process intended to trigger any latent ability to channel.

Larisa cupped her hands and gazed intently at her goblet. Violet light glowed above her palms, and the goblet gently lifted from the table and drifted to rest in her hands.

Alistar cast a quick glance around, but didn't see anyone else visibly channeling. His eyebrows rose in surprise. "You didn't draw from the lines." Even after testing, it was remotely possible for someone to develop the ability to channel from the mahiy lines. He had never seen someone move an object without linking to the magic first.

Larisa shook her head. "It's not from the mahiy lines, sir. I'm not quite sure how to explain—I can't reach *out* to pull from the lines, but I can reach *in* and draw it out." She steadied the goblet and took another sip. "I didn't even know it was possible until I met Cemar, sir, but now that I do… it's amazing."

Cemar smiled. "I only opened the door, Larisa. You chose to enter it."

"But I didn't even know the door *existed* until you showed me," she said, gazing at Cemar with the adoration of a subject to a beloved lord.

Is this an elaborate show? A scam? Or is it real? What I just saw contradicts all I've learned about how people use magic. How can she draw it from within? And what triggered this discovery? The questions were growing, and he had no answers yet.

"Such talents are never spoken of," Cemar said quietly. "Concealed, like everything else that does not benefit the House of Feyblade."

"You assume that they know of it at all," Alistar countered.

"Yes," Cemar said flatly. "I assume that very much." He walked to the stained glass windows and lifted a latch. A section of the window swung open on concealed hinges, and he stepped onto a low balcony. It stood no more than six feet above the ground, offering a view of the snow-covered garden.

Alistar followed, surprised to not feel the bite of winter's chill. Like the benches in the city park, a bubble of warmth encased the balcony. Cemar rested his elbows on the railing and quaffed his wine.

"I apologize for the sharp words, As'enel. I do not know for certain whether talent such as Larisa's is known or not. I cannot think I'm the first to discover it, but perhaps it has never been seen, or never understood before." Cemar shook his head. "But I hate the thought that youth such as Larisa could be denied their place simply because someone refuses to acknowledge that they, too, possess a unique skill."

"I understand," Alistar said. "But it's too easy to be blinded by anger or distrust of a person or institution, and assume malice when the truth may be ignorance instead." *He still hasn't told me if or how this relates to his alternate method of manipulating magic.*

Lady Sunward slipped out and joined them. She handed Alistar a goblet. "It looks like yours is empty, sir."

"Thank you." He accepted the fresh glass of icewine and sipped. Lady Sunward slipped her arm around Cemar's waist. Seeing a chance to escape his hosts for a bit and speak to the rest of the guests, Alistar excused himself and walked back inside.

Several of the attendees had found instruments and set up a makeshift stage. They seemed to know what they were doing. Evidently, this was not the first time they'd played here. Other people were clearing space for dancing, and the room brimmed with excited energy. Alistar took another drink of his wine, letting the flavors roll over his tongue. They seemed sharper, more defined than his first glass.

Larisa walked to him. "I hope you are enjoying yourself, Lord As'enel."

"I am, and I am learning many things I never imagined," he answered. "When I first arrived, you asked for my invitation. What did you do?"

"Oh. I was making sure that it was genuine. Invitations are

imbued with a touch of magic, and one of my skills is an ability to detect that signature. If an invitation doesn't have that, it's a fake."

"I see," Alistar murmured. "If I may ask, how did you discover your skill? It's clearly not the traditional method of channeling."

Larisa shifted uncertainly. "It takes… the right trigger to wake the talent. I can't explain it very well, I'm afraid. But Cemar offered me the catalyst, and without that, I know my skill would still sleep and I would remain ignorant and lost."

"What was this catalyst?" Alistar asked.

She shook her head. "I can't describe it. You would have to feel it to understand." Her eyes were bright and a little wide. "Will you try, Lord As'enel? Cemar offers it every time we gather. Some accept, some do not. It does no harm if you don't have the talent, and if you do, the awakening is unlike anything I can put in words. Like the touch of Rechmal on your soul."

"I… don't know," Alistar said. *A drug, perhaps?* A chill ran down his spine. *Ambrosia? Or am I jumping to conclusions? If Ambrosia caused this, we should have seen others with Larisa's ability by now.*

The musicians tuned their instruments and started an energetic tune. Larisa swayed with the music, eyes half closed.

"Do you dance, Lord As'enel?"

He almost declined, but the music tugged at him. Harmony, discord, resolution, all flowing from the strings. He wanted to move with it. His questions eased their persistent jabs, and he could relax. "It would be my pleasure." He offered her an arm.

Larisa gave a startled laugh at the gesture, and let him lead her to the dance floor. Other dancers had already begun, but they made space for Alistar and Larisa. There was no formal arrangement to the dance, just couples spinning about to the music, laughing and enjoying themselves, more akin to a rural festival than a ball. Alistar relaxed, joining in the revelry as the music drove his worries back.

CHAPTER 32

After several dances, Alistar begged a pause to catch his breath and wet his throat. A young man swept in and provided Larisa with a new partner. Alistar retrieved his glass and drank the rest of his wine. A pleasant glow hung around him, though he was certain two glasses of wine was not nearly enough to make him tipsy.

When he set his glass down, someone slipped it from his fingers and refilled it. Alistar blinked in surprise and found Lady Sunward beside him. She watched the dancers, smiling. "I hope you are enjoying the company, Lord As'enel."

"I am." Alistar sipped his wine and swirled the liquid in the glass. A bit of sediment settled on the bottom. "I'm glad I accepted the invitation."

"I hope you will consider accepting the other invitations you've been given this evening, both Cemar's and mine." She watched him from the corner of her eye.

"I… am keeping them in mind," Alistar hedged. "I have made it a personal rule never to accept marriage proposals at parties."

She laughed. "That's reasonable enough. I don't normally offer such at parties either—you are a rare exception, sir."

Alistar smiled, but did not reply. He watched the dance, swaying slightly in time with the music. The song ended and another began, then another after it, no one showing signs of stopping.

I wonder what time it is. Alistar reached toward his pocket watch, and brushed the lump of Dahr's speaking stone. *Hope they found the manor without too much trouble. Doubt I can use the stone here, if this is their base of operations.*

The reminder that he was here for a purpose pushed against the pleasant glow that clouded his thoughts. It didn't quite pierce through, but left him restless, feeling that there was something he should be doing, but he couldn't quite place what. Forgetting the pocket watch, he tried to pin down the sensation.

Cemar strode over to him and rested a hand on Alistar's shoulder. Alistar started, realizing that he hadn't seen the other in some time. Cemar looked to Lady Sunward first. "Celyn, would you lead the ceremony this evening?"

"Of course," she said. Glancing to Alistar, she added, "The finale of our gatherings. Among other things, any who wish to may attempt to waken latent abilities."

Before Alistar could decide whether to accept or decline, Cemar spoke. "As'enel, my friend, you simply must come with me on a drive this evening. It's a perfect night. The ceremony will be crowded, hot, stuffy, and you look like you're in need of some air. The snow in your face, the wind through your hair, you've not felt anything like it!"

When Cemar said it, Alistar became aware of how warm the room was. The thought of cold, fresh air drew him like a lodestone. He could step outside, clear his head. Enjoy the night.

Still, something nagged at his thoughts. *If I leave now, I'll never know what they're doing here. How they're drawing magic without the mahiy lines.* In spite of the appeal of escape, Alistar shook his head. "That is a kind offer, Cemar, and a welcome one, but I would rather stay and witness the ceremony."

"Come now, you're practically ready to climb the walls, As'enel. You need an outlet. Believe me, I've seen it before. You should know that I do not make an invitation like this lightly or often. You might not have another chance! You simply *must* come. I insist." Cemar tugged on Alistar's arm, a gentle but insistent pull. "The fresh air will do you good. I promise you will love the drive. You will feel as if you are flying."

Why is he so determined? The persistence of Cemar's cajoling left Alistar all the more stubbornly decided against capitulating. He pulled his arm free. "No. Thank you, but no, I must decline, Cemar. I apologize; your offer is very generous."

Cemar seized hold of his arm again, his grip tighter and demanding. "I *must* insist, As'enel," he said, a note of steel in his voice.

"Really." A dry voice cut over the music and the conversation. "You *must* insist? And why is *that*, old *friend*? So you can force the reins into As'enel's hands when your carriage smashes through another gathering down Dockside? Or maybe this time you'll careen through an orphanage."

Alistar started, jerking free from Cemar once again and turning toward the speaker. Tiyron Onyxflame leaned casually against a marble pillar, a wine glass in one gloved hand and Alistar's coat draped over his arm. He'd wrapped a dark scarf around his head, one strip covering his right eye like a pirate from some half-chip novel. His dark clothes cut a sharp contrast to the vivid colors around the room. He stepped forward, and attendees flowed back from him like the retreating tide. The music faltered and sputtered to a stop.

"Don't you think this party has dragged on long enough, Alistar? I really think it's time to make excuses and say farewells."

Alistar blinked and gave a quick shake of his head, trying to clear it. Onyxflame shouldn't be here—he knew that, though he couldn't quite place the reason why. But if Onyxflame was here and saying they needed to leave, he was probably right. "Yes... yes, we should go," Alistar agreed, stepping away from Cemar.

"You....," Cemar hissed, eyes fixed on Onyxflame. "How? You're *dead*, Tiyron! *Dead!* I killed you myself!"

Onyxflame fixed a baleful gaze on Cemar. "You *tried*," he said, voice cold as ice. "You tried and you failed, just like every other incompetent scheme you invent, you worthless, blind, writhing gutter maggot."

The visage of an affable host shattered as Cemar's face twisted in fury. With a scream of rage, he lunged toward Onyxflame, hands outstretched to strangle the elf.

Alistar shoved a chair into Cemar's path. Cemar stumbled with furious curses. The others in the room stared, frozen in shock and confusion.

Onyxflame dodged around Cemar and grabbed Alistar's arm. "We need to *go*," he hissed, voice tight.

"Block the doors!" Lady Sunward ordered. At her voice, people jumped, and a handful uncertainly moved to stand at the entrance.

Onyxflame tugged Alistar toward the stained glass window and balcony. Alistar followed, hoping that something would start to make sense soon. A couple of men made a half-hearted attempt to intercept them. Onyxflame shoved them aside with barely a break in stride. The unlatched balcony doors swung open when Onyxflame hit them with his shoulder.

Pounding footsteps pursued them, accompanied by Cemar's near-incoherent shouts. Onyxflame cast one look over his shoulder and vaulted the balcony rail. Alistar didn't bother with a backwards glance, leaping over the rail as if he was jumping from the deck of a ship. He barely noticed the sting of cold as he left the heat bubble and landed in the snow. Alistar closed his eyes and drew a deep breath of fresh air. The scent of pines filled his lungs, with the faint odor of horses and carriages. Closer, he smelled the sweat clinging to Onyxflame.

"Get up. Alistar, get up! What in perdition are you *doing?*" Onyxflame pulled at him urgently. "We need to *go!*"

Alistar straightened with a nod. The hue and cry rising from inside the manor enforced the immediacy of danger.

The snow came halfway up their shins at its shallowest, rising to nearly knee-deep in spots, slowing Alistar and Onyxflame to a hasty slog across the grounds. Onyxflame's breath was quick, as if he'd been running. "Don't know height of the walls, but I don't trust Cemar not to put nasty protections on them. Gate's our best bet, if we can get there before the guards."

"Guards?" Alistar repeated, pulling his wandering thoughts away from admiration for the clear night. "I didn't see guards."

"They kept out of sight and away from the upstanding citizens, but there are guards. Plenty of guards. Thugs." Onyxflame stumbled, caught himself, and shoved Alistar's coat into his hands. "You probably want this."

Alistar didn't feel cold, but obligingly pulled the coat on, since Onyxflame had taken the trouble to grab it.

They reached the low fence around the garden and pulled themselves over, finally reaching the drive and thinner snow. At one end of the drive, gates stood open, and at the other, a carriage awaited a team near the front door of the manor. Men stood around the carriage, heads bowed in conversation. They turned toward Alistar and Onyxflame. Shouts rose and several grabbed crossbows from the ground.

"Run!" Alistar pushed Onyxflame toward the front gates.

The elf needed no encouragement. Behind them, Alistar swore he heard the men cranking the shafts on the crossbows, no matter the distance between them. He was absolutely sure he heard the thump of bolts being fired, and veered to the right. Light glinted on the steel heads as bolts flew past.

They dashed through the gates and into the empty street, followed by shouts and pounding feet. Alistar picked a direction and ran, pulling Onyxflame after him. When the houses grew closer together, Alistar ducked into the alleys. Finally, he slowed and, hearing no immediate sounds of pursuit, stopped. Moisture seeped into his boots from melting snow and puddles of freezing water on the cobbles.

Onyxflame slumped against the wall, sucking in ragged gasps. Alistar barely felt winded. Cemar had been right about the fresh air clearing his head. A rush of frenzied energy from their escape pumped through his blood. Every nerve felt alive, as if he'd been living his whole life in a dream until now. Strength and speed raced in his veins.

He looked at Onyxflame. "You know, despite what the half-chip dramas claim, eyepatches aren't really common wear for privateers."

Onyxflame pushed the scarf up, uncovering his right eye, and fixed Alistar with a dubious look. "Really, De'seneth? *That* is the first thing you comment on?"

"Where's Dahr?" Alistar asked. He should have noticed the guard's absence long before now.

"Damned if I know," Onyxflame sighed, tugging at his shirt collar. "With any luck, following. I *think* I managed to get out a warning when the ward expired, but he was speaking to someone on the stone and sounded pretty concerned."

"Wait, the ward expired?" Alistar cut in. "It hasn't been six hours!"

"Going on seven now, De'seneth," Onyxflame said. "How drunk are you?"

"I'm not drunk!" Alistar said, indignant. "A couple glasses of wine, that's all."

"Well you're certainly not at top form," Onyxflame said flatly. "So either you drank more than you thought, or something else is going on. Did someone slip you something when you weren't looking? Did you pour your own drinks?"

Alistar frowned. "No. Not all of them, at least." He shook his head. "But I would have noticed…"

Onyxflame cursed under his breath. "Hematic perdition. De'seneth, at any point did you notice sediment, or bits of crystal, or *anything* odd in your drink or food?"

The implication chilled Alistar as the winter air did not. "You think I've been drugged."

"Given that I know you normally have more wits than a bale fly, yes, I do," Onyxflame said.

"Fresh air helps clear my head," Alistar said. "I'll be fine."

"Fine?" Onyxflame barked a sharp laugh. "Of course, fine. You're only drugged most of the way out of your wits while Cemar's thugs want to kill us, and we don't know if or when backup is coming. No reason to worry. I'm sure we're *fine*."

"Backup…" Alistar repeated. He fumbled into his pocket and pulled out the speaking stone. "I tried to use it before we left the first manor, but something blocked the communication." He cupped the stone in his hands and held his breath as it glowed. "Dahr, are you there?"

"Sir? Where are you? What's happened?" Dahr spoke quickly, his voice tight and urgent. "Where is Onyxflame?"

"Here," Alistar said. "We're somewhere in the Venture neighborhood, probably being pursued. I'd like to get out of here as soon as possible."

"Star has the carriage. She'll come for you with all haste," Dahr said. Alistar heard muffled shouting in the background from Dahr's side. "I cannot speak long, sir. I'm needed here."

"What's going on?" Alistar asked.

"The Successors have risen in revolt. I must go." There was a loud crash that sounded uncomfortably close to Dahr, an angry curse from the guard, then the stone fell silent.

Alistar blinked. "The Successors?" he repeated dully. "Why would they…" He trailed off. *Sok'lof spoke of another engagement. Could this be his doing? Why? To what end?*

"He didn't say how far out Star is, did he?" Onyxflame said.

"If she drives like Dahr, shouldn't take too long," Alistar said.

"No, he didn't say." He cocked his head to one side, hearing a distant rumble of carriage wheels. His brow wrinkled in a frown. "But that seems *too* soon."

"What does?" Onyxflame straightened. "You hear something?"

"You don't?" Alistar asked. "A carriage." He tried to guess the direction.

"From the manor," Onyxflame said. "I'd wager marks on it, if I had any." He paused, listening. "I hear it now. Think it's coming this way."

Alistar took the lead as the carriage rumbled closer. He thought that the alley was too narrow for a carriage, but he didn't want to test that theory.

"Tiyron! I know you're here!" Cemar bellowed. "You can't hide forever! I'll find you again. You know I will, whatever rat hole you crawl into. I'll lop off your *feet* first next time!"

"You know Cemar," Alistar said. *I should have recognized that far sooner.*

Onyxflame gave a short laugh. "I love these little drug-induced understatements, De'seneth, but this really isn't the best time."

"Later," Alistar said.

"If we get out of here alive, I swear on my blood I will give you the whole story," Onyxflame promised. "Can we run now?"

The alley opened onto a street lightly dusted with snow. Alistar looked both directions, wishing he knew the area. The buildings were tall and close together now, without expansive grounds. Townhouses, intended to support a growing community of common-born citizens come into wealth. Sounds echoed, and he couldn't be certain where pursuit was. Leaving the cover of the alley, he and Onyxflame ran across the street for the next narrow path between buildings.

Horses screamed as the carriage flashed around a corner and thundered toward them. On the driver's bench, Cemar raised a crossbow, his aim far too steady for a man seated on a jolting carriage with a team running at full gallop. Alistar shoved

Onyxflame aside and felt the bolt graze his cheek. They hit the cobblestones and rolled. Alistar found his feet first, and pulled Onyxflame up. They scrambled into the relative shelter of another alley.

"Damn, De'seneth. That drug might dull wits, but it certainly hones reflexes," Onyxflame panted.

"Mine or Cemar's?" Alistar asked.

"At a guess, both. Can't speak for the state of his wits, of course. They've never been terribly good." Onyxflame's bantering tone was forced.

"Judging by his screaming rage, not at their best, I'd wager," Alistar said, levity as forced as Onyxflame's.

Cemar pulled the carriage to a halt. "Come to get your toy back, Tiyron? Don't you want to see what I've done with it?" he bellowed.

Onyxflame's hands clenched in fists and his jaw tightened. "Gutter-born sheep-lover."

Questions tumbled through Alistar's mind, but he held them back. Men armed with blades and cudgels spilled from the carriage, and more followed in the carriage's wake. They rushed into the alley after Alistar and Onyxflame. Cemar sat on the seat of the carriage, winching back another bolt on his crossbow, cold, hard stare fixed on Onyxflame. Rarely had Alistar missed his cutlass more. A boot knife was no weapon for a sword fight.

They didn't wait for Cemar to ready his weapon, ducking into the next alley. Onyxflame took the lead, weaving between alleys like he knew where he was going. "Been here before?" Alistar asked when they paused.

Onyxflame looked up and down the side street their alley opened onto. Wind and the shelter of buildings left it relatively clear of snow. "Never in my life. But I know how Lewarden lays out alleys." He paused. "Hear anyone? Can't have lost them that easily."

Alistar listened. "Some behind us, some coming from the left.

Right sounds clear." Right also put them on the street and exposed with no immediate shelter.

Onyxflame cast glances both directions. "We're being herded?"

"Maybe," Alistar said. "They know this area." He knew he didn't want to march into the open.

"Alternatives?" Onyxflame wiped sweat from his brow.

Alistar cast looks all around, then pointed. A narrow ladder ran up the side of the building. "Up."

Onyxflame didn't argue, though he cast uneasy glances over his shoulder as sounds of pursuit drew closer. Alistar grabbed the ladder and climbed. The cold metal stung his hands, but he didn't stop for his gloves. Onyxflame dragged himself up after Alistar, nearly losing his grip twice on the way. Alistar caught his arm at the top and helped him onto the sloped roof. Onyxflame braced his hands on his knees and sucked in deep breaths, but straightened well before his sharp breathing eased.

"Which way?" the elf asked.

Alistar moved to the south end of the roof, where a narrow beam spanned the gap to the next building. It was slick but sturdy, and he crossed it like a spar in a storm. Onyxflame gave the beam a long, dubious look, but edged over it.

"Where'd they go?" The words, spoken in a low voice, barely carried to Alistar. "Check doors and windows. Watch the exits."

Alistar signaled Onyxflame to be as quiet as possible. The elf nodded and picked a careful path along the roof, trying not to knock loose the snow on the lip. Alistar peered down at the street. He wasn't surprised to see Cemar's carriage turn the corner onto the street they'd nearly taken.

Which way will get us away from him? And where is Star?

Cemar raised the crossbow. "I see you, Tiyron. You think I don't know your tricks?"

Since Onyxflame's entrance, Cemar has all but ignored me. I think I'm a little offended.

The crossbow twanged. Alistar heard a quick hiss of pain from

Onyxflame, then the elf called, "Your aim is as poor as your insults, Cemar."

Cemar's expression twisted in fury. "They're on the roofs, you incompetent lambs!"

Men in the alleys scrambled to find ladders. Alistar cursed under his breath. Cemar loaded another bolt, and several other men joined the carriage with crossbows of their own. Alistar hurried to Onyxflame, smelling blood. Onyxflame waved him off.

"He winged me; I'm fine." Onyxflame pointed to a beam spanning the gap to another roof. "Shall we?"

Onyxflame's chosen beam left them exposed to the crossbowmen only briefly. Alistar nodded and took the lead. On the beam, he paused a moment, as if hesitating. Several fired their weapons, and Alistar darted the rest of the way across.

"Save your shots for the other one," Cemar ordered. "You won't hit a man flush with Ambrosia."

He did drug me. That bottom-sucking barnacle!

Onyxflame abandoned caution and scrambled across the beam with a hissed string of profanities. Alistar steadied him, and they hurried along the edge of the roof. Behind them, someone fell, crashing to the ground with a cry cut short. Alistar cast a glance over his shoulder. Dark shapes crept across the rooftops toward them. They were at least out of Cemar's immediate sight. The climbing men appeared not to carry crossbows. Alistar counted at least eight, not including those on the ground.

"Think you can run?" he whispered to Onyxflame.

"On *this*?" Onyxflame hissed, eyeing the icy roof tiles. "More likely to break my neck."

Overhead, the mahiy lines flickered. Alistar glanced up in alarm an instant before the lines flickered out, plunging them into darkness. The moon was a faint sliver, offering little illumination.

"Blood and sand!" Alistar snapped. Across the roof, startled profanities joined his.

Onyxflame caught his arm. "De'seneth, this is our best chance to elude them. Back to the ground."

Elven eyes were better suited to darkness than those of humans. "Where's the ladder?" Alistar asked.

Onyxflame guided him to a narrow ladder and Alistar half climbed, half slid to the ground. The alley was entirely in shadow. When Onyxflame reached the ground, he caught Alistar's arm and broke into a run. Alistar kept his feet, but running blind disoriented him, especially after the clarity he had been enjoying. The rest of his senses remained sharp, though, and he heard the thump of feet on the ground behind them. Only one set.

"You lack vision, Tiyron. See what I have done, how I've put your work to use?" Cemar laughed. His voice drew toward them. "No, you still stumble in the dark."

What's he done, and how is Onyxflame connected? Is he claiming to cause the blackout?

"Doesn't he ever shut up?" Onyxflame snarled. "Persistent bastard!"

Behind them, Cemar pursued. Ahead, Alistar heard distant hooves and a carriage. When Onyxflame started to veer left, Alistar pulled him to the right instead. The elf's breath was quick and ragged. Alistar still wasn't winded.

"Who stitched you back together, Tiyron? The Silver Prince? Rillwater pirates?" Cemar called. "I'll skin you alive and carve you into pieces this time!"

The end of the alley loomed ahead of them. The steady pound of hooves was too even to be live horses. Alistar's hopes rose. *Rechmal, please let this be Star!*

Behind them, a crossbow clinked as a bolt was ratcheted into place. Alistar didn't know if it was aimed at him or Onyxflame. He pushed Onyxflame toward one side of the alley and dodged to the other. Onyxflame stumbled and tried to catch himself. The bolt thumped into flesh. Onyxflame screamed, a high, shrill sound.

The smell of blood filled the air. Cemar shouted in wordless satisfaction.

Alistar lunged to Onyxflame. The bolt jutted through Onyxflame's shoulder. He pulled the elf's good arm over his shoulder. Onyxflame's gasp was nearly a scream. He clutched Alistar's coat and stumbled into a staggering run. They burst from the alley onto the street. A carriage charged toward them, swinging at the last moment to turn the door toward them. The door opened and Star sprang out.

"Light," Onyxflame gasped. "Light the alley."

"Shine light on the mouth of the alley," Alistar ordered Star.

She didn't question the instruction, nor did she hesitate. The guard grabbed a lantern from the carriage and directed a beam of light into the alley.

Cemar staggered to a stop with a shriek of pain, one arm rising to shield his unspectacled eyes. He scrambled back into the darkness. Star took a step after with intent to pursue, but she cast a look to Alistar and Onyxflame. She stiffened. "Sir, you're bleeding."

Blood stained his coat. "Aspendark's," Alistar said. And the steady flow of it needed care soon. He hated to let Cemar slip away, but he wouldn't let Onyxflame bleed out.

Star helped him lift Onyxflame into the carriage and closed the door. The carriage started moving when she touched a panel on the wall. "I'm not certain who the closest trustworthy healer or doctor is from here, sir," she said.

"Coiled Dragon Clinic," Alistar said. It might not be the closest, but he knew he could trust Doctor Tan'shyo. "Take us there."

Again, no argument. If anything, Star looked relieved to have the decision made for her. "Yes sir!" She entered instructions on the panel, and the carriage sped to a gallop.

"Sir, I am sorry. We saw the vehicles leave the Da'ness estate, but not which one you entered. I regret to say that in spite of our efforts, we lost our trail on the one we followed." Star drew a box from under her seat and pulled out bandages.

Onyxflame slumped against Alistar, head drooping and breath quick. The crossbow bolt jutted from his right shoulder. His dark clothes hid blood, but they were wet to the touch. The sharp, coppery scent of blood hung in the air. Alistar took the bandages and applied pressure around the wound. He didn't try to remove the bolt.

"Dahr spoke of the Successors," Alistar said as he tried to staunch the bleeding.

"Yes sir. While we searched for the trail, we received a summons calling all available members of the Royal Guard. The Hollows rose in riot and are marching on the city. Redpine Generator was one of their first targets. I don't know if the technicians were able to escape before the rioters set it ablaze."

Alistar sucked in a sharp breath. "They did what?"

Star nodded. "When the ward expired and Aspendark took off, Dahr ordered me to follow. Unfortunately, Aspendark's route was… more direct than the carriage could accommodate. I should have abandoned it and followed on foot."

"If you had, all three of us might be trying to elude pursuit," Alistar told her. He let out a breath. "If there is anyone at all to spare, you need to send them to one of the manors in that district. I don't know exactly which one, but it should be the only one that shows signs of passage through the snow. That's where the gathering moved. I think most of the attendees probably have no idea what's going on, but you want to capture Lady Sunward and a half-blood man named Cemar. He wears dark spectacles most of the time—that was him in the alley. They're tied to the thefts from the mahiy lines. I don't know exactly how, but they are definitely involved. Might even have connection to the uprising in the Hollows."

"Lady Sunward." Star nodded grimly. "Understood, sir." She drew a speaking stone from her pocket.

"And as soon as possible, before they scatter," Alistar added.

"Of course." She activated the stone and spoke in low, rapid words. Alistar recognized the use of a code, though he couldn't decipher it.

Alistar shook Onyxflame gently. "Stay awake. You hear me?"

Onyxflame's eyelids fluttered and he grunted faintly. "Tired…"

"Stay awake," Alistar repeated. He wasn't entirely sure how important it was, but instructions to keep the injured person conscious consistently accompanied treatment of major injuries aboard ship.

The carriage stopped. Star sprang to her feet and opened the door, checking their surroundings before helping Alistar lift Onyxflame from the carriage. In spite of the hour, lights glowed inside the Coiled Dragon Clinic. Alistar draped Onyxflame's good arm over his shoulder and half-dragged him to the threshold. Star pounded a fist against the door.

The door opened. Alistar stumbled inside. Onyxflame gasped in pain, clutching Alistar's coat to remain upright.

Saskia stood at the door. Weariness ringed her eyes with dark shadows, and long strands of hair had come loose from her tight braid. Her dress was stained with blood and dark splotches. "Bring them in; we're still…" She blinked at Alistar, brow wrinkling in confusion and alarm. "Alistar? What are you… Who… Rat's Disease?"

He shook his head quickly. "Crossbow."

"Slee's Heart, don't tell me the rioters have crossbows now!" Her eyes were wide and she shook off weariness. "Bring him this way. I have an open room."

The clinic smelled of death and an unpleasantly familiar stench of decay, barely masked by harsh chemicals. Alistar carried Onyxflame after Saskia into the second patient room down the hall. Onyxflame's head lolled against Alistar's shoulder and his breathing was quick and ragged. When Alistar eased the elf down to lie on his side, Onyxflame clutched Alistar's arm.

"Where are we?"

"The Coiled Dragon Clinic," Alistar told him. "We're safe."

"No. No, no, no." Onyxflame tried to sit.

"You're bleeding. You need care." Alistar knew reason wasn't likely to overcome Onyxflame's phobia, but he tried to calm him.

"No. I can't—" The elf panted, eyes glazed with pain and panic.

Alistar pushed him back down on the bed. Saskia grabbed a bottle and filled a mug. She hurried to Onyxflame. "Drink."

Onyxflame's wide, panic-struck eyes fixed on Saskia without comprehension. She held the mug to his lips, and Onyxflame swallowed the liquid. "It's all right," Saskia soothed. "You're all right."

"No, no, can't," Onyxflame whispered. He pulled against Alistar's hold. "Please… don't…"

"Shh," Saskia soothed. "Alistar, please find my father. He should be in the examination room. Go."

Alistar looked uncertainly at Onyxflame. *Should I use a ward? Bind him to the bed?*

Saskia touched his arm. "I've sedated him, Alistar. Go."

He released Onyxflame. The elf made another attempt to sit, but fell back weakly. Alistar hurried to the examination room. Doctor Tan'shyo was washing his hands and instruments under steaming water. He turned at Alistar's arrival. "Mr. De'seneth? What's happened? What brings you here at this hour?" He glanced at the wall, where the clock read a little after three-thirty.

"Injured elf," Alistar said. "Crossbow bolt in the shoulder."

The doctor grabbed tools and quickly loaded them on a tray. "Is the bolt still in place?"

Alistar nodded. "Didn't want to remove it on my own."

"Good." Doctor Tan'shyo looked closely at Alistar. "Mr. De'seneth, pardon the question, but have you used some form of narcotic?"

"Without my knowledge or agreement," Alistar said. "But it seems that way. It's called Ambrosia."

"I've heard of it," Doctor Tan'shyo said, collecting his tray and striding from the examination room. Alistar followed. "If time and circumstances permit, I would like to examine you once our other patient is stable."

Alistar nodded agreement. The doctor entered the patient room. "Is the patient sedated, Saskia?"

"He is," Saskia answered.

Alistar stepped toward the door, but stopped at a tap on his shoulder. He turned to see Star.

"Sir, by your leave, I'll join the available guards in searching for your assailants and the gathering. I've informed Dahr that you're here and safe."

Alistar nodded. "You have my leave. Thank you, Star."

She bowed and left the clinic at a swift stride.

From Onyxflame's room came the sound of cloth being cut and torn. Alistar winced slightly, recalling that Onyxflame had been wearing the clothing sent from Rillwater. Saskia drew a sharp breath, and Alistar quickly looked into the room. They'd cut

Onyxflame's shirt off and were packing bandages around the bolt. The elf's back was to Alistar, and he saw another thick bandage wound around Onyxflame's upper chest. He blinked, trying to think of any other injury Onyxflame might have taken, and recalled none. Then he flushed and glanced aside, embarrassed to be witness to the breach of elven taboo on exposed skin.

"I am going to remove the bolt," Doctor Tan'shyo said. "The sedative should dull the pain some, but I'm afraid it will still hurt."

Onyxflame's head jerked in what seemed to be acknowledgment. His hands gripped the edge of the bed. The doctor cut the bolt off close to the skin, then eased it out. Alistar winced. He'd seen battle wounds tended before, but previous experience didn't make the present any more pleasant. Onyxflame gasped ragged breaths that barely restrained screams, then slowed to unconsciousness. Saskia quickly pressed bandages to the wound as blood flowed faster. She reached for more, hand searching as her eyes remained on her patient. Alistar slid fresh bandages into her reach and saw her quick, distracted smile of thanks.

"De'seneth, third shelf of the cabinet, grab the green bottle," Doctor Tan'shyo instructed.

Alistar found the bottle and unstoppered it. A sharp smell of antiseptic hit his nose. He handed the bottle quickly to the doctor before the odor riled his stomach. Saskia lifted the bloody bandages and her father poured a generous dose of clear liquid over the wound.

"The exit point as well?" Saskia asked, pressing fresh bandages in place.

"To be safe, yes," Doctor Tan'shyo said.

They carefully maneuvered Onyxflame onto his back. Alistar studied a point on the wall to one side, trying to at least somewhat respect the elf's modesty in a situation that offered very little. Something glimpsed from the corner of his eye struck him as wrong. Concern countermanded abidance by elven taboos, and he looked at the bandage wrapped around Onyxflame's chest.

Heat flushed Alistar's cheeks before his conscious mind, still battling the drug haze, recognized why. Comprehension came, and he quickly looked away. Under clothing, the wrap worked well to conceal breasts, but lacking a shirt, they were evident.

The elf he'd known as Tiyron Onyxflame was a woman.

Saskia and her father finished tending the wound and pulled a blanket over Onyxflame. "This is Aspendark, isn't it?" Saskia asked.

"Actually…" Alistar hesitated a moment, then gave up the idea of lying. "I *believed* this elf to be Tiyron Onyxflame, as did Dahr, the Silver Prince, and the warden and staff of Chirrod Prison. Evidently, she is not." That last came out hard and chill.

Saskia blinked. "Onyxflame? The criminal? But why would you—"

"I was… am investigating incidents related to sabotage or theft from the mahiy lines. Prince Cero authorized me to conscript Onyxflame to assist, and provided the Aspendark persona," Alistar answered.

"So, not really from Rillwater," Saskia said.

Alistar shook his head. "A Family-approved cover story."

Doctor Tan'shyo cleared his throat. "De'seneth, the examination."

"The what? Oh. Yes. Of course."

Doctor Tan'shyo took his arm and steered him from the room. Saskia settled on a chair beside Onyxflame's bed.

The doctor led Alistar to the examination room and conducted a thorough check of his vitals and reflexes. "You have remarkable response time, De'seneth," he observed. "How do you feel? Please be as specific as possible."

"Confused, angry, frustrated… I feel like this is the first time in my life I've been truly awake, and everything before tonight has been dulled and muffled. Heightened awareness. I'm not tired. When we were eluding our pursuers, I was barely winded even when Onyxflame was panting like a bellows. It's challenging to stay focused, though, and I know I'm not picking up on things as quickly as I should."

Doctor Tan'shyo scribbled notes on a pad. "Your description is similar to those I've collected from members of the lower class in regard to a drug that has made a recent appearance. You referred to this as 'Ambrosia'?"

Alistar nodded. "How many of the people you spoke to have fallen to Rat's Disease?"

The doctor's face grew grim. "Too many."

"It's killing them. The drug sold to the slums. It's the dregs, the waste. The poison."

Doctor Tan'shyo was silent for a long moment. "You know who is responsible?"

"I don't have proof. I don't know for sure. But I think the people who drugged me and tried to kill Onyxflame are connected to it." Alistar shook his head. "I shouldn't be telling you this. It's all confidential information."

"This isn't the first Crown secret this room has heard, De'seneth, and I doubt it will be the last. Your confidences are safe with us." He stood. "You should rest. I'll prepare a cot for you in my office."

"I'm not tired," Alistar said.

"You may not feel it, but your body needs rest. That is my diagnosis as a physician. Also, Saskia and I are both in need of sleep. It has been a very long night."

Alistar let out a long breath and nodded. "All right. I won't keep you up."

The doctor led Alistar to his office and set up a cot on the floor. Alistar wondered how many nights Doctor Tan'shyo had slept here himself.

Saskia stepped into the office after her father had left. "Are you all right, Alistar? Father said you'd been drugged."

"Restless, worried… and trying to figure out who in perdition that woman is."

"That question will have to wait until she regains consciousness," Saskia said. "And that's not likely to be soon. She lost a lot of blood. We can try to find a healer to come in tomorrow, but tonight, we all need to sleep." She rested a hand on his arm.

Her touch ran through his skin like a thousand gentle prickles of pure wonder. Alistar drew a sharp, startled breath.

"Alistar? Are you in pain? What's wrong?" Saskia asked, alarmed.

Alistar pulled her close, his lips finding hers in absolute, indescribable bliss. His arms wrapped around her and she pressed against him. He could taste her, feel the pulse of her blood, the racing of her heart. He wanted the moment to last forever. He wanted her with him always. He… wanted. More than anything he had ever felt before, he wanted her.

Their lips parted, and he felt the heat of her flushed face. "Alistar…" Her voice was a whisper. "Not now."

"Saskia, I love you. I want you. Please, stay with me." His words came in a breathless rush.

The pounding of her heart, the quickness of her breath, the response of her body to his touch. Alistar knew she wanted as much as he did. Yet she stepped back from him, keeping her hands in his but breaking the embrace. "Alistar. I will stay by your side until you sleep, but… until we are wed, that is all."

"Damn the wedding! Damn my family and yours, and damn the rest of them!" he burst. "Why not?" His voice cracked, and he thought tears might break free.

"Because you're not yourself right now, Alistar," she said. Her voice trembled, but she was resolute. "I will not leave you, but I will not sacrifice that moment."

He didn't say anything—there was nothing he could say.

She drew him to the cot. He lay down alone, reluctantly. Saskia pulled a blanket over him and held his hand in hers. "Close your eyes, Alistar. Just close your eyes and rest."

He complied and, to his surprise, sleep came quickly.

CHAPTER 34

Every muscle in Alistar's body ached. He sat up gingerly. When he steadied himself on the edge of the cot, his bruised and tender palms protested violently. A dense sea fog clung over his thoughts and dulled his senses. He found a basin tucked in a corner and washed his face, trying to banish the haze. He ran fingers through his black hair and left the office in search of the privy.

Once his bladder's needs were dealt with, his stomach made itself known. Alistar stood in the hall, debating where to go. Though they didn't live at the clinic, Doctor Tan'shyo and Saskia had quarters upstairs for occasions when the clinic needed staff on site at all times. He assumed they had retired there for sleep. He searched for his pocket watch and checked the time.

Ten thirty. I never sleep this late. Except, apparently, when I've been drugged and nearly murdered.

A door opened and Doctor Tan'shyo entered the hall. "Good morning, De'seneth. How do you feel? Do you notice any lingering effects? Loss of memory?"

"I feel like I got dragged down the road by a runaway horse. Sore, aching, and everything feels… dulled." Alistar thought back to the previous night. "No memory loss that I can tell. In fact, I would say quite the opposite. Every detail is clear and sharp." *How could I not have seen that I'd been drugged? It's so obvious now—Lady Sunward brought me a fresh glass on the balcony.*

"Good. That's in keeping with the other reports," Doctor Tan'shyo said. "Another common side effect is heightened emotional response. You may find yourself more easily angered, frustrated, amused. The reaction is normal and will pass. If you're hungry, help yourself to anything in the kitchen upstairs. I can at least offer eggs and sausage. Your elf is still asleep, and I have no good estimate of when she'll wake. I will let you know immediately if she stirs."

"Thank you. I'm sorry. Last night was… chaotic." Alistar ran his fingers through his hair again.

Doctor Tan'shyo nodded, face serious. "Not for you alone. The morning's broadsheets are upstairs as well."

Alistar climbed the stairs and found the kitchen. While he brewed a strong mug of tea and heated sausages on the stove, he picked up the broadsheet folded on the table.

"Rioting in the Streets!" The headline blazed across the front page. Alistar read quickly. The Successors of Heiset had marched from the Hollows and burned Redpine Generator. The technicians on duty escaped, but both suffered serious burns.

And any evidence at the generator, like those afflicted flowers, has been destroyed. Did the team that went to the generator preserve samples?

From Redpine, the mob split. One portion headed into the slums to incite residents to rise up against their oppressors. The rest carved a swath of chaos, looting, and rioting through the city toward the noble district. The broadsheet reported that many rioters proclaimed an intent to assault the Royal Palace itself and overthrow the king, declaring their mission blessed by Rechmal and his prophet, Zhrets Vonn.

"His *prophet?*" Alistar burst indignantly. "How can anyone call that lunatic a prophet?!"

The majority of the rioters never got as far as the noble district. The full force of both King Feyblade's and Prince Cero's Royal Guard herded them away from densely populated areas and subdued them. Those Successors who accepted the order to surrender were taken alive. Those who refused... weren't.

The Successors in the slums proved more problematic. At the time of the broadsheet's printing, conflicts continued. The broadsheet implied connections between the riot and the Dockside attack. The writer remained vague as to whether the attack spawned the riots or the Successors instigated the attack.

Alistar scanned the rest of the broadsheet for any mention of incidents or arrests elsewhere in the city, but if Star and her crew caught anyone from the gathering he attended, the news hadn't made even the depths of the broadsheet.

He remembered his sausages before they burned completely, and ate them with his tea. Mug in hand, he walked to the window. Frost etched the panes and icicles hung from the eaves. A few people moved on the street below, but not many.

Alistar drew Dahr's speaking stone from his pocket and activated it. Dahr answered promptly. "Sir. Are you safe?"

"Safe as I can be, I think," Alistar answered.

"And Onyxflame? Star told me he was injured."

Alistar opened his mouth, words on his lips, then stopped. "Unconscious, at the moment. Crossbow bolt to the shoulder, and required heavy sedation before the doctor could treat it. But, no longer in danger of bleeding to death." He wasn't ready to say more about the elf yet. Not until he knew who she really was. "Did Star have any success last night? Did she find the manor?"

"She found it, and some of the attendees. The principal parties, however, had already made their escape."

Alistar grimaced, but wasn't surprised. "They had time enough, unfortunately."

"Star is uncertain how much information those apprehended will have. Evidently, those who remained were thoroughly involved in an orgy when the Guards arrived. They expressed more distress over being interrupted than over the fact that they were being arrested."

"Sadly, that doesn't surprise me," Alistar said. "Not if they indulged in Ambrosia. They might have a different perspective by now." *If I'd stayed there, would I have joined them?* "What about the rest of the city?"

"Many injured, sir, and not all of them Successors. The Guard fared well, but civilians don't possess our armor or weapons. There have been deaths among them. Successors continue to run rampant in the slums, where they are more difficult to contain."

"Are you all right?"

Dahr's pause seemed one of surprise to be asked. "I received some bruises and lacerations, but nothing serious, sir. At this time, I'm not able to rejoin you, but may be able to do so later, nearer evening. Are you in need of anything?"

"Fresh clothes," Alistar said. He still wore his evening clothes, now rumpled, dirty, and stained. "Something less conspicuous. And I need more news than I'll get from the broadsheets."

"Understood, sir. If you need anything else, inform me at once."

"I will," Alistar told him. "Be careful, Dahr."

"Of course, sir."

Alistar dropped the stone into his pocket and let out a breath. He began to pace around the kitchen. *Cemar and Lady Sunward are still on the loose, as is Sok'lof. We have to find them and stop whatever they are planning. These aren't random events; there's a connection, and I'm not seeing the full picture yet. Onyxflame knows something, that's for certain, but will I be able to trust whatever he... she tells me? She could have said something about Cemar before—she had plenty of opportunity. But who else can I turn to?* Alistar stopped. *Lamorage. Where would I find... When did he ask to meet? Three days from Lord*

Proudmoor's event, which means... tonight. Tonight at 8:00, at Dockside. I am definitely not going alone this time.

Light steps climbed the stairs. "Alistar?"

"I'm here," he answered.

Saskia entered the kitchen. Shadows around her eyes and lines on her face told of weariness, but she smiled at him. "How are you this morning?"

"Aching, but all right, I think. Last night—I'm sorry, Saskia."

She slipped an arm around his waist and rested her head against his shoulder. "You don't have to apologize."

"Can I do anything to help here?" Alistar held her close.

"You already are," she murmured. "But with the clinic, always. We haven't received many victims from the riots, thankfully, but we get more and more instances of Rat's Disease. Father's one of the few willing to take them; he's certain it's a poison and not contagious, but most healers and doctors just aren't willing to take that chance." Saskia closed her eyes. "We can't cure them, but we can make their final moments easier."

"I think your father is right about Rat's Disease," Alistar said. "And I may know who's responsible."

Saskia raised her head, looking into his eyes. "You do? Who? Where?"

"I don't know for sure," he said. "This is still speculation. But I think the man who tried to kill Onyxflame and me last night is connected, if not responsible. His name is Cemar... or at least that's the name he told me. He's mixed blood, and has a following." Alistar briefly outlined the previous evening to Saskia.

When he finished, Saskia's eyes narrowed. Her voice was low and angry. "This man drugged you, tried to kill you, and may be responsible for the agonizing death of every victim of Rat's Disease?"

Alistar nodded. "And he's connected to Onyxflame somehow. I need to know what in blackened shoals Onyxflame knows! Cemar and his cronies are running unchecked about the city!"

"I'll check on her," Saskia said. "If she's awake and coherent, I'll tell you. If she knows something that can help you catch Cemar, you need it." She let her head rest against Alistar's shoulder a moment longer, then slipped away. Alistar listened to her footfalls down the stairs and resumed his restless pacing around the kitchen.

Saskia returned nearly ten minutes later. "Alistar? She's stirring. Father said you can go see her whenever you'd like. She's likely to be groggy when she first wakes up. I used the strongest dose of sedative last night. So, give her a bit before launching the interrogation, all right?"

Alistar nodded. "I will, I promise."

He followed Saskia down to Onyxflame's room. Someone had dressed the elf in a shapeless, loose patient's gown that did an admirable job of disguising her curves, as did the warm covers drawn over her. Bandages wrapped her shoulder and her arm rested in a sling. Her breathing was deep, but it caught and hitched with pain, and she shifted.

"You're not faking sleep well," Alistar said once Saskia left.

One eye opened, found him, then closed. "Blight, plague, rot, and ash," she cursed softly. She drew a deep breath and pushed herself up to prop against the headboard, wincing. Plastering on a familiar, sarcastic Onyxflame smile, she opened her eyes. "Good morning, De'seneth. Or evening—damned if I know what time it is. I'd get out of bed, but I don't think it would be wise to try."

Alistar folded his arms and leaned against the door, hard stare fixed on the elf. "Who are you?"

She raised an eyebrow. "The same person as I was yesterday."

Alistar's eyes narrowed. "*Who* are you, because you are *not* who you claimed to be."

"I *am* Onyxflame!" she snapped, indignant. "I'm just... not *Tiyron* Onyxflame."

"I'm not asking again," Alistar told her.

"Oh, come, De'seneth, you've surely had time by now! Haven't you already sent the Silver Prince's archivists scrambling to dig up every scrap of information they can find? Don't tell me that you don't have the record of my birth stashed in a folder somewhere, ready to wave in my face if my answer doesn't match it!" She scowled at him. "You, the Silver Prince, his staff, and half the guards in the city know who I am by now!"

Alistar's eyes narrowed. "No, actually, we've been rather more distracted by the fact that people are *dying in the streets* because of Cemar's drugs and by the entire Hollows rising in revolt and rioting across the city! So *who in Slee's frozen balls are you?*" His voice rose steadily to a roar.

Color drained from Onyxflame's face. "What?"

"The Successors have launched open rebellion." Alistar enunciated each word. "People are dying."

"And you want to blame *me* for that?" Onyxflame sat straighter, then winced.

"Cemar is involved somehow. Someone who I had never heard of until yesterday. Someone you are apparently quite familiar with, yet never mentioned."

The elf closed her eyes and drew a deep breath, then looked at Alistar squarely. "So are you looking for an answer, or someone to throw to the sharks, De'seneth? Because this sounds a lot more like the second than the first."

"Answers. Now." Alistar's hard gaze didn't relent.

Her mouth opened, but she hesitated. "You really *haven't* gone digging yet. Hematic perdition." She let out another breath. "All right, all right. Rykka Onyxflame, at your service, De'seneth. Four years younger than my brother Tiyron. Had the misfortune to be born to parents who didn't much want another mouth to feed, but couldn't quietly get rid of me without causing a stir with the neighbors. Which is a crappy reason to not drop a child at an orphanage, if you ask me."

Alistar said nothing.

"Tiyron made sure I had food, gave me his clothes when he

outgrew them, took me along with him pretty much everywhere. And when he left our parents' house and didn't go back, he took me along then too. But the people he got involved with on the streets weren't exactly the sorts you'd introduce to your little sister. So, we decided they wouldn't know about me. We looked enough alike that with a little preparation, I could pass as Tiyron, and none were the wiser. That's how we worked."

"And he took all the credit," Alistar said. *So many of Onyxflame's exploits seemed impossible for one man to do, but he always claimed that he worked alone.*

"Being overlooked was a life skill I'd embraced long before then, De'seneth," she said. "Tiyron was fascinated with the mahiy lines. I tinkered in artificing. Self-taught. He found someone who taught him, and by extension me, to read and write. We pulled heists. We made a name for Tiyron. Had a number of one- or two-time partners. I usually spied on meetings Tiyron held with them, though sometimes I took his place. We turned down a lot of offers of alliances." She closed her eyes a moment, and her voice grew tight. "Eventually, Tiyron was approached by a half-breed named Cemar."

Alistar straightened and took a step away from the door. "Cemar."

She looked Alistar in the eyes. "He must have studied everything he could about Tiyron. He knew *exactly* what to say, how to gain our attention and sympathy without raising suspicion. Appealed to the injustice of the rigid class system, the restrictions of the Path and the Tenants, the Silver Prince's stranglehold on the mahiy lines..." She gazed at Alistar. "You heard Cemar, De'seneth, and I heard him working on you. He makes it all sound *so* good, and he speaks with such *passion*. If he'd had a couple more hours, you'd have started to believe him too, even without the drugs. When I listened to him speaking to Tiyron, I believed him. I wanted to believe in everything he offered."

Alistar scowled, but he did admit that her description of Cemar was accurate. "So, he talks a good talk."

"And he plots a good plot, too. An ambitious one."

"What *did* he tell you?" Alistar demanded.

"Equality. The downfall of corrupt leaders. You name a promise that would appeal to Onyxflame, and Cemar was ready to offer it. He perfected an air of disdain and scorn for the upper classes." Her jaw tightened. "It was convincing enough that even when your evidence pointed in his direction, I dismissed the possibility. I didn't think that he *could* be involved in *this* plot because there was too much evidence of noble connections. Not until I saw the bastard with my own eyes last night."

Alistar's eyes narrowed. "What is he plotting, Onyxflame?"

"He had an idea for a machine that would siphon power from the mahiy lines and convert it to a condensed, solid form. He wanted Tiyron to make it. Presented the idea as an opportunity to break the Silver Prince's hold and provide a new form of magic. The concept absolutely fascinated me. I worked on the crafting and artificing, while Tiyron and Cemar schemed. Cemar didn't know about me, of course, though the longer we worked with him, the more I began to think he could be trusted with the secret. Tiyron scavenged up the materials for me, and I don't know where or how he got some of them." She paused. "That... includes his venture into sailing."

"This would be the device you spoke about when you claimed to have heard 'rumors' about one that could convert magic to a stable form," Alistar said. "Except your 'rumors' said it was incomplete and the designer was murdered."

She flinched as if he'd jabbed a knife in her injured shoulder. "It *is* incomplete and the designs *were* destroyed. It's not siphoning power; it's draining the lines dry! If it was working like it *should*, you wouldn't even *notice* the loss."

Alistar waited.

She was silent for several minutes. When she spoke, her voice was tight. "Cemar and Tiyron got into an argument over how to best use the device. Tiyron gathered all the plans and gave them to me. Told me to memorize as much as I could and burn them. Said it would be better to leave it incomplete than to let Cemar use it."

Alistar raised an eyebrow. "What did he say Cemar intended?"

"He didn't tell me. I'm not sure if he knew for certain, but he refused to debate the matter with me. Said there wasn't time, and that he was, moving the device from the hideout we shared with Cemar to somewhere safe." She drew a steadying breath and looked down at her hands as they twisted the edge of the sheet into knots. "I burned the notes and schematics, as he'd told me. When I returned, the hideout was ransacked. Tiyron and Cemar were both gone, as was the device. I first thought the Crown's soldiers had found them, or one of the crime gangs had taken them."

Alistar remembered Cemar's screaming, furious rage, and a chill ran down his spine. "It seems that wasn't the case."

Her hands clenched in fists. She raised her head, meeting Alistar's eyes. "I hunted shadows and phantoms for nearly a month. Finally, a contact dropped me a tip about men dumping a body outside the city, in an area where... well... bodies and parts of bodies aren't so uncommon." Her voice went flat. "I found Tiyron dying in a ditch. He'd been tortured. Brutally tortured, and I had no means of saving him." She fell silent, jaw tight.

She dropped clues, but I assumed Tiyron Onyxflame's secret partner was dead, not that the partner stepped into the role with Tiyron's death. "How long ago?" Alistar asked.

"Spring, last year. I buried him near Planter's Field. And I'm not telling you, the Silver Prince, or anyone else where." Her eyes gleamed with determined defiance against something Alistar hadn't planned to ask.

"Cemar was responsible?" he asked instead.

"Tiyron managed to tell me that much," she said. "But Cemar

had vanished without a trace, taking the device with him. He might never have existed for all I could find."

"And when the outages began, you didn't suspect that device was causing them?" Alistar asked dubiously.

"*I* was sitting in a cell in Chirrod Prison when the outages began, De'seneth," she retorted. "And no, I didn't, because that isn't what I designed it to do. Even incomplete, that's not how it should operate. Someone's altered the design drastically."

Alistar was silent for a time. "When you were arrested, you chose to keep the persona of Tiyron."

"It's his legacy. His name. His legend. So yes, I stood as him, and I spat his words in the faces of King Feyblade and Prince Cero when they tried me in secret."

"You could have gotten the charges dismissed by proving you weren't Tiyron," Alistar said.

She barked a sharp laugh. "Oh, yes, I'm *sure* that would have worked well. Instead of being tried for theft and sabotage, I could have been tried for heresy. That's *so* much better." She saw Alistar's dubious expression and plunged on. "Yes, heresy. Have you ever *read* the Tenants? The bit about 'proper place'? Not aspiring above your station? How about stepping outside the 'approved' roles for a woman? And don't even *start* to say that shouldn't matter, because it *does*." Her lip curled in a sneer. "Nobles can do whatever they want. They can pay a priest to justify anything as a privilege of their place in life, but some street rat? No, we should be 'grateful' for scraps tossed our way." Her hands clenched. "This is why Cemar is succeeding, De'seneth: because he's offering something people *want*."

"He claims he is, at least," Alistar said.

"And he makes it sound good. And what do you, the Silver Prince, the nobles offer? Table scraps?"

"What do *I* offer?" Alistar asked. "Searching out those responsible for the outages isn't good enough for you? Helping street children who would probably have died otherwise?"

"That is your *job*, De'seneth!" Onyxflame snapped. "Just like it's your *job* to inform your employer of this entire rotting conversation. So is Dahr standing outside taking notes, or do you just have an active speaking stone directly to the Silver Prince?"

Alistar's eyes narrowed. "Is that what you think?" His voice was flat and hard.

She threw up a hand in frustration. "You think I'm going to *forget* who's holding the cards? That I'm going to forget that I am under your hold and at your mercy? You can walk out of this building and I will come crawling down the street after you whether I'm fit to move or not because I *have* to!"

"And you would probably prefer that to remaining under the care of a doctor," Alistar countered.

She stiffened, breath growing sharp at the reminder of her surroundings.

Saskia opened the door and entered the room. She looked at both Alistar and Onyxflame. "This conversation has passed the point of meaningful dialog, and if the two of you keep yelling, you'll disturb other patients. Also, I need to change the bandages."

Onyxflame tensed as if considering trying to bolt. Alistar watched her and activated a ward. Onyxflame hissed in discomfort and tugged at the invisible chain between her wrist and the bed. Alistar felt her glower even as he strode from the room.

Saskia didn't chide Alistar for the sour end to his questioning of Onyxflame. Instead, she provided him with a list of tasks. He accepted them, glad for the distraction. He occupied himself with cleaning and sterilizing tools, folding linens, refilling bottles, and, eventually, washing Onyxflame's blood out of his coat.

He was hanging the sealskin coat to dry when Doctor Tan'shyo found him. "Mr. De'seneth, you have a visitor."

Visitor? Who? Did someone follow us? The thoughts tumbled rapidly through his mind until he remembered that Dahr said he would come in the afternoon. Alistar dried his hands and rolled down his sleeves. "Thank you. I'll be right out."

"I sent him upstairs," the doctor said. "I doubt you wish your conversation overheard."

Alistar paused. "How are your patients doing? Aside from the one I brought."

"Most of my patients have Rat's Disease," Doctor Tan'shyo said simply. "We've had one pull through today, so, better than yesterday."

One survivor, and that's an improvement. We have to stop this. Alistar nodded understanding. He headed upstairs, and found Dahr seated at the kitchen table.

The guard rose quickly. "Sir. I'm glad to see you well."

"You also," Alistar told him. Dahr looked no worse for wear. "What's the news?"

"We've cleared the rioters from everywhere but the slums at this point," Dahr told him. "Those who surrendered continually babble about divine signs and the downfall of the Crown. They claim that Rechmal openly bestowed his blessings on the Hollows when the wards failed, and that Zhrets Vonn is a prophet of Rechmal who will curse all the unfaithful."

"Are you familiar with the name 'Sok'lof'?" Alistar asked. "A human nobleman. He called himself 'Sir Sok'lof'."

"I do not recognize it, sir," Dahr said.

"I think he might be our 'Zhrets Vonn.' He was at the gathering last night, but left early, and it sounds as if the rioting began not long after that. Also, the buttons on his coat matched the one I found, and he's missing one."

"I will request someone to look into him immediately," Dahr said. He continued with the news. "Some midcity areas sustained heavy damage from rioting and looting. Several markets are completely untenable at the moment, and many others are closed for fear of further unrest."

"I know normal practice is to repay those who suffer losses from the purses of those responsible, but given how most Successors are poor as dirt, it would be a positive gesture if the

Crown offered some token recompense to those affected," Alistar said.

"Indeed, sir. I will pass the message on," Dahr said. "Shale Lane was not significantly struck, and your house is in good order. Your neighbors reported no sign of suspicious activity in the area, and they clearly kept a watch for trouble. Fortunately, they recognized me as a frequent visitor to your house. I retrieved fresh clothing for you and Onyxflame." He indicated a large bag at his feet. "How is Onyxflame?"

A simple question, yet fraught with so much danger. Anything I tell Dahr will reach Prince Cero. What will they do if I tell them what she told me? Probably drag her off to interrogate her about Cemar, her brother, and this device. Almost certainly not allow her to continue as my assistant, nor honor the agreement that she be released at the end of the investigation.

"I spoke with Onyxflame earlier," Alistar said. "He was foggy from sedatives, but..." he shrugged slightly. "He was Onyxflame. Don't know if the crossbow caused any permanent damage to his arm at this point. Cemar seemed to know him, and I have questions that need answers. But I doubt Onyxflame can answer them all, especially regarding Cemar's activities since Onyxflame's arrest. I'm certain they are not allies, given that Cemar was quite intent on trying to kill Onyxflame last night."

Dahr considered Alistar's words gravely. "Do you know of another source, sir? The guests detained from the gathering have been uncooperative thus far, and we have had no luck locating Lady Sunward."

"I need to speak to Veril Lamorage," Alistar answered. "He and I have been friends at work for quite a while, but he only knew me as De'seneth. I knew he'd gotten into some manner of questionable circumstances, but I now believe that Cemar has some kind of hold over him, either debt or blackmail. Last night, I found out that he's attended some of Cemar's gatherings. When we attended Lord Proudmoor's event and Lamorage learned that I'm the

As'enel heir, he asked my help without giving any details, and arranged a meeting. That meeting falls tonight, Dockside."

"You are not attending such a meeting alone!" Dahr said quickly.

"No, not if I have any choice about it," Alistar agreed. "Are you and Star available?"

"I will ensure that we are, sir," Dahr said. "Are there any others you wish to have in attendance?" He stopped abruptly, looking toward the stairs.

The steps creaked softly. Saskia stepped into the kitchen. "Oh, pardon me. I was going to grab a bite to eat. Am I interrupting?"

"Not at all," Alistar told her. "I was telling Dahr that Lamorage asked my help and wanted to meet tonight, Dockside. That was arranged before all this madness erupted."

"And I wish to know if he believes my sister and I will be sufficient accompaniment for this meeting," Dahr added.

Star is his sister? Oh. Well, that explains why he's so certain he can trust her.

Saskia blinked. "Dockside, tonight? Of course it shouldn't be just the three of you. I'm going as well."

Alistar just smiled. Dahr straightened, taken aback. "Milady, it will be dangerous."

She looked at him evenly. "Dahr, I make weekly house calls to Dockside and the surrounding neighborhoods. I am aware of the hazards. And I know my way around the area. Besides, my future husband is going, and if this is going to be an aspect of his career going forward, I want a proper idea of what is involved."

Dahr glanced at Alistar, who just grinned. "My fiancée says that she's going with us tonight, so, she's going with us. I'm not worried—she met my parents and received their approval; hooligans and crime lords aren't likely to scare her off. Although that reminds me... can I borrow a cutlass? Unless you put mine in that bag."

"I… did not see a cutlass in your room, sir," Dahr said. "I will acquire one for you."

"I keep mine packed away," Alistar said. "Don't usually need it. But tonight, I'd like a familiar weapon at hand."

"Of course," Dahr said, dipping his head in a bow. "And for you, milady?"

"I have what I need, thank you," Saskia told him. "What time is the meeting, Alistar?"

"Eight," Alistar said.

She nodded thoughtfully. "All right. I should have time to catch a nap beforehand, then. I'll let Father know what we're planning."

Dahr bowed to both of them. "I will make the necessary arrangements, and will return by six."

Alistar nodded. "Good."

After Dahr left, Saskia asked, "What did you tell him about Onyxflame?"

"Just that 'he' seemed to have some bad blood with Cemar," Alistar said. He let out a long breath. "I'm not sure I believe Onyxflame when she says she didn't suspect Cemar was involved. And even if she didn't, she should have still told me about him as a possible suspect. But I'm not going to condemn her to the court interrogators for that."

"So, as far as Dahr knows, she's still Tiyron Onyxflame," Saskia said. She nodded slowly. "All right. I'll abide by that."

"Thank you, Saskia." Alistar pulled her close and kissed her.

CHAPTER 35

Dockside stood dark and silent. Snow dusted the cobbles, tossed about by the wind. Piles of rubble shadowed the sides of the street, pushed aside and forgotten. No lights shone from the shuttered windows, and no voices sang boisterous, drunken anthems from the taverns. Alistar might have been alone with only the ghosts of the slain. The wind seemed to carry whispers of restless spirits.

He looked around, searching for signs of Lamorage. *Is he here? I haven't heard anything from him since Proudmoor.*

He glimpsed a faint glint of light, and approached. A metal disk etched with the image of a kurowa flower dangled from a doorknob. The etching glowed softly, and would be nearly indistinguishable under normal light. The building was as dark as those around it, but the door swung open when he turned the knob. The placard swaying in the wind proclaimed it to be a gambling hall.

Alistar looked up the street and raised his hand as if to brush the swirling snow from his hat. He didn't see Dahr, Star, or Saskia, but he trusted that they could see him and his signal. Cautious and alert, he stepped into the building.

The air was pleasantly and unexpectedly warm, and smelled of stale beer, old tobacco, and years of greasy food. A lamp glowed on a table toward the back of the room. Alistar stepped around the unoccupied bouncers' station, where patrons paid their entrance fee. The gambling tables lay empty. The building was eerily quiet. He could hear the wind whistling through an alley. Floorboards creaked with each step.

It's too dark. Lamorage would never leave a room this dark. There should be three or four times as many lights.

Wary as a cat, Alistar moved toward the table, searching the shadows. "Lamorage?" He activated lamps on the tables as he passed them, chasing back some of the darkness. Reaching the table, he found a sealed envelope. He glanced around suspiciously, then picked up the envelope and turned it over, checking for a name or seal.

The floor creaked under another pair of feet. "I didn't think you'd come, As'enel—or whatever your name really is."

The voice was not Lamorage. Alistar's eyes narrowed and he searched the darkness. "You doubt my claim?"

"I don't doubt you're associated with the pirates of Rillwater, but the As'enel heir? Unlikely."

"Where's the elf?" Alistar demanded, voice cool. He picked out a short, wiry form in the shadows. *Marus Ko'hut.*

"He's here," Ko'hut said. "Cemar was convinced you'd show for this meeting. Insisted that I wasn't to kill the elf unless you didn't turn up, so this makes the second time you've saved his life. Pity he won't get a chance to repay you for it."

"The second time," Alistar repeated. "What was the first?"

"Proudmoor's party," Ko'hut answered. "Lamorage was becoming a liability. I was to arrange his unfortunate, guilt-driven suicide. However, you took an interest in him, tilting the scales in his favor, from liability to potentially useful."

"As bait," Alistar growled. *Does he have any idea just how much he's telling me? I thought villains only gave gloating monologues in half-chip dramas.*

Ko'hut laughed. "As if he had some *other* use? And he did accomplish that purpose, at least."

Alistar tucked the letter into his shirt. "What do you expect to happen now? Are you done gloating?"

"I'm willing to offer a trade," Ko'hut said magnanimously. "Tell me where Onyxflame is, and I'll show you where to find Lamorage."

Does he think I'm going to accept that? Alistar eyed the man. *Blight, I think he actually does.* "As if I'll believe a man who just told me he intended to murder someone and stage it as suicide? You tell me where to find *Cemar*, and I might consider it."

"No need—I'll be more than happy to bring you to him myself." Ko'hut smirked.

He must have thugs with him. I don't think he's stupid enough to think he can take me alone. Where's his backup?

The floor creaked near the bar, and again near the cold fireplace as Ko'hut's thugs shifted and tensed for action. At the back of the room, behind Ko'hut, Alistar saw a quick flash of amber light, repeated twice—Dahr's signal that they were ready.

Alistar launched forward, lunging at Ko'hut. The man yelped in surprise, falling back and grabbing for a weapon. Thugs rushed from hiding, clubs raised. Alistar seized Ko'hut's arm and flung him into a table. The smaller man grunted and scuttled away from Alistar.

"Don't be foolish, As'enel," Ko'hut warned. "You're outnumbered."

"For the moment," Alistar said, drawing his cutlass. The weapon was a welcome weight in his hand as the thugs closed around him.

Someone grunted in surprise and thumped to the floor. Ko'hut cast an alarmed look over his shoulder. Alistar didn't waste the moment of surprise Star gave him. He slashed at the closest thug.

The man grabbed his bleeding arm, dropping his cudgel. The next one held his weapon to block Alistar's blade, but his stance betrayed a lack of confidence, as if he wasn't certain how to react when his opponent wasn't cowed.

Cemar and Sunward certainly didn't send their best for this task.

Realizing that the shadows worked against them rather than in their favor, the thugs activated more lights around the room. Star and Dahr swept through them, blades flashing, making no effort to avoid lethal force. Ko'hut scuttled to the far end of the room and raised his hands. For a moment, Alistar thought the gesture one of plea or prayer. Then he saw tendrils of violet light stream down through the ceiling.

Channeler! What's he doing? Alistar fought toward Ko'hut, but couldn't break free from the men around him.

Flickers of lightning danced around Ko'hut's fingers. He drew back his arm to hurl a bolt.

Saskia slammed her wrist clutch into the back of his skull. Ko'hut staggered, and she hit him again. Alistar knew the clutch was packed with sand and pebbles, dense and hard as any sap while being unremarkable in a woman's hand. A third strike finally sent Ko'hut sprawling to the floor. Saskia pulled a sharpened hair comb from her bun and held it against the man's throat as she checked whether or not he was conscious.

Alistar eyed the thugs before him. "Ko'hut's down. You sure you want to keep fighting me?"

They glanced at each other, then at their fallen comrades. "Who in perdition *are* you?" one growled.

"Alistar As'enel, heir to Rillwater and its fleets," Alistar said. "And my future wife just took down your boss. You think *you* can take us?"

The man swallowed hard and lowered his cudgel. "I don't know nothing about none of this. But I ain't getting paid enough to fight pirate lords. You won't kill me if I surrender?"

The remaining thugs held their weapons defensively, trying to watch Alistar, Dahr, and Star all at the same time. The two guards stood ready, but didn't attack.

"If you surrender, I will not kill you," Alistar agreed. "And if you show me where Ko'hut hid the elf, I might even allow you to leave, provided you *never* make contact with the ones who hired you again."

Dahr scowled at the idea of releasing the men, but said nothing.

The thug nodded slowly and swallowed hard again. He dropped his cudgel to the floor. The others followed his lead. "I'll show you where he took the elf. Sir."

"The rest of you, sit over there," Alistar ordered, pointing to a clear area at the far end of the room, away from any potential weapons. "Star, watch them."

"Yes sir." The guard herded the thugs into a clump and loomed over them as they sat, ready to cut down any who moved wrong.

Alistar looked to Saskia. She waved him on. "We have this under control, Alistar."

Dahr followed Alistar and the thug into a long hallway. All three of them carried lamps from the main room. Dahr glanced back at Saskia, then whispered to Alistar, "Sir, pardon my frankness, but if you do not marry that woman, I will consider it my duty to knock you senseless."

Alistar's lips twitched in a smile. "Only if she doesn't beat you to it, Dahr. Rest assured, I foresee no danger of such action being necessary."

The thug glanced at them uneasily, not certain what they whispered about. They passed closed doors, which Alistar guessed led to private rooms used either for gambling or prostitutes. The thug looked back at Alistar.

"I dunno for sure what Ko'hut gave the elf, sir, but I think it mighta been koshmar."

Alistar's jaw tightened. The drug was known to induce hallucinations—often unpleasant ones. *Still, better than giving him Rat's Disease. Probably.* "How certain can you be?"

The thug shifted uncomfortably. "Well, it was a vial of green liquid, and that's how I always seen koshmar look. And the elf started screaming not long after we shut him in the dark."

Alistar's eyes narrowed. Even without the addition of hallucinogenics, Lamorage feared the dark. "How long ago was this?"

"Maybe… about noon or so?" the thug answered uncertainly. He stopped at a door. "He's in here."

The door was locked. At Alistar's direction, the thug put his shoulder to it and forced the door open.

The only light in the room came through the broken door. A figure hunched at the foot of the bed. Wide, panicked eyes fixed desperately on the lamp glowing in Alistar's hand. Lamorage strained against the ropes that bound him to the bedpost, but he flinched when Alistar rushed to his side. Sounds of fear came through Lamorage's gag. His wrists were bloody and raw from struggles.

Alistar set the lamp on the floor, drew his dagger, and sawed through the ropes. "It's all right, Lamorage," he said. "I'm here to help. We'll get you out of here."

He didn't see recognition or comprehension in Lamorage's eyes. As soon as the elf's hands were free, before Alistar could even release his feet or remove the gag, Lamorage snatched the lantern and clutched it like a protective talisman.

Alistar cut the remaining bonds and pulled the cloth from Lamorage's mouth. "Lamorage. Veril, are you listening to me?" Alistar asked.

Wide, glassy eyes fixed on Alistar. "Radyn?" Lamorage whispered. He seized hold of Alistar's arm. "Radyn, don't leave me here. Matra's coming back. She has to come back. Don't leave me here! The light will go out!"

"Radyn? Matra? Who are you talking about, Veril?" Alistar asked. He shook his head quickly. It didn't matter at the moment.

"We aren't leaving you here, but we need to go. Come on. Can you walk?"

Lamorage tried to stand, but his limbs were uncooperative. Alistar lifted one of Lamorage's arms over his shoulder, half carrying and half dragging him into the hall.

"Matra's coming back, Radyn," Lamorage repeated. "There's her light, see?"

"All right, Veril." Alistar didn't try to argue with him. Wherever Lamorage thought he was, it seemed to be far from a Dockside gambling hall in Lewarden. "We've got lights." *How long does koshmar's effect last? Is he still hallucinating, or is this something else?*

Lamorage shuddered. "Don't let them go out." He sounded like a frightened child. "Don't let the chunya reach us."

Dahr's hand fell to his sword and he looked sharply up and down the hall. "What is this chunya?"

"A creature of the western mountains," Alistar told him. "Light burns it. It hunts in darkness, and elves are one of its favorite prey. It doesn't come so far south as Lewarden."

Lamorage leaned heavily against Alistar, and clutched the lantern in his free hand. In the main room, his eyes darted about quickly, searching the shadows. Alistar pulled him into the largest pool of light and took stock.

Marus Ko'hut sat on the floor, bound and groggy. The remaining thugs were quiet enough that Alistar wondered what threats Star or Saskia issued in his absence. The two women oversaw the room with an air of confidence.

Saskia moved to Lamorage. He was compliant as she looked into his eyes and bandaged his wrists. "Do you know where you are, Lamorage?" she asked him.

"We're looking for Matra," Lamorage said.

"Who's Matra?" Saskia asked gently.

He gave her a distressed look. "My sister. Matra."

"All right," Saskia soothed. "We'll help you look for her. Just stay with us."

Lamorage nodded quickly. His gaze fell on Ko'hut, and he flinched. "Don't want his help."

"Rest assured, sir, he will not accompany you," Dahr said. He addressed Alistar. "Star has called a team, sir. They will take Ko'hut into custody and examine this place. Do you wish the rest released before their arrival?"

Alistar fixed a hard look on the thugs. "If any one of you returns to your boss, I *will* know, and all promises are void."

Fortunately, none of them questioned *how* he would know, since he had no idea. Heads bobbed in agreement and voices spoke rushed promises and pleas.

"Get out of here," Alistar ordered.

They scrambled out the door and into the night.

The promised team of guards arrived not long after. Dahr and Star spoke to them and handed Ko'hut into their custody. Alistar overheard argument regarding Lamorage—the team wanted to take him as well, and Dahr objected. Alistar pulled the Silver Prince's badge from his pocket and joined them.

"Veril Lamorage will remain in our care," he told the leader of the team.

She eyed him. "By whose authority?"

Alistar presented the badge. "He's remaining in our care."

She was silent a moment, then bowed. "Yes sir."

Dahr nodded to Alistar. "We can leave at your word, sir."

"Good. Bring the carriage, please." Alistar addressed the leader of the team. "I leave the rest in your capable hands."

If Lamorage had coat or gloves, they were lost. When Dahr brought the coach to the door, Alistar and Saskia hurried Lamorage from the gambling hall into the vehicle. Star remained with the new team—in part, Alistar suspected, to ensure that nothing conveniently "disappeared."

"Make sure we aren't followed," Alistar told Dahr. "I wouldn't put it past those responsible to sacrifice Ko'hut in the hopes that we'll lead them to Onyxflame."

"Understood, sir," Dahr said.

Anyone who managed to follow the carriage on the twisting, reckless drive back to Coiled Dragon Clinic could only have done so by flying. When they finally stopped, Saskia peeled her fingers free from their grip on the bench and asked, "Is this... normal?"

"I'm of the opinion that Dahr should only be allowed to drive in the middle of the night, when the streets are empty," Alistar answered. "However, he hasn't gotten me killed yet."

When they opened the door, Doctor Tan'shyo rushed into the waiting room. His demeanor relaxed when he saw Alistar and Saskia. "You are safe. Thank the Reyker." His attention turned to Lamorage. "Your friend, I presume."

"Yes. He needs care," Alistar answered. "I'm sorry to be adding to your burden, Doctor."

"Think nothing of it, Mr. De'seneth. Come. I have a room prepared." Doctor Tan'shyo led them into an available patient room.

Lamorage's eyes darted around the room. He'd been all but silent during the carriage ride. Now he clung to Alistar's arm. "Radyn, where's Matra?"

"Sir, you must rest," Dahr said. "Allow me to locate her and see her to safety." The guard's manner was entirely serious, giving no hint as to whether he put stock in Lamorage's ramblings or not.

Lamorage hesitated. "But—"

"My duty is to see you safe," Dahr said. "I will do no less for her."

Lamorage relented and allowed Alistar to lead him to the bed. Alistar gently disentangled the elf's fingers from his coat. "The doctors need to check you over, Veril. All right?"

Lamorage nodded and sat on the edge of the bed.

Alistar turned to Doctor Tan'shyo. "He was restrained and locked in a lightless room since near noon. Also drugged. The man who told me thought he was given koshmar, but if you can, please watch for any symptoms of—"

"I understand," Doctor Tan'shyo said, before Alistar said "Rat's Disease." He shooed Alistar and Dahr from the room and closed the door for privacy.

"Sir, is there anything else you need from me at the moment?" Dahr asked.

"None I can think of. Thank you, Dahr. Contact me if there's any news."

Dahr bowed and departed. Alistar paced up and down the hall. He paused at Onyxflame's door, but didn't enter. He didn't hear any sounds from inside, and couldn't guess whether she was awake or not.

Doctor Tan'shyo and Saskia finished tending to Lamorage. When Alistar heard their steps and low voices, he joined them.

"Your friend should make a complete recovery," Doctor Tan'shyo said. "He's sleeping now. His current state is a reaction to drugs and trauma, but I am confident that it's temporary. He believes himself to be in his family home, perhaps at some earlier time in his life. To judge by the scars, his early years were not without encounters with the denizens of cold and dark."

"He told Saskia that Matra is his sister. I've never heard him speak of family other than his father during my time as his coworker," Alistar said.

Doctor Tan'shyo and Saskia nodded, guessing the same conclusion as Alistar. After a moment of silence, the doctor said, "The clinic is quiet for the moment. We would all benefit from some rest, and I think we should claim this opportunity while we have it."

"Agreed," Alistar said. "I wish you both peaceful rest."

"You as well." Saskia kissed him, then followed her father upstairs.

Alistar retired to Doctor Tan'shyo's office, but didn't lie down immediately. From his pocket, he drew the letter he'd taken from the gambling hall. He broke the seal and unfolded the parchment.

"I, Veril Lamorage, write this as my confession and my final statement."

Alistar drew a sharp breath. *What is this? It must be Ko'hut's work, a forgery. The script is similar to Lamorage, but it doesn't look quite right. It's... too legible. I don't think I've read a single report from Lamorage where I didn't have to guess at some of the words. This has to be a forgery. Ko'hut claimed he was planning to stage Lamorage's suicide.* He continued to read.

"I take full and sole responsibility for the deaths in what has become known as the attack on Dockside."

Alistar's mouth fell open in disbelief. *Lamorage? Responsible for that? Impossible.*

The letter continued, laying out a guilt-stricken narrative of a reckless noble that nearly obscured mentions of another person's presence, and that the other individual owned the carriage that was used. Alistar read it through twice and sat back, mind racing.

I don't believe the story this tells—not for a minute. If Lamorage was involved, it wasn't like this. And who else could have been in the carriage... Cemar.

Alistar jumped to his feet, grabbed a lantern, and raced down the hall. He marched into Onyxflame's room without knocking. The elf groaned and blinked blearily in the light. "Whatever it is, I didn't do it," she mumbled.

"When you confronted Cemar, he was trying to convince me to leave the gathering with him, go for a drive. You asked if he was planning to run down drunks Dockside or drive through an orphanage. What do you know about the Dockside attack?" Alistar demanded.

"De'seneth?" Onyxflame rubbed her eyes. "What are you talking about? Someone drug you again?"

"I'm not drugged and I'm not drunk," Alistar said sharply.

"And I'm not awake. Blood and sand, would you give me a minute to at least get *that* far?" Onyxflame snapped.

Alistar's jaw tightened. "The Dockside attack, Onyxflame. What do you know?"

"I know it sounds like a great way to blackmail someone." Onyxflame pushed herself up against the cushions, then growled in frustration when the ethereal shackle stopped her arm from moving farther. "Drug them up, take them for a ride, and don't give them the reins until it's too late to stop or turn. Then convince them that it was their idea and their fault, and let that take hold in a drug-addled mind. Sounds like something Cemar would do. Can I go back to sleep now?"

"You think Cemar set up the Dockside attack," Alistar pressed.

"Damned if I know! Maybe he thought it sounded like a good idea and intended to copy it. Who would he have been blackmailing, anyway?" Onyxflame pulled the edge of a blanket up to shield her eyes from the lantern light.

"Veril Lamorage." Alistar pulled the letter from his pocket and slapped it down on the table beside Onyxflame's bed.

Onyxflame slowly lowered the blanket. "Perdition... Wait. That was the night he begged the marks from you, isn't it?"

Alistar nodded grimly.

"He's Silverline's information leak?"

"Perhaps," Alistar said. "But if so, he's not the only one. Things went missing long before then." He cursed softly. "Cemar intended to set me up that night. Get a hold in the Family."

"Radyn?"

Alistar spun around, startled. He'd thought Lamorage asleep, but the western elf stood in the doorway, clutching a lamp. "You shouldn't be up. What's wrong?"

"I was cold, and it was too dark." Lamorage sounded like a frightened, lost child. He looked past Alistar to Onyxflame, and drew a startled breath. "Matra! You're safe!"

"Matra?" Onyxflame repeated. "Who in perdition—"

"His sister," Alistar interrupted. "I've been 'Radyn,' and I'm still not sure who that is."

"I'm not his sister!" Onyxflame protested. "And unless *you've* been telling him, how in Slee's Heart would he know I'm a woman?"

Lamorage looked between them. "Are you and Matra fighting, Radyn? Why are you mad at her?"

Alistar shook his head. "Don't worry about it, Veril. It's not about you."

"You shouldn't be fighting." Lamorage looked at Onyxflame again, then turned indignantly to Alistar. "You didn't tell me Matra was hurt!"

Alistar blinked. "I didn't know I was supposed to."

"Radyn! I can't *do* anything if I don't *know*," Lamorage said, hurt.

I have no idea what he's talking about now. Alistar let out a frustrated sigh. "It's been a long couple of days, Veril. Just… show me."

Lamorage nodded. He set his lamp on the table beside Onyxflame's bed and reached out, resting his hand on Onyxflame's injured shoulder. The light flickered and wavered, then a thin stream of purple light snaked down through the ceiling. It wrapped around Lamorage's arm then flowed down his hand, vanishing into his skin before it reached his fingers. Onyxflame inhaled sharply.

Alistar couldn't speak. He just stared.

I read the list of all registered channelers in the city, both the arcane and the healers. I saw names on there that I would never have guessed. But I know, with utter certainty, Veril Lamorage was not on that list. By the Reyker… he's a healer. My friend is an unregistered channeler within Silverline Power.

"Does it still hurt, Matra?" Lamorage asked with concern, looking at Onyxflame.

Onyxflame opened her mouth, closed it, and tried again. "It feels much better. Thank you." She cast a look at Alistar. She'd read the same list. She recognized the same absence.

"Radyn, you and Matra have to stop them." Lamorage's tone grew urgent. "You have to!"

"Stop who, Veril?" Alistar sighed, expecting another nonsense answer.

"The shining men."

Alistar stiffened.

Lamorage grabbed Alistar's arm. "You *must* stop them, Radyn! They're trying to… They made me do… something horrible." He shuddered. "I wanted to tell you, but I was afraid."

"You had good reason to be afraid," Onyxflame said. "Cemar isn't to be trifled with."

Lamorage flinched at that name. "I know they did something. I know my head is full of fog and the words are all sideways."

"You need to rest," Alistar said firmly. "Tomorrow, after you've slept, we can see if the words are working the way they should, all right?"

"You and Matra will stop those men, won't you?" Lamorage insisted.

Onyxflame said nothing. Alistar took Lamorage's arm and steered the elf back to his room. He activated a second lamp in the room. Lamorage curled up on the bed and closed his eyes. Alistar pulled the blankets over him. "Go back to sleep, Veril."

Lamorage's head moved in a small nod. "Yes Radyn."

Alistar walked back to Onyxflame's room. She folded the letter he'd left by the bed and gazed at him. "So, what are you going to tell the Silver Prince about him?"

"I'm certain either Dahr or Star have already reported the pertinent details of his kidnapping by Cemar's minions," Alistar said. "I wouldn't add much to that report."

"Unless Dahr is waiting very quietly outside this room, what just happened is not going to be in that report," Onyxflame said.

"No," Alistar agreed. "It's not."

"And you're not going to add it."

"No, I'm not," Alistar said. "When he's lucid, I plan to have a long talk about failing to register as a healer, though."

"And Dockside?" Onyxflame asked. "This letter?"

"Lamorage didn't write that. I don't believe it's an accurate presentation of the events," Alistar said.

"But you believe he was there, don't you," Onyxflame said, not really a question. "You don't think *that* is information some people very much want to know?"

"I think that ultimately, Cemar is responsible," Alistar said.

"You know that's not my point, De'seneth."

Alistar closed the door and strode to Onyxflame's bed. "And you are missing mine, so let me state it as clearly as possible, with no misunderstandings, Rykka Onyxflame. I do not betray my kin or my friends to anyone. Not to prince, not to king, not to country. I will not hand over a scapegoat to be sacrificed to the rabid mob."

Onyxflame blinked. "And here I thought you an upstanding, law-abiding, loyal lackey of the Silver Prince."

Alistar raised an eyebrow. "Onyxflame, exactly how often do you hear the phrase 'upstanding, law-abiding privateer'?"

"About as often as I hear about the Silver Prince giving one his personal seal and authority," Onyxflame retorted. "So what happens to your friend, then? Going to say nothing and hope the author of this letter doesn't talk?"

"If Lamorage can tell me where to find Cemar, it may never get that far," Alistar said.

Onyxflame fixed a long, dubious look on him.

"If I were inclined to inform the Silver Prince of every transgression I discover, someone else in this clinic is far more likely to become the subject of strenuous inquiry and investigation." Alistar met her gaze without blinking.

She shifted uncomfortably. "Seems Cemar isn't the only one who wields blackmail fodder when he wants something."

Alistar stopped cold. "Is that what you think I meant?"

She jerked at her shackled wrist. "Should I think otherwise? Because that certainly *sounded* like a threat, and when I can't so much as leave this *bed* without your leave, I'm in a poor position to negotiate. What is it you want, De'seneth?"

Alistar folded his arms. "Two questions. First, how in black reefs did you avoid discovery this long? I can't believe you were never searched when you were imprisoned."

She blinked, momentarily confused by the question. "Why do you want—never mind. Of course I was searched. First when I was tossed in the dungeon, and again when I was admitted to Chirrod Prison. Stripped and searched in every possible, humiliating way—inside a closed room, by an automaton. It cared only about what it was designed to care about: was I trying to smuggle anything in with me. It did not care in the least whether I was man or woman. Even prison guards deserve enough dignity to not be subject to such a breach of taboo." She shuddered. "After that, all prisoners wear shapeless clothes. I could remain concealed in Chirrod Prison." Onyxflame paused, studying the blanket. "The Skelocs, though… I wouldn't have been able to hide long. A woman, there? Wouldn't last two weeks."

Alistar believed her. And it certainly wasn't as if some other prison mine would be better. He paused, a thought striking him. "The shoes. Those provided with your clothes didn't fit."

Onyxflame grimaced. "The shoes. The shoes His Highness so graciously provided were clearly sized to Tiyron's feet. I'm sure they'd have fit him wonderfully. Probably cobbled based on footprints; certainly no one cared to take my measurements while I was incarcerated. Unfortunately for me, my feet are smaller than his."

"You couldn't just stuff some extra stockings into the shoes?" Alistar asked, dubious.

Onyxflame shook her head. "Tried that. They still rubbed my feet raw. Something about the shape and where they hit my feet." She let out a thin half-laugh. "Never thought that shoes, of all things, risked giving me away." She drew a breath and met his eyes. "What's the next question?"

"Why didn't you tell me any of this before?"

"I *was* going to tell you after we got away from Cemar, like I said I would," Onyxflame said. "Unfortunately for me, the 'bleeding out and in need of immediate medical care' destroyed any chance of controlling *how* it all came out. And before that... Well, please excuse me for saying this, De'seneth, but do you *really* think it would have gone well for me to tell you 'I'm not really Tiyron Onyxflame, I'm his sister. I'm just as skilled as him, and really, don't feel at all awkward about being an unmarried man alone in your house with an unmarried woman who you can liter- ally *shackle to a bed* with a couple words. I'm *sure* that wouldn't have made things uncomfortable at *all*!"

Alistar drew a sharp breath, outrage surging through his veins. "You think I would have forced myself on you?"

"That's—no!" she said quickly. "That's not what I meant! Perdi- tion, De'seneth, what I *meant* is the appearance of the matter. You told me how rumors can destroy a noble's reputation!"

"Oh, and you have shown great respect and concern so far for noble propriety," Alistar scoffed. "I shouldn't have *any* reason to doubt that as your motivation."

"It came out wrong. I'm sorry. I didn't mean it like that." Her words were rushed. "Does it help if I say that... No. No, it doesn't help at all to say that it's a fear not limited to just you."

"No, it doesn't," Alistar agreed coolly. "Sit up."

Uneasy, she sat up straight, tucking the blanket around her. Alistar untied the sling, allowing her full movement of her healed arm, then canceled the ethereal shackle. She didn't look reassured, especially when Alistar moved where he could see the back of her neck. Her breath was quick. "De'seneth?"

"Let me see the collar, Onyxflame."

Her hands trembled as she shifted the back of her shirt down and pushed her hair aside, allowing him to see the amber collar.

The runes marking its surface matched those on the pendant he wore. So long as Onyxflame wore the collar, she would be compelled to remain within fifty yards of the pendant, and she could not remove the collar herself.

Alistar expected a more complex latch. It yielded after several moments of manipulation and several whispered key phrases. He removed the ring from Onyxflame's neck.

She drew a sharp, startled breath and twisted around to stare at him.

"Arms," Alistar ordered.

"What?" She blinked, then pushed up the loose sleeves of her clinic gown. The inhibitors coiled around her forearms like bracers. They too were etched with runes. They too loosened their hold at his instruction, until Onyxflame could slide them free. They thumped into her lap.

She looked from the inhibitors to Alistar. "What is this, De'seneth?"

"No shackles, no restraints. No guards outside the door. You're not even injured anymore. You want to escape, I won't stop you. Do what you want." Alistar fixed a hard stare on her.

"My abrupt disappearance would send every guard in Lewarden on my heels. I don't want to escape, De'seneth. I want to avenge my brother and take back the work that Cemar stole from me," she said. "And I don't think I can take Cemar alone." She eyed the inhibitors in her lap. "I'll put those cursed things on myself if you make it a condition of continuing to work with you."

"If it was, I wouldn't have removed them in the first place," Alistar said. "What I want is the truth. Is there anything else you want to tell me?"

"Not a thing, but in the interest of not keeping secrets, I'll pretend the question was actually 'Is there anything else I need to know?' Because the answer to *that* question isn't the same." She sighed. "Your friend Lamorage isn't the only unregistered channeler in this clinic."

Alistar started. "What? You? I never heard so much as a *hint* that Onyxflame could channel." The news should have shocked him more, but he was starting to feel numb to revelations.

"Tiyron couldn't," she said. "We were *very* careful to avoid starting any such rumors because of that. It's far easier for a channeler to pretend that they can't channel than the reverse."

He recalled Onyxflame's reaction to Tatya and escorting the child to receive training. *How different would your life have been if someone had swept you off the streets and into the gilded halls? And if they had offered to take your brother as well?* Alistar absorbed the news. "Can your skills help locate Cemar?"

"What, no lecture on the necessary evil of registering? Truly, I'm shocked, De'seneth."

Alistar just gave her a look.

"I'm no bloodhound; I can't track. Gods know I would have found Tiyron if I could." She shook her head. "But I can say that Cemar is likely to make his move soon. He thinks that I'm Tiyron, and he wouldn't have taken my brother out if he didn't think him a threat. If we wait too long, the problem won't be finding Cemar, it will be stopping him before he takes the crown for himself." She grimaced. "Not going to lie, I despise the Crown, the Silver Prince, the nobles, the entire system. But letting Cemar take control would be worse."

"Different motives, same end goal," Alistar said. He collected the inhibitors. "I expect to hear from Dahr in the morning. I'll let you know what he says."

Onyxflame rubbed her wrists. "De'seneth… thank you. I'm sorry for what I said. You're an honorable man. Good night."

"Good night." Alistar retired to the study. *I don't know if this was a good idea. She may be long gone by morning, and I may be a fool to trust her and not turn her in. But this is my ship, and this is the course I've plotted. No turning back now.*

CHAPTER 36

The chime of the speaking stone jolted Alistar awake. He sat up quickly and fumbled it from his pocket. "What news?"

"Less than an hour ago, an attempt was made on Ko'hut's life, sir," Dahr announced. "The attempt was unsuccessful; however, the assassin was a member of the Royal Guard."

"What?" That news tore the last vestiges of weariness from Alistar. "A Royal Guard tried to kill him?"

"By His Majesty's orders, Ko'hut is now under constant watch by no less than two guards at all times, and only those who are personally recommended by certain trusted individuals. My name is on the list, but I have been granted leave from the roster by His Highness. Star, unfortunately, will not always be available to assist, though, because of this."

Cemar, or someone, has agents even in the Royal Guard. "Dahr, how certain can you be that the guards who are personally protecting the Royal Family can be trusted?"

"They are undergoing testing as I speak, sir," Dahr said. "Any disloyalty will be revealed."

That sounded ominous, and Dahr's tone discouraged him from pressing for details. "Has Ko'hut said anything?"

"No sir. Not a word. He refuses to so much as say his name." Dahr paused. "I found a little time to look into the names Sir Lamorage used last night. According to the scant records I found, Matra was his elder sister. The name Radyn appears to have belonged to his cousin."

"I'm surprised you found them at all," Alistar admitted. "Lewarden doesn't keep many records of the mountains."

"They keep death records, sir," Dahr said plainly. "Both are deceased. By the dates, it appears they died the winter before Sir Lamorage left his home and came to Lewarden. I conferred with an archivist, and learned that no prior arrangements had been made for him to come to the court."

Implying that Lamorage's decision to come to Lewarden had not been planned in advance. A response to the deaths? Alistar thought of the healing Lamorage performed last night. *A decision driven by guilt over not saving them?* "I see. Thank you. Any news from the rest of the city?"

"His Highness has instructed that, given the recent unrest, only essential personnel are required to report to work at Silverline Power. He has also instructed that employees will not be docked pay for not reporting to work. The rioters have been quiet for the past few hours, and have not made headway out of the slums. Many factories have chosen not to operate today, and unlike His Highness, they are not paying their employees for the forced leave, leading to fears among their workers that they will not have funds to feed their families. The more vapid of the nobility have expressed concern that recent events may interfere with the Ice Blossom Festival celebrations, and request reassurances that they will not be inconvenienced."

"And the louder the nobles complain, the more those people resent them," Alistar said. "The next riots might not need the Successors to stir them up. Burn the factories, and more people starve. Placate the nobles, and those with nothing grow more angry. Ignore the nobles in favor of the masses, and the nobles bend their political sway to attack." He shook his head. "I stayed out of political games for a reason."

"That is the news as of the moment, sir," Dahr said. "How are Onyxflame and Sir Lamorage?"

"Doctor Tan'shyo thinks Lamorage will make a full recovery. If he's lucid this morning, I hope to learn more about Cemar and his cronies. Onyxflame… consented to a healer's treatment last night. He should be fit to be up."

A sound of surprise from Dahr. "I was not aware the clinic had a healer available, sir."

"They don't, most of the time," Alistar said, avoiding offering further details. "Let me know if anything changes."

"Yes sir." The stone fell dark.

A push here, a shove there, and everything could collapse. The balance is too precarious. Rechmal preserve us, if I wanted to, even I could put Lewarden in a state of chaos. Cemar's opportunity is just waiting for him to nudge another piece over. This has been building since the fire in the factory last summer. He paused. *That was sabotage. I wonder if his hand was in that, too. Just how far is his reach?*

A light knock on the study door was followed by Saskia's voice. "Are you up?"

"I'm awake and decent," Alistar said, combing fingers through his hair and beard. "Come in."

She opened the door and stepped inside. "I checked on Onyxflame. She related an abbreviated explanation of last night. She tried to keep it focused on her shoulder, but I noticed the absence of certain… ornaments."

Alistar nodded. "I removed the collar and suppressors," he confirmed. "I'd appreciate it if you didn't mention that to anyone else."

She made a sound of agreement. "Also, Lamorage is awake and lucid. He recognized me, at least."

"Did Onyxflame tell you that he healed her?" Alistar asked.

Saskia nodded. "I don't know if Lamorage remembers doing

so, though. He was confused as to how he got here, and even what day it was. Father is upstairs making breakfast. Since everyone is fit to be out of bed, we can all eat there."

"Nothing like state secrets discussed around the breakfast table," Alistar commented. He looped his arm though hers. "Shall we?"

The two elves and three humans sat around a table and broke their fast with eggs, sausage, and tea. Onyxflame had reassumed her male persona. Apparently, the plain workman's clothes had been among those Dahr retrieved from Alistar's house, because Onyxflame wore them. Lamorage was dressed in clothes borrowed from the clinic, and toyed with the hems of the ill-fitting sleeves. Alistar could read his unease and discomfort. Doctor Tan'shyo and Saskia carried themselves as if nothing was out of the ordinary.

Finally Lamorage asked, "How did I arrive here, and... how long have I been here?"

"Just since last night," Alistar told him. "I went down Dockside to meet you, and brought Saskia and a few others as backup. Marus Ko'hut was waiting for me at the gambling hall."

Lamorage tensed and swallowed hard. "I'm sorry. I didn't mean to get you involved like that."

"I was already involved," Alistar told him. "We stymied his ambush. Ko'hut is under arrest and in the keeping of the Royal Guard."

"The Royal Guard?" Lamorage repeated, more alarmed that reassured.

"We found you locked in one of the rooms in the gambling hall," Alistar continued. "You'd been drugged and weren't coherent. We brought you here to the clinic."

"Did Ko'hut... tell you anything?" Lamorage asked.

Alistar chose to misinterpret the question. "He hasn't said anything while under arrest. This morning, an assassin tried to kill him. The attempt was unsuccessful, but he's a target. I suspect that you may be one as well, if they can find you, Lamorage. We were careful not to be followed when we came here, but please be careful."

"I'm not sure why he didn't kill me earlier," Lamorage said softly, staring at his plate.

"Cemar insisted on live bait," Alistar said.

Lamorage's head jerked up. "You know about Cemar?"

"Some. Not as much as I need to, and anything you can add will help," Alistar said. "Are you aware that there have been blackouts in the mahiy lines this winter?"

"I heard rumors," Lamorage said.

"The special assignment I was given was to investigate the cause of them," Alistar told him. He gave Lamorage a very brief outline of his assignment and how it led him to Cemar. When Alistar spoke of the gathering he'd been invited to join, tension crept through Lamorage's shoulders. At the mention of drugs, Lamorage paled, and when Alistar told of Cemar's insistence that Alistar accompany him on a drive, the elf's face lost all color.

"I'm guessing this sounds familiar," Alistar said quietly.

"Yes," Lamorage whispered.

"I'm fortunate that Aspendark managed to follow, and chose that moment to intervene," Alistar continued. He skimmed over their escape, up to Onyxflame's injury.

Lamorage frowned, looking to Onyxflame and seeing no sign of a wound. His brow furrowed as if he was trying to remember something. He cleared his throat awkwardly. "De'seneth, last night, did I... think you were someone else?"

"You called me Radyn," Alistar said.

"I got the distinction of being Matra," Onyxflame added.

Lamorage flushed vivid red. "I am *so* sorry, sir."

Onyxflame waved it off. "You were clearly not intending offense. And I can excuse mistaken identity when it's accompanied by healing."

"Healing?" Lamorage shook his head quickly. "You must be mistaken."

Alistar's eyebrows rose. "I was there as well, Lamorage. You healed Aspendark."

Lamorage shook his head more emphatically. "I dreamed that I saved my sister, nothing more! I can't heal others, De'seneth! My ability to channel isn't strong enough to rate even a mention. Not enough to save my sister or my cousin when we were caught outside of shelter and attacked. It was barely enough to keep me alive."

He sounded sincere. Alistar said nothing. Onyxflame spoke. "You've been involved with Cemar for a little while now, haven't you? Taken Ambrosia?"

Lamorage tensed. "What does that have to do with anything?"

"Quite a bit, potentially," Alistar said, guessing Onyxflame's line of thought. "Have you?" He knew the answer before Lamorage nodded in silent answer. He'd witnessed it at Proudmoor's gathering.

Doctor Tan'shyo listened with interest, especially at the mention of the drug. Alistar tried to formulate an explanation that didn't delve into technical details. "Our theory at the moment is that Cemar is draining power from the mahiy lines. He's developed a method of refining and crystallizing it, converting it to a solid form. He's diluting the power enough that ingesting it doesn't cause immediate death, and he's providing it as Ambrosia." Alistar let out a breath. "That drug *is* magic, Lamorage."

Lamorage shook his head. "That defies nearly every theory of magical energy!"

Alistar nodded. "Believe me, I know. But I met a six-year-old street child who woke as a channeler after tasting a piece of the toxic dross. I met a young woman who claims to draw magic from within rather than from the mahiy lines."

"I know her," Lamorage said. "And you think that it's... given me healing."

"You already *had* healing," Doctor Tan'shyo interjected. "A weak form of it, evidently, but, assuming you consumed this drug on more than one occasion, the additional magic enhanced your ability."

Lamorage picked up his mug of tea and stared into the depths as if he could read his fate there. "I'm not a healer."

"Fine," Onyxflame said evenly. "But you are someone who Cemar sunk his claws into. What's his goal? And how much do those around him know?"

"Lady Sunward… I think she's involved in all of it. Probably knows everything. Sok'lof… he and Cemar act like they're old friends, but… I don't think he knows as much as he thinks he does. I feel like… when he isn't around, Cemar and Sunward always seem like they have something going on that they aren't telling him."

"You think they're setting him up?" Alistar asked.

"Maybe. I don't know. Maybe they just don't want to share the results with him. I don't know. I certainly wasn't privy to any useful information." Lamorage swallowed hard. "Sok'lof might have a connection with the Successors. He talked about them sometimes, like he had some authority over them."

"And Cemar," Onyxflame prompted. "What do you know of his plans?"

Lamorage opened his mouth, then closed it again. He turned to Alistar. "De'seneth, are you really the heir to the As'enel house?"

"I am," Alistar promised. "You said that you needed help my family might be able to provide." He leaned forward on the table. "I know you're being blackmailed, Lamorage."

Lamorage looked at him, eyes pleading. "Do you know why?"

"Because you couldn't stop Cemar when he put the reins in your hands," Alistar said, voice low. "And you didn't have time to do anything else." He didn't know that for sure, but he watched Lamorage's face and saw the wave of guilt mixed with relief. "I know why you asked to meet at Dockside."

"He said that I did it, that I could have stopped or turned us away, but I couldn't. I tried. I tried!" Lamorage's voice shook.

Saskia's face went carefully blank, but her eyes burned with anger as she inferred the meaning of their words. Alistar hoped that fury was directed at Cemar rather than Lamorage.

"Of course you did, and of course he set it up so you couldn't prevent the situation," Onyxflame said. "But why did he want that hold on you?"

"He wanted Silverline people," Lamorage said, voice trembling. He stared down at his plate. "I… I know I'm not the only one, but I don't know who else he has. He wanted reports from me—about the health of the generator plants. And he gave me a list of projects he wanted to know about, or know who was working on them. I don't know where he got the list. From someone else in Silverline, certainly. The information was confidential. I gave him some of what he wanted." He paused. "The boring pieces—the reports where the generators were operating without issues. When I saw that one had problems, I just… didn't include that information. Cemar knew I wasn't giving him everything. Things got very unpleasant quickly. I thought he was going to have me killed." Lamorage drew a steadying breath. "I heard some things I wasn't supposed to. He's planning to disrupt the mahiy lines completely—all of them at once."

"*All* of them?" Onyxflame repeated. "How in Slee's Balls does he intend to do that?"

A chill ran down Alistar's spine. "Lamorage, has he figured out where the heart is?"

Lamorage nodded.

Alistar cursed. "If he knows that, he can disrupt the mahiy lines." He turned to Onyxflame. "There is one central point, one core for all the mahiy lines in Lewarden. Cemar takes his device there, and he can drain every line in the city. It's the central feed."

"So where *is* this point?" Onyxflame demanded. "Silverline Power?"

"Close," Alistar said. "You know what's behind the Silverline Power headquarters?"

"Prince Cero's estate," Onyxflame said. She stopped cold. "*There*? Cemar is going to break into the Silver Prince's personal estate? Gods, De'seneth, I think I want to see him try!"

Alistar shook his head. "No. No, this is bad. The Royal Guard are spread thin, between combating the riots, protecting Ko'hut from assassins, and taking steps to ensure that the members of the Royal Guard are, in fact, loyal, since one of their own was the would-be assassin. They're spread out all over the city."

Onyxflame grew grave. "And we only have two on our list who we're confident we can trust. Perdition. All right, it's more of a mess than I thought."

"Perfect conditions for Cemar," Lamorage said quietly. "Everyone's looking everywhere but at him."

"Except for us," Alistar said. "So we need— "

He was interrupted by the chime of the speaking stone. Alistar frowned and stood, activating it as he stepped into the next room. "Yes?"

"Sir, we have a problem." Dahr's ominous words were accompanied by loud crashes in the background, then a burst of shouting.

"What's going on?" Alistar demanded.

"Successors are attacking the garrison, sir." Dahr sounded far too calm for the news he was relaying, though Alistar did catch some hints of worry in the guard's voice. "It's possible they are being led by Zhrets Vonn."

"The *garrison*?" Alistar repeated. "Are they insane?!"

"From what I see, that seems the most likely explanation, sir," Dahr said. Another loud crash. "They are screaming about bearing Rechmal's blessing and bringing death to the unbelievers. They have, however, acquired weapons."

Alistar cursed, a sinking feeling in his gut. "Does that leave *any* of the Royal Guard free?"

"One moment, sir." A loud clang, then a scream. Dahr spoke again. "Any who are available have been called to quell this ill-advised attack."

And leaves the barest minimum guarding King Feyblade and Prince Cero. "Dahr, get to Prince Cero's estate. We'll meet you there."

He expected argument, or at least a demand for an explanation. Instead, Dahr simply said, "At once, sir. Should I wait for you before entering?"

"Yes," Alistar said. "Be careful. Our evidence points toward Cemar using this chaos as cover to make his move."

"Understood, sir."

All eyes turned to Alistar when he returned to the table, and no one spoke. Alistar looked around the table. "Aspendark, we need to go, now. Lamorage, I'm going to ask you to stay here, at the clinic. Saskia…" He longed to ask her to join them, but at the same time, the thought of putting her in such immediate danger terrified him. And if she joined him, Doctor Tan'shyo would be the only one present to both protect Lamorage and manage the clinic. "Will you keep Lamorage safe? If something goes wrong, he's one of our few surviving witnesses. I want to be sure that if I fall, everything we've learned isn't lost as well."

Saskia jumped to her feet. "You are *not* getting yourself killed, Alistar! That's an order!"

"What's happened, De'seneth?" Onyxflame interrupted.

"Successors are attacking the garrison, quite possibly led by Zhrets Vonn. The Royal Guard is fighting them off. *Everyone* is focused on the city and the fighting. What better time for Cemar to strike?"

"He won't be alone," Lamorage said. He swallowed hard. "De'seneth, Cemar loves to hear himself talk, and he loves having a captive audience."

"Literally or figuratively?" Alistar asked.

"Both."

Onyxflame headed for the stairs. "Then we have little time to waste, De'seneth." She turned and gave Saskia a quick bow. "I will do everything in my power to ensure your future husband returns unharmed."

Saskia caught Alistar's arm and pulled him close for a long, hard kiss. "You'd better come back," she whispered. "We'll keep Lamorage safe while you're gone."

"Thank you," Alistar whispered back. "I love you."

CHAPTER 37

Streets that should have bustled with traffic stood empty and far too silent. A handful of people rushed about, heads down, not looking at one another, as if they broke some great taboo by leaving their homes. Alistar and Onyxflame walked quickly. Alistar prayed for a carriage, but didn't see a single taxi on the street.

"Just to be sure, De'seneth, we haven't actually died and fallen into some spirit world equivalent of Lewarden, with all the buildings and none of the people, have we?" Onyxflame asked softly.

"No, we're not dead," Alistar said firmly.

"Good. I'd hope I'd have noticed if I was, but thought I should check." Onyxflame's gaze swept the empty street. "People are scared."

"And most don't see any indication that those in power are taking action," Alistar said. "That's when fear turns into anger." He cut through an alley, up several side streets, and finally reached one of the main thoroughfares.

They were in the loose border between Lower City and Midcity. Smoke hung in the air, dark clouds still billowing up from smoldering buildings. The market across the street was dead, no movement but a pair of dogs scavenging for scraps.

How many people have lost their livelihood? How many have died, or have yet to die from sickness or hunger? Even if we stop him now, how much of the damage Cemar has inspired cannot be undone?

A lone carriage rattled listlessly down the street. Alistar raised a hand to hail it, and the driver stopped to consider him, gaze cautious. "Headed somewhere, milord?"

"Can you and your team take us to Silverline Power?" Alistar asked. "I'll pay extra the faster you can get us there."

The driver heaved a sigh and leaned forward, cart whip resting across his lap. "I told the others, an' I'll tell you. I ain't having no part in protests, not even gettin' you there. Them folk do good work. Help a lotta people."

"Not to protest," Alistar said quickly. "I work there."

"Aye? Do you now?" The driver tilted back his cap to look at Alistar. "Oye, ain't you the fellow who paid to help a couple ladies find their kin after Dockside?"

Alistar didn't recognize the driver, but he nodded. "I did, though I hope I'm not the only person who did so that day."

"Only one I know," the driver said. "I'll take the pair of you. Better than listening to the talk of folks wanting to start new protests at Silverline, like it's their fault the Successors have gone crazier than usual." He hopped down from the driver's box and opened the carriage door.

Alistar and Onyxflame stepped inside. The driver resumed his seat, and his team set off at a trot. The interior of the carriage was drab but serviceable. Onyxflame gazed out the window and fidgeted with the fraying edge of the curtain.

"We're going into this blind, you know," she said in a low voice. "We don't know how many he has with him, or whether he's taking hostages, or even, for certain, what he intends to do."

"On a stormy night, in unfamiliar waters, everyone's on alert," Alistar said. "This isn't much different."

"And how many of those have you sailed with a crew of three?" Onyxflame countered.

Alistar gazed at her. "Cemar's rushing. He's throwing everything into causing distractions. He's going to make mistakes. And he already thinks that he's made one. He thinks that Tiyron Onyxflame is alive and bent on revenge."

Onyxflame shivered. "You didn't see what he did to my brother."

"No, I didn't," Alistar acknowledged. "But you did. And you can dispense the justice Cemar deserves."

She looked at him sharply. "If I dispense the justice I think he deserves, Cemar won't be standing trial before any mortal judge."

"Good," Alistar said. "No arrest means no chance of him escaping or someone rescuing him. Or worse yet, someone using him as their political pawn. The gods will judge Cemar."

She gave a thin laugh. "You sound so confident, De'seneth."

"It's a captain's job," Alistar replied. He pulled a sheathed long knife from his belt and held it to her hilt-first. "My armory is unfortunately thin at the moment, but we don't have time to stop at my house."

She blinked, surprised. "Are you sure?"

"You're not a prisoner anymore, Onyxflame. And you ought to be armed."

She accepted the blade and hooked it to her belt. "Thank you."

With little traffic, the carriage arrived at Silverline Power sooner than Alistar expected. The driver opened the door for them. "Silverline Power, milord. Three chips."

Alistar handed him a full mark. "Thank you. Keep the rest."

The driver inclined his head in a nod. "Kind of you, milord. Take care."

Alistar saw no indication of organized protest outside Silverline's gates. Even the usual handful of people were absent. He strode for the front gate.

"De'seneth?" Onyxflame asked, hurrying after him. "I thought we were bound for the Silver Prince's estate."

"We're getting backup," Alistar said.

"You *do* remember that I can't just walk in, don't you?" Onyxflame protested. "No badge. It's at your house."

Alistar didn't swear out loud. "You'll have to wait at the gate, then. I'll be as quick as possible."

The gate ogre stood at his post. He leaned down to sniff Alistar, then opened the gate with a grunt. "Associate De'seneth, pass."

"Can Aspendark wait in the guard house?" Alistar asked.

"With you?" the ogre asked. "Can enter."

"He can?" Alistar asked, startled.

"Director approved guests." The ogre waved Onyxflame after Alistar. "Said we protect families and friends if workers feel not safe at home."

The Silverline Power headquarters is one of the better defended sites in Lewarden that doesn't rely on the Royal Guard. And I defy anyone to bribe the ogres or gargoyles. The thought lifted his spirits slightly.

The gargoyles roamed restlessly as Alistar and Onyxflame strode toward the building. Some pedestals stood empty, their normal occupants stalking about the grounds or perching on thick tree branches. Morath prowled, growling softly when Alistar held out a hand.

Dahr had said that employees had been offered the day off, so Alistar was startled to find the lobby busy with people. The majority, he quickly realized, were not Silverline employees. Alistar wove around clumps of children playing with marbles and other toys to reach the front desk.

Assistants Torrent and Goldleaf both sat at the desk, scribing notes in their respective ledgers. Assistant Goldleaf greeted him. "Good morning, Associate De'seneth. Work or shelter?"

Alistar's brow furrowed. "Pardon me?"

"Ah, work, then." She made a note. "Director Strey'mend issued an offer to any Silverline employees who don't feel safe at their residences, inviting them to bring their families here until the unrest is resolved. As you can see, many have accepted." She shifted and settled on her chair, wings folded against her back. "What can we do for you, Associate?"

"Do you know the status of Prince Cero's estate?" Alistar asked her.

"I've not received any reports of unusual activity." She tilted her head to one side, then frowned. "Several protective wards and alarms have been disabled. And they must have been disabled by someone with the proper authorization, because anyone else doing so should have triggered several safeguards and secondary alerts."

"Who's authorized to do that, other than the prince himself?" Alistar asked, stomach sinking.

"Immediate kin, and members of the Royal Guard ranking Captain or higher." Assistant Goldleaf still had that distant look. "Two such ranked members of the Royal Guard are currently at His Highness's estate, as is His Highness."

Alistar spoke in a low voice. "I have reason to suspect that the loyalty of some members of the Royal Guard has been compromised. Would disabling these alarms allow someone without authorization or permission to enter His Highness's home?"

"Yes. And with them disabled, I cannot determine whether or not the estate has suffered an intrusion. This implies that the choice of the wards was deliberate and planned—none of the wards that would trigger notices to us here have been disabled, only circumvented. I will inform the Director of this news immediately." Her gaze focused on Alistar. "What do you need?"

"I need to borrow any available ogres," Alistar told her. Beside him, Onyxflame blinked and gave him a startled look. "Gargoyles as well, if any are amenable. As soon as possible."

Assistant Torrent turned to him. "We can send four ogres with you without overly degrading Silverline Power's defenses,

Associate De'seneth. You wish them to meet you at His Highness's estate, correct?"

Alistar nodded.

"They are on their way. Most of the gargoyles are unresponsive to requests at this moment. I will continue attempting to contact them, but the current situation had unsettled them."

Gargoyles were notoriously stubborn and averse to change. Alistar nodded understanding. "Thank you. What's the best entry point?"

"The western gate of the estate is unwarded, sir," Assistant Goldleaf said.

Alistar nodded again and waved Onyxflame to follow. They crossed the lobby, weaving around people, and returned to the frigid winter day. Onyxflame glanced over her shoulder as the door closed. "Not asking help from fellow Silverline employees?"

"The ogres *are* Silverline employees," Alistar said. "And I trust their loyalty to Prince Cero."

"They aren't very subtle," Onyxflame said.

"You'd be surprised," Alistar said. He pulled out the speaking stone and activated it. "Dahr, have you arrived?"

"Yes sir. I await you near the north gate. However, I just saw four ogres leave Silverline Power, heading to the west gate," Dahr answered.

"Good. We're headed that way as well," Alistar said.

"Are you sure, sir? The west gate is reserved for officials and diplomatic guests. It will be warded, and I do not have the authorization to open it."

"It *should* be warded. According to Assistant Goldleaf, at the moment, it's not," Alistar said. "We're on our way."

"Official guests and diplomats?" Onyxflame repeated. "Cemar does think highly of himself."

"No surprise there," Alistar said.

They followed the path to Silverline Power's back gate and entered the alley between Silverline Power and Prince Cero's estate. Onyxflame fished in her pocket and pulled out a strip of black cloth. She wrapped it to cover her right eye. Alistar gave her a questioning look.

"Even the best healer can't cause an eye to regrow," Onyxflame said, voice hard.

The statement puzzled Alistar for a moment, then he understood. *Tiyron must have lost that eye to Cemar's tortures.* "Can you still see well enough?"

"The cloth is thin," Onyxflame said. "It's not much hindrance."

Four ogres waited at the west gate. They saluted Alistar, fists to their chests. Alistar returned the salute. "Thank you."

"Assistant Goldleaf said not all guards to be trusted. What about this one?" one ogre asked, pointing.

Alistar followed the gesture and saw Dahr pacing restlessly, hands clearly away from his weapons. "Yes, he's trustworthy," Alistar said. "It's the ones already inside who I'm not so certain about."

Dahr joined them with a polite nod of respect to the ogres. The guard bowed to Alistar, and simply nodded a greeting to Onyxflame without any commentary.

Onyxflame raised an eyebrow. "No remark on how disappointed you are to see me still alive?"

"The garrison is under attack. Members of the Royal Guard have broken their oaths of service. I do not know whether my prince is safe or if he has fallen into the hands of criminals. A thief might come in handy now," Dahr replied.

"That's the closest thing to a compliment I've heard you say to me. I'll take it as one. Good to see you too." Onyxflame grinned.

Dahr rolled his eyes and shook his head. "Clearly, you are recovered from your injuries. You have the right shoes this time?" His voice carried a sharp hint of sarcasm.

Onyxflame smirked. "My shirt was ruined—the shoes survived, fortunately. And these are excellent for walking. Or running, as I was doing when that damnable spell dragged me off to go find De'seneth the other night."

Dahr walked to the gate and put a hand to the tangle of wrought iron vines. They uncurled and peeled away, leaving the gateway open. The guard was clearly uneasy. "This should not be unsealed. Even attempting to open it should trigger alarms."

Alistar stepped through, followed by Onyxflame. "Thus why I am concerned as to the loyalty of the members of the Royal Guard already inside. Because someone had to disable the protections."

Countless tracks churned the muddy snow around the gate. A short cobbled path led from the gate to a wide covered walkway, which split in several directions, offering access to the outbuildings as well as the palatial manor. Alistar had never entered the manor. He had, however, heard rumors and stories of the breathtaking splendor of the ballroom from those few fortunate enough to acquire one of the highly desired invitations to the Silver Prince's Ice Blossom Festival Ball.

"What we looking for?" the lead ogre asked.

"A male of mixed blood named Cemar, and His Highness," Alistar said. "If you find the prince, protect him. If you find Cemar, let me know. If you find any of your fellows, engage them in the search if possible."

The ogres all nodded with grunts of understanding and marched under the cover of the walkway, where they split up. The boards creaked under their heavy treads. Alistar, Onyxflame, and Dahr took the path toward the back of manor. The route took them past the Silver Prince's fabled gardens and the greenhouses where he bred and experimented with varieties of kurowa flowers. Alistar looked toward the greenhouses, and stopped abruptly.

"De'seneth?" Onyxflame asked.

Alistar held a finger to his lips and pointed to the tracks in the snow. Three sets, with a heavy tread, as if they had been burdened, led toward the greenhouses. Alistar followed. They could simply be gardeners, but he didn't want to risk potentially leaving enemies in position to flank them.

Dahr tapped his arm and pointed to crimson stains seeping under the door from one of the greenhouses. The tracks entered, then left again. Alistar's jaw tightened and he jerked his head in a quick nod. Dahr edged the greenhouse door open and stepped inside. He returned a moment later, closing the door behind him.

"Two apprentice gardeners, sir," he said in a low voice. "Both are recently dead."

Ahead, a door banged. All three of them froze. Steps thumped in the snow. "Is it the right spot or not? Not a lot of time left!" a male voice demanded.

"Almost… There! The middle of the courtyard by the fountain —that should do it," a female answered. Several voices grunted with effort and metal scraped on paving stones.

Alistar frowned and cautiously moved around the side of the greenhouse until he could see the source of the sounds. A fountain sprayed mists of water skyward in a cloud of steam. The droplets froze as they fell, forming a thin dome of shimmering ice over the fountain. Two men and one woman dragged a metal device as half as tall as a man, fitted with coils, tubes, and tanks across the stones toward the fountain.

Alistar sensed someone beside him, and turned to see Onyxflame staring at the trio, her eyes cold and her hands clenched in fury. "They dare manhandle my work so carelessly?" she hissed.

One of the men checked his pocket watch. "Seven minutes. Is that enough time to set up?"

"It'll have to be," the woman said. She pried open a panel and reached into the device.

"Idiot," Onyxflame growled. "She has no idea what she's doing."

Dahr marched into the courtyard, hand resting on the hilt of his sword. "What are you doing?"

The woman glanced over just long enough to see the uniform. "We're almost ready!" she said. "We'll meet the deadline, don't worry. Took longer than expected to find the center."

The men looked at Dahr and stiffened. "Praska, that isn't one of our—"

Dahr's blade flashed from the sheath and jabbed. The speaker fell back, blood spilling from his chest. The second man lunged at the guard with a shout. The woman jerked away from the device and flung her hand toward Dahr.

A flash of light struck Dahr and he froze, paralyzed by the touch of magic. The guard's eyes burned with rage, but his body did not respond, even as the man slammed into him. Elf and human both fell to the ground.

"Why are you here? Who else knows?" the woman demanded.

"If you expect answers, you really need to ask questions *before* you paralyze someone," Onyxflame observed dryly, stepping around the other side of the greenhouse and turning eyes away from Alistar.

The two stared at Onyxflame with wide-eyed recognition. "Impossible! You're dead! Cemar killed you himself!"

Onyxflame sneered. "Your idiocy never ceases to amaze me. Your 'leader' failed at something as simple as killing me, yet you trust him to take control of the *nation*?"

"You were dying!" the man burst, jumping to his feet and leaving Dahr where he lay. "I saw it!"

"Did you? Or did you see what you wanted to see?" Onyxflame's eyes narrowed. "Did you see what *I* wanted you to see?"

One thing was certain: Cemar's people did not see Alistar move up behind them until it was far too late. His cutlass plunged into the woman's back. Onyxflame's dagger slashed at the remaining man's neck. He caught the strike with his arm, gasping in pain as the blade bit deep.

"None of you deserve a death this quick or clean," Onyxflame snarled, ripping the dagger free.

He stood fixed to the spot, staring at her. "Revenant."

"You only wish that I was something so easily banished." Onyxflame stabbed the blade into his chest.

As the man fell, Dahr gasped and pushed up to his knees, finally able to draw breath again. Alistar crouched beside the guard. "Dahr?"

The elf waved him off, coughing. Onyxflame moved to the device, using the blood-stained blade to pry loose additional panels and expose the guts of the device.

"What are… you doing?" Dahr demanded.

"I built much of this device before Cemar stole and perverted it. I'm getting to the core and removing *my* work from Cemar's hands," she said sharply.

Reaching inside the metal casing, she ripped tubes and wires loose with no effort to preserve the inner workings. With a sound of triumph, she tore a tube of dirty gray metal free. Onyxflame untwisted the cap and tipped out an amber colored cylinder the length of Alistar's hand. The twisting runes etched into it pulsed with an inner glow. Onyxflame nodded in satisfaction and quickly returned it to the tube. She screwed on the cap and handed the tube to Alistar. "Be careful if you open it. The bar is hot."

Alistar accepted it cautiously. "What is this?"

"The power source." Her voice dropped low. "It's an artifact infused with the essence of a dragon. Don't ask where or how we got a hold of it, because I don't exactly know the details. However, avoid mentioning it around foreign dignitaries unless you're willing to risk an international incident."

"Acquired from somewhere reached by a Narnan merchant ship, perhaps?" Alistar asked.

Onyxflame didn't answer.

Alistar eyed the tube. Scratches marred the surface, and he

could see the outlines where clamps had secured it inside the device. "What does it do, and why give it to me?"

"I'd rather give it to you than to Dahr, and we both know he'd object to my keeping it. If you're so inclined, you can give it back later. I'd highly appreciate it if you forgot to mention it to anyone official when you make a report," Onyxflame said. She paused, plastering a pleasant smile on her face.

Dahr steadied himself, considered the bodies, then the device, and said, "Sir, they indicated a deadline."

Alistar nodded. "Is it safe to leave this here, Onyxflame?"

She reached inside the device and ripped out more of the guts. Sorting through the components, she tucked several in her pockets. "Without the core pieces, it's a garish lawn ornament, and His Highness is welcome to it. You know this place, Dahr. Where do we look for a power-hungry lunatic?"

"Follow me." Dahr set off at a swift walk, nearly a jog, around toward the back side of the manor house. "*You* built that device? For what purpose?"

"I made most of it, before Cemar and I had a disagreement on how it should be used and he stole it," Onyxflame answered. "And I might add, he did a piss-poor job of redesigning it without me and my plans. I intended it to siphon a thin stream of magic from the mahiy lines. Hadn't perfected the method of converting the magic into a solid, stable state. I planned to conduct other experiments with that magic. Cemar, on the other hand, apparently decided it was best used to make *drugs*."

"What about the claims these men made that he killed you?" Dahr pressed.

"I have some very unpleasant scars from the experience," Onyxflame told him, gaze hard. "I'd like to repay them in kind."

All the right implications, building a lie in such a way that Dahr was unlikely to ask too many questions. The guard nodded slowly. His expression said he was not completely convinced, but he accepted the answer for now.

Onyxflame spoke to Alistar in a low voice as they hurried after Dahr. "The artifact absorbs magic. The story I heard claims that if it gains enough power, the dragon's spirit will break free of its imprisonment and return to life. Since it was supposedly a very angry dragon that laid waste to continents during its life, try not to test that theory." She indicated the cylinder in Alistar's hand. "The tube was crafted specifically to contain it. The alloy blocks the magic so it can't be absorbed by the artifact, but when it's activated, it doesn't interfere with the artifact's draw."

Alistar frowned. "So it draws magic, but cannot absorb it. What happens to that power?"

"I designed my device to harness that. It amplified and directed the artifact. On its own, the core draws the magic around it, but the radius is diminished. Probably not more than a couple of rooms' range at most. I crafted dampers, which Cemar disabled, to limit how much the device pulls. Magic flows through the conduits and, to skip the technical details, is compressed into a solid form. That's how I intended it to work, at least. I didn't have time to sort through all the ways Cemar butchered my design."

Alistar turned the tube over in his hands. "How is it activated?"

Onyxflame whispered a word in his ear. "The first use activates it, the second deactivates it."

"Will it draw Ambrosia crystals as well?" Alistar asked.

Onyxflame frowned. "I don't know, though I would suspect so." She paused. "If someone had just swallowed the crystals, that could potentially leave some nasty holes, depending how quickly they dissolve."

They entered the manor house through the kitchens. The blast of hot air left Alistar sweating, and he quickly shed his coat and winter gear. He looked around for servants, but no one attended the ovens or prepared meals. The halls were similarly empty.

How close are we to the time? I should have checked my watch. Has it been seven minutes yet?

Despite the lack of people, the manor didn't feel empty. The air was heavy and oppressive. Alistar searched for shadows as they advanced—despite all the lamps, darkness lingered close. Dahr hurried his steps, almost jogging.

"I hope you appreciate the effort I've made to provide a suitable audience for the collapse of your empire." The voice carried down the halls.

Onyxflame hissed in anger. "Cemar."

Dahr was already turning down a hall in the direction of the voice. Alistar ran after him, silently cursing.

Cemar's voice rose. "My friends, today we witness the end of the oppression and corruption that has ravaged our homeland!"

"This arrogant traitor dares?" Dahr growled. "He *dares* say such a thing within His Highness's very home?"

"Where are they, Dahr?" Alistar asked. "I don't know where we're going."

"The drawing room," Dahr answered, grim. He turned a corner and pointed to an ornate door. "He sounds like he's on the stage."

"Witness the power that the gods have granted us!" Cemar shouted. Voices rose in frenzied cheers, but then trailed away in confusion.

"Such a fascinating display of power," the dry, flat voice of Prince Cero observed.

Blood and sand, that's not good. Not good at all. We need to get him out of there.

Alistar grabbed Dahr's arm to stop him from charging through the door. "Wait! Onyxflame, how many are in there?"

Onyxflame edged the doors open a crack and peered inside. "Cemar, strutting like he owns the place. I can see a dozen, but expect there's more. Can't see Prince Cero from here, but Cemar is glaring daggers at someone."

Across the room, a door crashed open and an ogre battle shout rattled the walls. Onyxflame jumped back from the doorway and added, "The ogres just arrived."

Dahr pulled from Alistar's hold and rushed into the room. Alistar swore under his breath and followed.

The drawing room could comfortably hold at least thirty. It boasted a fireplace on either side of the room and a small stage for hosting performances. Plush couches and chairs circled card tables and lined the edges of the room, placed so that guests could appreciate the portraits and statuary around the room. The floor tiles formed elaborate geometric patterns in silver and violet.

Cemar stood on the stage like a circus ringmaster waiting impatiently for his performers to begin. His dark spectacles didn't hide his growing outrage. Before him, two dozen people clustered around the raised stage. A handful more lingered around the room to watch the doors. All carried weapons, and half held themselves with the menacing air of street thugs. Alistar didn't recognize any of the thugs, but did see several people he remembered from Cemar's gathering. Neither Sok'lof nor Lady Sunward were present.

Prince Cero sat facing the stage, bound to a chair and guarded by a man and a woman, both elves. The Silver Prince's face was without expression, but Alistar read fury in the tension of his body. Alistar tried to place the man guarding the prince, but couldn't until Dahr snarled names in rage. The two guards looked at Dahr and dropped into fighting stances facing him.

They're members of the Royal Guard. The man brought the human-hating healer on the night Technician Bar'rege died. A chill ran down his spine. *His choice wasn't an accident, then.*

Cemar looked from the ogres to Alistar and Dahr. Jabbing a finger toward his thugs, Cemar indicated the ogres. "Take care of them!"

The thugs rushed the ogres with shouts of their own. Cemar focused on Alistar. "You dare interfere here? I'll rip your secrets from your flesh!"

"Oh, but aren't you forgetting someone, my *dear* old friend?" Onyxflame interrupted. "Do you want to dance with him, or me?"

She stood in the doorway. "Let me slip away now, and there's no telling when, where, or how I'll turn up next." She smirked.

Cemar vaulted off the stage. "Take care of them!" he snapped at his followers, running after Onyxflame.

"Kindly catch up when you've dealt with the rabble, De'seneth?" Onyxflame called as she vanished through the door. Cemar thundered after her.

For half a second, Alistar considered following. But doing so would leave Dahr unsupported and the Silver Prince in danger. Cemar's followers stared after their leader, confused to be abandoned. Alistar recognized the glaze of Ambrosia in their eyes. Unfortunately, he did not see the same in the eyes of the two elven guards.

Dahr and his opponents circled, gazes locked. The woman spoke. "You could join us, Lakewatch. I know you were another foundling abandoned to the orphanage by your parents when they couldn't afford to keep another child."

"You dare think I would betray my lord and my homeland?" Dahr growled.

"Don't bother with him," sneered the man. "Lakewatch is a loyal lapdog through and through. He can't even *think* anything but what he's told by his 'betters'."

Dahr quivered with fury, but he was not reckless. As Alistar moved to engage the clump of drugged disciples, Dahr advanced. His only response to the taunts came in the form of sharp steel.

Numbers were against Alistar, but the majority of the youths had clearly never seen battle, and some didn't even know how to hold their weapons with a proper stance. Alistar gave them his best cold privateer's smile—the one he normally reserved for the crew of a ship he was about to plunder. *My ship, my command.* "Well, come on then. Who's first to try their luck against the heir to Rillwater?"

If they all attacked him at once, they could overwhelm him with numbers. His words were a calculated risk to implant the idea that the only *right* way to fight him was single combat. He saw the thought take hold, and Alistar could clearly see that no one wanted to be first before his blade. He advanced, and they fell back. Reaching the stage, Alistar swung up, claiming the high ground and looking down on them with a sneer.

"No one? You were all so eager to claim the rewards Cemar promised when you didn't actually have to *work* for them. Will you roll over and surrender? Give up? I thought you *believed* in all those promises he spouted."

Rechmal, let me be reading them right. Let me only have to cut down one to break their will. I don't want to wash this room in the blood of the deluded.

Alistar heard clashing blades and shouts from both men and ogres, but he didn't dare move his gaze from the youths before him. He couldn't risk breaking the image of scorn and derision he was weaving. He couldn't let them see his worries.

A tall human pulled himself onto the stage. Alistar guessed him to be nearly twenty, probably from a merchant family. He had wide shoulders and arms that could toss hay bales or lift crates of cargo. By far, he was the fittest and probably the strongest of the group, and he even held his rapier with a degree of skill. "I'll take your challenge."

He settled into a fighting stance facing Alistar. Alistar gave him a brief nod. "Willing to fight for what you believe. Good lad. Rechmal guard your spirit."

The young merchant didn't last thirty seconds.

Terrified silence fell over the rest of the group when Alistar turned from the dying youth to face them. "Who's next?"

Weapons fell to the floor.

"No one?" Alistar asked.

"Lord As'enel, we… please, sir," a young woman babbled. Alistar didn't recognize her, and didn't think she'd attended the gathering he'd gone to. She dropped to her knees, hands raised in plea. "I'm sorry!"

Alistar let his gaze move past her to locate Dahr and his opponents. The battle between the three guards had moved away from Prince Cero, and Dahr was blocking his opponents attempts to edge closer to the prince. Beyond them, the ogres were cutting through Cemar's thugs. Alistar's eyes snapped back to the clump of youths. "Release Prince Cero," he ordered.

The Silver Prince cast Alistar a dubious look, but the young woman obeyed the instructions, teasing loose the knots on the silkweave cords. Prince Cero rose, and the young woman skittered back as if he might bite. From the prince's expression, the fear might not have been unwarranted.

"Leave this house," Alistar ordered. "Turn yourselves in to the guards at Silverline Power." His eyes narrowed. "If you do not, I *will* find you."

Heads bobbed rapidly and voices babbled compliance. They scrambled away under Alistar's hard gaze. He didn't know whether or not they would do as he instructed once they were away, but he had greater concerns. Alistar jumped down from the stage. "Your Highness, are you injured?"

Prince Cero stood stiff and indignant. "Your timing is impeccable, As'enel. I am unharmed. I do, however, question the wisdom of allowing that rabble to escape."

"Your Highness, with the questionable loyalty of members of the Guard, I didn't see a practical way of detaining them here," Alistar answered, voice tight. "I'm far more concerned with the instigator of this attack. You should get to safety."

"I will not allow peasants and criminals to drive me out of my own home," Prince Cero snapped. He strode to the abandoned weapons before the stage and snatched up a sword.

"Fine. Your choice," Alistar said.

"Your objections are noted," Prince Cero said stiffly.

"And undoubtedly ignored," Alistar retorted. He knew he should express proper respect, but he couldn't muster the words.

His mind was running far more in the paths of an As'enel captain than an associate engineer of Silverline Power.

The floor trembled and the windows rattled as one of the ogres collapsed. The other three roared in fury, crushing the remaining thugs with no more effort toward taking prisoners.

The female guard broke away from Dahr and lunged at Prince Cero. The Silver Prince was not a young man, and though he remained fit, his guards trained to be the very best. He met her attack with an angry grunt. "Traitor."

"You betrayed us first," she snarled. "Letting our people starve and freeze for your own profit." A vicious chop snapped the inferior sword in Prince Cero's hands. "We will not forget."

Alistar's slash opened a deep gouge below her ribs. She gasped in surprise and pain. Before she had a chance to react, the ogres reached her. She scored a glancing blow to one before falling to their assault.

Dahr parried his remaining opponent's attack. "Surrender."

"Die." The guard jerked a dagger from his belt and stabbed it into Dahr's thigh. Dahr staggered, then smashed the pommel of his blade into the other's face. The other guard collapsed, ripping the dagger free. Dahr sagged, blood rushing down his leg.

Alistar jumped to the guard's side, easing him to the floor. Dahr was bleeding too quickly—the dagger must have hit the artery.

Dahr panted for breath. "De'seneth. Go. Find Onyxflame before that damned spell makes him come scampering back to you. I will guard His Highness."

Dahr was in no condition to be guarding anyone, and he needed a healer immediately. Alistar pressed his hand against the wound, trying to staunch the bleeding. He turned to the ogres, who had already dealt with Dahr's opponent. "Get His Highness and Dahr to safety, now. Call a healer for Dahr immediately."

Prince Cero fixed Alistar with a hard look. "I will not be driven out of my own home!"

"Your Highness, your loyal guard is *dying*," Alistar snapped. "Have the decency and respect for his sacrifice to not join him!"

Dahr gripped Alistar's arm. His voice was soft. "No time for a healer, De'seneth. It's been an honor."

One of the ogres lifted Dahr, holding his massive hand to the bleeding wound. The other two flanked Prince Cero, and from their stances, they had every intention of ensuring that he left with them. With obvious ill grace, the prince conceded. "Very well."

Ignoring propriety and all etiquette's dictates on excusing oneself from the presence of a member of the Royal Family, Alistar turned his back to the Silver Prince and ran back into the hallway in pursuit of Onyxflame and Cemar.

CHAPTER 38

Alistar saw a door hanging open, and followed it down another hall. A long rug ran down the hall, muffling footsteps. It also offered evidence that others had passed in more haste than he did—the rug was rumpled and bunched in spots, as if someone had slipped while running. He didn't see bloodstains, at least.

The hall took a sharp right, continued several yards, and reached a door. Alistar pushed it the rest of the way open and stepped into one of the most famous, lavish rooms in the manor.

The Silver Prince's ballroom could host well over one hundred of Lewarden's finest, not counting servants, attendants, and guards. The weak winter sunlight brightened as it flowed through the dozens of twenty-foot tall stained glass windows, each depicting a unique scene from Lewarden's history. Preparations for the Ice Blossom Festival had been underway. Garlands of ice blossoms, enspelled to remain fresh, hung around the room and ran in woven strands between the chandeliers. The stage could hold a full orchestra and rivaled the Royal Theater House.

In the middle of the massive room, two people performed a dance that had no music, a dance with deadly intent. Onyxflame's dagger looked pitiful compared to Cemar's two-handed sword, yet her stance was casual, almost bored as she ducked and dodged his swings, then darted in to draw blood. Focused on their efforts to kill each other, neither of them noticed Alistar. The panes of stained glass splashed colors over them—crimson, emerald, amber, violet, azure. They almost made Onyxflame's drab clothing look suited to the finery around them.

Alistar scanned the room for any other enemies. He hadn't questioned Prince Cero as to whether more of his guards had turned traitor, or how many remained in the manor. He saw no signs of movement, and no one challenged or attacked him as he advanced.

Cemar's blade smashed against the floor as Onyxflame darted back. Rage twisted the mixed-blood's face. "Enough of this! You will not continue to mock me! Who are you *really*? I *know* that Tiyron Onyxflame is dead. I killed him myself."

"Did you now? Are you so sure, Cemar? You certainly didn't leave anyone standing watch after dumping me in that ditch. Have you checked? Did you send someone to search the bones?" Onyxflame countered.

Cemar hesitated a fraction of a second, but that was enough to imply that he'd tried to find Tiyron's body. "So you dragged off his rotting corpse. Maybe you're one of those northern face stealers, taking a dead man's flesh and wearing it like a mask. It doesn't matter. You'll die like he did, first begging for your life, then begging and pleading, willing to promise anything if you'll just be granted death." He sneered.

Onyxflame's expression twisted in fury. "Liar."

Cemar laughed. "I broke his bones, crushed his will. He told me every secret he knew. Did he mean something to you? He must have. I will enjoy finding out just who you really are."

Onyxflame trembled with anger, but she did not lunge at Cemar. Instead, her mouth twisted in a familiar smirk. "If you have to ask, then clearly you don't have *all* my secrets."

Cemar growled.

Onyxflame straightened, her eyes sweeping across the room. They touched on Alistar for a moment, and Alistar was sure she saw him, but she did not give a hint of that when she spoke again. Alistar stood still, not wanting to draw Cemar's eye.

"Why don't we stop playing games, Cemar?" she said coolly. "You like pretending you know how to use that weapon, but honestly, it's a glorified club in your hands. Your 'Ambrosia' might grant strength, but it obviously doesn't impart skill. Nor does it increase your intellect, as you prove more times in a day than I care to count. Where is your creativity? The artistic flair you keep trying to flaunt? Oh, and if you're interested, you can't continue to produce your drug. I destroyed the device, and burned all the notes long ago."

"You wouldn't dare. You cannot possibly be Tiyron. He would never destroy his precious creation," Cemar snarled.

"Then why was a destruction method built into it?" Onyxflame grinned. "You don't know nearly as much as you think you do. Especially about me."

What are you doing, Onyxflame? What are you up to?

"You will not stop Ambrosia, no matter what you think," Cemar scoffed. Violet energy flowed out of his hands and across his sword.

Alistar's stomach knotted. *He's not drawing from the mahiy lines. The source is internal, as Larisa's was. Is this an effect of Ambrosia? Can prolonged use trigger such ability in anyone?*

With a shout of rage and unnatural speed, Cemar swept his sword in an overhead chop. Onyxflame raised her arm as if to block. Streamers of magic poured from the mahiy lines to her. Cemar's blade slammed into a barrier inches from her arm. Onyxflame staggered, sliding back several steps, but she still smirked.

"You? A channeler?" Cemar demanded in disbelief.

Not just any channeler. A shielder. Defensive channeling. That's among the rarest skills.

Furious, Cemar swung again, then sprang back, pointing his sword at Onyxflame. A glow of gathering power shimmered at the tip. Onyxflame braced herself, never losing the smirk. "Are you *sure* you want to do that?"

A burst of magic erupted from the end of the sword. Onyxflame swept her hand down in a curve, and Alistar glimpsed a shimmering in the air, following her movement. Rather than strike the shield, Cemar's attack rolled down it, following the path of Onyxflame's hand, and came flying back at Cemar.

Cemar cursed and dodged, letting the blast of energy smash into the wall and scorch plaster. Alistar ran toward the half-breed, but Cemar recovered too quickly for Alistar to take advantage of the distraction.

"Are *you* responsible for this?" Cemar demanded, glaring at Alistar. "Do Rillwater pirates dabble in necromancy and dark arts?"

"Is *that* what you think?" Alistar retorted. "Don't let me spoil your illusions, then. But I'm not responsible for Onyxflame being alive, useful though he's been." He advanced, cutlass held at the ready.

Cemar eyed him and Onyxflame. "You think you can take me? Block *this!*" He thrust a hand into his belt pouch and grabbed a handful of thin crystal shards.

Alistar swore, rushing at Cemar, but the half-breed swallowed the shards. The air around him blazed violently purple, blindingly vivid and pulsing with power. A force slammed into Alistar, hurling him across the room. He had a moment to recognize that Onyxflame had shielded him from the blast itself before he crashed to the floor.

Cemar roared with laughter. "You cannot stand against me!"

Alistar climbed to his feet. He ached, but anger dulled the pain.

He grabbed the battered, scarred metal tube that held Onyxflame's artifact. "Onyxflame! 'Ware!"

Onyxflame glanced at him, saw the tube, and realized what Alistar intended. With a startled curse, she scrambled back from Cemar and released her barriers.

Alistar held the tube aloft. "Dragonbane!"

The Ambrosia crystals ripped from Cemar's belt pouch, hurtling toward Alistar amid a pulsing mass of violet light that flowed from Cemar himself. Every sconce in the room fell dark. The garlands of flowers around the room drooped and wilted in an instant. Cemar screamed, either in fury or pain. He staggered toward Alistar.

Onyxflame ran to Alistar, stopping at the edge of the cloud of magic surrounding him. Her mouth quirked in a grin. "Nice trick. Suppose I could ask one quick favor of you?"

"What is it?" Alistar asked, watching Cemar clutch a chair for support.

"At my word, release the magic and run for the door," Onyxflame said.

"What do you intend?" Alistar demanded.

"Something incredibly stupid." She grinned. "It's been a pleasure working with you, Alistar. Kindly give His Highness my apologies for destroying his ballroom."

"Destroying his—" Alistar began.

"Now!" Onyxflame shouted as Cemar charged, murder written on his face.

"Dragonbane," Alistar breathed.

The cloud of magic evaporated, and the Ambrosia crystals fell. Onyxflame snatched a handful out of the air and shoved them into her mouth.

A channeler is limited only by their ability to draw magic. And Ambrosia is magic.

A shell of violet light rose around Onyxflame, expanding rapidly. Alistar backed to the doorway and stepped through as the barrier hit the ceiling. Plaster cracked and chipped. Cemar slammed against the barrier with a scream of fury. The cloud of magic flowed back to him, and his blows gained force and strength enough that Alistar could feel the impact through the floor.

Behind Cemar, a second barrier formed, growing to match the first. Both barriers hit the walls, and windows exploded out in a shattering rain of delicate colored glass. Cracks spidered across the ceiling. First dust, then chunks of elaborate molding broke loose and crashed to the floor.

Cemar pulsed with the glow of magic, and he unleashed on the barrier before him, roaring his fury as chunks of the ceiling rained down. With alarm, Alistar noticed that although the barriers struck the ceiling like solid forces, debris fell through them unhindered as Onyxflame focused on reinforcing the site of Cemar's attack.

The two barriers pressed together with Cemar between them. The mixed-blood's power flared, and for a moment he held them apart. Cracks ran across the face of Onyxflame's barrier, and Cemar's sweat-streaked face twisted in a smile of victory. He drew back his fist, violet flames flickering around his hand.

Then his power failed, and the two shells collided to the sounds of screams and crushed bones. A massive chunk of the ceiling fell nearly at Alistar's feet, and he sprang back.

The barriers dropped. Alistar caught one glimpse of a figure surrounded in purple glow standing amid the falling rubble. He thought she raised a hand in farewell. Then the ceiling caved in, burying the ballroom and everything within in dust, broken plaster, and chunks of over-strained stone.

Alistar staggered back, coughing and choking on dust. He shoved the tube into his vest and retraced his steps in a stumbling run as the house groaned around him.

Did Onyxflame make it? Is she trapped in there, buried under the rubble? Are her barriers strong enough to keep her from being crushed?

He didn't know the answers, and he couldn't go back to find them with the manor threatening further collapse.

When he finally stumbled outside, he sucked in deep gulps of clean, cold air. He'd grabbed his coat as he staggered through the kitchen, and pulled it on as the biting winter cold permeated his clothes. The manor grounds were empty. Alistar cast a look over his shoulder at the Silver Prince's manor, but it offered no answers.

As he neared the west gate, Alistar heard sounds of fighting. He pushed himself faster, gripping his cutlass when he heard voices rise in shouts. "Death to the oppressors! Rechmal's justice on the elves!"

Successors? Here? Alistar crossed the threshold and turned to the sounds.

A dozen members of the Royal Guard held position in the alley, facing a swarm of wild-eyed, screaming humans who flailed weapons about madly. The guards blocked the attackers' access to both Prince Cero's manor and Silverline Power. In the midst of the rabid hoard, a man raised a staff topped with a crystal shaped in the form of a spray of eight jagged petals, representing the frost's breath flower sacred to Rechmal. The staff glowed, and the leaves shimmered.

"Strike them down! Let the wrath of the gods guide your hands!"

The guards braced against the attack. Alistar joined them, though he recognized only one of their number. Elves glanced warily at him, but didn't attack him. The Successors were pushing them deeper into the alley, forcing a path closer to the gates.

Alistar tried to see the man wielding the staff, but glimpsed only the vestments of a priest. The staff pulsed with light, then flared, a shock wave tossing elves and humans alike off their feet. Alistar scrambled up and finally got a clear look at Zhrets Vonn. His eyes narrowed as his suspicion was confirmed.

"Is *this* Cemar's vaunted equality, Sok'lof?" he shouted.

The priest's head jerked toward him. His mouth curled in fury. "As'enel. You betray your people? Throw your lot in with the oppressors?"

Successors had begun to recover, and hateful gazes fixed on Alistar.

"Betray?" Alistar barked a laugh that almost became a cough. "Which of us was espousing equality? Even standing with the elves? Which of us stood beside a mixed blood man and declared the Reyker to be fickle and uncaring? It certainly wasn't *me*."

The Successors hesitated, looking to Sok'lof. Sok'lof sneered. "Are you trying to sow doubt among the faithful, As'enel? You think them so simple, so easily drawn astray?"

"Cemar set you up, Sok'lof," Alistar said.

Sok'lof sneered. "A pathetic effort at subversion and misdirection, As'enel."

"You wouldn't be the first partner he's betrayed," Alistar said. "Or didn't he tell you about Onyxflame?"

Sok'lof paused, just for a moment, and confusion flickered across his face. "What of that worthless thief?"

Alistar snorted. "You didn't think Cemar built the device, did you? He doesn't have the skill in artificing. That was all Onyxflame's work." Conscious of the Royal Guard around him, Alistar judiciously edited the narrative. "And when Cemar had no more use for him, he betrayed Onyxflame. Just as he has betrayed you."

Sok'lof shook his head sharply. "The worthless elf deserved whatever Cemar did. Cemar is my friend; he would never—"

"Found that coat button yet?" Alistar interrupted. "You lost it how many months ago?" Before Sok'lof answered, he pulled it from his pocket and flicked it toward the man. "Strange, then, for it to show up last week on a roof in Shale Lane the night of an outage."

Sok'lof stiffened. "You lie." He raised the staff and pointed it at

Alistar. "Enough of this. Bear witness to the power Rechmal has granted me!"

That crystal. It's magic, like Ambrosia. Alistar glimpsed Sok'lof manipulating the shaft of the staff, pressing recessed buttons. Triggering something. *Blood and sand, that's a device of some sort.*

The crystal glowed. Alistar grasped the artifact tucked in his coat. "Dragonbane," he whispered as the light on the staff flared.

Wood splintered. Light surrounded Alistar. Successors fell back with shouts and screams. Alistar braced for an attack, but when his eyes cleared, he saw the Successors on their knees. Sok'lof still stood, staring at his shattered staff. The crystal flower, ripped from its resting place, hung in the air before Alistar. He reached out and took hold of it, then whispered the key word again. The light dispersed.

Sok'lof looked around wildly, eyes crazed. "What are you doing? Stop him!"

Royal Guards flanked Alistar and spread to either side of him, weapons ready, but the Successors remained kneeling. Some raised their heads to stare at Alistar in awe. "Rechmal has rejected Zhrets Vonn. His favor falls on another."

"His favor—what?" Alistar repeated.

"The blessing and favor of Rechmal!" A wild-eyed man stared at the crystal in Alistar's hand. "The light and glory that sustained us through the darkness! The gift from the Lord of Magic himself! It has chosen *you*!"

"No!" Sok'lof roared. "You dare!" He lunged at Alistar.

The Royal Guard rushed forward. None of the Successors intervened as the elves seized Sok'lof and wrestled him down to the cold stones.

The guard nearest Alistar turned, considering him, then the crystal he held. His tone was surprisingly polite, even diffident. "Lord As'enel, our thanks to you."

They don't know what just happened any more than the Successors do. It probably looked like one of the gods really did intervene. Alistar nodded. "Of course." He lowered his voice. "Please make sure their leader lives to see his trial."

The guard nodded grimly. "It will be done, sir, I swear on my life. And the Successors?"

Alistar stood straight and tall, pitching his voice to a commanding boom. "Successors of Heiset, you will surrender."

To a person, they obeyed. The elves eyed Alistar with wary respect. Alistar nodded to the guards, and they hastily began collecting the Successors into custody. Once Alistar was confident the fanatics wouldn't fight, he spoke to the guard beside him. "Where is His Highness?"

"He is safely within Silverline Power, Lord As'enel. We were to see you to him with all haste, but—"

Alistar nodded. "I'll go there at once."

"I'll show you there, sir," the guard said quickly. Without waiting for agreement, he snapped rapid orders to his fellows and strode toward the Silverline back gate.

Alistar eyed Sok'lof, unsure whether he dared allow the man out of his sight. Sok'lof glared at him, eyes burning with spite.

The guard noticed Alistar's hesitation. "Lord As'enel, I swear to the gods that he will not escape, and we will permit no harm to come to him until he faces the Crown's justice." He pulled off his glove to show the seal of the Royal Family glowing on the back of his hand, sign of a newly renewed oath of fealty and loyalty.

Alistar accepted that, though his skin crawled and he felt Sok'lof's eyes trying to bore holes in his back. They entered the Silverline Power complex by the rear gate, then entered the main building.

CHAPTER 39

In a small foyer in a restricted area of Silverline Power, an elf in healer's robes fussed over Prince Cero, to the Silver Prince's obvious annoyance. Lady Syri stood to one side, worry and amusement warring in her eyes despite the gravity of the situation. Half a dozen members of the Royal Guard stood around the room. Dahr was not among them.

The moment Alistar entered, Prince Cero stood and banished the healer from the room. "Out! This is a matter of state and you are not cleared for this level of confidentiality."

The healer started to protest, and Alistar heard those protests continue as one of the guards escorted the man out, until distance finally silenced them.

Prince Cero's gaze fixed on Alistar. "As'enel. What in Slee's name just happened in *my home?*"

"Your Highness." Alistar bowed. "Cemar is dead. Onyxflame asked me to pass on his apologies for the mess."

The prince's eyes narrowed. "Where is Onyxflame?"

"Tiyron Onyxflame is dead, Your Highness."

"You are *certain*, De'seneth?" Prince Cero pressed, looking into his eyes. "You are aware of his talents."

"Yes, Your Highness. I am certain that he is dead. He died battling Cemar and defending Lewarden." Alistar knew he stretched the truth with that last part. Tiyron's motives had undoubtedly been less altruistic, but he had delayed Cemar's schemes, whatever his reasons had been. "What of Dahr, Your Highness?"

"Dahr Lakewatch survived until His Highness safely arrived at Silverline Power, sir," one of the guards said. "However, the healer was not able to reach him in time."

"I see," Alistar said quietly. "He was a good man." Further words failed him.

"He was, and his sacrifice will be honored," Prince Cero said. "The report I received from Assistant Goldleaf indicated that the damage appeared to originate from the ballroom. How, exactly, *did* Onyxflame accomplish that? Did you allow him access to explosives, As'enel?"

"Your Highness, Onyxflame could have made an explosive with a bottle of wine, two napkins, and a spoon," Alistar responded.

A ghost of a wry smile touched the Silver Prince's mouth. "I suppose there is some truth to that. I expect a full report."

"Of course, Your Highness," Alistar said. He was not looking forward to that, nor to deciding which pieces to include and which to leave out. "What's the status of the garrison? I encountered your guards fighting Successors when I left the manor, Your Highness."

"We held the Successors off at the garrison," answered a guard. "A group, including their leader, broke from the attack and we were unable to follow them."

The guard who had escorted Alistar spoke. "Zhrets Vonn has been apprehended, thanks to the assistance of Lord As'enel, Your Highness." He nodded at the crystal in Alistar's hand. "He succeeded in removing the symbol of leadership from the man, through means unknown to me, and the Successors surrendered."

Lady Syri moved closer, studying the crystal. "Associate, might I see that?"

Her question distracted both Alistar and Prince Cero. "I… of course," Alistar said. "I'm unsure of its exact nature, if it's Ambrosia or—"

"I don't think that it is," she said, taking the crystal from his hand. "Based on the appearance and crystal structure, I suspect it may be crystallized magic. Pure, rather than the bastardized form employed in the drug. Not naturally occurring, though. Curious."

Alistar had no idea how she could determine all that from little more than a look, but accepted her assessment. "I'll leave study of it in your hands."

"My thanks, Associate." She nodded, then turned to Prince Cero. "If my supposition is correct about this crystal, it's possible that something similar had been employed to power that manor. And if that is the case, it's possible that we are looking at an entirely new branch of magic theory."

"Perhaps," Prince Cero agreed. He considered Alistar. "Given the circumstances, we have not yet had opportunity to investigate the manor house that those reprobates used as their base."

Alistar nodded. "The concept is fascinating. I wasn't able to learn the details when I was there; I'd be very interested to learn more, given the opportunity. I don't know how much the leader of the Successors knows about the underlying principles, or how much he will be willing to reveal. To be honest, I'm not sure I would believe anything that he *does* say."

The Silver Prince answered with a curt jerk of his head. "He'll be questioned, but I do not hold high expectations that doing so will gain much, given the need for haste. He will stand trial publicly, and soon. The people deserve the chance to see the man who led the uprising. And to see him executed."

Alistar nodded understanding. Cemar was dead, but people needed someone to blame. Someone they could see, rather than being told to trust that the instigator was dead and buried under rubble.

"There is also the matter of your reward," Prince Cero continued.

Alistar paused. "My reward?"

A servant entered the room, carrying a tray with glasses of wine. Prince Cero took one and considered Alistar. "Yes, your reward, As'enel. You deserve public recognition for your work in this matter. And given certain aspects of the current political climate and the tensions in Lewarden, it is better still that the praise and reward go entirely to a human. I will send a formal letter of apology to Admiral As'enel for acknowledging your family's actions."

Alistar stopped. "No. Your Highness, my family will not accept that. Better that the As'enels never be mentioned, and certainly not in a situation that gives the appearance that you intentionally called my family to Lewarden to handle this matter."

The Silver Prince's eyes narrowed at Alistar's refusal.

Alistar continued, "Additionally, there's no need to bring my family into the matter at all."

"Oh? How so?" Prince Cero asked, voice cool.

Alistar met his gaze without flinching. "Your Highness, Alistar De'seneth is an Associate Engineer, Third Degree, in the employ of Silverline Power, and he recently successfully completed the investigation at the automaton factory. You don't *need* the As'enel family involved in the matter at all. You have a human, a resident of Lewarden, already in a position where *no one* is going to find it odd that he could be assigned to an investigation. There's no need to complicate the matter with As'enel involvement."

He couldn't read the Silver Prince's expression. "I will consider this suggestion, Senior Engineer De'seneth, Fifth Degree."

Alistar blinked. "Third, sir. And if not, what happened to Fourth?"

"I chose to bypass it. Senior Engineer, Fifth Degree."

Alistar was silent for a moment, then inclined his head in acceptance. "Thank you, Your Highness."

"Under such circumstances, the Crown would, of course, ensure that Senior Engineer De'seneth was richly rewarded for his service," Prince Cero said. "Beyond simply a promotion recognizing his work within Silverline Power."

He's very focused on the idea of a reward. Why is it so important... Oh. He doesn't want to be indebted to the Family. Alistar inclined his head in a nod. "A man would be foolish to decline such a reward, Your Highness."

"He would indeed," Prince Cero agreed. "What reward would he ask?"

Alistar blinked. "I... do not know, Your Highness. I've had little time to give the matter thought. Two men who worked just as hard as I did and who provided invaluable aid during this investigation are dead. I must ask your pardon if I am not thinking of rewards at the moment." When he said the words, the enormity of the matter finally crept up on him. Cemar was dead. Zhrets Vonn, proven to be Sir Sok'lof, was in custody. Lady Sunward's location was unknown. Some of Cemar's followers were in custody, others remained on the loose. Lamorage might face charges for his part, under duress or not. Dahr was dead. Onyxflame might be dead or trapped under the rubble. He had no idea how much remained of Cemar's drugs, and how many more people might still die from Rat's Disease. He was numb and exhausted, and the last thing he wanted was further interrogation.

The prince studied him. "Very well. We will discuss the matter when you make your report." He paused, then added stiffly, as a man unaccustomed to saying the words as more than empty platitudes, "You have my thanks for your work and for the release of my person from that... man. You are free to leave if you wish."

"Thank you, Your Highness." Alistar bowed and walked to the door they had entered.

"Bring a carriage for De'seneth," Prince Cero ordered.

"Yes, Your Highness!" One of the guards sprang to attention and followed Alistar outside.

"Ideally, one that won't stand out *too* much in the rest of the city?" Alistar asked him with a weary smile.

"Of course, sir," the guard agreed. "Where are you bound? To your home?"

Home appealed, but only for a moment before he thought of sitting alone in the empty rooms. "Do you know where the Coiled Dragon Clinic is?" Alistar asked.

"Are you injured, sir?" the guard asked in immediate concern.

"No, nothing serious. My fiancée is there."

"Ah. As you wish, sir. I will drive you there."

He didn't see the guard use a speaking stone, but the carriage arrived within minutes. The driver hopped down with a quick salute, and the guard assumed the driver's seat. Before climbing in, Alistar asked, "Out of curiosity, how is your driving compared to Dahr's?"

The guard paused, then laughed. "You let him drive, sir? I am so sorry. He is… was notorious for his skills at the reins. I believe that, while I am far from the best driver among us, I am less reckless than he tended to be." He grew more sober. "We will miss him greatly."

"It was an honor to have his company," Alistar said. He climbed into the carriage and closed the door. Sinking onto the bench, he let his head rest against the wall.

He wasn't sure if he dozed, or simply passed the trip in a daze, but it seemed only moments before the carriage stopped and the door opened. Alistar blinked, then climbed out, casting quick glances around, wary that he was being led into a trap.

The Coiled Dragon Clinic stood before him. Alistar caught the guard giving him a concerned look. "Are you all right, sir?"

"Just… tired," Alistar said.

The guard shadowed him to the door and inside, still

concerned. The waiting room was empty. He heard Saskia's voice coming up the hall. "I'm sorry, we're only seeing emergencies at the moment, but if you need—Alistar!" Seeing him, Saskia ran across the room and threw her arms around him, holding him tight.

Alistar clutched her, not wanting to let go. He heard an embarrassed cough and throat-clearing behind him. Reluctantly, he turned to the guard. The elf's gaze was firmly fixed on a piece of artwork on the wall as if it was the most fascinating image in the world.

"Will you need a ride anywhere else, sir?"

"No. I'll stay here right now." Alistar paused, dredging up his courtesies. "Thank you."

"Of course, sir. Good day."

As the door closed, Saskia stepped back, eyes worried. "Alistar, where are Dahr and Onyxflame?"

Alistar shook his head. "They're both gone. Dahr is dead. Onyxflame… might be."

She took his arm and led him upstairs. "Tell me."

Alistar cast a look around. "Where's your father? And Lamorage?"

"Father is tending to patients, and Lamorage is resting. He's been testing his healing abilities and, like many a new healer, is very poor at judging his limits. His help has been a blessing, though. We've managed to save several more victims of Rat's Disease." She steered Alistar to a couch and sat beside him.

Alistar leaned against her, wrapping his arm around her. "We started at Silverline Power," he began. He related the events, from Silverline Power to Prince Cero's estate. At some point, Doctor Tan'shyo entered the room. Alistar paused, but continued the narrative. His voice cracked when he told of Dahr's fatal injury, but he pressed on to Cemar's death and the collapse of the ballroom.

When he finished, no one broke the silence for a time. Doctor Tan'shyo finally spoke. "You need to rest, De'seneth. You're exhausted."

Alistar rose, not wanting to sit still. "I can't rest. There's more I still need to do."

"Can it wait a few hours?" Doctor Tan'shyo asked.

He didn't ask what Alistar needed to do, to Alistar's relief. Alistar couldn't actually think what answer he would give, but sitting still felt disrespectful to his comrades' memories, as if he was letting them down after they had fought and bled to stop Cemar. "Can I borrow parchment?"

"Of course. You'll find it in my office, ready and waiting after you've caught a short rest," Doctor Tan'shyo answered.

Alistar walked down to the office and considered the parchment he found. Considered the report he needed to write. Considered the half-truths he'd need to tell and the details he needed to omit to preserve both Onyxflame's and Lamorage's secrets.

Doctor Tan'shyo is right. I need a clear head before I write this.

He lay down on the cot and closed his eyes. It seemed only moments before someone gently shook his shoulder. "Alistar. Dinner's ready."

He groaned and sat up gingerly, feeling muscles ache in protest. "Already? All right. Didn't think I slept that long."

Saskia smiled. "You barely stirred when I came in earlier. Feeling a little better?"

"A little," he acknowledged. "Thank you."

Lamorage joined them for dinner. The elf was subdued, and hesitated to meet Alistar's eyes. After the table was cleared, however, he followed Alistar downstairs to the office.

"De'seneth, are you going to turn me in?" he asked quietly.

"For what?" Alistar asked. "Failing to register as a channeler? From what you said, you had a talent that was known and judged not strong enough to warrant registration. It's been heightened through use of Ambrosia, and you'll need to register now, but that's not worthy of official sanction."

"Not that," Lamorage said. "Or, well, not *just* that. I mean Dockside. Cemar. Everything."

"You used Ambrosia, but so did half the young nobles at Lord Proudmoor's party," Alistar said. "You were kidnapped because Cemar's people identified a connection between you and me, and they were trying to get hold of me. That is all I intend to say in my report."

"But you know that's not… not all of the truth," Lamorage said. "And someone will investigate the incidents. And they will need to know more if they're going to catch Cemar."

"*I* am investigating the incidents," Alistar said. "Lamorage, I'm the investigator assigned to this. *This* is the 'special project' I was given. And you don't need to fear Cemar any longer. He's dead."

"Dead?" Lamorage's head jerked up. "He's dead? You're certain? How? Did you see it?"

"I saw it," Alistar promised. "I am certain that he is dead, without a doubt. Very messily dead."

"And the others?" Lamorage's voice trembled.

"Sok'lof has been captured. I don't know about Lady Sunward. Are there more?" Alistar asked.

Lamorage shook his head. "Those three were in charge. The rest followed their lead." He looked at Alistar. "If you are leading the investigation, and hide information…"

"Lamorage, I don't throw my friends into the water when the sharks are in a feeding frenzy. Right now, it would be impossible for you to receive a fair hearing. People are scared and searching for someone to blame." *And I believe the Crown would weigh justice for one man, especially one with so few political ties, as less important than appeasing the city.* "Please trust me on this."

Lamorage bowed his head. "Thank you, De'seneth. I don't deserve this, but, thank you."

Alistar clapped him on the shoulder. "If you need anything, I'll help how I can, Lamorage."

Lamorage nodded and withdrew. Alistar sat at the desk and pulled the stack of parchment to him. He stared at the page, wondering where to start.

Cemar's gathering. Start there.

Once he began, the words came more easily than he expected. He focused on the areas he knew would catch Prince Cero's attention: the manor's power drawing from a source other than the mahiy lines, the internal channeling displayed by Larisa, Cemar's claims about magic. He kept his description of Onyxflame's arrival and Cemar's pursuit brief, including Onyxflame's injury and Star's arrival. Alistar scribbled himself a note to request a copy of Doctor Tan'shyo's report on Onyxflame's injury. Hopefully his future father-in-law would be willing to leave out mention of Onyxflame's sex. Alistar did include a summary of the history between Onyxflame and Cemar as one-time allies who experienced a falling out over philosophical differences.

He continued on to the rescue of Lamorage, leaving out any mention of the "suicide" letter Ko'hut had left. He had no way of knowing what Ko'hut would or would not reveal when he was questioned, but hoped that his own report would carry more weight than the word of a kidnapper and would-be murderer.

Alistar got up and walked around the room, flexing his cramping hand and stretching his legs. He had only the final confrontation with Cemar left to record.

From his pocket, Alistar drew Dahr's speaking stone. No power remained in it; like every other enchanted object in Prince Cero's ballroom, it had been drained when he'd activated the artifact.

There's no one to contradict my account. He wavered between relief and guilt. *I don't have to worry about Dahr's report or what it will say. I don't have to worry about what any other witnesses will say. Sok'lof isn't likely to talk, and Ko'hut hasn't revealed anything yet. I know Prince Cero wants the conspirators charged and executed with all possible haste, before the people grow more restless, so the interrogators won't get extended time with either man. How much does either one of them know about Onyxflame? About the device, and the artifact that powered it? Did any of them understand how it worked? Rechmal knows I do not.*

Alistar reached into his pocket and pulled out the metal cylinder that contained and constrained the artifact. *What other power does it hold? How else could it be used? Do I trust this power in anyone else's hands? I'd hesitate to tell even Father about it.*

After a long moment, Alistar tucked the artifact away and returned to his report. He recorded Onyxflame disabling the device by destroying key components. No doubt the Silver Prince would have the remains of the device thoroughly analyzed in an effort to reconstruct it. Someone might notice the absence of a power source, but if questions were directed to Alistar later, he would deal with them then.

He slept another night at the clinic, but after breakfast the following morning, Alistar caught a taxi carriage and went home. For the first time in what felt like forever, he climbed the steps and unlocked his door. Shale Lane showed no sign of looters or riots, to his relief. The house was quiet. Mrs. Ke'lyn had left a note for him, indicating that she would be absent until the situation in the city calmed enough for safe travel.

Alistar climbed to his room. He saw evidence that someone had gone into his closet, but Dahr had been as respectful of his privacy as possible, and nothing but the clothing had been disturbed. Alistar stood looking around the room for a long moment, then walked to the guest room. He caught himself about to knock, and opened the door.

The chest containing Lord Aspendark's clothes and effects stood closed. Alistar pushed open the lid. Silkweave clothes, trays with cosmetics, accessories, and some papers, greeted him. "I suppose someone will need to collect these," Alistar mused. "Or maybe they're mine to dispose of as I want. They'd probably sell well. Someone would buy them." If the sumptuary laws didn't forbid dressing above one's class, he'd offer the clothes to the poor on the streets.

He frowned slightly. He didn't see any of the noble-style shoes he'd purchased for Onyxflame, and didn't recall seeing them in the bag Dahr had brought. If any additional clothes were missing, he couldn't tell—he'd never inventoried the contents of the trunk. Alistar briefly looked around the room and under the bed, but let the question of the shoes slide, though in the back of his mind, he wondered how much someone could pawn them for.

Finally, assured that his house was in order, Alistar reread his report, tucked it into a portfolio, and left again, catching a taxi to Silverline Power.

Little had changed since the previous day, except that temporary housing had been arranged for the families who sought shelter, and the lobby held only a few remaining non-employees. One of them, a brown-haired human man with a toddler, hesitantly approached Alistar.

"Excuse me, sir? Are you Associate De'seneth?"

"I am," Alistar said. "Can I help you, sir?"

The man swallowed. "I'm Nikolae Bar'rege. Technician Bar'rege was my wife."

"I'm sorry," Alistar said. "My deepest condolences for your loss, sir." The words felt insufficient.

Bar'rege shook his head quickly. "I was told, sir, that those responsible for my wife's death have been caught, and that their fall came at your hand, sir. I simply… want to thank you, from myself and my son." He held a hand to Alistar.

Alistar clasped it. "I know it's no compensation for her death, but the knowledge she shared with me was invaluable."

The man drew a deep breath and nodded quickly. "It wasn't in vain, then. That is all any of us can ask when we stand before Lord Starbinder. Thank you, sir."

He released Alistar's hand and withdrew. Alistar approached the front desk deep in contemplation. Assistant Goldleaf awaited him. "Good day, Senior Engineer De'seneth. How may I direct you?"

"I need to deliver a report," Alistar said.

"At once, Engineer." Her eyes grew distant as she engaged in silent communication. Her gaze focused on him again. "His Highness has requested that you bring your report to him directly. A carriage will arrive shortly to bring you to the palace."

Alistar glanced at his clothing quickly. He was not dressed for a court appearance. "The palace?" he repeated.

"His Highness's manor suffered severe enough damage as to be deemed unlivable until repairs are complete," Assistant Goldleaf said. "Your current dress is acceptable; I have already confirmed with the palace assistants."

The carriage arrived promptly, whisking Alistar to Feyblade Palace. Inside the carriage, he found a long brocaded suit coat. The tails nearly reached the floor, and it fit Alistar comfortably. It also added an elegant flair to his otherwise unsuitable dress. He felt slightly more confident when the carriage door opened and he stepped out.

Prince Cero stood waiting for him, accompanied by two dozen guards. Alistar noticed Star among them. Her expression was stoic, but she met Alistar's eyes and dipped her head in respect. Her eyes were red and puffy from tears.

Heavy lines marked the Silver Prince's face, but he stood straight and tall. He studied Alistar, then spoke. "Senior Engineer De'seneth, thank you for answering my summons."

Alistar bowed deep. "Of course, Your Highness."

Prince Cero gestured for Alistar to follow. "You have done a great service to us and to our nation. Have you given thought to the matter of your reward?"

"I have given thought to my report, Your Highness," Alistar countered, offering the portfolio.

One of the guards started to reach for it, but Prince Cero intercepted the document himself. "Thank you. I appreciate the prompt nature of this. You included everything?"

"Everything I thought relevant, Your Highness," Alistar answered.

Prince Cero led the way into the palace. "I have heard rumors of individuals able to channel without use of the mahiy lines, as well as the manor house engineered to use another power source."

"Both are mentioned in my report," Alistar said. "What little I learned of them."

Prince Cero eyed him as they walked. "You still wish to study the matter?"

"I find the idea fascinating," Alistar acknowledged. "I don't know if it would be possible, but yes, I would appreciate being given opportunity to do so."

"You will have the opportunity to study the manor, at least," Prince Cero told him. He raise a hand, and a servant approached, bearing a silver platter with a scroll. The Silver Prince took the scroll and handed it to Alistar.

Curious, Alistar broke the seal, to find himself holding a deed. He looked up sharply. "Your Highness?"

"The manor house that the ruffians claimed as their lair. The estate was held by a lending firm, as the original owner forfeited on her debts. It now belongs to you, with all debts paid and taxes exempted indefinitely. Report on whatever secrets you find within. It has, of course, been cleaned, but we have not pried into its depths yet."

Alistar blinked, and slowly nodded. "Thank you, Your Highness."

"I also understand that you are engaged to be wed," Prince Cero continued.

"Yes, Your Highness, to Saskia Tan'shyo. Her father runs the Coiled Dragon Clinic."

"I am acquainted with the good doctor," Prince Cero said. "A loyal servant of the Crown. I trust that I may expect an invitation to the nuptials."

Alistar stopped in his tracks. "We intended to have a small ceremony, Your Highness, with family and a few friends in attendance. The sanctuary we were considering has limited—"

"Then you will need to make use of a larger one," Prince Cero said. "You will allow me to cover the difference, of course." His eyes narrowed on Alistar. "A hero and champion of Lewarden should have a fitting celebration to commemorate such a joyous occasion as his wedding."

Alistar said nothing, because he was certain any words that came out would not be appropriate. *You intend to turn my wedding day into a political event.*

His expression apparently spoke his thoughts clearly enough. Prince Cero continued. "You are well aware of the tensions within Lewarden, De'seneth. The divisions between the classes and the races. As I told you, the Crown needs to offer a gesture that the people can accept. An indication that we are not what the Successors claim. We require a human who they can look up to as a hero, and who receives our accolades."

"All of which should be done before my wedding," Alistar pointed out.

"As it will be," the Silver Prince agreed. "But such a gesture is nothing if it is done and then forgotten. Your marriage to a woman not of noble birth strengthens our message."

Alistar's jaw tightened. "I see."

"I will, of course, offer a formal apology to Admiral As'enel," Prince Cero continued.

It was the second time the prince had made that offer. This time, Alistar did not speak against it, though he could only imagine what his father would say when he received the message.

"If you want to make a gesture to the people of the city, there's something additional you can do," Alistar said.

Prince Cero raised an eyebrow. "Continue."

"Memorialize those who died because of Cemar and his plot," Alistar said. "I don't mean just Dahr, Onyxflame, and the guards who were killed, though their names should be included. I mean everyone who died in the Dockside attack. Those killed when the Successors tried their coup. Every victim of Rat's Disease. *Show* the people that you know who they are and who they lost. Honor them."

He saw the Silver Prince's dark expression when he included Onyxflame in the list, but the prince's face became a mask as he listened to Alistar. "Very well, De'seneth. It will be done."

That means that I'm agreeing to the rest, doesn't it? So be it, then.

"In another matter that may be of interest to you, the identity of the apparent leader of the Successor uprising has been confirmed."

"Sok'lof?" Alistar asked.

The prince answered with a curt nod. "Indeed. A minor noble from the outskirts of Lewarden. Youngest of four, little inheritance to speak of. When he stands trial, the Crown will call on you to testify against him."

"Of course, Your Highness," Alistar said. Not a surprise, under the circumstances. After all, he had to explain the significance of a coat button. "Is there any word of Lady Sunward?"

"None. If her family knows her whereabouts, they are unwilling to reveal them. I have agents searching for her," Prince Cero said.

Alistar drew the prince's money purse and the seal from his pocket. "Your Highness, I have completed the investigation of the theft and sabotage done to the mahiy lines. Allow me to return these."

Prince Cero accepted the purse, but not the seal. "Keep that. I doubt this will be the last time I call upon your skills, young Lord

As'enel." His use of Alistar's surname was clear and deliberate. "It will save time if you already possess my signet."

That wasn't the response Alistar wanted to hear. His fingers curled around the seal as if he could crush it. "As you will, Your Highness."

"You have served your country well, Lord As'enel. Should the gods will it, you will continue to do so for many years to come."

In his study, Alistar sat at his desk and cupped his hands around a speaking stone. As it began to glow, he gently set it into the recess in its storage box. The day was still early, and he didn't know whether or not his father would be available, but he could not in good conscience let the news wait.

The stone shifted colors, indicating that someone had activated it. Alistar expected to hear his father's deep voice, and was startled to instead be greeted by an alto coarse from seasons of bellowing over wind and waves. "Alistar. What news?"

Alistar fumbled a moment for a response. "Mother?"

"The Admiral had to take care of some business at the docks. Hard to say how long he'll be. I'm writing replies to a few letters of inquiry regarding Taslor Aspendark. One of them implies possible interest in marriage. So. What news?"

The repetition of the question reminded him that he hadn't provided the code words to indicate that he was alone. "I'm well enough. The last few days have been… busy. And you?"

"Well enough," she agreed, presenting the code in return. "Aside from the current scuffling on the dock, at least. Bit of a disagreement about the distribution of goods."

Alistar winced. More often than not, if a disagreement over booty grew serious enough to require Admiral As'enel to resolve it, he settled the matter by claiming the disputed goods himself. "You'd think they would have learned by now to have that all worked out before they hit port." He shook his head. "You said you were answering letters of inquiry regarding Aspendark, though."

"Indeed. Your father told me something of the matter. Special assignment from the Silver Prince, keeping you in Lewarden for however long it takes to resolve." She didn't sound overly pleased with the notion.

Alistar's jaw tightened at her dismissive tone, then he forced himself to relax. "In case Father didn't mention, the Silver Prince chose me personally for this assignment because he believed me the most capable of his engineers to handle the matter. And the matter in question was nothing less than preventing complete subversion of the mahiy lines in Lewarden. Or, more bluntly, my assignment was to stop saboteurs from destroying the grid of mahiy lines and crippling the city."

"He mentioned something to that effect," Mother said blandly. "And that Aspendark, whoever he really is, supposedly hails from Rillwater, and has a bastard sister named Rozika Tide as his business manager."

"Aspendark has been forced to cut his trip to Lewarden short and return home unexpectedly," Alistar said. "Quite unfortunate, but the matter couldn't wait."

He could almost hear his mother's eyebrow rise. "Is that so? I see. Well, the remaining letters will have to reflect that bit of news. I could perhaps delay them entirely, but I've already had the pleasure of writing a scathing retort to Lord Oremeld and I would hate to let that go to waste."

"No, by all means, send it," Alistar said. If there was one matter he and his mother never argued about, it was their shared opinion of Lord Oremeld.

"So are you going to tell me why you're calling home, or are we just going to delay until your father is available?" Mother asked bluntly.

Alistar hesitated. Part of him wanted to keep delaying, keep putting off telling her that his assignment was complete. Part of him wanted to crow his achievements to the sky. He drew a deep breath. "I wanted to let you and Father know that Saskia and I have to make some adjustments to our original plans for the wedding."

"You're moving the ceremony to Rillwater?" Mother asked. Then she paused. "No, I suppose you probably aren't. What changes, then?"

"We're going to need the entirety of Night's Eve Sanctuary, rather than just the smaller rooms as we first anticipated," Alistar began. "A larger guest list, primarily from Lewarden. Probably some security. Oh, and the Silver Prince will be there."

Mother had started to make displeased noises about the changes, but the last stopped her cold. "The Silver Prince is attending the wedding of an Associate Engineer?" she asked.

"Senior Engineer," Alistar said. "Fifth Degree. That's as of... yesterday."

"Senior Engineer?" she repeated. There was long pause. "I see."

"The reception will be at my house," Alistar continued.

"The townhouse is rather tight for that, isn't it?" she asked. There was a note of caution in her voice.

"Not the townhouse," Alistar said. "A manor house in the Venture District. I haven't seen all of it yet, but what I did see was quite nice, and it certainly has the space for a celebration with family and friends. The manor was a piece of my reward for successful completion of the assignment."

Another long moment of silence. Finally, she spoke. "Alistar, there *are* less dramatic methods of demonstrating that you're not planning to move back home anytime soon."

"There are, but you didn't listen when I used them," Alistar responded, applying the same bland tone she had used. "I decided that dramatic might work a little better."

She sighed. "Stubborn boy." A sound of movement, and papers shuffling. "You're determined to sail this ship your own way, aren't you? I suppose I don't have a say over the wheel now."

Alistar's eyebrows rose slightly in surprise. It was perhaps the first time he'd heard her claim anything less than total command over the direction of his life. "I'm not going to say I'll never come back to the family trade. But right now, this is where I want to be. Where I'm meant to be." He sighed. "And, evidently, where the Silver Prince wishes to keep me, given that he declined to reclaim his token when I offered it."

"A promotion, a manor house, a royal presence at your wedding." Mother considered. "I will acknowledge that on this venture, you've acquitted yourself better than you would have on a ship."

"And I don't have to split my take with my crew," Alistar added. "Although… I wish that wasn't the case. Aspendark is dead, as is a member of His Highness's Guard who was invaluable to my assignment."

"That's a heavy burden to carry, Alistar," she said soberly. "A heavy weight for any captain, even one who doesn't get to choose his own crew." He heard her let out a long breath. "You know this isn't the course I charted for you, but you've sailed it, and you've claimed a new port as your home. You're a captain, Alistar, as true as your sister or brother. Seas guide your rudder, and storms take you."

To some, the words could sound like a curse. Alistar knew them to be a blessing. A weight lightened in his chest. "May the storms ever take you home," he said, the full version of the sailors' blessing. "Thank you."

The wedding guest list had swollen. It was impossible for it to do otherwise when the Silver Prince was attending. Every noble in the city had sent inquiries and polite, or not so polite, suggestions that it would benefit Alistar to invite them. At least all the missives had been directed to Silverline Power rather than his private residence, because more than one individual had also attempted to make their case to him directly when their efforts did not gain the desired response. As much as he'd taken pleasure in watching the gate ogres remove unwanted guests, Alistar was relieved to finally reach the end of four months of constant harassment.

He pushed aside a curtain to look down on the crowd outside Night's Eve Sanctuary. Elves who would normally never deign to set foot in a place of worship dedicated to the Reyker argued vehemently with unyielding Royal Guards, trying to gain access. The guards had strict orders to turn away anyone without an invitation, and they scrupulously checked each one, watching for counterfeits.

"De'seneth, is it *really* necessary to go barefoot?" Lamorage asked. Alistar had chosen his friend to be his attendant and assistant, the man who would walk beside him to the ceremony.

"It's tradition. Bad luck to break tradition," Alistar said. "Besides, the floors are warmed, and it's spring."

"Tradition also says that if someone attacks you at the wedding, I'm supposed to be ready to duel them in your stead," Lamorage said.

"Of course!" Alistar agreed. "A groom has far more important things to worry about than pesky duels. Though if you'd rather leave that to the Royal Guards, I'll understand. How do things look downstairs?"

"Everything's ready. Once you get your coat on, you can mingle a bit," Lamorage told him.

The wedding clothes, both Alistar's and Saskia's, had been paid for by the Silver Prince, who commissioned some of the best tailors in Lewarden for the task. Alistar's coat alone would have cost him two months' pay, even at his new salary. Prince Cero had probably paid with his pocket change. Alistar wore the De'seneth family colors, sea blue and oak brown, while intricate crimson embroidery covered the bodice of Saskia's silver dress and ran in two wide lines down the skirt, and lace of the same color made the sleeves. Alistar slipped his arms through the sleeves of the silkweave coat and let Lamorage help him with the buttons.

"I don't know if you heard," Lamorage said. "I turned in my resignation."

Alistar nodded. "I heard. Have you made plans for what to do next?" He wasn't surprised. He'd been able to protect Lamorage from official repercussions and from being studied and subjected to experiments regarding his healing ability and its permanent empowerment. Alistar could not protect his friend from the shunning of their colleagues.

"Not yet," Lamorage said. "I'm sorry, I shouldn't lay this on you today of all days."

Alistar rested a hand on Lamorage's shoulder. "You know I'll help if I can."

Lamorage nodded. "Thank you."

Alistar left the upper rooms and walked down the stairs to the reception area. The floor was comfortably warm under his bare feet. The air smelled of fresh lilacs and kurowa flowers. Many guests were already seated, but those few who lingered greeted him warmly.

An elven woman walked past him, dressed in a breathtaking gown of azure silk, long gloves coming up nearly to her shoulders to maintain propriety, since the sleeves of her gown were gauzy, and they shimmered like the wings of a dragonfly. She curtseyed, and Alistar bowed, trying to place her face. He knew he'd seen her before. A friend of Saskia, perhaps.

A guard frowned at the woman. "Your invitation, ma'am?"

She reached into her handbag. "Of course. Right here."

He frowned at it, as if suspicious. Alistar smiled. "It's all right; I'll vouch for her."

The guard looked up in surprise, seeming to only then realize who Alistar was. "Oh. Pardon me, sir. Of course. Go ahead, ma'am."

"Why, thank you." She nodded to the guard. "And thank *you* as well, Mr. De'seneth. I'm honored that you were so kind as to invite me to join in this celebration of your good fortune."

"I'm glad you can attend," Alistar replied, still struggling to place her and come up with the correct name. Before he succeeded, she had moved on, entering the sanctuary.

Admiral As'enel stood next to the doorway to the sanctuary. Today, out of respect for his son's effort to keep his professional persona separate from Family business, he wore De'seneth colors rather than As'enel. Alistar joined his father, who shook his head as he scanned the crowd. "One blighted political circus in that room, Alistar."

"I know," Alistar said. "But they're mostly my choices, and there are plenty without a drop of noble blood in them. Friends."

"I had words with the Silver Prince about using my son's wedding for political posturing."

Alistar smiled. "I thought you might."

"I was surprised you didn't push back on the matter more firmly," his father said. "At least until I learned that you'd already argued him out of openly acknowledging Family involvement."

"After winning that battle, I didn't want to test just how far I could stretch his patience," Alistar said.

"I suppose," his father allowed. "And you did come through with a respectable take. I like the new house."

"Thanks." Alistar grinned. "The bar should be fully stocked by the time we get there."

"Bankrupting yourself on your wedding day, Alistar?"

"Not at all!" Alistar assured him. "All the refreshments at the party are being provided and paid for by the Silver Prince. No need to hold back on that account."

"Ah, now there's a proper privateer. Good job." Admiral As'enel chuckled and clapped Alistar on the shoulder, then ambled into the sanctuary to join the rest of Alistar's family.

When the bells tolled, the remaining guests found their seats. Alistar waited, and was rewarded when the upper door opened and Saskia flowed down the stairs to him. He'd seen the dress before, but never seen her wearing it. He forgot to breathe until she teasingly elbowed him in the ribs.

"Bad luck for the groom to pass out," she said, eyes twinkling.

"You're beautiful," Alistar told her.

Lamorage and Star followed. The fact that both Alistar and Saskia chose elves as their attendants had caused some stir. Alistar had avoided listening to any political spin put on the topic, and told any who asked simply that it was how they both chose to honor those who had helped them. After them came Kaz and Tatya carrying the boxes with the wedding bands. The orphans didn't get many opportunities to leave the Silver Watch, but an exception had been made for Alistar's wedding. Both children stepped carefully, overly aware of their finery. Kaz especially stood straight and tall, taking his role extremely seriously. Tatya's eyes were wide in silent wonder at everything.

The tolling of the bells ended, and the opening strains of the choir's song began. Alistar held his arm to Saskia. She took it, and they entered together, arm in arm, and walked around the outer edge of the room. At each statue, they stopped to offer their prayers to the god. Lamorage and Star followed, while Kaz and Tatya waited in the doorway. When Alistar and Saskia completed a full circuit of the room, returning to the doorway, they walked down the center aisle, flanked by Lamorage and Star. Kaz and Tatya brought up the tail.

The ceremony itself passed in a blur. Alistar knew they spoke their vows before the gods, but none of the details stuck in his mind except Saskia's beauty and the knowledge that she was willing to spend the rest of her life with him.

"Those who have been united under the blessings of the gods, let no mortals sunder," the priest declared.

Thunderous applause shook the sanctuary. Alistar took the band from Kaz and slid it over Saskia's finger, and she did the same with the band Tatya carried. They kissed—a quick, rushed meeting of the lips before guests swarmed them.

Alistar's family and Doctor Tan'shyo were first in the line, the right of family coming even before the Silver Prince, though he followed immediately after them.

"Thank you for inviting me to join you on this joyous occasion," Prince Cero said to Alistar.

"Thank you for your generosity," Alistar replied.

Prince Cero turned to Saskia. "A pleasure to meet you, Lady. Your father's assistance to the Crown is ever appreciated."

"I hope that mine will be equally so," she replied. "Thank you, Your Highness."

Alistar's father cut in, addressing Prince Cero. "My son tells me that you're paying for the refreshments at the reception, correct?"

"I am," Prince Cero agreed cautiously.

"Good." The admiral smiled, a malicious gleam in his eyes. "We'll be sure to make plenty of toasts, then."

"I'm sure you will," Prince Cero said stiffly. "I trust that you will not drink the entire city dry in the process."

"I make no promises," Admiral As'enel said. "A newlywed couple needs opportunity to celebrate without making a political spectacle of their happy union."

Alistar cleared his throat firmly and gave his father a firm look. "If you don't mind, there are other guests waiting for a chance to speak to us."

Once Alistar and Saskia finally finished greeting all their guests, they made their escape through the priests' entrance and into the waiting carriage. Other people were tasked with collecting the gifts and transporting them to the couple's home, and with seeing the guests taken care of, and numerous other tasks that Alistar had no attention to give. He did think back, trying to remember if the elven woman he'd vouched for had come through the greeting line. He didn't recall seeing her there.

The reception was limited only to family and close friends. That guest list, at least, Alistar and Saskia maintained complete control over. The manor's dining hall easily accommodated everyone, and Alistar was eager to banish the ghost of Cemar's gathering by filling the room with laughter and fresh memories. Musicians played lively tunes and servants brought tray after tray of food and drinks. With Saskia at his side, Alistar regaled his siblings and brother-in-law with tales of Lewarden. They, in turn, recounted events from their respective ships. The stories rapidly grew, exaggerations flying like sea gulls around fish guts. Eventually, Alistar bowed out, letting his siblings continue their friendly rivalry without him.

Admiral As'enel had caught Lamorage and drawn him into conversation. Alistar listened in as he refilled his goblet with honey mead.

"Leaving Silverline, then," Admiral As'enel said.

Lamorage nodded. "Yes sir. It's… no longer the haven it used to be. But I'm not planning to leave Lewarden yet. Not certain what I will do next."

Alistar's father considered, thoughtful. "Alistar speaks well of you and your skills. It would be a shame to put those to waste. I'm short of trustworthy people in Lewarden after the winter's incidents."

Lamorage glanced into the depths of his goblet. "You're only offering because I'm Alistar's friend."

" 'Only'?" Admiral As'enel repeated. "Yes, Alistar recommended I consider you for a position. I know my son, and I know that as your friend, he wouldn't recommend you for a task he doesn't think you capable of. Think about it. Let me know. The offer is open, no time limit."

Lamorage hesitated, then nodded. "Thank you."

Alistar gave his father a smile and a small nod of thanks.

The celebration ran late into the night. Finally, Alistar and Saskia slipped away to their suite. Before they could reach the bedroom, they first had to navigate through a maze of gifts and packages piled in the outer room. Most they would open the following day, but tradition called for them to choose one gift to unwrap on the wedding night. Alistar's gaze swept over the dazzling array of colorful and elegant packages. Ribbons threaded with silver or gold glittered in the lamp light. Sprays of enchanted everblooms spilled in woven cascades down the sides of boxes. Yet one particular gift continuously drew his eyes back to it.

The silkweave wrapped around the box was dyed with all the colors and patterns of an abstract stained glass window—pinks, yellows, greens, blues, and purples. Three metallic ribbons wound around it. The widest, copper, waged war on the yellows in the silkweave. The second ribbon, silver, at least didn't actively assault the rest of the colors, but the thin cobalt ribbon made up for the silver's lack. Alistar found himself just staring at the gaudy thing as if taking his eyes off it would give it opportunity to attack.

Saskia eyed it as well. "What… who would… Who is that from?" she finally asked. From her tone, she wasn't certain she wanted to know the answer.

Alistar picked up the package and turned it around. It had a solid weight, but he found no tag, and no signature on any of the ribbons. "It's not signed," he said.

"Is it really supposed to be *here*?" Saskia asked cautiously.

Alistar opened his mouth, then stopped.

I promise you, De'seneth, I will bring the most hideous, garish, gaudy, blindingly ugly gift to your wedding, and in comparison, even the worst of the rest will seem mild and perhaps even attractive.

"Alistar?" Saskia asked.

"I know who it's from." His voice almost failed him. He tried again. "I know who this is from. Yes, it's for us. It's supposed to be here." *I saw her. That had to be her, outside the sanctuary. Onyxflame came, as she said she would, and I didn't recognize her.* "Saskia, do you mind if we open this one tonight?"

"I'm afraid I'll have nightmares about it eating the rest of the gifts if we leave it out here," she said, mouth curling in a wry smile. "You *will* tell me who sent it, won't you?"

"I will," Alistar promised. "Inside."

They entered the bedroom and untangled the ribbons from the package, then stripped away the garish silkweave. Saskia tucked the bundle into a basket, getting it out of sight. Alistar opened the box and drew out a large model ship. He recognized the design immediately—a small privateer craft, designed for raiding and meant to be manned by a crew of no more than five. At the prow stood a figure in As'enel colors with black hair and beard. Around the base of the model, "May the storms ever take you home" was inscribed.

Alistar lifted the model and handed it to Saskia. She gasped in surprise and examined it. "This is beautiful craftsmanship. The detail! And is that meant to be you at the prow? It looks like it." She ran her finger over the lettering, and something clicked softly. A panel swung open on the base, and a tightly rolled scroll fell out. Alistar picked it up from Saskia's lap and untied the ribbon.

"Thanks for the invitation, De'seneth. I did my best to keep my promise, and if anyone outdid me, they had to be trying much too hard. Good luck to you and your bride. And… thank you for not looking for me. Maybe we'll meet again, if the Reyker will it."

Saskia read over Alistar's arm. "Onyxflame?" she asked softly.

Alistar nodded. "She's alive, then. Alive and well." He let out a long breath and smiled. *Alive, well, and no doubt causing trouble somewhere. Storms take you, Onyxflame. May they ever take you home.*

ABOUT THE AUTHOR

Sanan Kolva lives in eastern Washington with her family. She is the author of Chosen of the Spears series and has short stories in several anthologies. She has worked as a technical editor for an electrical engineering firm for over a decade. Winterlight is the result of idly wondering how to apply her understanding of the electric system in a fantasy setting.

Sanan can be found at http://sanankolva.com, where you can also sign up for her newsletter.

If you enjoyed this book, please tell someone else who might like it, or leave a review on your preferred platform.

www.ingramcontent.com/pod-product-compliance
Lightning Source LLC
Chambersburg PA
CBHW051550100726
47898CB00001B/43